ALL TOO POSSIBLE

Frankie sighed. Her plan to keep him at arm's length was working, so far. But the longer she stayed cooped up in this cabin with him, the harder it was to not stare at him and want to touch his handsome face and explore his long, lanky body.

"If only we had a deck of cards," she said, rousing a triumphant "Ah-ha!" from him. He slid off the bunk and delved into the side of his valise for a small box that turned out to be playing cards.

They agreed on rummy and began to play. Several rounds of cards had Frankie well ahead in points and Reynard growing frustrated by her luck.

"Perhaps we should try another game," she said. "I've always been terrible at euchre, but I'll try it if you'll refresh my memory of the rules."

She turned out to be abominably lucky at euchre, too.

With a huff of disgust, he looked up at her.

"You, Frankie Bumgarten, are impossible."

It came out because she just couldn't keep it in any longer.

"That's the problem, Reynard Boulton. I'm all too possible."

His gaze locked with hers and lightning struck along that visual connection. Seconds later, he was up and launching himself across the cards, headed straight for her lips.

She didn't move, didn't brace to resist.

When his lips came down on hers and pushed her back, she wound her arms around his neck and held on.

He kissed her with a need and urgency that answered every question her heart could ask.

Also by Betina Krahn

A Good Day to Marry a Duke
Three Nights With the Princess

Published by Kensington Publishing Corporation

The
Girl with
the Sweetest
Secret

BETINA
KRAHN

ZEBRA BOOKS
KENSINGTON PUBLISHING CORP.

http://www.kensingtonbooks.com

ZEBRA BOOKS are published by

Kensington Publishing Corp.
119 West 40th Street
New York, NY 10018

All Kensington titles, imprints, and distributed lines are available at special quantity discounts for bulk purchases for sales promotion, premiums, fund-raising, educational, or institutional use.

Special book excerpts or customized printings can also be created to fit specific needs. For details, write or phone the office of the Kensington Sales Manager: Attn.: Sales Department. Kensington Publishing Corp., 119 West 40th Street, New York, NY 10018. Phone: 1-800-221-2647.

Zebra and the Z logo Reg. U.S. Pat. & TM Off.

First Printing: December 2018
ISBN-13: 978-1-4201-4349-2
ISBN-10: 1-4201-4349-2

eISBN-13: 978-1-4201-4350-8
eISBN-10: 1-4201-4350-6

10 9 8 7 6 5 4 3 2 1

Printed in the United States of America

For all the little girls in my life:

Kate, Sarah, Lauren K,
Regan, Sofia, Evelyn, Allora, Logan, Lula, Lucy, Gracie,
Norah, Cora, and Lauren V

You've helped my heart
grow bigger with each passing year!

Chapter One

"Never seen a man hold liquor like he can," Beulah MacNeal, legendary proprietress of the Chancery, said with a dark chuckle.

Reynard Boulton, heir to the Viscount Tannehill, stood on the mezzanine overlooking the gaming floor of Mrs. MacNeal's infamous gambling establishment in southwest London. The air was a haze of spirits and smoke, and crackled with the noise of a risky but lucrative pleasure trade. Below, a familiar barrel-chested figure in evening clothes was propped against a gaming table with only a couple of chips in front of him.

"He's a regular marvel of nature," Reynard said, wincing at the way Redmond Strait reached for a glass of whiskey on a passing tray and missed, dropping his arm heavily. "Stewed to the gills. Again." He frowned and turned to the massive but elegantly clothed woman seated on a grand settee behind him. "How much has he lost?"

"A bundle," Beulah said, opening her fan and appraising the action on the floor below. "Near two thousand."

Reynard gave a soft whistle from between his teeth.

"Third time this week." She accepted a glass of champagne from a tray presented by a uniformed servant, and sipped daintily. It was odd, Reynard thought, how a woman of such monumental proportions could seem so dainty at times. "He's lost similar amounts each time."

"Damn. And you sent for me because?" Reynard narrowed his eyes.

"He's a friend."

"Of yours?"

"Don't be difficult, Fox. I know you know him and his family. I know you'd not want to see him come to harm. He needs to go home."

"And you called me to be his cabbie." A barb lurked in that statement, but Beulah smiled, too familiar with the vagaries of his moods to be offended. Reynard frowned, not pleased at being read so accurately.

"Take him home," Beulah said flatly, studying her now empty glass. "And see he doesn't return for a while." Her broad but still lovely face was as determined as he'd ever seen it. "I've been hearing rumors."

Every nerve in Reynard's body came alert. News. Gossip. *Rumors*. Information was Reynard Boulton's stock and trade. Surely he hadn't missed a juicy bit. The possibility was downright unsettling.

"What kind of rumors?"

"About his losses." Beulah's all-seeing gaze bored into him. "And the family in trouble because of it. Despite what some may think of me, it is not my desire to see men wreck their fortunes and families at my tables."

Reynard turned to stare at jug-bit Redmond Strait. The hard-drinking old prospector from the American West was fast becoming either a colorful legend or a cautionary tale in London's jealously guarded upper crust. Either could spell disaster for Red's family of abominably perfect and pulchritudinous females—who were most likely ignorant of the threat his nightly entertainments posed to—

Good God. He blanched, caught in a squeeze between a long-ignored conscience and mortal dread. He had made a *promise*.

Curse Ashton Graham's hide. When heading for New York with his pregnant wife, Daisy, he had wrangled a promise from Reynard to look after her family in his absence. Her sisters were babes in the woods, he said. Too pretty for their own good, he said. London was full of snakes, rakes, and scandalmongers, he said. And if anyone could look after them and see that nothing wicked assailed them, it was the Fox himself . . . who was on a first-name basis with *wicked* and had the resources and cunning to intercept and deflect any harm that threatened Daisy's family.

He closed his eyes for a moment, fighting back the memory of Ashton's genuine worry and the liquor they'd consumed the night before Ash and Daisy left for America. He'd been near comatose by the time his old school friend pried that unthinkable vow from him.

What would it hurt? he had told himself when he sobered up. They were so fresh and innocent and their mother and uncle were so doting and protective, what could go wrong?

He glanced down at the gaming floor and frowned at the way Red stumbled and then laughed uproariously at his own misstep—drawing his fellow gamblers into the hilarity. *That* was what could go wrong.

A frisson of shame went through him at the way he'd abandoned his word on such a self-centered premise. Since that night, he'd done his best to avoid the Bumgarten women and their hard-drinking uncle.

Below, Red managed to capture a passing glass of

whiskey and down it. "Whoa, howdy, boys! That there's some fiiine Irish whiskey!" It seemed like the entire patronage joined his raucous laughter.

Reynard grimaced and then nodded to Beulah MacNeal.

"Fine," he said roughly. "I'll pry him loose from your table and carry him home." And he descended the steps to save silver magnate Redmond Strait from his own worst impulses.

Frances "Frankie" Bumgarten lay awake in her feather-plumped bed, staring up at the delicate canopy overhead. Light from the wheezing coals in the hearth moved sinuously across the silk-lined brocade, and the stylish townhouse was so quiet she could hear the chimes of the clock in the distant entry hall. Minutes that seemed like hours dragged by. For the third time that week, she had awakened in the middle of the night and found it impossible to go back to sleep. The reason was all too clear.

Elizabeth Strait Bumgarten, Frankie's mother, had given her an ultimatum: cooperate and make herself amenable to noble suitors or find herself packed off back to America.

Elizabeth was determined to see her daughters married and settled in matches that provided both status and comfort. As heiresses to a fortune derived from Nevada's silver mines, they deserved nothing less. Their older sister Daisy had married the penniless second son of a duke—a love match, of all things—making Elizabeth all the more determined to see her three remaining daughters married according to her expectations.

The fact that none of them were interested in marrying the boring, self-absorbed, duty-ridden sons of noble houses seemed to escape her.

Frankie turned over and pounded her pillows into a

more comfortable shape, wishing that her mother would prove half as malleable.

Minutes later, overheated, she threw the covers off.

The featherbed was too soft, the mattress below it, too hard . . .

She would have to find a way to endure and escape unattached through dinners, parties, and balls until the end of the season. She was not about to be railroaded into some half-baked arrangement with one of the matrimonial rejects that haunted tearooms and debutante balls.

Truth be told, she couldn't see any advantage in marriage, for herself or any other woman. It was a lot of fuss and bother, with vows to *cleave to, honor,* and *obey*. The man would get her marriage settlement, a housekeeper, bed warmer, and ultimately an heir and a baby tender. While she would get a belly full of duty, then of baby, then of even more duty.

The fact that she knew about the bed-warming, baby-getting part should probably disqualify her as suitable wife material, anyway. Her elder sister Daisy had been quite explicit with her on what to expect regarding marital nightlife, and, it all sounded more than a little off-putting. She hadn't seen or met a single man she would consider sharing bed and board with, much less her most intimate body parts.

That thought propelled her from her bed and set her pacing. It really was too warm in her room. She fanned her nightgown and a moment later headed for the door. There was only one cure for this kind of restlessness.

The great brick kitchen on the sub-street level was cool and mostly dark. She paused to let her eyes adjust rather than turn up the low-burning gas lamp. Cook was not overly fond of Frankie's nighttime journeys into her domain; no sense advertising her presence. She held a hand over the stove and smiled at the lingering warmth. It was just enough. She knew exactly where the little copper café-au-lait pot was shelved and where Cook kept milk in the icebox.

She had the milk warming and was reaching for a crockery cup from the shelf when a thump and a rattle came from the steps and short hall that led up to the alley door.

She froze and craned her neck trying to make out the alcove in that hallway. Young Bob the footman always dozed there until everyone—meaning Uncle Red—was in for the night. But the seat was empty. Then came what might have been a muffled groan and the sound of a lock being scraped. Picked? She staggered back against the sideboard. Someone was trying to force the alley door?

Thieves!

She looked around for something, anything with which to defend her home. Spotting an old wooden bread paddle hanging above the fireplace—the one Cook used to threaten any footman sneaking a taste from a serving bowl—she grabbed it and judged it hefty enough to make a dent in a robber's motivation.

The alley door swung open with a muffled bang, and it sounded like someone grunted and then muttered in annoyance. She positioned herself at the side of the steps leading down into the kitchen, paddle raised. The minute the two figures lurched into view, she swung the paddle at the nearest one and a top hat went flying.

"Aghhh!"

It was a glancing blow. She could have done better. But it sent the closest wretch stumbling and the other fellow sinking to his knees, then to the floor. Wait—a top hat?

The head gear rolled across the floor, and a deep voice growled, "Damn it!" She lurched back with a hand clamped to her mouth—she'd only managed to make the one she'd struck mad as a wet hornet. He clapped a hand to the side of his forehead, straightened, and turned on her.

"Jesus, woman, what are you trying to do? Kill someone?"

In a heartbeat, she recognized that patrician voice, that chiseled face, that . . . *oh, no.*

Clutching the bread paddle to her chest, she scrambled back, trying to make sense of the fact that Reynard Boulton, heir to the wealthy and reclusive Viscount Tannehill, was in her house in the middle of the night . . . with . . .

"Uncle Red!" She recognized the heap on the floor as he pushed up on one arm and shook his head weakly. She ran to him, knelt, and searched for signs of injury. "What's happened? Are you all right?"

The smell hit her the same moment Reynard Boulton's voice did.

"He's bloody fine. Just stewed to the gills."

Red reeked of whiskey. It wasn't exactly an unusual occurrence, but the fact that he was collapsed on the kitchen floor looking pie-eyed and incapacitated was alarming. His head hit the floor and his eyes closed.

"It's me that's in mortal danger," Boulton bit out. "What the devil possessed you to attack someone entering your kitchen with—"

"I thought you were a house-breaker," she replied irritably. He was testing the side of his forehead and glowering down at her. From that angle, he looked tall and intimidating. Light hair, gray eyes, and chiseled features. She didn't remember him being so . . . tall or so . . . handsome. She did, however, remember his condescending manner toward her and her sisters at Daisy's wedding three years ago. Insufferable *nob.* She rose, chin up. "Young Bob always locks the door and goes to bed when Uncle Red comes home, so I thought he was home already."

"Well, he wasn't." Boulton looked around the floor for something.

"What are you doing bringing my uncle home?"

"He was incapable of making it to his own door, so a mutual friend asked me to see him home." He drew his gloved hand from his injury, and inspected it, seeming relieved that no blood had been drawn. However, he was growing a nice little goose-egg above his eye. With any luck, he might even develop a shiner. She could only hope.

"Come on, Uncle Red." She stooped beside him, taking hold of his arm and straining to pull him upright. "You can't lie here. Let's get you up to bed."

Red was in no condition to contribute to his own relocation, and after several tugs and changes of grip, she gave an exasperated groan and looked up at Reynard Boulton. He was watching her efforts through narrowed eyes.

Judgmental ass.

Having to ask for his help was nothing short of humiliating.

"If you would be so good as to assist me in getting him to his bed," she said tartly. "My mother will faint dead away if she finds him on the floor of the kitchen in the morning."

It took a moment, but he jerked a nod, muttering something about good deeds going unpunished.

Red was pure dead weight as they pulled him upright, positioned themselves under his arms, and supported him around the waist. Frankie was aware of Boulton's arm against hers around Red, and of the fact that he was bearing the better part of Red's weight. Still, getting her uncle through the center hall and up the stairs took monumental effort.

She directed them along the upper hall to Red's room and managed to open the door. At the side of his bed, they let him go and allowed him to fall, facedown onto the pristine linen. Huffing annoyance, she heaved both of his feet up onto the bedcovers and started to unlace his shoes.

To her surprise, Boulton reached for the other shoe and a moment later set it carefully on the bench at the foot of the bed. Then he transferred his attentions to Red's suit coat, tie, and collar. Soon, she was able to pull the coverlet from beneath her uncle and lay it over him.

It was chilly in the room. There was no fire and the staff hadn't thought to draw the heavy drapes closed for the night. Moonlight coming through the window allowed her to see Boulton plainly as he stood nearby, his light eyes wandering over her. She suppressed a shiver.

"What were you doing in the kitchen in the dead of night anyway, Miss"—he was distracted momentarily— "which Bumgarten are you?"

"Frances. Frankie to my friends and family. You can call me *Miss Bumgarten*," she answered, feeling an annoying tightness in her throat. Increasingly self-conscious in her nightgown, probably because she was naked beneath it, she wrapped her arms around her waist. "I couldn't sleep, so I went downstairs to make some warm milk."

She looked up, met his gaze, and nearly dropped to her knees. His gray eyes had warmed to silver, his lips were parted as if he were about to speak, and his features glowed with an arousing kind of heat. Speculation weighted that silver gaze as it roamed her and lingered boldly on the skin bared by the drawstring neck of her nightgown. She felt it like a physical touch. What the devil was happening to her? She felt prickles all over, like she had been plunged into hot water.

"He's not usually like this," she said, pulling from his gaze to glance at her wayward uncle.

"I'm afraid he is. More than you know," Boulton said coolly. "He's what you Americans call 'a drinkin' man.'"

"Well, he's not usually this—what you Brits call—'into his cups.'"

He made a rumbling sound deep in his chest that might have been a laugh.

Her fingertips tingled.

"I suppose I should thank you for bringing him home." She raised her chin and started around him toward the door, but he stepped into her path, facing her, now even closer.

"Yes," he said, his voice oddly lower, softer. "You should."

Then he stood watching her, seeming expectant.

Every nerve in her body vibrated with a delicious sort of tension.

"Very well. Thank you, Mr. Boulton," she said through half-clenched jaws, irritated by her reaction to his presence as much as his ungracious attitude. The sooner he was out of the house, the better. "Let me show you out."

She stalked down the hallway and down the stairs, refusing to look behind her to see if he was following. The minute she reached the kitchen she picked up the bread paddle from the floor and pressed the handle to her as she began to look for his hat. A moment later, he arrived in the doorway and watched as she retrieved his headgear and held it out to him.

"I'm afraid it's damaged," she said as he took in the dented side and broken brim. "I'll see that it is replaced. If you will give me the name of your hatmaker . . ."

"No need," he said tersely, holding it up and appraising the dangling piece of brim with an irritable squint.

"I insist."

His mouth twitched as if he were suppressing a stronger reaction.

"Fine. Scott's." He grimaced and grabbed his forehead as if pain had just speared through it again. "In Bond Street."

She felt an alarming urge to soothe that forehead and touch the light hair that fell in a soft wave over it, but managed to keep her arms tucked.

"I suppose I should apologize for your head," she said.

"Yes. You should." He clipped energy from each word as if saving it to deal with the pain.

"I could mix you a headache powder," she said, astonished that those words came out of her mouth. She was trying to kick him out the door, wasn't she? "Cook keeps a supply of medicinals here."

"I believe you've done quite enough." He donned the damaged hat with a wince and headed for the alley door. At the step, he paused.

"A word of advice." He slashed a look at her from beneath that droopy, broken brim. The sad-looking hat didn't dampen his allure or dent his dignity. "Next time you decide to go rambling about the house in the middle of the night, be so good as to put on a few clothes."

She stood for a moment staring at the alley door after it slammed, feeling scalded by his dismissal.

Put on a few clothes.

She took a swing with the bread paddle, imagining a satisfying "crack" it would make as it connected with the other side of his swollen head. Who did he think he was, making comments on her person, like he'd never seen a woman in her night—She froze.

He'd seen her in her nightgown. A trickle of illicit excitement slid through her, followed hard by a wash of embarrassment.

Sweet Lord, what had she done?

He was the Fox—collector of secrets, spreader of gossip, master of whispers—and she and Red had just handed him a whole bushelful of humiliating tidbits.

He wouldn't dare, would he? Ruin her reputation over something as harmless as being caught making warm milk in the dead of night . . . in her own kitchen . . . in her nightgown?

She returned the paddle to its place above the great hearth, forgot all about the milk warming on the stove, and fled up the stairs to her bed.

The sheets now felt cool against her flushed skin as she climbed between them and clamped her hands over her eyes. Uncle Red's favorite description of a certain kind of unscrupulous Englishman came to her: *low-down, kipper-suckin' sidewinder*. Reynard Boulton was that, all right.

But she had the unsettling feeling that there was more to the viscount-in-waiting.

She relived the entire episode, trying not to dwell on the memory of his every feature, every expression, every word. It was nearing dawn when she finally succumbed to sleep, but even then, she was plagued by dreams of arrogant gray eyes that shone silver in the moonlight.

Chapter Two

"Sink me. Would you look at that."

Reynard Boulton stood with his back to the ballroom, a week later, and was not tempted in the slightest to turn from the punch table and learn the source of Milroy Stevenson's wonder. Milroy, after all, thought indoor plumbing a miracle of God.

Reynard did, however, pause in the midst of topping off his cup of punch with a shot from his flask and glance up into the reflection of Sir Marion Tutty's gaudy ballroom. The place was stuffed with mirrors, in imitation of either the palace of Versailles or his host's favorite bawdy house . . . hard to say which. He sighed. He despised these cursed debutante do's—had gladly quit them years ago. If it weren't for the possibility of a confrontation between his heavily indebted host and a mysterious business rival, he would never have put in an appearance.

"No, look, Fox." The big fellow elbowed Reynard. "She's the prettiest—no, the most gorgeous creature I've ever seen."

A female had caught his eye? That wasn't exactly noteworthy, considering Stevenson had spent most of his life in a Yorkshire village surrounded by ham-fisted farmers' daughters and the pigs they tended. Reynard shot a glare at Milroy before spotting Carlton Laroche on the other side of Milroy, gawking in the same direction.

"A walking dream." Laroche sighed. "Just look at those eyes." Apparently, he'd been struck by the same creature. But he had spent the better part of his life in London—his standards had to be higher.

With a huff of disgust, Reynard turned and followed their gaze across the ballroom to a clutch of bright-eyed young things gathered around a young woman with chestnut hair and eyes as big and blue and decadently fringed as any he had ever seen. He froze. She wore a rich blue gown that enhanced her eyes and a corset that enhanced a figure that needed no correction. Just standing there she seemed fluid and graceful and utterly—*what the hell?*

"Dammit, Stevenson—" His tone became uncharacteristically fierce as he grabbed the big fellow's arm and turned him away from the sight of her. "Don't go near that one."

"What?" Stevenson gave a half laugh as he strained to turn back to that feminine vision. "Don't be absur—"

"I said, don't go near her." The pressure Reynard exerted on the Yorkshireman's thick arm finally reached the fellow's thicker head. "I'd hate to have to pound you to pig feed to make you see reason."

Stevenson was taller and more muscular than Reynard, but it was a wood-cutting, plow-pulling kind of strength. The Fox, as both friend and foe alike called Reynard Boulton, possessed a more refined sort of power. He was a formidable swordsman, a dead-on shot with a firearm, and a tireless bare-knuckle fighter. Half of his physical prowess came from years of training under Europe's elite blade masters, the rest was the result of risky escapades in London's underbelly. Those who underestimated his elegant appearance and mannerly demeanor did so only once.

Stevenson's response was a confused laugh.

"What's got into you, Fox?" Stevenson stared at him, then back at the young woman with widened eyes. "You know her! Who is she?"

"No one you need to know." Reynard abandoned his grip on Stevenson, sensing his reaction had drawn too much attention.

"C'mon, Fox," Laroche chimed in. "Who is she?"

"Someone who will get that fine Roman nose of yours rearranged if you don't keep it to yourself." He turned back to his spiked punch, sensing mounting interest in the looks Stevenson and Laroche exchanged. They weren't going to let it drop.

Laroche raised his eyebrows and strode away. He returned after a quick word with their host, wearing a mischievous smile.

"Bumgarten," he said to Stevenson. "She's one of those Bumgarten females. Sir Marion wasn't sure which one."

The pair turned to him expectantly.

"You know the Bumgartens, Fox—those rich American girls." Laroche was clearly the foolhardier of the two. "Come on—tell us about her. You wouldn't be keeping her for yourself, would you?"

Reynard glanced up into one of those mirrors that gave him a view of what was happening near the door. Several young stallions had descended on that covey of females and Frances *too-pretty-for-her-own-good* Bumgarten was flirting with those devastating eyes of hers.

"Very well." He turned back to his companions, downed the rest of his doctored punch, and leveled an icy gaze on them. "Word is, she practices dark arts to entice reckless young idiots into her arms—then sucks the life from them and discards them like locust husks. Others say she turns into a deer at night and runs naked through the forest, participating in wild animalistic rituals. Still others say she becomes a banshee at will and slithers through the city's gutters collecting secrets with which to ruin the high and mighty. Personally, I have seen her mesmerize grown men with a single glance at fifty paces." He glared pointedly at the pair. "Just now, in fact."

He had them hanging on every word. The horror on their faces was proof of how gullible they were—especially regarding canny young virgins—canny young *American* virgins.

It took a moment for them to react to the fact that he was having them on. They scowled and drew back.

"I am trying to save you from yourselves. Take it from me—ignore your curious and lusty impulses and walk away unscathed." The pair were hardly the worst London's elite had to offer, but he couldn't imagine either being up to the challenge of mating Frances "Frankie" Bumgarten. And he was sworn to protect her family. And her.

He poured another cup of that execrable punch and strode off in search of Sir Marion's library, or whatever retreat the beleaguered tycoon had fashioned for himself in his house full of horse-faced females.

Stevenson and Laroche watched Reynard Boulton stroll away—a slow, controlled prowl that seemed as natural to him as breathing. The Fox knew things. Hell, the Fox knew everything. He had eyes and ears in noble houses and bawdy houses, in government offices and gambling dens, in bank vaults and boardrooms, back alleys and bedchambers. He was London's foremost information broker, the unofficial keeper and sometimes dispenser of society's secrets. If he said the Bumgarten girl was poison dressed as pie, they had reason to believe it.

With a glance at each other, then back at her, the pair headed straight across the ballroom for those mesmerizing blue eyes.

Moths to a flame.

"There he is. Isn't he marvelous?"

"Not even tolerable." Frankie Bumgarten cut a dark glance across the Tuttys' ballroom at Reynard Boulton, who seemed to be lecturing two nicely turned-out young gentlemen. So full of himself.

Arrogant wretch.

Why on earth would the Fox deign to appear at Ardith Tutty's coming-out party? Surely, he had better things to do. Like being fitted for a new hat. That custom-made silk topper she had ordered as a replacement had cost her a bundle. It wasn't easy to come up with the funds without alerting her mother, which would have opened up another whole bag of worms. She'd had to hit up Uncle Red and shame him into contributing to the purchase.

She glanced furtively at Boulton's elegant figure, telling herself she was looking for evidence that the goose-egg on his forehead had turned into a black eye. She couldn't tell; his left side was turned away from her.

He behaved as if he were already the viscount and outranked every other man in the room. Much as she would like to find fault with him, it couldn't be with his appearance, he was too easy on the eyes. His perfectly tailored evening clothes conformed to every angle of his tall, lean body. Then, of course, there was that hair, every wheat-gold strand in perfect order. *Yes, well,* she shook herself back to reality. His appearance had to be the reason the man was invited everywhere, because his constant air of superiority and relentless observation were enough to put off the most charitable of hosts.

She had learned his prickly, difficult nature early on. He was an old schoolmate of her sister Daisy's husband, Lord Ashton Graham. They had been introduced at Daisy's wedding three years ago, and since then he had pointedly avoided her entire family.

Bounder. She had finally put his distaste for her and her sisters down to the fact that they were new American money and he was old English nobility with all of the judgment and superior airs that status implied. If she had any delusions that his opinion of them might have mellowed over time, her encounter with him in the kitchen a few nights past had dispelled them.

What she wouldn't give to see him taken down a peg or two.

"And soooo talented." Claire, Frankie's younger sister, leaned close to whisper: "His every movement creates a melody."

"His—what?" Frankie turned to Claire and found her staring at the orchestra—no, the *conductor* of the orchestra. That tall, smartly clad figure directed the flow of delightful music from a twenty-piece ensemble.

Her heart sank.

Him. Julian Fontaine was Claire's developing passion. She had heard his chamber orchestra perform at an exhibition and now secretly scoured the *Times* and the society pages for mention of him. So, this was why Claire had been so eager for their mother to accept an invitation to the disagreeable Tutty girl's ball.

Claire read disapproval in her frown and grabbed her arm. "Don't tell Mama. Please, Frankie."

"He's a musician, Cece. For God's sake—Mama will lock you in the cellar when she finds out."

"*If* she finds out. Please don't tell her. Promise me you won't tell her." Claire squeezed her arm. "I'm desperate to make him see me. If you can just keep her out of the ballroom for a little while . . . pleeeeease."

Frankie stared at her, seeing in her soulful eyes a yearning that Frankie had never experienced but recognized as something fundamental to her younger sister's sensitive spirit. She groaned quietly.

"You're not going to do anything scandalous, are you?"

"No." Claire feigned affront at the notion, but melted a moment later under Frankie's interrogating glare. "Well, not exactly." Claire nodded toward a sideboard where a servant stood watch over a violin case.

Oh, Lord. Frankie groaned. Cece was going to play and draw attention to herself, smack in the middle of London society. It was not only going to catch Fontaine's eye, it was probably going to ignite an unquenchable flame of attraction between them. He'd be madly entranced by her beauty and talent and in coming days there would be a flurry of private communiques and assignations—all of which she'd be sworn to secrecy about. But sooner or later, news of their scandalous romantic entanglement would reach her mother and all hell would break loose.

She would be blamed for allowing it to happen and Mama would rail about the betrayal and the indignity and the gossip, not to mention the ascribed immorality of it. Romance had always been tainted with sin in her mother's mind. As the storm subsided, they would be banned from balls and parties, packed up and whisked off to some cottage in the back of beyond—worse, back to New York—even Nevada! And while she loved horses and could tolerate the ranch hands' rough ways, the cows and sagebrush made her itch and her nose always ran and her eyes swelled—

"Frankie, *please*." Claire now gripped both of her hands tightly and the intensity of their exchange drew a few glances. She allowed Claire to pull her back toward the nearby entrance, and before she could refuse, the raw hope in Cece's angelic face and sea green eyes demolished her defenses. Her beloved younger sister was a true romantic. It came with her uncommon sensitivity and talent for music. So, who was she to deny something that was probably a fundamental part of Cece's soul?

Damn it. She sagged. She was probably going to regret this.

"Give me a few minutes and I'll find a way to steer Mama to the retiring room. When you see us leave, you'll have a quarter of an hour to enchant your musician."

Seconds later they were engulfed by a gaggle of tittering girls fresh from primping and gossiping in the ladies' room, and there was no escape. She glanced around, hoping her mother couldn't see them. Elizabeth Bumgarten was clear on her instruction to avoid such situations: "No man wants to have to wade through a clutch of giggling ninnies to pluck out a desirable maid for a dance." Frankie sighed quietly, seeing in Cece's pained expression that she was recalling it, too. The whispers of excitement and girlish intrigue all around them that made her feel older than her twenty-two years.

Ardith Tutty, nineteen and the deb of the hour, had completed the obligatory first dance with her father and the second with her godfather, and had taken the floor with two other gentlemen since—neither of whom was under age fifty. Still, she didn't seem in the least beset by such a dismal start to her life in society. Moments later, Frankie understood why.

Several smartly attired young men descended on the group and spirited girls away to dance, giving lie to her mother's social wisdom. Soon, the only one left standing with Frankie and Claire was Ardith, who had made herself all but unavailable during the pairing . . . turning aside to greet a nearby matron and brandishing her fan in a way that forbade any approach. Now, however, she fluffed her bodice frills and applied her fan, staring over it at two gentlemen making their way across the dance floor toward them.

"He's mine," she said to Frankie, under cover of her fluttering fan.

Frankie blinked, wondering if she'd heard correctly. "I beg your pardon."

"The one on the right. Carlton Laroche. He's mine." She gave Frankie an icy little smile. "You two can fight over the other one."

Stunned, Frankie watched Ardith appropriate Laroche's arm and bat her eyes in a calculated way. The gentleman escorted the deb of the hour onto the floor, but not, Frankie noted, without a backward glance at her.

Conniving heifer. When vexed, Frankie reverted to colorful ranching lingo, peppered with Uncle Red's miner slang—to her mother's dismay. She stared at the departing pair, thinking that Ardith might be young but she was already a determined competitor in the marriage sweepstakes. She had sized up Frankie as competition and brashly warned her off as she staked a claim to one of the more handsome men in the room. *Silly cow.* As if Frankie would ever be interested in jumping such a claim.

The other fellow presented himself before Frankie and Claire with a stiff bow, muttering his name with a heavy north-of-England accent. "Milroy Steve'son, a' yar service. Would either of you farr ladies, um, carrre to dannce?"

Frankie edged back a half step, which left Claire closer to the fellow. He flushed slightly as he offered his arm. Claire gave her a look before accepting the invitation and proceeding to the dance floor.

That left Frankie standing alone, or so she thought. A moment later a girlish voice whispered, "A lot of good that will do her."

She turned with a start to find a stout, frizzy-haired young woman in a too-tight bodice leaning in to speak to her. Hazel Something. They had been introduced at Lucinda Mazur's coming out party. Plain and self-effacing, Hazel hadn't been especially memorable, except for the way Ardith and some of the other girls had belittled her.

"What will do who no good?" Frankie frowned, turning to the girl.

"Ardith." Hazel glanced around to be certain no one was paying attention, then nodded to the evening's honoree as she whirled past. "She's set her cap for Laroche, but it will come to naught. Her father won't give her permission to wed until her older sister Marcella is married."

"Really? He demands his elder daughter be married first?" Frankie said. "Why would he do such a thing?"

Hazel looked puzzled for a moment, then realized she didn't know. "It's an old custom in noble houses and the Tuttys have always aped fancy manners. Barbaric if you ask me." She grinned wickedly. "Especially when the eldest is Marcella Tutty."

Frankie felt even more at sea and her face must have shown it. Hazel produced a tight little smile. "She's so plain and disagreeable, where would they ever find someone to take her on?" She shot a satisfied look Ardith's way. "Ardith will die a spinster if she can't change her father's mind."

Frankie glanced at arch-competitor Ardith with new eyes.

"Of course, there are ways," Hazel added. "And Marcella and Ardith Tutty are nothing if not determined."

Before Frankie could respond, Hazel was discovered and bustled off by her irritable lady mother.

Frankie watched the dancers and the knots of conversation going on around the edges of the dance floor . . . the furtive glances to see who might be in earshot, the whispers and quiet exclamations of surprise or indignation, the hearty laughter and back-slapping of those who endured these honored traditions of camaraderie, connection, and engagement.

It was a sea of intrigue, she thought, watching the couples on the dance floor and those populating the sides and the conversation nooks. How many of them had secrets that would cause their lives or social connections to unravel if they were to be uncovered?

Already tonight she had been made privy to three confidences that she would rather not have heard. What was it about her that made people tell her things? She turned to go in search of her mother, knowing there were seating areas filled with mamas and matrons outside the ballroom and on a mezzanine balcony overlooking the far end of the ballroom. That was most likely where—

Two gentlemen blocked her path and she was surprised to find their host, Marion Tutty, in company with another man, staring down at her.

"Sir Marion." She took a half step back and used her fan, uncertain what she had done to draw their host's notice. "Such a lovely party."

"Miss Bumgarten, I believe." Sir Marion's smile had a

tension about it. "Such a delight to have you here, my dear. You have brightened our gathering with your presence and acquired admirers this evening, one of whom I bring for an introduction." He turned to the man at his shoulder, who stepped forward and caused Frankie to inhale sharply. "Your Grace, may I present Miss Bumgarten, of America."

Chapter Three

The gentleman clicked his heels smartly as he bent his head in a gracious nod. He was tall, dark, and expensively dressed. A blue-rimmed white satin sash held in place by a gold medallion lay diagonally across his broad chest. It was a Continental look, she had learned from her London associations. That all took a moment to sink in, along with "*Your Grace.*"

This was a *duke*.

Her hand extended, seemingly of its own accord, as she sank on weakening knees into a well-practiced curtsey. She rose into the glow of a smile beaming at her from beneath large brown eyes that glinted with amusement. He had short dark hair and square, solid features that were ennobled by an aquiline nose and a firm mouth.

"Maximillian, Duke of Ottenberg has been so good as to grace us with his presence this evening," Tutty continued, a bit too eagerly.

"Miss Bumgarten." The duke's voice was deep and pleasant around her name as he gave her hand a kiss and a surprising bit of pressure before returning it to her.

"Your Grace, it is an honor to meet you," she managed, reeling a bit.

She glanced at the far end of the room, wondering if her mother was watching.

"The pleasure is mine, dear lady," he said with a throaty accent that marked him as being from the north of the Continent. "Our host speaks the truth to say that you brighten this gathering with your radiance. I hope you will make this evening all the more memorable for me by accepting my invitation to dance."

"I would be pleased to, Your Grace." She gave him her hand and accompanied him to the dance floor where couples were answering the music's call for the next dance. It was a waltz, a dance Frankie had not only been tutored in, but actually enjoyed. As he put his hand to hers and clasped her waist, she felt the stares of the room collect around them and experienced a trill of excitement.

The duke was as impressive a dancer as he was a figure. His every movement seemed confident and calculated to put his partner at ease. She fell into the rhythm of the music and steps, feeling her skirts sway pleasantly in the turns. She couldn't imagine a more perfect partner.

"And where is Ottenberg, Your Grace? I'm afraid I have not had time to study the geography of the Continent as much as I would like."

"Prussia," he said tautly, watching her for a reaction. "The north of Germany. My lands border the Mecklenburg."

She nodded, making a mental note to find a map somewhere.

"And what brings you to London? Business or pleasure?"

"Business is ever in a German's mind," he said with a laugh. "But not in his heart. There we find room for . . . sweeter pursuits." He collected her gaze in his and smiled warmly.

Oh, he was a charmer.

As they whirled through another round of steps, he

made her feel as if they were the only two people on the dance floor. He spoke of his interest in shipping and acquiring contacts in international commerce and she told him of her first home in the great American West and how she came to be in London. He confessed that he longed to visit the United States, land of cowboys and gold mines and endless opportunity. When she asked if his duchess enjoyed London, his gaze took on a canny edge.

"I am unmarried, *Fräulein Bumgarten*." He increased the pressure of his hand around hers. "I have only myself to blame. I search the world for the perfect woman. Nothing less will do. One with eyes of sky blue, hair the color of polished mahogany, and a fire in her heart." His hold on her hand grew tighter still. "But where am I to find such an angel?"

She reddened at the implication of the bold words that he clearly intended to describe her. Perhaps she was misreading his flattery. Lord knew, she was no expert on Continental customs. It could be that German nobles were raised to different standards of propriety from Brits or Americans.

"Well, if I run into such a lady, Your Grace, I will be sure to send her your way."

He chuckled, drawing her into a mischievous laugh as the waltz drew to a close. He surprised her by continuing to hold her hand discreetly after the music faded away. He asked earnestly for another dance, being "so reluctant to part with you after only having found such a rare and companionable young beauty."

She was a sucker for blatant admiration.

The next dance was not as lively, but the slower pace gave them more of a chance to talk.

"Horses," she informed him, were her family's trade at

her Nevada home. "Well, horses and silver. We were—are—mining people."

"Horses and silver." He mused on that. "We have a great tradition in Prussia—excuse me—*Germany*, of breeding horses for battle and for show. If someday you come to my country, you must see the Lipizzaner stallions. They are silver and white horses that are trained to do the most remarkable things . . . to perform the dressage and do the airs above the ground. You know this, yes? The airs?"

"I don't believe I've ever heard of them."

"Remarkable things. To stand on hind legs and jump and lunge through the air . . . is most extraordinary. These horses were bred first by the Hapsburg royalty for battle. Spanish and Arabian stock increased the strength and endurance." He studied her. "You ride, then?"

"Do I ever. But there are so few places in London for a truly pleasurable ride. Hyde Park's 'Rotten Row' and Serpentine are always so crowded and scrutinized. I am used to open spaces where you can give your mount his head. I love flying across the countryside with the wind in my hair and the sun on my face. So much better than sitting primly and having to match pace to every other horse and rider on a simple path."

She halted. He was watching her keenly and his hand had once again tightened on hers. "I'm sorry, I didn't mean to go on so."

"Think nothing of it," he said with a smile that didn't quite reach his eyes. "You Americans, you have the reputation for living free, yes? And I would love to see you riding so—with your magnificent hair unbound and your face to the sun. You have the free spirit, Fräulein Bum—"

"Frances, please." She dared correct his address in the name of forming a more interesting connection. "Or Frankie. Family and friends call me that."

"A 'little name'?"

"We call it a 'pet name.'"

"Ah. You honor me with such permission. Then you must address me as Maximillian. Alas, my family had no 'pet name' for me." He made a moue of a face that bordered on the adorable. "They were serious and dutiful people."

"Something tells me you are of a different stripe," she said, smiling.

He blinked. "Stripe? I have no stripes."

She laughed softly. "It just means you are different from them. Like a horse of a different color."

"I see." He seemed to relax and whirled her around in an elegant spin that required him to hold her tighter. "Alas, I am indeed my parents' son. Ottenbergs breed true. Duty and determination are passed on in the bone and sinew. That and a burning desire for beauty."

She could have sworn his eyes glinted, but the next moment the music ended and she spotted her mother standing at the edge of the dance floor, making a show of conversing with friends but in reality, watching Frankie and her intriguing partner. Frankie felt the duke's presence in the firm pressure of his hand around hers.

Without a word, he conveyed that he intended to have her for a third dance, and she felt oddly conflicted. One dance was simply custom, and two was a display of enjoyment or interest. But three in a row was considered too exclusive, too familiar. It was possible the German duke was unacquainted with the nuances of England's social niceties. Lord knew it took *her* a while to catch on to them, even with the Countess of Kew for a guide.

Thinking of the beloved countess who had tutored her and her younger sisters in society's expectations, Frankie wondered what she would think of the duke's forward behavior. Was this the start of something she would come to celebrate or to regret?

When the music began, the duke took her into his arms, then halted with a start and looked over his shoulder. He removed his hands from her and stepped back, his expression dark and his mouth suddenly a hard line. Reynard Boulton came fully into view with a wicked little smile and a gloved hand presented for hers.

"Forgive the intrusion, old man," Boulton said with more than a hint of insolence. "But I believe this dance was promised to me."

The duke stepped back, gave a stiff bow accompanied by a forced smile—"until later, fräulein"—and strode off the dance floor.

"What the devil do you think you're doing?" she hissed as the Fox set a hand to her waist and steered her into the flow of dancers.

"Saving your reputation," he said with a smile that was clearly meant for everyone but her. "People are starting to talk." He met her eyes for a moment. "Primarily your mother. Good God—that woman. Another dance and she'd have had you wedded and bedded before banns."

She glanced toward her mother's last known location, remembering the suppressed excitement in Elizabeth's face as she watched Frankie with the duke. The *S* in Elizabeth S. Bumgarten did not stand for subtlety.

Curse his hide, Boulton was probably right.

"I should think you would know better, Miss Bumgarten. Displaying such simpleminded fascination with a Prussian."

"Simpleminded—" She bit back few ranch-hand words in favor of something more ladylike. "My dance partners are none of your business."

He was totally unaffected by her censure.

"In fact, you should thank me," he continued, "for preventing you from squandering your reputation on a man you know nothing about."

"And I suppose you know everything there is to know about him. Your stock and trade, right? Knowing everything about everyone."

There was a slight hitch in his otherwise flawless steps, and his features lost some of their customary hauteur. It was then that she realized just how close he held her and how easily they moved together. She slid her hand to his shoulder, meaning to increase the distance between them, but discovered an unexpected muscularity beneath that elegant tailoring. Distracted by the realization that the Fox was hard in more than manner, she looked up and straight into his gaze.

"He is Prussian," he declared, looking away sharply. "That is all one needs to know."

For a moment, his dove gray eyes had seemed softer, more accessible. She was relieved to see only a hint of old bruising on his face.

"And what about being 'Prussian' should disqualify him as a dance partner?"

"They are a hard and militaristic people. They have a passion for guttural consonants, cuckoo clocks, and fat liver sausages. Their nobility rule with an iron hand, and when they see something they want, they take it." He glanced away, checking their progress on the floor. "There. You now have all you need to know about Prussians and your fascinating duke."

Something in the tenor of his voice and the way he avoided looking at her made her wonder if something more than just outraged propriety caused him to intervene so crassly. After he brought her uncle Red home the other night, she had considered that he actually might feel some responsibility, however reluctantly, toward their family because of his ties to Daisy's husband. But this—stepping in to save her from herself—this was beyond the pale.

"Good to know you're such an expert on nationalities," she said, determined to show him she wouldn't be intimidated. Since there were a number of measures left in the dance and they had to talk about something. "What can you tell me about the French? One Frenchman in particular. I believe his name is Julian Fontaine. He is the maestro of the orchestra providing this lovely music. What do you know about him?"

He put another inch between them, and she noted the way he retreated into superiority.

"Why should I know anything about him?" he said, glancing away. "He is a *musician*."

"A very talented musician. The conductor of a fine and sought-after chamber orchestra."

"It sounds as if you've already made a thorough study of your own."

"Not nearly as thorough as I would like," she said, making a point of looking through the dancers toward the orchestra.

"You do have eccentric tastes, Miss Bumgarten," he said frostily. "Dukes. Musicians. Prussians. Frenchmen."

"Not all Prussians, just Maximillian. And not all Frenchmen, just Julian." They happened to be passing the orchestra at that moment and she turned her head to glimpse the handsome conductor, knowing that Boulton watched her with a frown. He was under the impression that she was asking about Fontaine for herself and didn't like it. *Ooooooh*. A trickle of excitement wound through her. "Do you think he's handsome?"

"I don't think about him at all." He was growing downright testy. "He is a musician."

She craned her neck to look past his shoulder at Fontaine, and felt Boulton broaden the distance between them yet again.

"I think he's absolutely dreamy."

He left her at the edge of the dance floor, with an irritable nod that gave her a twinge of guilty pleasure. She'd managed to rile him. *Mr. Know-it-All. Mr. Smooth-and-Worldly. Mr. He-Stoops-to-Conquer*. Why would her presumed interest in other gentlemen concern him in the least?

Unless he had taken a more personal interest in her reputation.

In the midst of those musings, her mother appeared at her elbow and drew her out the nearest door and up the stairs to the ladies' retiring room.

"A duke, Frances. *Heaven above*, what splendid luck! You must be on your best manners here—none of your Nevada nonsense tonight." She pulled Frankie closer on the stairs and lowered her voice. "No flirting or dallying with other gentlemen—especially not that impossible Reynard Boulton. What were you thinking, abandoning the Duke of Ottenberg for a turn around the floor with that miscreant?"

"I didn't exactly have a choice," she said, bracing for a barrage of advice intended to turn her into better matrimonial bait. "Mr. Boulton cut in and insisted I had promised him the dance. Objecting would have caused a scene."

Elizabeth looked around to be certain no one could hear them.

"Of all the nerve. The man's not yet a viscount, and he has the gall to interfere with a *duke's* choice of partner."

She put her arm through Frankie's as they climbed the stairs and traversed the upper hall to the ladies' retiring room.

"Well, no matter. It's clear the duke is smitten with you. And why wouldn't he be?" She patted Frankie's hand. "You're a prize, Frances. A perfect gem of a prospective bride."

Frances. Frankie cringed. When her mother used her given name, she was either being wrapped in praise meant to confine her on a pedestal or was in trouble and headed for much worse. In this instance, it was probably both. Her mother now saw her as a potential duchess and wouldn't give her a moment's peace until she was wedded, bedded, and the subject of bragging rights. And despite the duke's obvious attractions—she flexed her hand, remembering his forceful grip—she wasn't yet certain that becoming the Duchess of Ottenberg was desirable.

I've never even tasted a liver sausage.

Chapter Four

Cheeky little flirt. Reynard Boulton watched Frankie's mother appropriate her and usher her out of the ballroom—no doubt for a lecture on how to hook and land a Prussian duke.

He had been fiercely aware of Frankie Bumgarten from the moment she stepped into the ballroom. Those flashing blue eyes . . . that lustrous chestnut hair . . . that curvaceous little body that had ridden his thoughts like a thoroughbred, again and again in the past few days.

Since that night in her darkened house, when he'd caught her in the kitchen in her nightgown, he had had the most unsettling physical reaction to her. Even an incidental recall of those moments earned him a revisitation of the heat and arousal he'd felt. Those eyes, that full mouth, the swell of her breasts—she'd been bare as birthing day under that nightgown, he'd stake his reputation on it. Standing in her uncle's room, bathed in moonlight, she was the most luscious female he'd seen in—hell, he'd never seen any woman who could make him respond like that. You'd think his john thomas was Prussian—it practically clicked its heels in salute.

He hadn't been himself, since. Irritable and feeling like

he was never in the right place or doing quite the right thing. Distracted and overly aware of his body and all manner of heightened sensations. The woman bashed him in the head with a bread paddle, for God's sake, and just tonight, he had warned off randy suitors and interrupted the attentions paid to her by that arrogant Prussian that Tutty was toadying to—only to have her fix her fickle attention on a musician!

Enough! His promise to watch over her family did not extend to suffering turmoil in his flesh and hazarding his sanity every time he encountered her.

He pulled down his vest, brushed his sleeves, and determined not to think of her again this evening. He strolled through the halls and down to the parlor of Tutty's ridiculously mirrored house. *One would think, with daughters like his, the man would keep reflected images to a minimum.* As he walked, keeping an eye out for tonight's host and any encounters Tutty might have with guests, he took in snippets of conversations.

"... terrific on the rail, but can't come from outside ..." Horsemen.

"... ghastly green with all of that frumpy tulle ..." Fashion mavens.

"... can't afford the losses, then he shouldn't play ..." Ahhh.

He paused and made a show of checking his pocket watch. Here was a conversation he needed to hear. But before the subject of the gossip was made clear, a uniformed servant appeared with a note on a tray. The young fellow stood in the middle of the salon, looking confused, clearly having difficulty locating the person he was sent to find. A note for whom? Reynard caught the fellow's eye and beckoned him over.

"I believe that is for me." He snatched the note and the servant withdrew, seeming relieved to have it off his hands.

It was a message from Tutty inviting someone to a meeting in one of the upstairs rooms. A private meeting under cover of his daughter's come-out ball. This was no doubt the confrontation he'd come to witness.

Tutty was known to be deeply in debt and Reynard had received word from a mutual friend that Tutty vowed to rectify that untenable situation shortly. He tucked the note into his inner breast pocket and strolled at a leisurely pace into the great hall and toward the stairs.

The ladies' retiring room was full to overflowing with women seeking relief in the porcelain-lined bathing room's "necessary." Under the stress of waiting to be relieved, women chatted openly about the dancing, those in attendance, and the occasional intrigues they witnessed.

Elizabeth Bumgarten finished covertly lecturing Frankie on protocol and agreeability and fussing over Frankie's hair and complexion. She used her fan vigorously as she listened to the other women's gossip and complaints, muttered, "'A wholesome tongue is a tree of life,'" and decided to exit. Frankie demurred, saying she would stay a few minutes more to rest her feet before joining her mother in the ballroom . . . ready for another round of dancing with the duke.

Elizabeth searched her daughter with a critical eye, unconvinced of Frankie's appreciation for the marvelous opportunity that had just dropped into her lap. But she departed, and in so doing, seemed to spark an exodus. Half a dozen women followed her out and harried housemaids began to straighten the chaotic room and attached bathing chamber.

Frankie sighed and tucked herself into a chair by an open window. She found herself rubbing her right hand, wondering at the memory of the duke's grip. It was oddly tight and restraining . . . as if he thought she might try to flee in the middle of a dance. What was it Boulton had said about German nobles? "*When they see something they want, they take it.*"

Was his touch a sign of . . . ?

The thought that he might have marked her as a matrimonial prize as surely and emphatically as her mother had marked him was unsettling. What if she didn't want to get married? What if she found the duke overwhelming? What if she hated clicking heels and cuckoo clocks?

Would her mother care how she felt or listen to her objections? She thought of the steely purpose just now in Elizabeth Bumgarten's eyes. For the first time since they came to London, Frankie felt the true threat of her mother's relentless determination to—

"He kissed you?"

The door had burst open and in flooded Ardith Tutty and a trio of other young women, including the speaker.

"He did!" The deb of the hour was flushed and walking on tiptoes, radiant with the pleasure of her romantic progress. "Though I had to make it easy for him. Carlton Laroche is not the most forward of gentlemen." She rolled her eyes, drawing titters from the others.

"But what about your father?" another girl asked. "If you can get a proposal out of Laroche, will he really turn it down?"

"What about Marcella?" the third girl chimed in.

So, Tutty's rumored declaration that the eldest must marry first was real, and these girls thought it as barbaric and impossible as that girl Hazel had. This was yet another secret she would rather not have had confirmed.

"Oh, I'm not worried," Ardith said with a saucy air. "Marcella has a plan to take care of that. Fairly soon, in fact."

The others were surprised by her confidence.

"Really? She has her cap set for someone?"

"Who has she selected as her victim?"

They laughed while Ardith just smiled, her eyes twinkling with mischief.

Secrets. Everywhere. Frankie crept around the tester bed when they entered the bathing room as a group, and she kept to the cover of the bed drapes, trying to purge their wicked laughter from her mind. She was going straight back to the ballroom, even if it meant dancing with the duke under her mother's scrutiny. Then she remembered . . .

Cece! She was supposed to keep her mother busy for a while. She didn't know how long they had been gone from the ballroom, but she hoped it was long enough for Cece to accomplish her mission.

Reynard reached the upper hall, checked first one room, then another, finding most locked and quickly realizing he had the wrong hallway. He quickened his step and proceeded through the great hall, into the other wing. The first room was open, but dark and unoccupied. In the next, he found lamps burning and a couple of old cods with their feet up, smoking cigars. He left them to their privacy and continued to the third room, which showed evidence of recent use—full ashtrays, drained whiskey decanters, and a collection of straight chairs gathered around a table. He strolled around the room, finding no cards or chips, nothing to hint at the identity or purpose of the men who had spent time here.

Had he missed it? Was he too late?

Whoever the note was meant to fetch probably knew where the meeting would be held. He just had to continue his search. He exited the room and hadn't taken two steps before he saw Frankie Bumgarten step out into the hall several doors away.

Her again! That was probably the ladies' retiring room. At the most inconvenient—he did not want to have to deal with her while in the midst of an important—

He grabbed the next doorknob he came to and ducked into a dimly lighted room where he paused with his eye to the crack he left open to watch her pass. Only she didn't pass, at least not right away. He held his breath until somebody behind him spoke and startled him into turning.

"Well, hello there." It was a woman's strident voice and it took a moment searching the room to locate the speaker. On the bed. His eyes widened. In *dishabille*. His jaw dropped as he recognized the woman reclining on the end of the large tester bed. Marcella Tutty.

"Miss Tutty?" he said so quietly he wasn't sure he'd spoken aloud.

"Who are"—she squinted, searching—"oh!" Apparently, she was expecting someone else. "Reynard Boulton, as I live and breathe." She sat up holding a bit of sheet to her, and he realized her shoulders were bare. Ye gods, was she naked beneath that sheet?

"I beg your pardon. I've intruded. I was simply—"

"Reynard, you rascal, I know exactly what you were doing." She pulled at the sheet until it came untucked and he watched in horror as her naked legs and bony feet slid to the floor. She bunched up the fabric around her, holding it in place with her thin arms at her sides, and came toward him. "You got my note."

With whatever she had planned interrupted by his appearance, she apparently decided to seize the opportunity he presented. In a heartbeat, she was inches away and reaching for his vest buttons. He grabbed for the door handle, but a moment later had to abandon it because he needed both hands to fend off her astonishingly agile fingers.

"Miss Tutty—Marcella—really! Cease this immediately."

She tried to push his coat from his shoulders and had half his vest buttons loose before he realized stronger measures were required. "Marcella!" He seized her by the shoulders, trying to hold her off, but she apparently thought it quite the game and redoubled her efforts to disrobe him and drag him toward the bed.

Frankie saw him as he stepped out into the hallway, watched him spot her, and recognized the "aw, hell" look on his face as he opened the nearest door and slipped inside. She halted, glaring at the door he hadn't closed fully behind him. How dare he be so blatant in his attempt to escape her? Would it have killed him to nod or say, "We meet again, Miss B?"

Raising her chin, she continued down the hall, determined not to let his foul temper and bad manners spoil her evening. There was, after all, a charming duke downstairs, one who would take her into his arms and dance her into exhaustion. This time if he wanted a third dance, she would see he got it.

Her step faltered as she came even with the door—left open a good three inches. Sloppy of him to forget to close—

"Ohhh, Reyyynnard." A woman's breathless voice floated out into the comparative silence of the hall. "I'm yours."

Shocked, she was at the door before she could stop herself. She did, however, manage to halt at the opening. Her heart beat faster as she heard his muffled voice say something like "yrmaddmrcella."

"Everyone knows what a wicked boy you are." Her

voice sounded more determined and there was a scrape of movement. "Come and turn me into a wicked girl. I'm yours, Reynard. All yours."

"Let go, Marcella." His voice was louder now and stern.

Every instinct Frankie possessed said she should walk away, and just let him have his hideous little tryst with—Marcella? The secrets she'd been privy to that evening converged in a rush of insight, and she scowled and widened the crack to peer inside the room.

Reynard was in the process of being divested of his garments by a rail-thin, half-naked woman coaxing him to take advantage of her "charms." It was such a shocking scene that she didn't know whether to flee, interrupt, or just laugh. The latter won—albeit a half-strangled version that came out as a hiccup-gasp that resounded in the room.

Both Reynard and Marcella turned to the door and saw her staring at them. Reynard lurched back, trying to take advantage of the young woman's surprise to escape, but Marcella grabbed the tail of his coat and held on for all she was worth. They stared at each other, then at Frankie in horror. Neither gave an inch until Frankie's voice shattered the stalemate.

"What on earth?"

Marcella, seeing that her seduction was a failure, released Reynard's coat, sank to the floor, and began to scream bloody murder.

Frankie froze, but Reynard quickly buttoned his coat and held out his hands, trying to quiet Marcella.

"Shhhh, Marcella! Good God, woman, you'll bring half the city down on you!" Every word he spoke and each move he made toward her caused her to scream all the louder.

Frankie found herself thrust abruptly into the room and off to one side as several men shoved past her to enter. Sir

Marion, the head of that delegation, stopped dead, staring in shock at the shameful tableau that greeted them. One of the men turned up the gas lamp, and the yellow light washed the rumpled bed, disturbed rug, and half-naked female on the floor in stark, pitiless relief.

"Oh, Father—he—it was his fault!" Marcella cried, lifting her head long enough for Sir Marion to glimpse the agony in her pinched face. "He seduced me—"

Sobs took over again and as she lay on the floor in a pitiful heap, Frankie had difficulty believing that such a display of misery and despair would possibly be faked. If she hadn't seen what happened with her own eyes, she would think Reynard a monster for seducing and shaming the poor, vulnerable girl. But only a moment before she had seen with her own eyes Marcella trying to strip Reynard Boulton of his clothes and drag him bodily to her bed.

Sir Marion's face was pale and his lip trembled, but he made no move to comfort his disgraced daughter. When Reynard headed for the door declaring, "She's mad as a hatter," Tutty's friends came out of their shock to grab and restrain him. Outraged, they snarled threats, insults, and accusations of all manner of foul, unprincipled deeds.

A moment later, Ardith Tutty rushed into the room and, after surveying with dismay the room's occupants, rushed to kneel by her wailing sister. "What has he done to you, my sweet Marcella?"

"He tried to have his way with—" Marcella allowed herself to be pulled into Ardith's arms. "He p-promised to m-marry me."

"My poor, dear, innocent sister," Ardith moaned, rocking her gently.

Tutty hurried to close the door to prevent the people collecting in the hallway from hearing more of what was happening. One last figure forced his way through the door before Tutty sealed it: the Duke of Ottenberg.

Tutty collected himself and turned on Reynard with a display of righteous fury. "How dare you? What kind of monster would enter a man's home under the guise of friendship and seduce his precious daughter?"

"I did not touch your daughter, sir," Reynard declared. "I was looking for a meeting—I was sent a note summoning me to—I thought it came from you. It's in my breast pocket."

"I sent no such note."

"See for yourself," Reynard demanded. "It's there in my pocket." One of Tutty's friends delved into his pocket and handed the note to Tutty.

Sir Marion opened and read it, and his face paled. His gaze flicked back and forth as if he were searching for a response, then he drew himself up and crumpled the note in his fist.

"It means nothing. Anyone could have written this."

"This is an outrage." Reynard struggled against his captors, but after a moment, seemed to come to himself and planted his feet to face his accusers. "I opened the door—seeking the meeting I was summoned to—and found Miss Tutty reclining on the bed in the very state of undress you see now. She obviously mistook me for someone else." He jerked a nod at the wailing seductress. "I had no idea she was in the room."

His denials did nothing to convince Tutty and friends of his innocence. Frankie, who was pressed against the wall beside the door, watched the furtive glances Ardith and Marcella exchanged. This, she was convinced, was the "something" Marcella had in mind to snare a husband.

Lord, what a nasty piece of work she was; prowling

alley cat one moment and pathetic mewling victim the next. And unless someone spoke up, Reynard Boulton might very well be railroaded into a lifetime of misery, married to the deceitful witch.

"He's telling the truth," she said, stepping out from the wall, raising her chin as the men turned on her in disbelief.

"Who are you?" one of Tutty's friends demanded. "And what in blazes are you doing here?"

"Frances Bumgarten. Sir Marion knows me." She glanced at their host and his face darkened in displeasure. She hurried on before they could banish her from the room. "I was coming down the hallway when I saw Mr. Boulton approach and open the door. As I reached the door, I heard raised voices and noticed the door had been left partway open. I confess to a shameful curiosity—I peered inside." She braced, determined to speak the truth of what she saw.

"Miss Tutty, Marcella, was entreating Mr. Boulton to join her on the bed, using language I cannot repeat. He tried to leave, but she insisted and"—she swallowed hard—"and she tried to remove his coat."

There was an audible intake of breath.

"Why would you say such a thing?" Marcella wailed. "She's jealous—they're all jealous of me."

Frankie blinked, astounded by the charge, and looked from one man to another, trying to read their reactions to her testimony and Marcella's accusation. One by one, they looked at Reynard and then at Marcella, who had ceased her vigorous sobbing in order to watch her future unfold. Under their scrutiny, she did her best to look bereft and wronged, but came off looking simply peevish. Sarah Bernhardt she was not.

The last face Frankie glimpsed was that of the Duke of

Ottenberg, standing at the back of the room, leaning against the fireplace mantel, seeming rather amused. That twist of a smirk did nothing for his looks. Did he not believe her? What was he doing here, anyway?

"I can tell you, gentlemen," she declared, focusing on Sir Marion, "that Mr. Boulton could not have had time to disrobe Miss Tutty, much less disgrace her before I came upon them. I don't know why she was naked in bed up here, while her younger sister's party was going on downstairs, but from what I heard her say, I believe she was as surprised to see Mr. Boulton as he was to see her."

She looked at Reynard and then at Sir Marion, holding her breath as a pregnant silence descended. One of the men restraining Reynard released his arm, and a second later, the other dropped his hold. Their faces showed sympathy for Sir Marion's plight, but they furtively eyed the door as if wishing to be done with the whole distasteful incident.

She could have sworn Sir Marion's lip curled slightly as he turned to stare at his daughter. Marcella pulled the sheet higher around her, as she felt the mood in the room changing, and she began to show alarm.

"Papa, you must help me." She must have realized it sounded too much like an order, for her voice softened and became a girlish whine. "You must do something—make him pay for what he's done—he must make it right. Oh, pleeeease, Papa. You must rescue me and see my honor restored." In a stroke of theatrical genius, she flung herself toward her father's feet, reaching plaintively for him. "Help me, Papa . . . else I cannot live with this shame!"

Unwittingly, Marcella had just reminded him that her shame would be *his* shame as well. After such a humiliation, Sir Marion would be the scorn of all of London. And if they hoped to keep such a scandal quiet, Marcella had chosen the wrong man to accuse. Reynard Boulton could and likely would destroy them with a few well-placed words.

Recognition, betrayal, and desperation trailed across Sir Marion's face before he straightened, squared his shoulders, and turned to Reynard with grim determination.

"I do not know what happened here, but I cannot allow my daughter's honor to be questioned." He flung the crumpled note he still held at Reynard's feet. "You, sir—I shall have satisfaction from you."

The walls themselves seemed to inhale in shock.

"What?" Reynard was stunned. He looked at Frankie, then at Sir Marion as if he'd been sucker-punched.

"See here, Tutty, you can't mean that," one of his friends declared.

"That is madness," the other said, rushing to Sir Marion's side. "No one has dueled in England in fifty years! It's a relic—archaic—not to mention bloody illegal!"

His stunned companions attempted to dissuade him from the challenge he had just issued, but Sir Marion was firm in his decision. He would defend his compromised daughter on the field of honor. He would pit his lifeblood against Reynard's. Nothing less would erase the stain Marcella's predicament had brought on her family's good name.

Frankie could scarcely breathe. She stared at Reynard, whose gray eyes were now silver with heat. His smile grew slowly.

"I shall show you more consideration than you have just shown me," Reynard said with icy calm, stepping closer to Sir Marion to engage his eyes. "As the challenged party, it is my right to choose the weapon. I choose pistols." There were gasps and murmurs of dismay; pistols were deadly. As he stared at the older man, his expression could have frozen the Thames in July. "With a blade, I assure you, you would have no chance with me. My second will contact yours."

Following that, he strode out the door, his eyes on Frankie the whole way.

Chapter Five

Frankie watched the glow of Claire's face in the family coach on the way home later, and she scowled. She prayed it was dark enough to hide the pleasure radiating from her sister. Thankfully, their mother was too absorbed in the evening's strange ending to pay attention to Claire—the only one of her daughters who never caused her a moment's worry.

"What could possibly have caused the Tuttys to withdraw from their own ball? It's unprecedented. Unthinkable." Elizabeth shook her head. "It must have been something drastic. Lady Audrey Kessing said she heard servants say that one of Sir Marion's daughters had taken ill. But Admiral Lofton insisted there was a confrontation between some prominent gentlemen. He said he heard raised voices and saw some men rushing for the doors.

"What did you hear?" she asked, pinning Frankie with a look.

"Very little." She struggled to look sincere. "I was too busy dancing and being agreeable to our titled brethren." She smiled, knowing she had just dragged a major distraction into her mother's mind.

"Yes. A pity the duke left so early. But at least he did

take leave of you and suggest he wishes to see you again. That's something." She sat back, thinking on that, but soon returned to the mystery of the Tuttys' withdrawal. "Well, I'll find out what happened, sooner or later." She looked back at Frankie. "I bet that rascal Reynard Boulton knows."

That he does, Frankie thought, *and for once he probably wishes he hadn't a clue.* Personally, she was glad that the part she played at the evening's demise was unknown, and she prayed it would stay that way. As they rolled through the darkened streets, she closed her eyes against the brief flashes of light provided by the streetlamps they passed and lay her head against the frame of the coach window.

Still under the spell of the look Reynard gave her as he exited the bedchamber, she felt her entire body taut as a bowstring and starting to ache with tension. Those silver eyes, so full of anger, passion, and recognition, had bored right into her soul. Sweet Lord, she'd never had a man look at her like that. He was highly mannered, clever, and socially adept, but that look revealed a ferocity and raw male power that she would never have guessed lay beneath his oh-so-refined public face.

It had only taken an instant for her to memorize a look that she sensed would stay with her for the rest of her life. She had exited the bedchamber after him and had seen him make his way down the grand stairs. There, he corralled Carlton Laroche and that Stevenson fellow he had been with earlier, and dragged them with him out the front doors.

A duel. He'd been challenged to a fight. Was that like a Main Street draw-down between gunslingers? An image of Reynard Boulton lying dead in the dust of the OK Corral made her stomach do a slow grind. Was that how they did it here? Face each other and see who can shoot first? It was Reynard who chose pistols and said that Sir Marion should be glad he hadn't chosen swords—Sir Marion wouldn't have stood a chance.

Dear God. Would they really try to kill each other over that scheming, deceitful Marcella? Meet each other at high noon and fill each other full of lead? What if they both died? Much as Reynard annoyed and dismissed her, she couldn't bear to think that something would happen to him. And just when did he become *Reynard* in her thoughts? No doubt he would be appalled by such familiarity.

She hurried straight to her room when they arrived home, prepared for bed, and was a little surprised when Claire crept into her room a short while later with a sweet, dreamy smile. She had all but forgotten her secondary mission of the evening.

"Thank you, thank you, Frankie—a million times over!" Claire hugged her tightly, and then took her by the hands and pulled her to a seat on the bed. "Oh, my gosh—if you only knew—I don't know how to tell you how wonderful it was. It was simply *magical.*"

"You played for him?" Frankie asked, knowing the answer before she asked.

"*With* him, Frankie. *With* him." Cece looked as if she might float above her seat on the bed. "He and his orchestra were playing a concerto—Max Bruch's Violin Concerto in G Minor, one of the best violin concertos ever written, it's so complex and melodic—which they do sometimes as a break for the dancers and to showcase some of the musicians. Oh, my God, Frankie, what a violinist he is!"

Frankie groaned. This was worse than she expected.

"What did you do?"

"I was spellbound at first, listening. Every legato, every adagio, was pure Heaven. I closed my eyes and the music took me over. The next thing I knew I was playing counterpoint to his lead and he turned and stared at me in surprise.

I thought at first that he might stop the music and order me out of the ballroom. But after a moment, he smiled and continued to play his part with occasional pauses to allow me to pick up the main theme. It was like he *invited* me into his music. It was amazing. I don't think I've ever played so well in my life."

That was saying something, for her younger sister was nothing short of a virtuoso with a violin. Her talent astounded all who heard her play.

"So, what happened after that?" Frankie prodded. "Did you talk to him? Did he ask your name or compliment your playing?"

Cece's sweet face was radiant as she delved into priceless memories.

"When the piece ended, he handed the lead to his first violin for a lovely Brahms quartet that is so lyrical you can almost see the fawns frolicking in the—"

"The man, Cece, tell me about the man! Is he as handsome up close as he seems from a distance?"

"Ohhh, yes." Cece fell back on the bed, arms flung wide in ecstasy, and practically melted on the counterpane. "He is divine. His hair is nearly black and his eyes are the most beautiful russet brown. He's tall and gallant and has a lyrical French accent. Every word he speaks sounds like it belongs in a love letter." She sighed. "He invited me to a rehearsal next week." She looked reverently at her hand. "And he kissed my hand as we parted."

"Lord above." Frankie winced. "Rein it up, will you? You've hardly even talked to the man."

Claire sat up sharply and fixed a surprisingly lucid gaze on her.

"We more than talked, Frankie. We *played* together. We shared part of our souls with each other. It was so much more than speaking—it was *communion*." She straightened, squeezed Frankie's arm, and declared, "I'm going to spend the rest of my life learning the depths of the love and the music in Julian Fontaine's heart."

Frankie studied Cece's determination and groaned.

She knew this was going to be trouble. Lord help her, she couldn't bring herself to heap any one of a thousand possible objections on Cece's optimism. There were plenty of others more than willing to stuff her sister's sweet, imaginative spirit into a rut of tradition and duty.

"Promise me you'll be careful and not do anything rash."

Claire's expression took on a lucidity that surprised Frankie.

"I have both feet planted firmly on the ground. I know what I want and what I'm fated to do. And I'll do my best to make it happen with as little commotion as possible. I promise."

"Oh, Cece—sweet Cece—I want only what's best for you." She reached out to stroke her sister's soft cheek.

"I know, Frankie." With her own news spent, Cece now sensed the tension that Frankie carried like a bad kipper in her stomach.

"So how was your evening?" she asked, jiggling Frankie's hands.

"Not nearly as special as yours." Frankie shrugged, trying to seem casual. "A duke, a few dances, and another of Mama's lectures on how important it is to be gracious and accommodating to our marriageable 'betters.'"

"Oh." Cece grimaced. "Sorry."

"I'll survive. There was one dance with Reynard Boulton—that gossipy fellow who was so arrogant and inhospitable at Daisy's wedding." She wrinkled her nose.

"Two left feet?" Claire asked with genuine sympathy.

"No, just one of each. He is actually a good dancer.

But he still acts like I'm a country bumpkin who has to be ordered to behave."

Claire sighed. "I'm so sorry you had a difficult time while I—"

"Don't you dare let my disappointment spoil your wonderful evening, Cece." She opened her arms and gave her sister a warm hug, praying that she hadn't made a terrible mistake by enabling Cece's musical rendezvous. "But I'm warning you, if that fiddle player breaks your heart, I will personally break that handsome nose of his."

Cece laughed, but Frankie was suddenly back to thoughts of grievous bodily harm and the peril to "that gossipy fellow."

"Say, did you see Uncle Red downstairs?" she asked. "I wanted to ask him something."

"No, but I bet he's in the study," Cece said. "He's there most nights."

Minutes later, Frankie found Red in the book-lined study he had taken over as his sanctuary in recent months. He sat behind a large walnut desk with his feet up and the cold remnants of a cigar clenched between his teeth. The gas lamp by the door was turned down, and his sun-weathered face looked worn and lined in the glow from the lamp on his desk. Civilized living was taking a toll on him. He looked up and smiled.

"What are you doing up this time of night?" He pushed back from the desk and patted his knee like he had when she was six. "I thought you all went to bed an hour ago. How was the shindig?"

"Fine, I guess." She crossed her arms and settled on the edge of the desk, facing him. She hadn't climbed onto his lap for a story in twelve years. Sometimes he forgot that she was a woman grown. "I met a duke from Germany who seemed to like me."

He gave a wry smile. "Bet that made Lizzie's night."

"Well, it gave her someone to chew on besides me."

He threw back his head and laughed in a way she realized she hadn't heard in a while. The twinkle in his eyes made her think how much she'd missed his scandalous good humor.

"I couldn't sleep, so I thought I'd come down to ask you something."

"Yeah? Fire away, girlie. But there ain't much I know that you don't, these days."

"What is a duel? I mean, how does it work? Is it like a Western gunfight?"

"Duel? Why would you ask—" He shot upright in his chair searching her visually. "Dang an' hang me! I missed some fun tonight, didn't I?" His grin grew as wide as the Missouri River. "What happened?"

"Well, I'm not entirely sure." She prayed she would be forgiven for that small lie. "But the Tuttys—they were the hosts—got upset over something and withdrew from the guests, sending word via servants that they would not return. It was clear the dance was over, so we all called for our carriages and headed home. As we waited, I heard talk that somebody might be fighting a duel."

"Spit an' roast me!" He looked away for a moment. "A real duel. There ain't been one here in years. These pinkie-up English got laws against it." He thought about it for a moment, scratching his grizzled chin. "From what I hear—two blokes with a grudge face up with either swords or guns. If it's guns, they take turns shootin' at each other. If it's swords, they go at it and whack and jab until somebody draws blood. Unless they're *real* mad at each other, in which case they fight until somebody's dead."

"But how does it work? And where do they do it?"

"Don't know all the dots an' tittles, but they have to do it someplace the law can't see, that's for sure."

"That sounds crazy to me. They just stand there and take turns shooting at each other until one of them gets lucky? That makes no sense."

"No crazier than high noon in the streets of Abilene or Tombstone. Gunslingers just get it over faster. I guess these English blokes like to prove their steel by staring down bullets one at a time." He studied her as she digested his conclusion.

"What are you up to, Frankie? You got that 'I'm about to do somethin' Mama won't like' look about you."

"Who, me? You know better than that, Uncle Red." She slid off the desk and leaned down to give him a peck on the cheek. "Good night."

Red watched with narrowed eyes as she exited into the darkened center hall. He knew Lizzie's girls better than Lizzie did. And *that* one knew something she wasn't supposed to know—he'd bet his best saddle on it. He needed to find out what it was before her mother did.

There was one bloke in town who knew everything about everybody, and he had a pretty good notion where to find him.

Red was often a guest of members in the best gentlemen's clubs in London. As a class-blind American, he had bestowed his Nevada stories and ribald wisdom on the doormen and night porters who controlled access to their members' elite premises. He had become a favorite among them, and when he arrived at the side door of the Athenaeum Club asking for Reynard Boulton, the porter not only admitted him, but personally ushered him to the bar, where he found Reynard in the company of two gents he recognized but couldn't have named with a gun to his head.

"Aww, hell." The Fox saluted with a half-empty glass of whiskey. "Red S-Strait. My n-night's now com-plete."

"Boy howdy. You fellers look like you had a heck of a night." Red slid into a seat across the table from Reynard, taking in his reddened eyes and sloppy diction. "I musta missed a chance for a real rip-snorter."

"D-dood ye ebber," said a tall, beefy fellow with a York-shire accent. Red knew it was Yorkshire because he had a farrier from York tend to his horses' hooves, and he could barely understand a word the man said. This bloke looked like he was about to slide underneath the table.

"What's this I hear about a duel?" he asked.

Reynard groaned. "News travels fas-s-st."

"And bad news travels faster. So, who's doin' the honors?" Red charged ahead, figuring that since the Fox was all liquored up he could skip the niceties. The boy seemed to be in a royal mood. "Where an' when?"

Reynard looked up from his glass, studied Red for a minute, and heaved a hard breath. "A couple o' days, I guess. S-somewhere constables are deaf an' blind."

The big fellow collapsed senseless on the tabletop with a thud, and the other bloke looked like he'd be joining him shortly. After a minute Red fixed his stare on Reynard. The boy could sure hold his liquor.

"Well?" Red prompted.

"Well what?"

"Who?"

"Guess" was all Reynard would say. And he stared right back.

It slowly dawned.

"*You?*" Red practically jumped out of his chair. "You're one of th' poor bastards?"

Reynard nodded miserably, looking like there wasn't enough whiskey in the world to make him forget that fact.

"Who's the other fella?"

It took a minute and another gulp of whiskey for Reynard to respond.

"Marion T-Tutty."

"The bloke that gave the party tonight? Jesus—this just gets better an' better." Red beckoned the waiter over and ordered a gin and tonic. Reynard raised one eyebrow, apparently still sober enough to question Red's uncharacteristic choice of liquor. Red sighed and explained, "I'm cuttin' down."

He studied Reynard for a minute. "I figure you got more sense than to try settlin' anything with a pistol, so I'm guessin' he did the callin' out. What'd ye do to make him want to put holes in yer hide?"

"I wouldn' marry his horse-faced daughter."

Red burst out laughing and then called out to the barman. "Forget th' gin, Wally. Bring me a glass and a bottle o' fire-breathin' *Irish*."

Chapter Six

It was chilly, damp, and still mostly dark three mornings later, as Frankie hid in the alley beside their house and watched Uncle Red exit the front doors onto the quiet tree-lined street. As expected, he headed in the direction of the stable where they kept their horses. She waited just a minute, searching the predawn murkiness, before stepping into the street.

She felt conspicuous in her disguise and oddly exhilarated by her mission. Cece's assurance that no one would know she wasn't an upper-crust youth in her trousers, stiff collar, and bowler hat, wasn't enough to relieve her qualms. Cece, after all, was only just awakening to the fact that there were two sexes walking the earth.

She told herself that she was excited to see a secretive part of the world of men. From what she'd learned, Red was right, there hadn't been a confirmed duel in decades. This was an historic chance to learn something about men's private dealings. But down deep, she knew more was involved and she suspected that "more" had to do with Reynard Boulton. She wanted to see what he would do with such a challenge, and to learn if that look he gave her at Tutty's truly came from tempered steel at the core of him.

A small part of her admitted to excitement at seeing him again, watching him move, seeing his eyes silver with emotion, sensing the power and potency in him. Deeper still, there was a concern that something bad might happen to him and she might never—what? Figure out the coil of passions that drove him? Decide whether she liked him or loathed him?

Once Red was out on the street, she slipped into the stable, handed the groom his payment, and mounted a dappled gray hire that was saddled and waiting. She had planned carefully and feared that Aramis, her sure-footed roan, would give her away to her uncle. What she hadn't counted on was the rough seams of her newly purchased trousers chafing the insides of her thighs as she rode. She soon spotted her uncle riding at a brisk pace toward the edge of town, and struck off a safe distance behind him.

Red's course took them out of town, along a river and past a village that was only beginning to stir. Farmers were heading for pasture to bring in cows for milking, smells of pan bread and sausages cooking drifted by on the breeze, and the jingle of harnesses being rigged for hauling and harvesting could be heard. After a time, they entered a mist-laden wood of tall oaks and slender lindens. Red slowed and Frankie reined up in order to avoid running into him. She sensed they were getting near the location when he dismounted and led his horse off through the trees.

She followed suit and soon came upon an oval-shaped clearing in the trees that spanned a rutted path occupied by four coaches with a number of riding horses hitched to the rear of them.

Red walked his mount over to a coach, exchanged a few words with the driver, and tied his mount to the rear of the vehicle. Then he joined several men in a group at one side of the clearing, greeting them solemnly, talking softly in the rising light.

She led her mount around to the same coach and learned from the driver that it was Reynard Boulton's hire. She tied up her mount on the far side of the coach and tried to imitate a typical male swagger as she made a wide circle through the trees and came up behind several spectators to watch.

She had arrived just in time. A gentleman garbed in undertaker black, wearing a silk top hat and black gloves, took the center of the clearing and called the challenger and challenged forward. After a brief meeting where the rules were explained, both principals—Reynard and Tutty—nodded agreement and were forced to shake hands. They retreated eagerly to opposite ends of the oval clearing.

Reynard was accompanied by the two men she'd seen him with at Tutty's ball. Uncle Red stood with them, his feet spread and arms crossed, looking as serious as she had ever seen him. Tutty was accompanied by two men also, and a couple of additional fellows stood halfway between the two parties, one wearing spectacles and bearing a medical bag.

The men with Reynard and Sir Marion were "seconds," whose job it was to try one last time to negotiate a resolution to the problem, a tidbit from the information she'd gathered from Uncle Red. The seconds met briefly at the center of the field and shook hands, looking none too friendly as the black-clad referee presented a wooden case containing two ornate pistols to them. The guns were inspected by the seconds and declared to be acceptable before the men retreated to their principals.

It was then that Frankie noticed yet another observer, positioned several yards into the woods, nearly hidden in the shadows surrounding a massive tree trunk. She squinted and made out dark hair and a square, muscular build. It took a moment for her to realize it was Ottenberg. The duke was supposedly Tutty's friend. Why wasn't he with Sir Marion's men? And why cloak his presence here in shadows?

Reynard stepped farther into the clearing and she moved to the end of the row of onlookers to get a better view of the proceedings. He removed his coat and unbuttoned his vest, handing both off and then running both hands back through his dew-dampened hair. He paused, hands on his waist, feet planted with determination.

His shirt was stark white in the burgeoning light and his perfectly cut trousers emphasized the lean grace of his form. On the other end of the clearing, Tutty was refusing to remove his coat as his seconds requested, declaring it wasn't necessary. The physician in attendance was summoned to persuade him and explained that a white shirt would make it easier to see and treat any wound that occurred. Paling, Tutty removed his coat but refused to give up his vest. In the end, they let him have his way and the combatants were called to the center of the field of honor.

Frankie couldn't take her eyes from Reynard. He rolled his shoulders and coolly surveyed the spectators as if memorizing those present. Then his gaze fell on her at the side of the group, and it halted, looking her up and down, focusing with growing intensity on her face.

She felt it the moment he recognized her—a bloom of combustible heat like lightning striking dry grass erupted in her core and her knees went weak. Those eyes, those dove gray eyes glowed silver again and half a dozen emotions crossed his face before it settled into a fierce scowl. She could do nothing but nod to him—a lame wish for good luck, but it was all the moment could afford.

The referee presented the weapons to Tutty and Reynard, allowing Tutty as challenger to choose first. Tutty grabbed the closest pistol and Reynard was left to take up the other one. The referee positioned them back to back and instructed them to take ten paces on his mark, then turn at his signal, and fire at will. Early turning would be considered a breach of honor and satisfaction would be awarded to the non-offending party.

Frankie's heart pounded and her hands curled into chilled fists in her gloves as she watched Reynard's steady strides and the way he held the pistol upright by his shoulder. His manner was contained and assured.

Sir Marion, on the other hand, appeared to wobble a bit with each step, as if his knees were about to give out. She could have sworn the barrel of his pistol shook as he reached his mark.

"Turn!" the referee barked. When they'd done so he added, "Fire at will."

Tutty frantically raised his pistol and fired at Reynard.

The report of the gun stopped Frankie's heart for a second. As the smoke from the barrel dissipated, Reynard remained planted, facing his adversary shoulder first to present a smaller target.

Her knees went weak at the sight of his undamaged form standing straight and true. A shocked murmur went through the spectators.

Tutty's shot had gone wide. He missed!

Not a breath was taken or let as Reynard lowered his pistol, took careful aim at Tutty's form, and fired.

Sir Marion flinched and fell back a step, then another. His eyes were wild and his hands flailed about his chest as panic rioted in his ruddy face. His seconds rushed to see how badly he was injured and after a frantic inspection, they turned to stare at Reynard in disbelief.

"The bullet sliced a path across his chest!"

Tutty's legs buckled and a second later he hit the ground

like a wet sack of potatoes. Confusion broke out as the physician and Reynard's seconds rushed to Tutty's inert form.

Frankie was horrified to hear onlookers say that Reynard would likely be charged with murder if Tutty died, since dueling was illegal. Several men headed for their conveyances, eager to be away from any possible legal repercussions.

Reynard strode forcefully into the middle of the group surrounding Tutty, seeming unconcerned by the confusion and Tutty's collapse.

"Is honor satisfied?" he demanded of Tutty's first second. "I will have an answer now or require you to take up Sir Marion's pistol and finish the job yourself."

The second paled and stammered as the physician ripped open Tutty's sliced shirt and vest and inspected him front to back, declaring, "There's not a drop of blood on him. Just a burn track where the bullet passed close enough to singe his skin."

They leaned in to look and, true enough, there was a horizontal red mark across Tutty's chest, but no broken skin and no blood. The physician held his hand to Tutty's nose and then glanced up with a wry expression. "It appears Sir Marion has fainted."

The second reddened as a few chuckles expressed the group's nervous relief. The physician produced smelling salts from his bag and tested his supposition. Tutty turned his head away from the strong smell, showing he was not critically injured.

"Well, sir?" Reynard pressed the second. "Is honor satisfied?"

"It is, sir," the second declared, accepting Reynard's offered hand.

Reynard strode over to the referee, shook the man's

hand, and offered the required fee, which was accepted with a doff of the man's top hat and a look of admiration.

Frankie heard Red's laughter as he and Reynard and his seconds took swigs from Red's flask. She froze for a moment and prayed that they wouldn't notice her as she darted back into the edge of the woods. As she retraced her circular route to her mount she felt almost dizzy with relief.

Red was heading for his horse when she came out of the trees. Mercifully, he was looking away from her as she crept behind the nearest coach . . . which suddenly began to move. She scrambled to keep it between her and her uncle.

When it rolled out of range and she could no longer use it for cover, she saw that Red had retrieved his mount and was talking with Reynard's seconds. She ran for her horse, only to have an obstacle move into her path and a hand clamp onto her arm. She looked up in alarm to find herself facing one very angry-looking Reynard Boulton. A second later he dragged her to his coach, practically tossed her up the steps, and then barked orders to the driver. The moment the door closed behind him, the coach lurched and the driver was heard shouting encouragement to his team.

Frankie, who had just stumbled onto the tufted-leather bench, was thrown back against the seat and struggled to right herself. The look on Reynard's face made her scuttle back on the seat against the far wall.

"My horse—"

"What the bloody hell are you doing here?" he roared.

She swallowed hard and told herself she couldn't cringe any further and live with herself.

"I came to see what happened. I was there at the start,

if you'll remember, and I wanted to be there at the finish. It was quite enlightening." Collecting herself, she pushed up onto her knees to look out the small rear window and was relieved to see her hired mount—and only her mount— trotting along behind the carriage.

She let out the breath she was holding and slid down to the seat, causing her unfamiliar male attire to bunch and bind. The damned collar was a misery and the wool trousers had chafed her inner thighs raw and caused a devilish itch around her waist.

"That's all you have to say for yourself? You were curious about what would happen? Did it never occur to you that sneaking out to witness an illegal duel—dressed in men's clothes, no less—that if you'd been recognized, there would have been a scandal you'd never live down?"

He snatched the bowler from her head and threw it on the opposite seat.

She gasped and reached up to rescue the braid she had done hastily in the dark that morning and coiled atop her head. Some of the pins had worked loose and her mass of hair was tilting dangerously to one side.

She froze. He was lecturing her about her reputation? Again?

Curse his arrogant, condescending hide! She was sick of him treating her like a disobedient child.

"No more of a scandal than if you'd been caught dueling," she snapped back. "It's illegal in England, you know."

"I am very well aware of that." He fixed her with a look that said she was in dangerous territory.

She refused to be chastised for caring about—

"You could have gone to jail, perhaps even been hanged if Sir Marion had died," she charged.

"Fat chance of that." His tone was caustic.

"Oh, because you're such a crack shot and knew what you were doing?"

"Exactly," he bit out. "I always know what I'm doing, Miss Bumgarten. You, on the other hand, seem to have no notion of the trouble you would bring down on yourself and your family with such thoughtless, reckless behavior."

"Oh, but I do know what would happen if I were caught, *Mr. Boulton*. I would be shamed, shunned, and virtually unmarriageable." She paused to collect herself. He was right, blast him. But she realized he was not only right, he was actually disturbed by the possibility of her family— and just possibly herself—being damaged by her actions.

Why would he . . . what was behind his high-handed interventions in her actions and associations? He scarcely knew her mother or sisters, and Red was a coattail acquaintance. That left *her*. Why would he take it upon himself to intervene in her life and insist she behave according to his notion of what a lady should—

She turned to him with a speculative look.

"You don't suppose we could go back to make sure an infamous gossip could see me and blacken my name a bit?"

"Good God." He jerked his chin back, truly appalled.

"Oh, wait—that's *you*. You're a known gossip hawk. If you were to tell on me and start a rumor, you'd be doing me a favor."

"What?" The outrage in his voice was replaced by a tension that she sensed had to do with the way he turned his head to avoid looking at her. "Mad as a March hare," he muttered.

At least he was no longer on the verge of bashing her senseless or chucking her out the coach door.

"Not at all. My mother is determined to marry me off

to a nobleman of some kind and, personally, I'd rather be skinned alive. Or maybe dipped in honey and buried in an anthill. Or keelhauled under a garbage scow. Or dipped in a vat of—"

"I get the idea." He sat back in the seat, his hands clasped tightly enough to turn his fingers white. But he still managed to look down his nose. "Rather drastic alternatives. Such notions of marriage usually come from firsthand experience. What makes you so averse to matrimony?"

"Well, the way I see it, men stand to gain a lot more than women by marriage." She watched his features lose more of their tension. Lord, he had a perfect face—all manly angles around stunning gray eyes and richly curved lips—when he wasn't furious.

"A sentiment certainly not shared by the bachelors of London."

"You see?" She turned her entire body to face him. "They have their own best interests at heart. They don't want to be tied down, or forced to burden their resources, or to have to answer to someone for every minute of every day." She raised her chin. "Why shouldn't I have the same privilege?"

He exhaled a slow, steady breath.

"The best place for you would be tucked away in marriage to a man with a firm hand"—he looked away, adding—"and a hearing defect."

"Hypocrite," she charged, and saw him bristle. Oooh, he didn't like being called out. "Look how vehemently you fought going into marriage. Fighting a duel and frightening Sir Marion half to death."

"Being tricked and forced into marriage against one's will is an entirely different matter . . . a matter of honor."

"Really? And being packed off into a marriage and made

to share your life and your very body with a stuffy old wretch you can't bear—that would be more honorable?"

His eyes widened. Something she'd said struck him in a way that made his gaze glint with recognition. What had she just given away?

On impulse, she asked the question she'd been pondering for days.

"What if Marcella had been beautiful and clever and sweet-natured? Would you have been so outraged and abstemious then?"

Chapter Seven

For a moment, there was no sound but the clatter of coach wheels on bricks and the thudding of her heart in her ears. He was closer now, studying her with those fascinating eyes and making her feel a little out of her depth. Then he reached up and pulled a couple of pins from her drooping braid, and it fell in a jumble onto her shoulder. He looked it over and slowly pulled the ribbon from the tail of the loose braid.

He was so overwhelming and so sure of himself, she couldn't bring herself to protest. That, and to be honest, she wanted to see what would happen next. He was exploring, which meant he was as curious about her as she was about him. She recognized within her confusion a distinct feeling of wanting to be near him like this . . . a longing that was as irresistible as it was risky. This was the second time she'd felt this way.

Being so close to him made her body come alive, made her skin tingle and her lips grow sensitive. Every part of her experienced something new and delicious. It was attraction, she realized. This was what Daisy had been talking about when she described her overwhelming reaction to Ashton.

Maybe this man-woman thing wasn't so off-putting after all.

Except, it was happening with Reynard Boulton. Arrogant bounder. Gossip hawk. Keeper of secrets. If it was happening with him, imagine what it would be like with a man she truly cared about.

She refused to run from this awakening part of her, but neither did she know what to do with it. So, as she often did in confusing moments, she turned to teasing instead.

"What if rosy lips had said, 'Oh, Reynard, I'm yours'?" She leaned toward him. "What if comely curves had beckoned, 'Oh, Reynard, make me a wicked girl?' Would you have resisted then?"

His surprise faded into something she couldn't quite read. He stared at her as if deciding something before leaning to meet her with a determined gleam in his eyes. His nose was an inch from hers; she could almost taste the whiskey on his breath.

"Marcella is a gargoyle in women's clothing. As coarse and ugly on the inside as she is on the outside. But I wouldn't have married her if she had looked like Venus herself. I won't be coerced or bullied into a commitment that is abhorrent. There is nothing honorable in making a marriage I do not want."

"Exactly."

She should have felt some pleasure at scoring so definitive a hit on his arrogant male reasoning. But his gaze registered yet another thought she wished she were privy to.

She felt her throat constrict as he plucked another pin from her hair and inserted his fingers into her loosened braid, freeing her hair and drawing it out across her shoulder. Every strand seemed connected to the secret sensitivities of her body as he wrapped it around his hand and then studied the feel of it gliding through his fingers.

"You seemed awfully sure of yourself back there," she said, trying to drag her thoughts away from her excitement and the pleasure evident in his eyes. "Were you that confident in your aim or were you just lucky?"

"I am quite proficient with firearms."

"Proficient enough to slice a man's vest and shirt without slicing his skin?" She searched his angular face as he nodded, seeing a casual certainty in his gaze that masked other thoughts. "Wow. You'd make a heckuva gunslinger. Or a trick shot in a Wild West show."

"Gunslinger?" He made a soft noise that sounded like indignation. "I take it that was meant to be a compliment."

In the silence that fell, she studied his neatly shaped hands, long legs, and devilish eyes. Fair was fair, came a passing thought. If he took liberties with her hair, she was entitled to do the same. On impulse, she reached up to touch his hair, finding it every bit as soft as she had imagined. Then she touched the spot she'd hit, just above his left eye.

"Where did you learn to shoot like that?" she asked.

"Paris. Barcelona. Florence. Vienna."

His hand moved on to her face, stroking the curve of her cheek. She felt her blood rushing to meet his touch. Was she blushing?

"You fought duels in all of those places?" she continued.

Wonder of wonders, he produced a small, genuine smile. The unexpected warmth of it sent pleasure spiraling slowly through her.

"Hardly. I trained. There are contests here and on the Continent. Americans aren't the only people good with firearms, you know."

"You entered sharpshooting contests?" She shivered as the pad of his thumb crossed her lower lip. Lord, he was melting her skin, inch by vulnerable inch. She was going to be a puddle on the floor by the time they got to . . . wherever he was taking her.

"Nothing quite so common." He tore his gaze from her for a moment to glance out the coach window and assess their location. "Private lessons and selective competitions were arranged."

He trailed his fingers down her chin and throat but was stopped by her stiff collar and tie. Her toes were curling in her shoes. One word was all she could manage.

"Why?"

"Why what?" He was close enough for her to feel his breath again.

"Why would a future viscount want to become a dead shot?"

She could have sworn his lips were fuller, darker.

"As you said, I am reputed to be a 'gossip hawk.'" His attention focused on her mouth. "People take exception to having their closely held secrets uncovered. There are times a man must defend himself, and the availability of weapons is not always what one would wish."

"Really? I wouldn't have taken you for such a dangerous fellow. In what other ways are you 'proficient'?" She looked down and searched his hands, finding and tracing a scar on his knuckles. "Fisticuffs?"

"Really, Miss Bumgarten, are you always this nosy?"

"I confess, I am." She laughed softly. "We have that in common, I'm afraid. I can't seem to keep my nose to myself." She explored the backs of his hands and then their hardened palms and sensitive fingertips. "A grave failing in a young woman, according to my mother. But then, her nose is always in everyone's business—especially her daughters'—so she's not really one to talk." She tucked one leg under her on the seat and wove her fingers experimentally through his, feeling the gentle pressure of his in response. "So, fisticuffs?"

He sighed with exaggerated forbearance.

"Lacking other means, I have been known to defend myself with bare fists."

"That I would pay to see."

He raised one eyebrow.

"I wager you would, reckless hoyden that you are."

For the first time in days, she felt the tension in her core melting. And with it, went her defenses and discretion.

"You should be thanking your lucky stars that I was reckless enough to speak up for you the other night." She looked up into his gaze. "In fact, you owe me."

"For what?" He seemed less outraged than she might have expected.

"For saving you from a fate worse than death: matrimony."

He studied her, then gave a short laugh. "I believe your well-intentioned interference merely pushed Sir Marion to extreme measures."

"You owe me, Reynard Boulton," she said emphatically.

"Just what price do you think your *invaluable* assistance is worth?"

She tried to think, but—distracted as she was—everything that came to mind involved his lips, his hands, or his lean, muscular body. Hardly something she could demand at the moment.

"I'll have to think about it. I'll take your marker."

"God forbid I ever give you a chit. You would pauper me in days."

"Oh, I'm not interested in money. I have plenty of that." She rolled her eyes toward the roof of the coach as if thinking. "However, there are times a girl needs help."

"As I have seen," he quipped. "Dallying with Prussians and Frenchmen . . . snooping at doorknobs . . . attending duels . . . dressing as a man . . . you do need help." One eye narrowed. "At the very least, you need advice on headgear. That bowler you were wearing is hideous. Ready-made, I wager."

"See there—half a dozen excellent reasons I shouldn't be married. Not a man alive would want his wife dallying with Prussians, snooping, spectating at duels, and dressing like a man, all in the same week. But it seems to me the pot is calling the kettle black. Why aren't you married and begetting heirs? You must be at least *thirty*. Surely there have been a few young ladies nearsighted enough or desperate enough to show interest in you."

"Barely thirty," he declared, indignant. "Not a codger yet, by any stretch. And there have been a few sighing maidens—though, fewer than one might expect, given my charming nature and lucrative prospects." He leaned a shoulder back against the seat with a faint curl to his nose. "It may have to do with my reputation as a scandalmonger."

He hadn't had time to fully button his shirt and vest. A slice of skin dusted with light hair captured her attention. She licked her lower lip.

"I won't marry until my uncle dies and I bear the title myself." He removed one of his hands from hers and ran it back through his hair.

"Does your uncle require that?"

He paused for a moment, riffling through inner thoughts that drained some of the pleasure from his expression.

"My uncle requires nothing. And everything."

"Must be the side of the family with all the charm," she muttered.

The set of his jaw made her regret bringing up the subject. Their delicious teasing, their tantalizing brush with intimacy was over.

Moments later, so was the ride.

The coachman shouted to his team and the hum of the wheels on a brick street stopped as the carriage rocked to a stop. She blinked and lurched to the window. This was her street.

"We're here." She tried to collect her hair as she strained to see who might be on the street in front of her house. Then she stopped, struck by another thought. "My horse— I have to return it to the livery."

"Which livery?" he asked, grabbing her hat and pressing the oversize bowler down over the messy coil of her hair.

"The one on Trinity Road," she answered.

"I'll take it back for you." He watched her straighten her coat and trousers and tug at her collar, and smiled. "And we'll be square."

"Ohhh, no." Her eyes narrowed. "I'm saving your marker for something bigger than letting my mount trot behind your coach to a stable. I'll hide the horse in the alley and take him back to the livery myself."

He bounded out of the coach ahead of her, and when she paused in the opening, he reached up for her with both hands.

"I thought you were in a hurry." He beckoned emphatically and as she made to step out, he lifted her down. When her feet touched the ground, he didn't release her.

* * *

Reynard looked down into eyes as deep and blue as a Swiss mountain lake and couldn't make his hands give her up. Even wearing men's clothes and that ridiculous hat, she was something to behold. Rosy lips, flushed cheeks, lashes that framed those heart-melting eyes . . . he felt just the way he had the first time he encountered a Rembrandt in a museum: fascination that turned to awe that turned to gooseflesh. He'd never met anyone like her. She was beautiful and desirable enough to capture his senses, and fresh and forthright enough to turn his self-possession inside out.

What the hell was he doing? He had no business enjoying the fact that a mere swatch of cloth separated his hands from her delectable curves, or the warmth that she exuded with every breath, or the devious charm of her no-holds-barred conversation.

But he did, God help him.

"You should thank me," he said, his voice tellingly husky.

"For what?" She made no move to escape his grasp.

"For keeping your scandalous secrets, and for shielding you from the infamy you so richly deserve."

She chewed the corner of her lip, sending a wave of something like longing through his chest. "I will."

He was unprepared for her to grab him by the lapels and pull him down to her, but was even more unmanned when she planted a warm, lingering kiss *on his cheek*.

Before he could react, she had pulled away and headed for her horse. A moment later, she and the horse were trotting side by side down the alley toward the kitchen door—the location of the encounter that started this madness in his mind and body.

He touched his cheek where sensation lingered. That

was his thanks? A buss on the cheek that was suitable for a father, an aging uncle, or a younger brother? After what they'd just shared? The "sharing" part was the most embarrassing.

Accursed female. Somewhere in her family tree there had to be a witch or some other such practitioner of allurements and the diabolical arts.

He charged back into the coach, barking an order for the driver to take him to Tannehill House in Exeter Square. By the time his arse hit the seat, he was red-faced and his ears felt like they were on fire. A kiss on the cheek—she may as well have patted him on the head. *Good boy, Reynard.* The little witch roused his desires, then used them to blow a hole in his pride.

But as the coach rumbled through the streets and across the Cheswick Bridge, his irritation dissipated enough to allow a cooler analysis of the encounter. The way she'd submitted to his touch and entwined her fingers with his, the glow in her luminous eyes—he would swear she had been as fascinated by those sensations as he was.

One other detail came to mind: her disgust at the notion of sharing her body with a husband. It made him wonder about her experience with the opposite sex. Her unbridled conversation would give one to think she was as game and bold in sexual matters as she was in conversation. But given the ever-present scrutiny of her ambitious mother, that might not be the case.

In that light, her reaction made more sense. If she were a true novice at sensual games and physical pleasure, she might be testing the waters. That dance of will-she-or-won't-she could be the natural steps of a young woman exploring new sensations and desires. Innocent then provocative, sweet then sultry—it was a maddening dance that surely kept a man's attention.

Damn it! He was doing it again, letting her invade his thoughts and spin webs of now-what, what-if, and if-only. He had more important things to consider, like checking his sources, remaining solvent, and keeping body and soul together long enough to find out . . . what he needed to find out.

Chapter Eight

Tannehill House was an impressive brick and stone Georgian-style manse that faced Exeter Square. The entry was marked by massive black doors under a grand portico of a sort lacking on the other homes surrounding the green. Tannehill was built before the square came into being and as the initial property, retained room for a small garden and a carriage house that lay to the side and rear of the main house. It was the carriage house Reynard aimed for after the coach deposited him at the end of the drive; it was his prime residence—the space allotted to him by his miserly uncle.

But he was met in the central path of the garden by one of the footmen and redirected to the kitchen, where he encountered Bailey, his uncle's majordomo. The look on the aging servant's face was grave, almost regretful.

"He wants to see you, Master Reynard."

"As soon as I wash and change—" Reynard turned toward the door.

"Immediately, sir. He was most emphatic about that." The graying, but still rail-straight servant met his gaze briefly. "As soon as you set foot on the property, he said."

The entire kitchen staff, from cook to scullery maid, stopped their work to watch his reaction, some with anxiety, others with sympathy.

Reynard drew a deep breath, nodded, and checked his vest, coat, and shirt collar to be certain he was presentable. He had no tie, but "immediately" was not to be ignored. He followed Bailey out of the kitchen, up the stairs, and into the main hall where he was met by Sir Harold Rowantree, solicitor and trustee of the Tannehill holdings.

Sir Harold, tall, silver-haired, and impressively mutton-chopped, was a welcome sight. He had been around as long as Reynard could remember and had always offered discreet friendship and guidance to Reynard, despite his loyalty to Reynard's uncle. He was one of two people in Reynard's life who genuinely cared for him and did their best to temper his uncle's harsh and miserly treatment of him. But the lawyer's presence here, now, presaged something important happening in his uncle's affairs. Reynard braced for whatever was imminent.

"There you are." Sir Harold offered a hand and clasped his shoulder.

"Good to see you, Sir Harold, as always."

"We sent word to your club and discovered you had an 'early morning engagement.'" The look on Sir Harold's face said that he and Reynard's uncle knew about the duel. Such news traveled fast.

"Yes, well, that went as hoped. Resolved without injury."

Sir Harold clasped his forehead, relieved. "Thank the Almighty."

"What are you doing here?" Reynard looked around, finding all the same in the entry hall and the grand parlor beyond: the unused and out of tune pianoforte, the collection of paintings now yellowed with a lacquer of neglect, the rugs that showed more fading than wear from the last decades.

The Boultons were not a prolific lot in any sense: no children, no social circle or business alliances, no music, no expressions of joy or creativity. Dogged attention to balance sheets, properties, and investments produced a significant income that lay moldering in the family vaults, but little else. Tannehill House, he had come to believe, was the shell of a long-dead promise of Family. He and his childless skinflint of an uncle were the last of the line. Not for the first time, he wondered if that might not be for the good.

"Your uncle has been taken ill," Sir Harold announced gravely. "It seems to have been a stroke, yesterday morning. His left side was affected, though the physicians hold hope he may walk again . . . someday. He is not strong, but"—he looked down, avoiding Reynard's eyes—"he is coherent enough to summon me for instructions."

Reynard felt a spear of prescience run down his spine.

"What kind of instructions?"

"The *final* kind, I fear." Sir Harold sighed and waved a hand before him, ushering Reynard back through the hall toward his uncle's study. "He wished to delay until the outcome of your 'morning appointment' was known before instructing me in his wishes."

Reynard paused just outside the heavy mahogany door to prepare himself, and Sir Harold gave his shoulder a welcome clasp of support.

The large, book-lined study was dim from drawn drapes, overheated from a fire in the grate, and musty from the waning essence of its owner and sole occupant. Ormond Boulton, Viscount Tannehill sat in a wing chair before the hearth, covered with blankets and surrounded by ointments, elixirs, and medical paraphernalia. Reynard slowed at the sight of the old man's worn robe and the sleeping cap over his balding head. He had never seen his uncle out of his customary black suit. It was something of a jolt.

"So"—the old man's voice was changed, now damaged and hoarse with the strain of trying to speak—"I see you survived."

"I always do." Reynard moved closer and stopped near the old man's footstool, clasping his hands behind his back, steeling himself.

"Like a cockroach." The old man's habitual look of disdain was made grotesque by his drooping mouth and half-closed eye. His words came slowly, drawn out by disability. "Who did you kill this time?"

"I have never killed anyone in a duel, Uncle. You know that."

"Not that you hav-en't tried," the old lord growled, stirring uncomfortably beneath his covers. "What was it? Win-ning too much at cards? Mak-ing free with someone's wife? Spread-ding gossip about the wrong peo-ple?"

"It was a matter of deceit and honor—the deceit, his daughter's, and the honor, mine."

"Hon-nor?" Ormond's attempted laugh set off a round of coughing. Harold hurried to him and offered a handkerchief as he fought through the fit. Straightening at last, the old man glared at Reynard as if holding him personally responsible for it. "What would you know of hon-nor?"

He reached with a drooping hand for a glass of water on the table at his fingertips but could not secure a grip on it. His pale face became blotched with anger, and he struck out with that unresponsive hand, knocking the glass to the stone hearth where it shattered.

Reynard watched the impotent fury in his uncle, then picked up the pitcher from the medicine table to pour another glass, and offered it to him.

Ormond Boulton shot him a venomous look. Using the same stricken hand, he reached up and knocked the glass from Reynard's grip, sending it to join its shattered mate on the hearth.

"Don't pre-tend with me, boy. I know your true nature, your low asso-cia-tions and dealings, your under-hand-ed tricks. Don't think a show of false con-cern will change your fate."

"I am too experienced with *your* true nature, Uncle, to expect anything from you but scorn. But no matter what you do to me, I will not follow in your vengeful footsteps. We are nothing alike. I have learned honesty, determination, and decency in spite of your example. And your opinion will not, cannot make me less than I am."

The old man's faded eyes glittered with awful clarity.

"You learned man-ners and fan-cy words to cover your sins. Pretend all you want, but the truth is, you're more like me than you know. Alone. Friend-less. Trusting no one. And you hate me as much as I do you."

Reynard stiffened, but refused to give the old man the satisfaction of seeing the impact of his words. He turned toward the door, but spotted Sir Harold's aggrieved expression, paused, and turned back.

"I may indeed hate you, Uncle." It was a shameful truth, but perhaps balanced by the raw honesty that followed. "But that does not mean I do not also pity you."

As he reached the doorway, he was struck by the word that never failed to pierce his heart. The old man hurled it like a spear when he couldn't penetrate Reynard's fiercely guarded emotions any other way.

"Bastard!"

Reynard strode out through the hall and the front doors, turning into the garden. His hands were clenched, his shoulders were bunched with strain, and each step fell hard, as if he needed to punish the very bricks of the path he walked. He paced for a bit, barely seeing the lovely chrysanthemums, the fading asters, the shaggy boxwoods in need of a trim.

This was not his home. Not really. It was the place his father had grown up and the place he had been born. But he was never meant to stay here. He had thought often of leaving, of turning his back on all of this conflict and uncertainty. But the question that had been drummed into his core would only go with him if he did. He needed answers and was determined to stay until he got them, one way or another.

But right now, he had to spend the angry energy those few minutes with his uncle had generated in him. He realized where he had to go.

Mehanney's Gym was little more than an abandoned warehouse near the docks filled with roped fight rings, a motley collection of spectator seating, and a plank-paved level in the rafters for more penurious or daring patrons. The place was hot and smelled of old sweat, burning tallow lamps, and the sour tang of men engaged in violent exertion. The high, horizontal windows were too filthy to admit much light, and the shouts, grunts, and thuds of men sparring contributed to a miasma of fierce, competitive energy.

Reynard paused to let his eyes adjust to the light and spotted several shirtless men in a separate area toughening their fists against weighted leather bags and repeatedly hefting iron weights. Training, they called it, making bare-knuckle fighters and "boxers" stronger, harder, and faster. He strode around the equipment cages and lockers, watching the fighters and prospects working their muscles, privately glad that he didn't have to knock heads with any of them.

"Well, yer lardship, fancy seein' ye here." A scrawny, grizzled fellow with rolled-up sleeves and a hand-rolled cigarette tucked over one ear met him with a grin missing several teeth. "Slummin', are we?"

"Apparently." Reynard smiled. He and the enterprising fight manager went back a few years. "How's the game, Mick?"

"Roight as rain, guv." He cocked his head as he watched Reynard taking off his top hat, kidskin gloves, and coat. "Come to watch me make champeens o' these benighted lovelies?" He gestured to the fighters in various stages of learning measured mayhem at his tutelage, and then his smile broadened. "Or mebee ye come fer somethin' a bit more excitin'."

Reynard's grin matched Mick's, and soon he was stripping to the waist and having his hands wrapped in cotton bands. He fell to and hammered one of the weighted bags with a vengeance.

"What's ridin' ye, lad?" Mick held the cylindrical bag for Reynard to hit with potent one-two combinations. "Ye lose a bet?"

"An argument," Reynard spit out, panting, and dug in to punish the bag until more of his angry energy was spent. From there he did a bit of sparring. He got in a few good shots on a promising young fighter and took a couple of blows that rattled his teeth in their sockets.

"Out of practice," he said, collapsing on a bench later, letting Mick tend his face and check his ribs to be sure the pain he felt didn't represent true damage. He laid his head back against the wall and closed his eyes, feeling nicely depleted. Moments later, Mick chuckled and muttered he'd be back, and someone else settled on the bench beside Reynard.

"You should take it easy, old man," came a voice marginally more cultured than that of the toughs that populated Mehanney's.

Reynard's eyes opened. "I won't be old until I decide to be."

"There's the God's honest truth." Grycel Manse leaned back against the wall, copying Reynard's posture. "Got a tidbit for you, Fox." The fellow had a blocky face and bent nose that said he'd spent time at Mick's Mehanney's establishment, and a pin-striped suit that said he no longer needed to wield his fists to keep body and soul together. Manse had come to the same conclusion that Reynard had years ago: there was power and sometimes money to be had in the information trade.

"That Prussian bloke you asked about?" Manse said. "He's no longer at Claridge's. Movin' in with a business associate as we speak. Word is, his host ain't too happy, but didn't have no choice."

"And do I know this unfortunate 'host'?" Reynard asked, glancing around and finding no one else within earshot.

"You met him just this morn, I hear. An' he was so impressed, he fainted dead away." He grinned at Reynard, showing the stalwart remains of what was once a very fine set of teeth.

"Tutty? The duke has moved into Tutty's house?"

"Took it over's more like. Word is, he's bought up a bunch o' Tutty's debts. Now he owns Tutty's hospitality as well as his business."

By the time he left Mehanney's, the Fox had acquired a few more tidbits, including a reliable report that Redmond

Strait had not been seen at Beulah MacNeal's gambling hall in more than a week.

The mention of Red immediately brought Frankie to mind and the mention of debts brought to mind her assertion that she had plenty of money. He should check with another of his sources to see just how far Red had sunk into debt. Not that he cared.

Glowering as unwelcome tension gathered in him again, he caught a cab for the steam room and baths at his club.

Not that he cared. All his life, despite personal failings and difficult circumstances, he'd taken solace in facing facts squarely. Now, after one bloody week, she had him lying to himself.

Chapter Nine

T wo days later, as Frankie was preparing to accompany Cece to lessons with her "new violin teacher," Julian Fontaine, their younger sister, Sarah, burst into her room without knocking.

"So, Cece's got a fella and you're helping her sneak out to see him," Sarah Bumgarten said breathlessly. As the youngest and arguably the cutest of the Bumgarten girls, she had largely been given her head in whatever she wanted to do. Their mother tsked and tutted, but since Sarah was not considered old enough for the marriage market, she did far too little to correct Sarah's headstrong behavior.

"How did you—" Frankie whirled from the cheval mirror, horrified by her sister's brazen announcement. "Don't you dare let Mama hear you!" She rushed to close the door, then grabbed Sarah by the shoulders and pushed her to a seat on the foot bench of the bed. "How did you find out about that?"

Sarah bristled and crossed her arms, her huge gray eyes darkening.

"You and Cece think you're so clever—but you don't think to check keyholes before you prattle on about your big secrets. You really should be more careful. Bridges blabs to Mama about everything she hears."

Of course. Bridges was Mama's lady's maid. They were thick as thieves.

"And she's not above listening at keyholes. Just so you know."

Frankie stiffened, thinking—

"Don't worry, she doesn't know," Sarah said. "And I won't tell. But I'm more than peeved that you didn't let me in on it at the start."

"You aren't exactly known for your discretion, kiddo."

Sarah glowered. "Don't call me that. I'm not a kid anymore, I'm almost eighteen. Plenty of London debs are married by nineteen."

"Well, you better hope Mama doesn't take it into her head to marry you off to some old codger with a pedigree as long as his beard."

"She won't." Sarah raised her chin in arch defiance. "She's saving me to tend her in her dotage." She mimed squinting at needlework. "I'll be the old maid who stays at home and does needlework between Mama's megrim doses and lumbago plasters." Still squinting, she held a cupped hand to her ear and produced a dead-on imitation of an old lady's voice. "Until I need spectacles and an ear trumpet me-self."

Sarah's clowning made it hard to stay irritated with her for long, and lately she'd been less fractious and annoying than before. She was eighteen soon. Frankie's eyes widened. She was growing up.

"Very well. But if you let this slip to Mama, I'll haul you out to the shore, and stake you out on the rocks until the seabirds pluck out your eyes."

"Ewww." Sarah drew back. "Did you get that from

Uncle Red? The things he says—he can be so crude and outrageous."

"Colorful, sweetie. He's colorful. After you've met a number of these dull, pasty-faced Englishmen, you'll appreciate a little 'outrageous.'" Frankie rose and headed for the cheval glass again. "While you're here, make yourself useful and check the tapes on my petticoat. I'm not sure I got them all and I can't have petticoats sagging and dragging behind me this afternoon."

"You need a lady's maid," Sarah grumbled, getting on her knees to peek under Frankie's skirt and tug selectively at her petticoats. "When you're a duchess you'll have to have one to help with all your fabulous—"

"Duchess?" Frankie's heart nearly stopped as she stared at Sarah's reflection beside hers in the mirror. "Who said anything about me being a duchess?"

"Who do you think? Mama and Mrs. Conroy—she's Martin Conroy's mother—discussed it over tea yesterday. Lord, the things they say about people. And they act as if I'm not even in the—"

The door flew open and in rushed Elizabeth Bumgarten, her face flushed and eyes bright with excitement.

"Frances! He's here! You must come down straightaway." She seized Frankie by the shoulders and turned her around and around, scrutinizing and grudgingly approving her printed silk dress with the mutton chop sleeves and front drape drawn back into a demi-bustle.

"Who is here?" Frankie endured the way her mother corrected the lay of the crocheted lace around her square neckline and puffed her sleeves a bit more.

"The Duke of Ottenberg. Who else?" She turned her attention to Frankie's hair, tugging and tucking, though it needed neither, all the while delivering a Bible quote that set Frankie's teeth on edge.

"'Who can find a virtuous woman? For her price is far above rubies.'" She stepped back, surveying her handiwork. "And you, my dear, are worth more than diamonds." She paused, frowning. "Where is Claire? We must show our most refined and accomplished faces. We should have her play—"

"She is preparing for her lesson with her new teacher," Sarah said, hopping up from the foot bench, smoothing her dress and trying to look mature. "I'll take her place."

"Never mind, you." Elizabeth glowered at her youngest daughter. "Come, Frances." She gave Frankie a final inspection and pinched each of her cheeks to bring color to them. "We mustn't keep the duke waiting."

With that, she grabbed Frankie's wrist and hauled her out the door to the head of the stairs, where she released her and made a show of descending in a ladylike fashion that was intended to be an example. The reputed eyes in the back of Elizabeth's head failed to detect the curl of Frankie's lip as she followed.

Moments later she paused as she entered the parlor, struck by the impressive figure of the duke—hands clasped behind his back—framed by the sunlight from the parlor window. He was tall and handsome in a fierce, masculine sort of way. She should probably not dismiss him out of hand just because Mama was so determined to have him for a son-in-law. But she had to admit that thus far, it was his major drawback.

"Fräulein Bumgarten." He strode to take her hand and squeezed it as he delivered a perfect Continental kiss on it. He looked up to catch her gaze, and his smile didn't quite match the intensity of his eyes. Frankie found that observation a bit unsettling. And that hand squeezing habit of his was downright unpleasant.

Civilities were exchanged, coffee was ordered, and Elizabeth settled herself in the middle of one settee, leaving Frankie and the duke to share the one facing her. Frankie groaned privately. Her mother had been born with a gift for manipulation.

"It is so lovely of you to call, Your Grace," Elizabeth said with a smile and a nod to Frankie, indicating she should speak. *Now*.

"Especially since you must be quite busy with your commercial and property ventures," Frankie obliged. "I hope you're having success here."

"I am, fräulein. In fact, I am so successful that I have decided to spend more time here." He raised his eyebrows, implying something. What? That he would be around to grace her with his attention? "I just acquired a house in Kensington Square."

"Kensington Square?" Elizabeth tapped the side of her chin thoughtfully. "We have acquaintances there, I believe."

"Isn't that where Sir Marion Tutty lives?" Frankie asked.

"So it is." The duke seemed surprised by the realization. "A lovely place. Beautiful gardens in the center of the square. And my house is large enough to accommodate guests." He reached for Frankie's hand and, surprised by the abrupt movement, she yielded it to him. "I hope to show it to you soon, but I must make a few changes first."

"I'm sure it will be lovely, Your Grace." She tried to pull her hand away but he had a firm hold on it and she couldn't free it without yanking gracelessly. A long moment later, he released her hand and smoothed his coat, producing a stunning smile that only heightened her confusion.

"I have never been to Germany. I have seen only pictures,"

Elizabeth said, waving the butler forward with the linen-draped coffee cart. "I believe you have forests, great rivers, and castles set on mountaintops."

"Ah, yes. Mountaintops and forests. There is a jest in my country that walking up and down our many mountains is why we are so strong. And our castles are the most beautiful in the world."

Elizabeth poured and he accepted the coffee, declining cream and sugar, but selected a sweet biscuit from the plate Elizabeth offered.

"The tradition of Christmas trees was imported from Germany," Elizabeth continued, serving Frankie next. "Such a lovely custom. We had a tree here in the parlor last Christmas, didn't we, Frances?"

"We did," Frankie answered, relieved to be able to say something. "And we lighted candles all over it on Christmas Eve. It made a beautiful light by which to sing carols and exchange presents."

"Presents?" He cocked his head.

"Gifts," Elizabeth provided and he nodded in understanding.

"Does your family not exchange gifts at Christmas?" Frankie asked.

"In my country, Christmas is for children. The gifts, they reward good behavior." He lifted his nose. "There is coal in the shoes for those who misbehave."

"But surely you also exchange tokens of generosity and affection among friends and loved ones," Frankie prompted, cradling her cup between her chilled hands. She couldn't help imagining a young child's face as her Christmas hopes were dashed by the sight of a lump of coal in a shoe. Would they really do such a thing?

"There are other occasions to reward affection between

adults, fräulein." He settled a bold gaze on her face and hair and then let it drift downward. "You, of course, would be showered with both gifts and affection in my lands. Such beauty and spirit are rare. Who could resist showering you with an outpouring of generosity?"

Frankie could see her mother was wide-eyed and struggling to swallow a mouthful of coffee. After forcing her daughters to learn and conform to endless social nuances and cautions—she was shocked to have a noble suitor behave with such roving eyes and blatant admiration.

"You flatter me, Your Grace." Frankie felt her face heating.

"*Nein*, fräulein. Flattery is not in my nature. I have lived too long with the Prussian manner of speaking the plain truth." He glanced at her mother's surprised expression and checked his manner, producing a rueful smile. "I see I must be more English in my speech. I hope you forgive my boldness. I do not wish to discomfort you."

"Oh, goodness." Elizabeth fanned herself, uncharacteristically flustered. "It is true, we are more reticent in speaking of such things, Your Grace. But you are far from giving offense."

He seemed to relax, though Frankie sensed it was only for their benefit. There was an air of continual readiness beneath his reaction as he turned to her and put out his hand for hers. She surrendered it with less enthusiasm than he showed in reaching for it.

"Perhaps you will help me to learn proper English ways, fräulein."

"I have only recently learned them myself. But I would be happy to help you, Your Grace."

He drew a deep breath. "I am in good hands, then. To

thank you I wish to give you something you have said you most enjoy."

Frankie frowned, unable to remember ever speaking to him of—

"A ride in the country," he pronounced with a smile that was charm itself. "You did say you wish to ride freely and breathe the fresh air, yes?"

"I believe I did," she said, relaxing enough to smile.

"Then I will call—" He paused to amend his address. "May I call for you tomorrow at two and escort you into the country?" He transferred his dazzling smile to her mother. "I must first seek permission from your lovely mother, yes?"

"Riding?" Elizabeth was delighted at the prospect of more ducal attention for her daughter. "My daughters are avid riders, Your Grace. They spent their early years in the American West and they can be a bit daring on horseback."

"Your daughter has spoken of her family's fame for horses and of her love of riding. I, too, admire horses and would enjoy a stimulating ride in the open country." He turned to Frankie. "You will come, yes? I have a lovely mare that you might enjoy."

"I have my own horse, Your Grace," she said, wishing she had an excuse to keep from going, and unable to find one. A glance at her mother's glowing eyes gave words to her reluctance. She was being encouraged, pushed, *railroaded*.

"I believe I can make time for a ride."

"Marvelous." He smacked his knee like a judge banging a gavel, then rose and set his coffee cup back on the cart. Seconds later, he kissed hands and exited at an energetic pace, that slowed only as he accepted his hat and gloves from Jonas the butler.

The sound of the front doors closing penetrated Frankie's

jumbled thoughts. The next instant, her mother flew across the space to settle beside her with a girlish squeal.

"Frances—you're on your way!" she crowed, a bit out of breath.

"Yes, I am." She stood before her mother could continue. She needed desperately to escape the tightening vise of Elizabeth's expectations. "I promised to go with Cece to her first violin lesson with this new teacher, and I'm afraid we're going to be late." She only paused long enough for a glance at her mother's confusion. "It wouldn't do to make a poor first impression with the monsieur, now, would it?"

The orchestra practiced in a small theater that doubled as a lecture hall for a small college of the arts in south London. When they arrived—Cece carrying her precious violin and Frankie a load of misgivings—they were ushered inside by the theater's manager and found the handsome director involved in deep consultation with his musicians about the piece they were about to play.

Frankie and Cece took seats halfway back in the hall and watched as the musicians took their places and Julian Fontaine stepped onto the podium. Moments later, they were playing a lovely, dramatic piece that made Cece sit forward and grip the back of the seat in front of her. Something was happening and Frankie hadn't a clue what it might be. But tall, dark Julian had seen Cece enter and had given her a slight nod before taking his place and calling the orchestra to attention.

Did Cece know the piece? Frankie sat forward too.

"What is it?" she asked in a loud whisper. When Cece responded, her eyes had a luminous quality that almost shocked Frankie.

"It's Brahms's Violin Concerto in G major, Opus 77." Her smile would have made the *Mona Lisa* jealous. "My favorite piece. They're playing my favorite piece."

Lord, she was completely smitten. And he was luring her in deeper, using an entire orchestra as a tool of seduction.

"How does he know your favorite piece?" Frankie demanded.

"He asked the night of Tutty's ball and he remembered what I told him." There was a waver of excitement in her voice, and before Frankie could stop her, she had snatched up her violin and was striding down the aisle to the stage.

Julian turned to see what was distracting some of his musicians, and at the sight of her, warmed the entire hall with a smile. He left the podium and headed to the steps to assist her onto the proscenium. A moment later, she was taking a chair offered to her by the man seated beside the first violin. She found her place in the sheets of music and as the orchestra resumed, began to play. It may have been Frankie's imagination, but the music seemed richer and sweeter when Cece joined them. Even seated several empty rows back in the hall, she could see the spark that flared between Cece and Julian Fontaine.

One piece followed another and soon Julian gave the musicians a rest and invited Cece to play a simple duet with him. Hardly a breath was taken or let in the hall as they played, clearly for each other. Frankie sat spellbound, feeling a little guilty at her immersion in their pleasure. It was like eavesdropping on a personal intimacy between them. Every draw of the bow, every melodic phrase, every rich and vibrant tone spoke of a special bond developing between them.

Frankie wasn't the only one watching; the whole orchestra sat mesmerized by their performance and broke into fervent applause the moment it ended. It was clear they had respect for their maestro and now also for the lovely American with the stunning eyes and remarkable gift. Cece flushed with pleasure as they called for her to join them again.

By the time the rehearsal was over Frankie was in turmoil, torn between the apparent genuineness of the feeling between the pair and her certainty that they would face enormous obstacles in pursuing such a liaison. Later as they stepped into the cab Julian summoned for them, he kissed Cece's hand and held it as if it were something precious to him. Frankie felt her stomach drop. For a brief moment, she envied Cece the passion and sense of connection she already felt for Julian Fontaine.

She tried to imagine feeling such passion and connection. She batted aside her most recent memory of the duke. But she had felt such stirrings at Reynard Boulton's gentle touch, his handsome eyes, and his wry smile . . . she had been so caught up in his delicious presence that she pulled him down and planted a kiss . . . on his *cheek* . . . as if he were her uncle. It was her chance to experience a real kiss, a true man-and-woman moment, and she panicked.

Lost in her own conflicted and confusing thoughts, she was a bit startled when Cece turned to her and seized her hands as the cab began to move.

"I never imagined it would be like that. Music all around me and flowing into me, through me. All of those musicians with 'voices' of their own, blending their talents together to make something grander, finer than they ever could alone. It's a marvel, Frankie." Her eyes misted. "I have been to numerous concerts, but I never understood how it would feel to play in concert with other musicians."

Frankie smiled, stroked her sister's flushed cheek, and realized that this was more than just a romance. It had not occurred to her that Cece had never played with an ensemble before today. This was a stunning new experience for her sister. It was both wonderful and dangerous, for this awakening of her passions and emotions might never allow her to settle dutifully back under their mother's wings.

As much as she wanted to protect Cece and keep her safe, Frankie couldn't in all conscience deny her this chance to expand her experience and furnish her soul. Nor could she refuse to help her sister continue to see the man who might become her . . . patron . . . lover . . . soulmate?

There would be more meetings now, of that she was sure. Was she crazy for getting involved in such a scheme? What were the chances that her sister's joy would end in something sanctioned and socially acceptable, like marriage?

Frankie listened with sinking spirits to Cece's raptures. She herself had been swept away by the beguiling romance of the music and the passionate looks Julian and Cece had exchanged. He was clearly as infatuated with her sister as she was with him. But infatuations were not love, nor were they lasting.

Alarmed by the number of things that could go wrong in this subterfuge of theirs, she realized it was up to her to see that they didn't go wrong. She had to protect Cece and that meant learning all she could about this Julian Fontaine.

There was only one person she could go to for help. And he owed her.

"You cannot go alone," Elizabeth said, staring at Frankie the next morning at the breakfast table. She turned to her brother. "She cannot go alone."

Smells of eggs and ham and fresh-baked scones had

lured Red into the family bosom, and he had set aside his newspaper to eagerly tuck into a plate piled high with food. It wasn't the first time he'd used his dogged eating habits to ignore Elizabeth, so she knew his game.

"Redmond!"

He looked up, his eyes wide and mouth full.

"What?"

"Frances cannot ride alone with the duke. You must go with her as chaperone."

He swallowed. Hard.

"Aw, hell, Lizzie. I'm no good at nanny-sittin'. Look what happened when I chaperoned Daisy all over hell-and-gone."

"Too true," she said, fixing him with a look that said she still hadn't fully forgiven him for allowing her eldest daughter to let a duke slip through her fingers, despite the fact that Daisy was happily married and the mother of a precious young boy. "But in this case, you'll be doing it from horseback, which is your natural habitat. I cannot go and she doesn't have a proper lady's maid. Her sisters are either much too young or too . . ."

Elizabeth glanced down the table at her offspring. Frankie was watching them with arms crossed and glare forming; she hated it when they talked about her as if she weren't present. Cece was studying some sheet music, as usual, her left hand poised as if holding her violin, fingers curling in execution of an unheard melody. And, of course, Sarah had her nose in a book. Denied the excitement of a debut in society because her mother insisted she was too young, she spent her days riding, training the stray dogs she had adopted, and working her way through the library that came with the house.

Not, in Elizabeth's eyes, a proper chaperone in the bunch.

Then Frankie spoke up.

"I'd love to have you come, Uncle Red. I think we could both use some time on our saddle-bones."

Red chuckled at her genteel modification of his customary "ass in a saddle," and then nodded.

"All right, ye got me." He looked thoughtful for a moment. "So, this Prussian fella, he speak English?"

Frankie nodded as her mother launched into yet another soliloquy on the duke's handsomeness, impeccable dress, and exquisite manners—all of which were gilding the lily as far as she was concerned.

With sinking spirits, she imagined the impending ride . . . listening to him drone on about his beloved mountains and sober, God-fearing family . . . suffering another of his bone-crushing hand kisses. He would find a secluded place to stop and wangle a real kiss out of her. Next it would be gifts she couldn't refuse and that would simply entrance Mama. He would shock one and all by commanding every dance at every ball and every dinner at every party. People would soon expect to see them together and her mother would dither endlessly about when he would speak to Red for permission. He would propose and she would be trapped and speechless, which he would take for acquiescence, and then he would announce to the world they were promised.

There would be a wedding agreement Red would sign without reading, and a flurry of fittings and preparations. The wedding would dazzle society and she would be bearing His Grace's weight in bed each night while he tried to poke her full of babies, and before she knew it, she would be sitting on a mountaintop in Prussia eating liver sausages!

Hell's bells. She wasn't going to let that happen without

a fight. And to escape such a calamity, she was going to need an ally.

As they left the dining room later, Frankie inserted her arm through Red's and leaned her head on his burly shoulder.

"I have a favor to ask, Uncle Red. Two, actually."

Chapter Ten

Ottenberg called promptly at two o'clock that afternoon. Promptness, he declared as he stood with booted feet spread, commanding the center hall with his presence, was a Prussian virtue.

Frankie had chosen a dark blue jacket with scarlet piping and matching skirt, and to wear her hair in a simple chignon. Her hat was styled after a man's silk topper, with a demi-veil pulled to the back in a saucy bow of netting. The duke smiled as he examined her. The next moment Red appeared in his riding coat and English boots, hat and gloves in hand, and held out a beefy paw to the duke.

"Redmond Strait, Yer Grace." Red grinned as he pumped the duke's reluctantly offered hand. "Frankie's uncle. Her ma insisted I come. Said some fresh air would do me good."

"Good to meet you, Mr. Strait." The duke drew his hand back with a stiff expression, and Frankie thought to herself that she'd just caught him in his first lie. And not a very good one at that. "I shall do what I can to see you fully exercised." He turned to Frankie. "It appears we must make a brief visit to the Hyde Park first, but then we will proceed to the Guildsmere Battery, where I have sent my man ahead to arrange refreshments."

It wasn't a suggestion or proposal, it was a decision. His.

"Why Hyde Park?" she asked, hoping he would see her reluctance, remember what she had said about the place.

"I have a business matter to attend there. It grieves me, fräulein, that it intrudes on our pleasure, but it will hopefully prove worth the inconvenience." He looked less grieved than determined. The way he had seized her afternoon as if it were his to dispose of made her wish it was already over.

"Perhaps you would prefer to take care of your business first," she suggested, "and then return to collect us on the way to Guildsmere."

"Oh, no, my dear, it will only take a few moments. And the view of the place they call the Serpentine will surely entertain you."

Was he determined to annoy her or was he simply used to making decisions and having everyone around him kowtow? She felt her free-range-American hackles rising.

"I heard o' that Guildsmere place," Red said before Frankie could object further. "Military in olden days. Always wanted to see it."

The sun shone through a gray haze caused by London's countless chimney stacks, but it was still strong enough for Frankie to feel it on her face. A lifting breeze promised a comfortable outing. As her big roan gelding, Aramis, was brought up by a groom from the Trinity stables, she couldn't help rushing to greet him and give him a carrot she had snagged from the kitchen. He nuzzled her in joyful familiarity.

"You feed the horse before he does work?" The duke inspected her beloved mount with a skeptical air. She barely kept her jaw from dropping.

"He is my favorite and I give him treats to show I care for him."

The duke gave a slight frown, and then his gaze caught on the English saddle on Aramis's back.

"You ride astride?" He searched her skirts with a hint of shock.

"Always." She lifted her chin, determined to let him know his opinion was irrelevant. "It is the Nevada way, Your Grace. More secure and, frankly, more comfortable. Though, I have given up my Western saddle for an English one." What would he think if he knew she sometimes groomed and brushed her horse as well?

He seemed to be turning her peculiar habits over in his mind as he helped her to mount. He laced his hands to form a step, and soon they were riding three abreast through the streets toward Hyde Park. She caught the duke studying her and realized he was scrutinizing her seat with a sly smile. A knot began to form in her middle. This had not started off well, and now she was stuck pursuing his blessed itinerary for hours.

The cool, gray streets were full of carriages, cabs, lorries, and pedestrians, but within fifteen minutes, they were riding through the Hyde Park gate to join other riders on the sand-colored path lined with trees. Rotten Row was walk-slow-and-look-smart territory, the complete opposite of the unfettered, joyful exercise the duke had promised her.

Within two minutes of arriving, she spotted Mrs. Clayton Erskine, wife of a cabinet minister and a friend of her mother's, riding a stockinged chestnut and scrutinizing everyone who came through the gate. Mrs. Erskine smiled stiffly and nodded in greeting. Mama would surely get a full report before the day was out. Lord Bradford was nearby, showing off his fashionable daughters on horses that looked as bored as the young women on them. Another smile and nod. There were several gentlemen on horseback who nodded or tugged hat brims as they passed and stared covertly at her unconventional choice of saddle. Lady riders studied her seat as she passed and leaned to whisper to one another and their escorts.

Combined with the duke's sidelong glances, it was an invasive and unwelcome kind of attention that she had studiously avoided for the last two years. Whatever possessed the duke to publicize his association with her like this, to make sure they were seen together by all and sundry? Who would care that they rode together today?

"Well, well," came a familiar voice coming up behind her. "Imagine meeting you here."

Reynard had watched her arrive with Red and the Prussian, right on schedule. They made a striking trio, but his attention fastened on Frankie—beautifully turned out in her dark blue riding habit, in perfect control of her handsome mount, and looking utterly composed. At the moment, the duke was being distracted by a pair of gentlemen intent on speaking with him.

When he rode up behind her and spoke, she started and reined up sharply. Red halted and turned to see what caused her surprise and broke into a grin at the sight of him.

"Hey, Fox," Red greeted him with a mischievous grin and a buoyant wave of a hand.

"What are you doing here?" she demanded. Her eyes were set off by the color of her jacket and her face was flushed with either pleasure or surprise. He took a steadying breath. He had never seen her looking more vibrant.

"Riding, I believe." He responded with a nod to Red and then looked down. "Ah. Horse. Definitely riding."

"Why here?" she said, exasperated. "On the most

famous bridle path in the kingdom? I wouldn't think you engaged in such fashionable habits."

"Yes, but, being the curious sort, I love to see and hear the doings of the fashionable set, Miss B. And where better to do that?"

Turning her head so the duke couldn't see, she gave him a glare that could have set a haystack ablaze. Fortunately, he was made of less flammable stuff. He smiled and edged his mount forward as the duke turned from the gentlemen he had spoken with and spotted him.

"Rottenberg, I believe." Reynard leaned forward, nodding. "A pleasure to see you again. And in such fetching company."

"I do not recall the introduction," the Prussian said, though his narrowed eyes indicated he remembered the face.

"Yer Grace, this here is Reynard Boulton," Red inserted, resting his forearm on the pommel of his saddle. "Viscount Tannehill in the makin'."

"He was at the Tuttys' ball last week," Frankie added, annoyed by the duke's selective amnesia. Lie number two. "No doubt you saw him there." She leaned forward in her saddle to look past the duke. "Have you completed your business here, Your Grace?"

"Almost." The duke looked around restively. "I am to see a horse—one I may decide to purchase. They bring it around now."

"Conducting a horse purchase here?" Reynard raised one eyebrow and glanced at the grand company parading past. "Interesting."

"Actually, I had hoped to gain Miss Bumgarten's opinion before the purchase," the duke said, giving her a smile that conferred condescending approval. "Coming from a family that knows horses, I hope she will appreciate good riding stock when she sees it."

"Heh." Red gave a huff of a laugh. "She knows good stock when she sees it." He looked at Reynard. "Bumgarten gals take their own head when it comes to ridin'. But they know what they're doin'."

"I would love to see this animal you are considering." Reynard addressed the duke with a hint of challenge. Rotten Row was hardly the place to be seen trying out new mounts, and surely the Prussian knew that. That meant he intended to show off an acquisition in this public place, intending to impress Frankie. "And to hear Miss B's opinion of it."

If the duke's glare had been a knife, Boulton sensed he would lay dead and headless in the middle of the path.

A commotion occurred across the railing separating the row from the carriage lane. A mounted rider was having trouble leading a fractious horse through the carriages. A wave of consternation and comment accompanied the animal's attempts to free itself from the groom's callous use of the reins. As the horse neared their party, its eyes were wide and anxious and it seemed to be struggling with a sizeable curb bit.

"There he is, the grand stallion," the duke said, glowing with anticipation. "He has most unusual coloring, eh, *mein fräulein*?"

"Striking." She stared in open dismay at the way the groom used a crop and yanked the horse's head around.

In truth, the horse was stunning—a bit over sixteen hands, dappled white with a black mane and tail and a beautiful, if somewhat muscular, confirmation. Andalusian blood, no doubt. Reynard watched both the horse and

Frankie as the groom prodded the animal to the railing between carriages and boxed it in with his own mount. She gripped her reins tightly and her face was taut with self-control. Ottenberg concentrated so intently on his prize that he was oblivious to Frankie's tension.

"Bring him around so I can see him move," the duke ordered, jerking his head toward the entrance to the Row, near the Hyde Park Gate.

When the groom turned his own mount to drag the horse past the carriages and down the lane, the stallion took exception to the way the groom's horse brushed his hindquarters and kicked, hitting the groom's horse—which shied and bolted, tearing the stallion's reins from the groom's hands as he fought to stay upright in the saddle.

Reynard saw a disaster in the making as the black-and-white stallion spooked and reared. He grabbed Frankie's elbow to get her attention. "Back up—give him room—he's going to—"

The stallion was blowing in panic and confusion, and his hooves hit the metal railing with a clang that spooked him further. He twisted one way, then another, trying to find an opening to freedom. Frankie, Red, and Reynard wheeled their horses and scrambled out of the way, while the duke spat orders in German—his face red and eyes hot. Their withdrawal created space for the horse to escape and in a wild-eyed panic, he reared and lunged over the railing, clearing it by an inch.

As the stallion made for open ground farther down the lane, Frankie spurred her big roan with her heels and took off after him. Reynard was seconds behind her. Red was seconds after him.

Frankie bent to her horse, urging him after the stallion. Reynard tried calling out, telling her to let it go, but the wind and the thunder of hooves made it impossible for him to be heard. His heart crept into his throat as she pulled even with the runaway and leaned precariously from her galloping mount to reach the stallion's dragging reins. Twice, then three times she leaned and grabbed for the reins, and he could hear Red bellowing just behind him. On the fourth try she grabbed them and straightened in her saddle, and began to slow her mount.

The stallion fought the reins, his mouth open and neck arched. Frankie was having a hard time slowing him down and the panicked stallion kicked out at the big roan that was crowding him. Aramis reared, stumbled, and went down rear-first, throwing her off as he scrambled for footing.

Reynard was the first to reach her and dismounted at a run, slamming to his knees in the sand beside her.

"Miss B!" He grabbed her shoulders as she sat up and when she looked up, seeming a little dazed, he began to feel her arms for broken bones. Red arrived a moment later and she waved him after the stallion before he could dismount.

"I'm fine!" she shouted. "Get him before he breaks his fool neck!"

Red shot her a grin and kicked his mount into a dead run that was as impressive as any Reynard had ever seen. The old boy still had it in him.

"Stay where you are," he ordered, feeling her shoulders, neck, and the back of her head. "You could be injured—"

"Hardly," she said, propping herself up with her arms. "I've been thrown more times than I can count. I can tell there's nothing broken. Let me sit up."

"Are you certain?" he said, feeling a belated rush of anxiety he had held at bay while charging after her. Then she looked up with big blue eyes that were slightly out of focus, and he felt like he'd taken a haymaker to the gut. Her perky hat with its saucy bow was damaged; there was dust all over her riding habit; and her skin was flushed from her wild ride. Those moments the other day in the coach came back to him. It was all he could do to withdraw his hands and allow her to right herself as other riders arrived.

The duke slammed to a stop and dismounted like an avenging angel. "Are you injured, fräulein?" He stood over her with worry etched in his stony face.

"I'll be all right, Your Grace. Just a bit shaken up." She squeezed Reynard's arm as if to insist he stay beside her.

"*Mein Gott*, I will see that monster destroyed!" When he saw her trying to rise, he stooped to extend a hand. "Please, allow me."

"I believe she should go home and be seen by a physician," Reynard said as she reached her feet with assistance from them both, but swayed against him.

"I agree," the duke said, extending an arm as if expecting Reynard to cede her unsteady form to him. Reynard met him eye to eye.

"I have her, Ottenberg." His concern for her overrode his common sense. "Perhaps you could find someone to lend a coach?"

Ottenberg straightened, glancing at the well-heeled riders watching them, and tempered his reaction. Then he looked past Frankie to her horse that had regained its feet and stood, head down, beneath a nearby tree. His expression darkened and Reynard turned to see what had drawn his notice. There was a slash on the roan's right flank and his surprise was somehow transmitted through his contact with her.

"What is it?" She turned to follow his gaze. "Aramis!"

"The carriage, man!" Reynard barked at Ottenberg, who looked as if he would lash out at the impertinence, but he saw Frankie wilt against Reynard and stalked for the line of carriages, gripping his riding crop as if looking for something or someone to use it on.

She rushed to the horse and ran her hands over his head and neck, murmuring reassurance.

Reynard bent to look at the wound. "Not as bad as it looks. Shallow, but a bleeder," he said quietly as several onlookers dismounted. He glanced around, recognizing several faces, and stepped closer to her.

"Now would be a good time to faint," he murmured for her ears only. "If you're keen to escape this debacle with the Prussian, that is. Who could blame you? Being thrown and then the sight of blood . . ."

What were the options? Frankie was frantic. Giving the duke a piece of her mind in front of God and everybody . . . calling off the ride and searching for a way home . . . finding a horse doctor while fending off the duke's commands that were cloaked as concern . . .

Frankie looked at Reynard with sudden clarity and then collapsed in the most ladylike swoon he had ever seen, raising her arms, pressing the back of a hand gracefully to her forehead, giving him time to catch and collect her into his arms. The reaction of onlookers was immediate; they made a path for him and called for a carriage, any carriage to bear the young woman to safety. Confusion broke out as several people offered to see her horse to a veterinary surgeon and to see his mount returned to his stable. He spoke to a gentleman he knew, putting their mounts in his hands. A short, elegantly clad fellow wearing thick spectacles appeared to direct him to a carriage on which the footman was just putting up the hood.

"Mister Pelham." Reynard recognized him as a former MP. "I would be most grateful, sir."

"Think nothing of it." The old fellow hurried along beside him as he carried her across the bridle path to a nearby carriage. "I hope she recovers quickly. She is a most courageous young woman."

Reynard nodded, thinking she was more foolhardy than brave, but he had to agree with the old boy that there was something admirable in her willingness to take action even though it jeopardized her own safety. He was breathing hard and torn between holding her close and throttling her as he climbed into the carriage. The footman closed the door and took his perch on the back while the driver at the front took the address.

Reynard deposited her bottom half on the seat and kept his arms around her shoulders as they reached the streets. Mr. Pelham's barouche was a light, well-sprung carriage that made the ride surprisingly gentle. Still he couldn't bring himself to release her. For a moment, he just watched her breathing softly in his arms.

She popped one eye open, then the other, and sighed with relief.

"Where did you learn to faint like that?" he said. "Is that your mother's doing? Did you have a vapors-and-swooning tutor?"

"It may surprise you to learn that this is the first time I have pretended to faint in my entire life." She raised her chin but made no effort to remove herself from his lap.

"You're right, I am surprised. Mastering the art of genteel fainting is something of a rite of passage among upper-class girls."

"You forget," she said, eyes twinkling, "I'm upper-class by finance only. Down deep, I'm a hardy, rough-ridin', cattle-wranglin' female from Silver City, Nevada."

That startled him for a moment.

"Good," he declared. "Because I think I may have thrown my back out carrying you. I may have to have help getting into your house."

Chapter Eleven

"Gallant of you," she said with a wry tone, "carrying me all the way to the carriage by yourself."

"You *should* be impressed." He raised his chin to look down his nose. "I usually leave the hauling of damsels-in-distress to the servants."

She gave a soft gasp that turned into a giggle.

"You're as bad as Uncle Red."

He narrowed his eyes, indignant. "You dare to class me with that mendacious old codger?"

"He's also a generous, loveable, entertaining old codger. Are you sure you don't want to join him in my hard-won esteem?"

"Alas, I am neither generous nor loveable, though on occasion I have been credited with being entertaining. I do have in my repertoire the juiciest stories in the kingdom." On impulse, he raised one eyebrow and she laughed. The sound contained a drenching warmth that melted his tension and made him far too aware of the curvaceous form leaning across his lap. His sensitive and susceptible lap. He needed to get her off him and set her back—distance—he needed some damned distance!

But he couldn't make himself disturb her.

"What were you really doing there?" She shifted, seeking a more comfortable position for herself and creating an intensely uncomfortable one for him. God, she was lying right across—

"Out for my morning constitutional. Always been an early riser."

"That's a whopper if I've ever heard one. I seem to recall that you never appeared before noon when you were at Betancourt for the wedding. I can't imagine your habits have changed that much." She gave his chest a poke with a finger. "And you condemn Uncle Red for spinning yarns."

He studied her for a moment, then wagged his head in wonder. "The things that come out of your mouth. 'Whoppers and spinnin' yarns and square-dealin' and cattle wranglin' . . .'"

"Don't think you're going to distract me." She lowered her lashes, studying him. "You came to see *me*."

He gave a huff that sounded far too much like surrender to him.

"Red came to see me at my club last night, and between demonstrating the difference between a 'hondo knot' and a 'hangin' noose' he damn near cleared out the bar's supply of Irish whiskey. Before his head hit the table, however, he mentioned something about you wanting to see me. And he wanted to know why you would think I owed you a favor."

"What did you tell him?"

"That you're a hysterical female given to all manner of crazy notions and debilitating humors, and that he shouldn't listen to a word you say."

"So you lied."

"I did." He attempted an air of righteous justification, but couldn't tell if it was working. There was a captivating twinkle in her eyes. "It was pure self-preservation," he continued. "If he learned the truth about what happened at Tutty's and that you attended the duel dressed in men's clothes, I would be blamed for the whole of it." He sniffed. "I don't much fancy the idea of walking around on crutches for months."

"Uncle Red does have a temper," she said, nodding.

"And he seems to think his nieces are flawless flowers in life's grand garden." He shifted slightly, his voice lowering in a way that made him redden. "Your turn. What possessed you to go riding with Rottenberg?"

"Ottenberg," she corrected.

"I know how he pronounces it. Rottenberg is more accurate. I believe I warned you about the Prussian tendency to *take* whatever they take a fancy to. Today being a case in point."

She pursed a corner of her mouth and seemed to be measuring the truth of that statement against recent experience. "He called on us yesterday and my mother decided I should be deliriously happy to accept his attentions."

"Grievously poor parenting. But let's get back to this favor you're extorting from me."

"Okay." She took a deep breath, preparing herself. "I want you to skulk around or whatever it is you do to learn about people, and find out about someone for me. I need to know whatever you can learn about him."

"Him? Ottenberg?" His expression darkened along with his thoughts. She was asking him to investigate the Prussian for her?

"Heavens, no. The Frenchman, Julian Fontaine. The musician whose orchestra played at the Tutty girl's ball."

He felt like he'd just been smacked.

"For a woman dead set on avoiding matrimony, you

have a remarkably robust interest in men." He took her by the waist and shoved the rest of her off his lap and fully onto the seat. She righted herself and turned to face his now irritable expression. "Prussians. Frenchmen. You really should make an effort to meet an Italian or two to round out your—"

"I need to know where Fontaine studied; if he's married or otherwise attached; if he's a pauper or has resources; if he's a man of honor. I already know he's a gifted musician, but I need more."

"A musician." He crossed his arms to keep from tearing his hair out. She had a gift for mesmerizing him one minute and taking him to the brink of sanity the next. "I can tell you already that he's dramatic, temperamental, has expensive tastes he cannot afford, romances women for pleasure and profit, and never stays in one place for long."

She stared at him without blinking.

"I sincerely hope not." Worry crept into her face. It was the first time he'd seen her look uncertain about anything, and he wasn't sure he liked being responsible for that. "Cece would be crushed."

"Cece?" He scowled.

"My sister. You remember Claire—the one with the violin, whose music can make angels weep? It's Claire who has taken a fancy to him."

He turned and stared at her for a moment, recalling that there were three Bumgarten girls left at home, and one of them played a brilliant violin. Relief bubbled up in him, turning to chagrin a moment later.

"The violinist." He tugged down his vest, trying to bolster his self-possession. "You want me to investigate this Fontaine fellow for her."

"For *me*. I feel responsible for her and I can't abide

the thought that she could give her precious heart to a smooth-talking, fast-footed bounder. She's under his spell, and I want to be prepared in case he tries something shady."

"She's meeting him in secret?"

"I go to 'lessons' with her as chaperone and alibi. So far, they've just exchanged looks and sighs, and played violins so sweetly it would make a hangman cry. But that won't last forever. And Mama would have a fit to think her precious Claire is having passionate thoughts about any man, much less a musician. Claire has always been the sweetest and best of us. And I admit, I don't like keeping such a secret." She looked down at the fingers she was wringing. "Not that I would ever tell Mama. But . . . secrets get so . . . complicated."

"Yes," he sobered, watching her come to one of the central lessons of his life and feeling strangely drawn to her in that moment. "Secrets are complicated. And uncovering them . . . airing the truth . . . dealing with the consequences . . . is often quite painful. Give a sober thought to that as you proceed with aiding and abetting your sister's illicit romance."

She looked askance at him and he realized she was drawing conclusions about him and his reputation as a gossip hawk.

"So, that is experience speaking?"

"It is."

He clamped his hands firmly on his knees and leaned forward to see past the side of the carriage hood and gauge their location.

Traffic was terrible; wagons, omnibuses, pushcarts, and heavily laden lorries clogged the streets.

He sat back and gave a huge sigh. "I'm starting to feel a spark of sympathy for your ambitious mum. The two of you conspiring, sneaking behind her back, and plotting a romance that would give any proper parent the shivers . . . she has her hands full."

"Honestly, she believes her life will be complete if she can see one of her daughters wearing the title of 'duchess.'"

"I see." He scrutinized her erect posture, smooth skin, and delicate coloring, and couldn't help sharing his conclusion. "Daisy chose Ashton over Duke Arthur, so now it falls to you to make good on her life's desire."

"And along came Ottenberg." She rolled her eyes. "She thinks he's a gift from God."

He chuckled. "An opinion he no doubt shares." He watched her from the corner of his eye and a small, vulnerable part of him gave a silent cheer when she laughed.

God, but she was dangerous to be around. He had never felt so eager to see a woman—anyone, really—as he was to see her. She was bright, vibrant, outspoken, daring, and deliciously frank with her feelings and opinions. Frankness . . . from that day forward, he would never think of her as anything but "Frankie."

When they arrived on her street and spotted the entrance to her house, she surprised him by covering his hand with hers as it lay on the seat.

"Thank you for helping me escape what would surely have been an awkward situation and an even more miserable afternoon."

"My pleasure." He sincerely hoped she didn't know just how much of a pleasure it had been. He turned his hand over and felt her thread her fingers through his.

They finished the ride in silence, listening to the hum of the wheels and the clop of hooves on brick. When the carriage came to a stop, he rose, ordering the footman to see to the front door as he stepped down and collected

Frankie in his arms. With minimal groaning, he carried her up the steps and into the center hall of the stylish townhouse, past the gaping butler.

Frankie tried to look wan and stricken, but there was too much color in her cheeks as she clung to his shoulders. Those lean, muscular shoulders. She could feel his body moving against her as he carried her up the stairs. He was straining gallantly a bit by the time they reached the second floor and her mother and sisters came running to see what had happened.

Elizabeth took charge, directing him to carry her into her room, then rushing back out to send Claire for the doctor and a footman to look for Red—who was supposed to be chaperoning her.

Reynard gave a terse account of her being thrown from her horse, which included Red and the duke seeing to the horses while Reynard escorted her home. Elizabeth was visibly disappointed that the duke hadn't been the one to bring Frankie home, and annoyed that Red had thought more of "some blasted horse" than his precious niece's health. She sailed out of the bedchamber, over Frankie's feeble protests, to fetch headache powders and rally the household staff to her daughter's welfare.

When Reynard moved to the bed to say, "I see you're in good hands," she grabbed his coat, pulled him down until their noses were almost touching.

"Thank you," she said softly, and pulled him close enough for their lips to meet. Surprise made him hesitate for a moment, then he propped his arms on either side of her and let her take his mouth in a deepening, soul-shattering kiss. The possibility that her mother could rush in at any moment made that illicit contact so much more delicious. It was all he could do to keep from lowering himself against her and freeing his arms to hold her tight against him.

A sound near the door made him spring up and back away—though not without a last, hungry look at her flushed face and desire-filled eyes. His whole body was trembling. Elizabeth returned to usher him out without a word of gratitude and close the door sharply behind him. He was left to wander down the stairs and out the open front doors in a sensual haze that later would cause him more than a moment's panic.

Upstairs, Frankie was interrogated about the calamity, scrutinized head to toe, and diagnosed with signs of an oncoming ague. Elizabeth had her lady's maid, Bridges, come and help change Frankie into bedclothes, then administered cool cloths and a tincture of something god-awful-tasting and smelly.

The physician came and went, prescribing rest between the administration of more powders and tinctures. Elizabeth drew the drapes and assigned Sarah to sit with her sister in the darkened room, while she went downstairs to send messages to . . . whichever of her friends might be interested in or incensed by this bit of family drama.

Frankie fought the drowsiness from the medicines to go over and over that kiss in her mind. It was so lovely, so surprising. His mouth was by turns soft and hard, and his tongue laved her lips and—

"You kissed him," Sarah's voice came from nearby and when Frankie turned her head, she found her little sister leaning over the edge of the bed with wide eyes, biting her lower lip.

"I did not—"

"I saw you," she charged. "I was there just behind the door and you grabbed his coat and you kissed him. And he kissed you back."

It was no use trying to deny it.

"Yes, I did. And he did." She let out a pleasant sigh.

Sarah leaned closer and whispered, "What was it like?"

Frankie narrowed her eyes. "You have no business seeing that, much less asking about it." But the look of expectation, the curiosity, and girlish eagerness made Frankie recall all of her own curiosity and the way she had wrangled Daisy into sharing intimate secrets with her. Surely it couldn't hurt to tell her—

"It was lovely. His lips were soft one minute, hard the next. He felt warm and tasted oddly sweet. It was amazing." She grabbed Sarah's sleeve and pulled her closer. "And if you breathe a word of this to Mama, you're dead."

"Yeah, yeah," Sarah said, pulling her arm away. "Staked out on the rocks and all that malarkey." She grinned. "You really liked it?"

"I did," Frankie said, snuggling deeper into the covers and feeling her body alive with lovely new sensations. "Already, I want another one."

Red had always had a way with horses. Despite an inauspicious start with the duke's failed purchase, he had managed to run the handsome beast down and lead him to safety before he managed to hurt somebody or get hurt himself. Rogue horses on London streets were shown no mercy.

"Here ye are, ye stubborn four-legger. You were damn close to a date with the knacker man." He led the horse into a box stall at the Trinity Road stables, where the Bumgartens kept their horses. A stable hand brought hay and water and a few oats, eyeing the horse warily as he backed out of the stall. Red waited a while, watching the horse adjust to the calm surroundings, and then approached it to remove the bridle and heavy bit. He scowled at the dried blood on the bit and took a quick look at the horse's mouth. "Still tender there, are you? Not used to a rough hand. Well, yer Handsome Highness, you are one lucky bag o' bones."

When Red arrived home, he found Frankie in bed and the household in turmoil. Elizabeth gave him a verbal thrashing for being such a poor chaperone before he escaped to Frankie's room and found Sarah napping in a chair by her bed. He paused a moment, scrutinizing Frankie's face, and then shook her arm gently. Her eyes flew wide before settling into warm recognition.

"What's up, Frank? You said you were fine, else I wouldn'ta left you." He settled on the edge of her bed and took her hand in his. "Yer ma has you beatin' down death's door."

"I'm okay, Uncle Red. I just needed to get out of that mess, so I . . . fainted at the sight of blood on Aramis."

"Blood on Aramis?"

"The fancy boy kicked him, that's why he went down and dumped me off. We saw the cut later and I . . . fainted."

"Sorry I missed that." He chuckled. "Must have been a sight."

"Is Aramis all right? I heard Reynard ask someone to take him to a veterinary surgeon to get stitched up."

"I'm sure he's fine. I'll check with the Fox to get yer boy home." He paused for a moment. "I caught up with the runaway, but by the time I got 'im back to that Rotten Row, everyone was gone, so I brought him to Trinity for the night. He's got a tender mouth, and they put a nasty curb bit on him."

"So, he's fancy?" Sarah said, sitting up in the chair. She had obviously been listening. "What color is he?"

"A dapple white with black mane and tail. Purtyest thing ye ever did see. High-strung, though."

"I want to see him," Sarah said, coming to the edge of her seat.

"Go ahead." Red waved his hand toward the door. "Just don't let yer ma see you slip out. And be sure to get back in time for supper."

Trinity wasn't far away and Sarah took one of her dogs with her in the alleys she walked. Nero was a wolfhound mix who was devoted to Sarah and had been known to growl at Elizabeth when she chastised Sarah too vehemently. When she entered the stable, she spotted Marley, the head groom, and waved, asking where they had put the new boy.

"There you are," she said, climbing up onto the gate of the stall for a look at the stallion. She gave a low whistle. "They were right about you. You are a pretty boy." After a minute, she made Nero wait in the stable alley while she entered the stall to get a better look at him.

He was glorious. Perfect lines—a bit muscular—not a thoroughbred—something more interesting. She folded her arms and leaned her shoulder against the wall, letting him get used to her presence.

After a bit, he stretched his neck toward her and sniffed. She smiled. He wasn't beyond redemption, he was just sensitive. She edged closer, maintaining her casual, arms-folded posture. He took a single step toward her, sniffing again.

"You've got mats in your mane. And that fancy tail

could use a brush." She kept her voice low and soft. "How long has it been since you had a good grooming?"

He perked up his ears toward her and she laughed softly.

"If I didn't know better I'd swear you understood what I just said."

She found a stool and brought it into the stall. Perched and comfortable, she called Nero in and he instinctively gave the stallion a wide berth. He sat down at her feet and watched the horse, even as she did. She began to talk to the horse about her family and their other horses and their home in the States.

By the time she left, she sensed that he would allow her to approach, and she gave his neck and withers an affectionate stroke. Tomorrow, she vowed, she would find out who owned him and make them an offer.

Chapter Twelve

It was three full days before Frankie was allowed downstairs for meals and back to her regular routine. Even then, Elizabeth watched her carefully and cosseted her like a rich old relative. The arrival of several bouquets of flowers with a note of apology from the duke picked up Elizabeth's spirits. The game, she was heard to say, was still on.

Frankie, unimpressed by the grand floral deluge, muttered that the entire main floor of the house smelled like a funeral parlor. The dogs sniffed and sneezed and Sarah's pet ferret wreaked havoc on several blooms. Red winced at the pervasive smell of romance and took to his study, when he wasn't out finalizing a deal to buy an imported pretty-boy horse from a fellow with shady leanings. Sarah had a way with uncles as well as other animals.

Claire was the only one of the household who didn't complain about the inconveniences of having a sickbed in the house. Frankie was relieved at first that she was spared Claire's irritation at missing her "music lessons." Then as she spent her first afternoon in the downstairs parlor she noted a sway in Claire's step and a certain glow in her heart-shaped face. She waited until Elizabeth was occupied belowstairs, laying plans for the week's dinners, to approach Claire on her alarmingly fine mood.

"Oh, I've just mastered a new piece," Claire explained it away. "I feel such a sense of accomplishment whenever I do."

"Cece . . ." Frankie's suspicion was clear. "What have you been doing while I was indisposed? And don't you dare say 'practicing.' It's as plain as the nose on Red's face. Sooner or later, Mama will notice too."

Cece pulled her to the window seat and swore her to secrecy.

"I promise," Frankie gritted out. "Now tell me."

"I've seen him twice more." Cece squeezed her hands. "Once at the concert hall for practice and again at the tearoom in the Promenade."

"The Prom—Sweet Lord, Cece, why don't you just climb St. Paul's dome and shout to all of London that you're seeing a man without Mama's permission? Everybody in that place is looking for a juicy tidbit to trade over after-dinner coffee."

Cece looked a little taken aback at Frankie's reaction. "But we were there early, two thirty. And everybody knows the smart set doesn't go to tea until half past four." She looked concerned and appeared to recall the conditions of the rendezvous. "At least I didn't see anyone I knew."

That was a small comfort. Frankie's shoulders sagged.

"What's done is done. But from now on you don't go a step outside this house without me," Frankie insisted. "Especially if you're going to meet *him*." The pall her disapproval cast over Cece's mood gave her a pang of guilt. She wasn't above sneaking and meeting a man in secret herself. "Okay, tell me about it. What is he like?"

Cece perked up and became a veritable stream of biographical information on Julian Fontaine. He was bright and witty and amusing in a boyish sort of way. He was from Paris, learned the piano and violin from the age of five years, and studied under maestros in Vienna, which accounted for his love of the Three B's. When Frankie gave no sign of recognition, Cece tsked and said, "Bach, Brahms, and Beethoven."

Frankie nodded. She had heard of a couple of them.

"What about his family? Who are they? Where are they?"

"He doesn't speak much of his family. I gather they are estranged. They were not thrilled by his choice of profession, despite their early encouragement of his talent."

"And does he have a wife or fiancée tucked away somewhere?"

Cece drew back. "Certainly not." Then her indignation softened. "I don't think so." She frowned, uneasy at the only answer she had to give. "Surely he would have said something."

Frankie snorted. "Of course he would tell the girl he's romancing all about his wife and children across the channel."

"He's not like that, Frankie." She was more adamant than Frankie had ever seen her. "He's fine and good-hearted and a gentleman in every respect. He hasn't even tried to kiss me—well, except for my hand." She looked down at that hand with such fondness that Frankie groaned.

"Fine. He's a saint." Frankie couldn't help letting her lingering disbelief show through. "But I'm still chaperoning you with him until he presents himself to Mama and Uncle Red and does right by you. No more of this sneaking around to see him by yourself. Okay?"

Cece nodded and the color returned to her face.

"He's wonderful, Frankie. You'll see."

* * *

The duke called two days later to present Elizabeth and Frankie with a box of oranges, a ballotin of chocolates, and yet another armful of expensive flowers. He was invited for coffee and seemed every bit the restrained and gentlemanly suitor. His conversation was light and peppered with amusing anecdotes. At the end of the visit, he once again apologized for the disastrous turn of their previous ride. He said he had decided to have nothing to do with the wretched beast that had caused her fall from her horse. He gave no indication that he knew or cared about the horse's fate.

Frankie tried to be gracious without being too welcoming, and if the duke took no notice of her coolness, her mother did. The minute the front door closed behind the duke she turned on Frankie with fire in her eyes.

"The duke was obviously trying to make amends— though Heaven knows what for. It is my understanding that you took it upon yourself to go after that crazy beast and got your horse injured and yourself thrown." Elizabeth rose and clasped her hands before her as if she were trying to keep them from doing something she might regret. "He is a man of rank and stature. I will see a change in your attitude, young lady"—she shook a finger—"or there will be consequences."

Frankie sat for a while, turning the visit over in her mind and coming to the realization that she didn't trust what she saw in the duke today. Every instinct she possessed told her that the anger and arrogance she had seen on Rotten Row were the truth of his nature, that engaging parlor manners and bestowing thoughtful gifts were exceptions, not the rule.

Deep in thought, she wound her way to the music room at the rear of the house, where Cece practiced. She sat awhile, thinking of the difference between the duke and Reynard and of the way she felt in each's company. Cece's music always seemed to clear her thoughts and bring her to surer conclusions. As she listened and watched her sister play, she could almost see what Cece was thinking.

Him. She wanted to see and be with Fontaine. The slow, dolorous passages expressed eloquently her longing for him. Frankie thought of the duke and couldn't imagine ever wanting to be with him so passionately. Reynard, on the other hand . . . she could certainly imagine . . . and dear Lord, that was so much worse.

One of the upstairs maids arrived with a note that had been delivered to the kitchen door for Claire. Frankie shot to her feet and insisted on reading over Cece's shoulder. It was an invitation to Cece to meet Julian again at the tea-room, and afterward go for a stroll.

Cece gave her a soulful, plaintive look that vibrated every one of Frankie's heartstrings.

"All right," she said with reluctance, but without heat. "Get your hat and gloves. It's time I met this fellow and judged for myself."

The tearoom in the Promenade was less than half full, mostly pairs or small groups of ladies having refreshments between intervals of shopping. The room was decorated with lovely gilded patterns on the ceiling and walls. Potted palms and medleys of blooming hothouse flowers framed the mirrors and windows, giving the room a garden-like feeling. The tables were draped with layers of pristine white linen, and the chairs had carved rococo backs accented with gold. Large glass cases displayed the cakes, profiteroles, scones, and tarts that could be ordered, and each table bore a small vase of fresh flowers.

Julian was waiting for them at one of the tables and rose

to give Claire a chaste Continental kiss on each cheek. He murmured, "Enchanted," when introduced to Frankie and gave a courtly bow over her hand. At close range, he was as handsome as he was from a distance. Black hair, big, warm brown eyes, and an easy grace to his movement—it would be difficult indeed for a girl to resist such a combination, especially when it came with wonderful music and a stream of romantic-sounding French.

They ordered tea and Frankie noticed that he touched Cece's hand on the tabletop several times. She asked about his orchestra, his plans to stay in London, his favorite restaurants, and whether he rode.

His answers were quick and engaging, though he did stumble later when asked about his family. Once again, the word "estranged" came up and the subject slipped away as the food and tea arrived.

It was subtle things that gave away his financial condition. His suit, though nicely cut and well-tailored, showed signs of wear at the sleeves and elbows. His shirt, though immaculate, was starting to fray around the collar, and his tie was limp from enduring so many stylish knots. This was a man who took pride in his appearance and knew how to use limited resources to live better than his income might suggest. He ate eagerly, savoring every bite and glowing with gratitude when they encouraged him to finish the tea sandwiches and tarts on the tiered server.

He had been eyeing the violin Claire brought as part of her excuse for the afternoon, and he excused himself to speak with the manager briefly. When he came back he asked if he might borrow Cece's instrument for a few moments. She gladly handed it over, and the next few minutes, there was hardly a breath taken in the tearoom.

Everyone present could feel the warmth and light and

vibrancy of his talent blending with emotion to produce rich and nuanced sound. He played, Frankie thought, like a man in love. But was it Cece he loved or the passion for music she brought into his life? Did it matter?

By the time he paid the bill and they walked out on the street, Frankie had made up her mind. It did matter, very much, that he loved Cece for herself . . . for her talent and sweetness and hope and stubbornness . . . for all that she was and all that she could be.

That was a question no meeting in a tearoom, a concert hall, or even in a church on a wedding day could answer. That would only be proved by time and trial. And she prayed, in that moment, that he would be a man who valued honesty, faithfulness, and love above all else.

By the time she reached home and changed for dinner, she knew what she had to do. After dinner, she went to her room and penned a note to Reynard asking him to meet her the following afternoon at the tearoom in the Promenade. Granted, it had barely been five days, but she had to know what he had learned.

Red was stepping out for a drink at a nearby club, and she pulled him aside.

"Can you please drop by the Athenaeum Club for me, and give this to Reynard Boulton?" She thrust the envelope bearing Reynard's initials into his hand and he scowled and drew back his chin.

"What's goin' on between you two?"

"He promised to help me with something," she said. "Simple as that."

"Uh-huh." Red put on his top hat, stuffed the note into an inner pocket, and then looked her over. "Somethin's going on, Frankie. I got a nose for this stuff. When yer ma finds out, she'll throw a conniption."

"It's nothing, Uncle Red, I swear. He's just doing me a favor."

As he stepped out the front door she heard him mutter, "I hope it ain't like the one that actress, Vesta Tilley, did fer the Earl of Sapping."

At two o'clock the next afternoon she entered the tearoom on the Promenade that she had visited only the day before. It was almost deserted and she drew a breath of relief. The fewer the people who saw them together, the better. Unfortunately, she'd had to bring Sarah with her and stow her at the milliner's, two doors down, with permission to choose a new hat. This could turn out to be a rather expensive outing.

She ordered tea for two.

Half an hour passed and she requested a second brewing and more of those lovely berry tarts and cucumber sandwiches. Sarah would arrive in a few minutes to join her. And though she had told her little sister whom she was meeting and a version of why, she wasn't thrilled at the notion of engaging Reynard the Fox in front of Sarah.

Just as she was ready to collect her gloves and parasol, a shadow appeared at the door and resolved a moment later into a tall, elegant form that made her catch her breath. He sat down beside her, took in the ruins of an elegant high tea littering the tablecloth, and gave her an arch look.

"I see you started without me," he said, dangling a crust that had a curl of cucumber still attached and then dropping it with a rueful expression.

"I wasn't sure you were coming." She felt her cheeks redden as he surveyed the remnants of her repast. "I did say two o'clock."

"I didn't get the note until a short while ago. Apparently, it was left with the night porter who went off duty this morning without finding me." He waved a waiter over, ordered "more of the same, please," and then cleared space for his elbows on the table. "Now what is so urgent that I had to cancel a fencing bout?"

"Fencing?" She looked confused, imaging him riding a fence line, then recalled, "Oh, the sword kind." She drew a heavy breath. "It's Cece—Claire. Things are moving faster than expected and I have to know what you've learned about Julian."

"It's only been a few days." He seemed taken aback. "If it's that urgent, why not just invite the poor wretch over for dinner and interrogate him yourself? I imagine your mother has a store of devious methods for extracting information from reluctant victims."

"Does she ever." She grimaced. "Unfortunately, I don't want her to know anything about this infatuation of Cece's. Not yet, anyway. But I can't go on helping them without knowing he is sincere." She paused to sip her cooling tea as the waiter came to clear the table. The aproned fellow intruded again moments later with a fresh pot of Darjeeling and a plate of savory sandwiches.

"So?" she prodded as he creamed his tea and added sugar lumps. "What did you learn?"

"He's French."

Her face fell. "Of course he's French. And?"

"And he's been here for over three years, at first as a violinist, and later as first violinist with the London Symphony. When the conductor of the Soliel—that's the name of his orchestra—retired, he was recruited to fill that post and managed to bring a number of fine musicians with him from the symphony. As you might imagine, that didn't make him very popular with the lords of London music. They've been critical of his performances, but that doesn't seem to dampen the enthusiasm of the patrons. He's been barred from several larger halls, but finds plenty of work in smaller venues and at private do's like the one at Tutty's."

"So, he's not rich," she said, looking thoughtful.

"Not by a mile. But he pays his musicians first and regularly, which is itself an accomplishment, and they seem to hold him in high esteem. He's earning his spurs, so to speak."

"Spurs? But he said he seldom rides."

"Spurs, as in knights of old had to earn their spurs in battle; spurs were an honor. Meaning, he is earning his success, showing his worth, and claiming his rightful place in the music world."

"All of which means he's a good musician and has some grit and the determination to make something of himself. But what about the man himself? Is he a good and honorable man? Lord above, is he married?"

"As for honorable, I think paying his musicians before he pays himself says quite a lot. As to marriage, I'll have to do more digging. But I've not heard that he's been seen about with anyone. I don't think he's ever mentioned a wife. His family is in Paris—"

The door opened and a discreet tinkle announced the arrival of another patron . . . tall, dark, and elegantly dressed.

"I thought that must be you, fräulein. I saw you through the window." The duke came straight to their table and stood looking down at her expectantly.

"Your Grace." She almost stuttered. "What a surprise to see you here." Then after an awkward moment in which the two men locked gazes, she added with forced geniality, "Won't you join us?"

"Gladly, dearest fräulein." He caught the waiter's eye and waved to a nearby chair. He waited for the fellow to hurry over and pull a chair from another table to seat him with Frankie and Reynard. Then he surveyed the table. "Well, well, what have we here? A lovely little English tea party, yes? But where are the children?" He chuckled and glanced up to gauge Reynard's reaction.

To his credit, Reynard did not respond. He sat straight and reserved, concentrating on his cup, with only the occasional glance Frankie's way. She prayed it would stay civil between them.

"What are you doing in the Promenade, Your Grace?" she asked.

"I was told there is a fine watchmaker in these shops. And I have lost some minutes on my favorite watch." He pulled out a gold pocket watch that was set with diamonds and rubies in a family crest. "It was my grandfather's. And my father's after him. I would have it keep perfect time." He smiled and Frankie felt a chill as if from a draft. "I seek perfection in things I hold dear."

"Perfection is a worthy goal," she said, seeking to fill the silence, "but a hard standard to meet." She glanced at the tiered server. "Today, however, you are in luck. These raspberry tarts are perfect . . . in fact, divine."

Chapter Thirteen

Tensions eased as they sipped tea and ate, the duke eyeing Frankie and Reynard eyeing the duke. More than once she tried to start a conversation. Eventually she found a topic of mutual interest.

"The duke has acquired a house," she said to Reynard, who glanced at her coolly. "Where was it again, Your Grace?"

"Kensington Square," the duke said with a smile.

"The same square that Sir Marion Tutty lives on," she added.

"The same house, I believe," Reynard said, causing her to set her cup down with a clack.

"What does that mean?" She frowned.

"It means Sir Marion has sold his house to me." Ottenberg spoke up with a hint of purpose in his expression.

"So, the Tuttys have moved?" she asked, feeling the tension rising sharply between the men and having no idea why the duke's buying Tutty's house would cause it. Clearly, there was more to the story.

Yet another damned secret.

"Not yet. Maybe someday. For now, I am enjoying Sir Marion's hospitality while he enjoys mine."

Treacherous undercurrents were rising here. Clearly, Reynard and the duke didn't like each other. One step in the wrong direction could send the encounter into dangerous territory, and Reynard had already fought one duel this month.

At that moment, the door opened and Sarah breezed in with a stack of hatboxes bearing the name of one of the premier milliners in London. Frankie swallowed hard, forcing a smile for her sister.

"There you are. And, my goodness, you've bought up every hat in the shop!" Frankie's short laugh sounded brittle in her own ears. The men rose along with her. "You must excuse us, gentlemen. It is later than I realized and we must be home soon. We have guests coming for dinner."

"And who is this divine creature?" the duke said in sultry tones, his gaze fastened on Sarah's flushed face and sparkling eyes.

"My sister, Your Grace. Sarah Bumgarten." She quickly donned her gloves and gathered her parasol and purse. Before she could walk around the table to collect her sister, the duke had Sarah's hand in his and was clicking his heels. He delivered a charming kiss as Sarah delivered a charming curtsey.

"How wonderful to meet such a fresh young beauty. An unexpected pleasure, Fräulein Sarah."

Frankie expected a giggle from Sarah at the courtly address, but a quick glance at Frankie's tense face and Reynard's icy control must have warned Sarah that this was not the time to be flippant or girlish.

"Lovely to meet you, Your Grace," she said with surprising aplomb. "I have heard so much about you."

"Well, we must be on our way." She grabbed Sarah's elbow in a covert grip like the one her mother frequently used on her. The sly way the duke looked at her little sister made her want to step between them to shield her from his attention. It was all she could do to maintain her composure and measure her pace as they exited. "Good day, gentlemen."

Frankie waited until they were out in the Promenade and well out of sight of the tearoom windows before glowering at her little sister.

"I thought we were going to have tea," Sarah said, glaring back.

"No time for that. We have more important things to do."

"More important than tea with a duke?" She gave an irritable huff as Frankie propelled her along the street to the cab stand. "You'd better not let Mama hear you talk like that."

Reynard watched Ottenberg's face register amusement as Frankie collected her impressionable young sister and left. *Rotter-berg* was more like it. The man looked at Frankie's little sister as if she were a potential acquisition. He was a swine trumped up in fancy clothes and oily manners, and he was making it clear that he wasn't about to abandon his interest in Frankie.

They stood facing each other for a moment, neither willing to give visual ground. Then the duke produced another deceptive smile as he laid his napkin on the table and began to don his monogramed gloves.

"I really should thank you, Boulton." He drew a breath that expanded his broad chest even farther.

"For what?" Reynard braced for whatever was to come.

"For bungling your way into a trap that was set for me." His grin grew broader. "The invitation you intercepted was meant for me. Tutty's daughter was plotting to be my bride. She thought that she and her pathetic father could force me into it. As it happened, you saved me a good bit of trouble. I owe you, Boulton, and I always pay my debts." He reached for his hat. "Fair warning, I also collect what I am due."

He looked Reynard over, seeming less than impressed with what he saw. "You should know: had I fired the second shot"—he sneered—"the spineless Tutty would never have risen again."

That night, Reynard made his rounds in London, accompanied by the very useful Grycel Manse. His goal was to learn as much about the duke's dealings as possible, and he hit "pay dirt"—as Red Strait would have put it—when he found one of the directors of Coutts Bank drowning his marital sorrows in gin at the Cecil Hotel bar. Additional spirits and a thick beefsteak freed the man's confidence and he revealed that a certain German had been buying up debts of men prominent in merchant houses and industrial concerns for shillings on the guinea. And not just his bank, he related. He'd seen correspondence relating to similar action at Child's and Martin's . . . all private banks and generally well regarded, but pleased to unload some of their less profitable loans.

Persuasion was no longer required by the end of the meal. The German in question was Ottenberg. He was making a play to become a power in London commerce, and he was doing it on the backs of those who had outspent their means.

"Not illegal," Manse said to Reynard as they left the Cecil and headed across the Thames for London's southern precincts.

"Just business," Reynard said dryly as they hailed a cab. "Until your new creditor starts making demands for coin and starts selling off your shops or moving into your house."

"Or makin' free with your daughters," Manse said under his breath.

Reynard stopped in the midst of climbing aboard a hansom cab.

"Damn." He looked at Manse in the lamplight along the embankment. "You're sure of that?"

"Servant talk." Manse's blocky face was serious. "Most of Tutty's retainers have been let go, some with juicy stories to tell. Word is, the Tutty daughters aren't lookin' so good of late."

Reynard settled back into the cab seat as Manse climbed in beside him. "The duke is every bit as bad as I feared."

They visited a prominent music hall, a couple of gambling establishments, and ended up at Beulah MacNeal's Chancery. They were welcomed by the proprietress herself and offered seats and champagne on the mezzanine overlooking the playing floor. They sipped and gossiped and Beulah chuckled at a few of their stories and contributed a few racy bits of which she had personal knowledge. Just as they were getting comfortable, Beulah's keen eye spotted a familiar figure handing off his hat and walking stick to one of the servers.

"What is it?" Reynard detected the change in her attention and turned to follow her gaze.

Redmond Strait was headed for the bar, looking more subdued than Reynard had ever seen him. His shoulders were rounded, his hair was rumpled, and his chin bore a three-day growth.

Reynard glanced back at Beulah, who raised one eyebrow. He rose and handed off his glass to a servant. "I'll send him home."

Reynard found Red leaning on the bar, one foot on the brass railing, contemplating the play of light through a shot of golden Irish whiskey.

"Imagine seeing you here." Reynard leaned an elbow on the bar beside Red. "I thought you agreed to stay away from here and contemplate your losses for a while."

"Yeah, well, I ain't too fond of my own company just now," Red said, sipping the whiskey. "Thought I'd find somebody else's to keep me from dwellin' on—" He halted and grew downright morose. "I got problems, Fox."

"Don't we all." Reynard signaled the barman for a shot, and then settled an observant gaze on the Westerner. He was passing fond of the old prospector and didn't like seeing him like this. "What's got you off your drink?"

"I done somethin' stupid."

"Welcome to the human race, Red."

"I mean real stupid." Red set the glass of whiskey down without tasting it again, which set off an alarm in Reynard. Anything bad enough to put Red off his beloved Irish lightning was bad indeed. "I got a few markers out, you know." He paused and rubbed a spot on the mahogany bar with a meaty finger, then braced to make his confession. "More'n a dozen. A couple are big enough to choke a horse."

Reynard nodded. He had gathered as much from other sources.

"Well . . ." Red swallowed. Clearly, this was hard for the old boy to talk about. "They been bought up—at least some of 'em have."

Reynard felt his gut twist. Buying up debts. Mentally and physically he braced, thinking, *please, don't let it be—*

"The duke what's been courtin' Frankie—he's the one bought 'em."

"Ottenberg," Reynard gritted out, half expecting a thunderclap and sulfurous fumes to appear at the sound of the name.

"Yeah. Him. Anyway, I saw him out an' about today, down near Fleet Street. He took me for a drink, showed me my markers, and told me I owed him twelve thousand. Said he wants payment. I told him I didn't have it—straight out—but, if he'd wait 'til I hear about the new vein in our North Star mine, I might have it and more." The memory turned Red's face to granite. "The varmint smiled like a rattler gettin' ready to strike. Said he'd think about it, since we're likely on the way to bein' *family.* Then he said he might find another way for me to take care of my debt."

Reynard clenched his hands into fists and his stomach did a slow grind. Ottenberg wanted Frankie, that much was clear, and it didn't take a genius to figure out what he would propose to settle Red's debt. It was surprising the wretch hadn't come right out with it, there and then.

The idea of Frankie being forced into marriage because of her uncle's debts infuriated him. While she claimed to be averse to matrimony, she would do anything to see her beloved family safe—including marry a man unscrupulous enough to blackmail her into it.

He couldn't let it get that far.

Gritting his teeth, he turned to the whiskey waiting before him on the bar and threw it back in one gulp. The fire in his throat joined the one in his blood to set his gaze alight.

"The worst part?" Red shoved the still-full glass away from him on the bar top. "Facin' my girls. Lizzie will skin me alive. I prob'ly deserve that, pissin' away the family money. But Frankie and Cece and Sarah—I love 'em like my own. I'd rather die than see disappointment on their sweet faces."

Reynard nodded, unsettled by how deeply he was drawn into Red's emotion. He understood that protectiveness—was feeling an annoying bout of it himself. If he had resources of his own, he could give Red a loan or even pay off the marker altogether. His difficult financial situation was suddenly even more infuriating. He was kept constantly at the edge of insolvency by his spiteful uncle, despite the fact that he was the named heir and entitled to an income. Yet again, the secret behind his uncle's disdain for him was circumscribing and constraining his life.

"Go home, Red. Now." He took the old boy by the arm and ushered him toward the hat check and then the front door. The Chancery's doorman nodded and stepped outside to whistle for a cab. As they waited, Reynard looked into Red's troubled face.

"I promise you, Red, we'll find a way to deal with your debts—and see to it Frankie and the girls are safe and provided for."

As Red climbed into the cab Reynard paid for, the Fox realized he had made yet another promise he would have a hard time keeping. What was it about these blasted Bumgartens that made him want to pick up a blade and carve the world into a different shape for them?

Chapter Fourteen

Nearly a week later, the Bumgartens' townhouse was humming with preparations for the Earl of Kessing's dinner party and musicale. Elizabeth smiled as she watched her daughters prepare. Frankie and Claire were now well acquainted with the requirements for attending society affairs and chose dresses and hairstyles that were becoming and tasteful.

Lord and Lady Kessing, James and Audrey to their intimates, had heard Elizabeth speak of Claire's talent and asked her to have her daughter share her accomplishment at their soiree. Elizabeth was honored and thrilled to be able to show off her daughter's ability, so Claire had to be honored and thrilled as well.

She would need accompaniment, Claire had told her mother when the plans were being laid weeks ago: a piano and perhaps another violin. Of course, Elizabeth agreed. But as time passed, she forgot about it. On alarmingly short notice, Claire came up with the idea to invite her new violin teacher to perform that service for her.

Elizabeth, who had never seen the man, sighed with forbearance and declared that he should be honored and thrilled at such an opportunity.

That was how Frankie came to be trudging with leaden feet up the steps to the Kessings' impressive Georgian-style home alongside Claire, who was cradling her violin case and practically walking on air. Her accompanists tonight would be a pianist of some skill chosen from Julian's orchestra, and a violinist who happened to be Julian himself.

It would be the first time they were seen in public together, and that, Frankie knew, was the problem. When she played with the pianist, all would focus on her soaring talent. But the minute Julian took up his violin and began to play with her, the audience's awe would turn to surprise and speculation. It would be obvious that they not only played together as if reading each other's mind and heart, but that they had done so many times.

Even though Frankie had warned Claire to keep that moonstruck look off her face, she had no confidence that Cece would be able to carry it off. She was that far gone. All she had to do was look at Julian and she began to glow.

Truthfully, he wasn't much better. Being a musician and in tune with his emotional and creative spirit, he couldn't keep the passion he felt for Cece from his eyes as they played.

Their mutual desire grew stronger, deeper, and more obvious with every "lesson" Cece took with him. It was a disaster in the making.

Frankie could only hope to moderate whatever damage was done.

With that in mind, she had armored herself with her prettiest gown, which was turquoise satin with ivory trim and a demi-bustle, and had put up her hair with ivory combs studded with aquamarines. She helped Claire choose a stunning ivory satin gown without a bustle, trimmed with dark green embroidery down the bodice and a lovely hunter green sash pinned at shoulder and waist by her mother's favorite gold brooches. With her lustrous dark hair and sea-green eyes, she was in every sense stunning.

The introductions seemed endless as they arrived; the number of noble and wealthy guests was most impressive. Frankie silently chided herself for not attending to her mother's cautions about how important the event would be in the social calendar. Everyone who was anyone was here. She looked around, wondering if—and she saw him.

Tall and lean, impeccably dressed and wickedly handsome, Reynard Boulton made her heart beat faster. She smiled and turned to whisper to Claire, but came face-to-face with the Duke of Ottenberg.

"Fräulein," he said, reaching for her hand even as it offered itself to him.

"Your Grace, you surprised me."

She wished with all her heart that she could just faint and skip the next few hours, but her mother's gaze was compelling, even from twenty feet away. This was not a time for cold feet or trembling knees, that steely scrutiny said. There were impressions to be made, futures to be sorted. She had responsibilities.

By the time their host and hostess led them in to dinner, the duke had announced that he would sit with her during the performance to help her learn a proper Prussian critique of music. His arrogance, considering that the performer being critiqued be her beloved sister, and his assumption of her acquiescence, had her wound as tight as a watch spring. She wanted nothing more than to stomp on his foot and tell him to stuff his Prussian superiority where Red always advised that annoyances be stored: "where the sun don't shine."

To her great relief, there were two banquet-length tables in the cavernous dining room and she was not seated at the same table as Ottenberg. Her mother and sister were near the head of her table with the Kessings. She was not far away, but her dinner companions were an elderly statesman with a hearing deficit, his wife, and their granddaughter, who had recently made her debut in society. Reynard, as it happened, was seated several places down and across the table. If she leaned forward, she could see him regaling his dinner companions with scandalous stories.

She had never seen him quite so animated or so purposefully charming. The temptation to watch him was monstrous and she could have sworn that, as she gave in to the urge to peek, he winked at her. She shivered with pleasure and reached for her wineglass, hoping she could steal a few moments with him later. To find out what he'd learned about Julian.

The old knight, Sir Gregory Peters, had spent some time as an envoy to the German court and was delighted to hear there was a Prussian duke present. She promised to introduce them and turned her attention to the young girl, Mildred, who was about Sarah's age. They had a pleasant conversation, but Frankie found herself thinking that Sarah, for all her headstrong qualities, was a good bit more knowledgeable and mature than this girl, who was already out in society.

Halfway through the fish course, Mildred began to sneeze and dab her eyes with her handkerchief. When Frankie asked if she was quite all right, the girl stared at the peppery haddock with dismay.

"I am gravely sensitive to something in this fish," she said, eyes watering. "Perhaps the pepper. I have a delicate constitution, you see. Certain odors and foods have terrible effects on me." She turned with a plaintive expression to her grandmother, who nodded permission to her.

She turned to Frankie. "I fear I must excuse myself."

Watching Mildred slip in misery from the dining room gave Frankie an idea. She pulled out her handkerchief, covertly laid it over her lap, and covered it with pepper from the nearest cellar.

After the final course, their host and hostess rose and led them into the grand salon, which had been staged with palms and candelabra and set with chairs for the musical part of the evening. There was time for the ladies to refresh themselves, but guests soon began seating themselves for the performance. That was when the duke descended and clasped her elbow tightly, like her mother did when being emphatic, only harder.

"Dinner was quite boring without you, fräulein," he said, looking down on her. "Perhaps you and your family can join me for dinner some evening."

"It sounds lovely, Your Grace. However, it may be a task finding time to—Oh, I nearly forgot, I just met a lovely gentleman who served as envoy to the German court. He is quite keen to meet you." She pulled her arm discreetly from his grip to take his arm instead, and led him directly to Sir Gregory for an introduction. Moments later, as the duke was being interrogated about the latest happenings in the now unified Germany, she saw Claire looking around for her and excused herself to assist her sister.

In truth, Claire needed nothing but the sight of Julian to make her night. He had just entered, located her, and was coming toward the grand piano. He was dressed well, in a befitting suit of evening clothes.

"There he is." Claire groaned softly. "He is so handsome and so dear. Promise me you'll watch Mama's reaction to our duet. I want to know her every expression and everything she says."

"I will, I will." Frankie kissed her on the cheek and gave her a playful shove. "Now go and be brilliant."

Claire glided to the front of the room and took her place before the piano. Her violin case lay open on a small side table and she picked it up with a smile. Julian had opened it for her and laid her bow across the neck of the violin, as he did when she came to practice with him.

She settled the violin under her chin and stroked it with her bow. The sound was sweet and pure, awakening her heart's passion. She looked up into Julian's beautiful brown eyes and read the suggestion in them. The first bars of the sonata they had rehearsed came flooding into her fingers and onto the strings. She didn't have to try to recall the flow of notes and signatures; they came as if she read them in his eyes. Then, as if on a signal, they halted and he nodded to her with a hint of a smile. She felt a flush of warmth as she turned to face their audience.

She spotted her mother, with Frankie beside her, and the duke settling beside Frankie. Frankie looked determined to make the best of his presence and smiled at her. She nodded to them and then turned to her pianist for a few last-minute instructions. Julian smiled warmly as she looked up, sending her his love and letting her see his confidence in her. Calm spread from that sweet gift of faith, quieting her jitters and leaving in their wake the feeling of being filled with joyful music, of being ready to open her heart and let it out. This, his adoring eyes said, was her night.

* * *

Moments later, Lord and Lady Kessing appeared at the focus of the chamber and introduced Claire Bumgarten as a lovely young violinist, the daughter of Mrs. Elizabeth Bumgarten. They retired to seats at the front of the gathering and Claire nodded to her pianist to begin.

Within seconds Claire was demonstrating how inadequate the Kessings' introduction had been. Her first piece was a quick, complicated Paganini caprice that established her skill and made guests gasp with surprise. Her fingers flew and her body swayed with the joy of the music.

The Kessings looked at each other in surprise. They sensed after just a few bars that this was no ordinary exposition of a young woman's "accomplishment." If it had been anywhere else, the chamber would have exploded in applause after the first piece on the program, but in the upper-crust salons and grand parlors of London, applause was considered a woefully common response. Thus, it was something of a shock to have Lord Kessing shoot to his feet and call "Bravo!" There were echoes of it all around the room, bringing a flush of pleasure and a nod of acknowledgment from Claire.

The second piece was that lovely Bach sonata that she and Julian had practiced together. Their command of the instruments and bold interpretation of the demanding piece brought delight to their erudite audience.

Frankie watched in fascination as the listeners sat straighter and grew ever more attentive. Not one head nodded in boredom, and some guests leaned forward, into the music, with rapt expressions and clasped hands. Beside her, the duke inhaled sharply, and she glanced up to find him taut with attention as he absorbed every nuance of Claire's playing.

On her other side, their mother glowed with pride tinged with surprise. She had heard Claire play for years and had enjoyed an abundance of delightful music. But she had never heard such depth and complexity in her daughter's work or thought of her daughter's skill as anything to be celebrated and shared on more than a home musicale level.

Frankie's mother seized her hand and held it tightly as the dynamics of the music became more intricate and emotive. A moment later, the duke seized her other hand in his customary viselike grip, and she was trapped between them.

When she could stand it no more, she twisted slightly in her chair and her mother's hand tightened on hers as if commanding stillness. The duke's grip grew even more uncomfortable, and she finally yanked her hand from his to reach for her handkerchief.

Buried in peppered cotton, her nose prickled and then began to burn. She sneezed. Then again—as quietly as possible. Her eyes began to water and she pulled her hand from her mother's. Elizabeth cut her a scolding look and she shrugged in genuine dismay.

Inhaling pepper turned out to be genuinely awful. She dabbed her eyes and leaned to excuse herself to the duke. He made to accompany her, but as she motioned him to stay seated, he glimpsed her swelling nose and watery eyes and quickly transferred his attention back to the music.

Stifling sneezes and blinking away tears, she made her way to the rear doors of the salon. Thankfully, the other guests were fixed on the music and barely noticed her exit. With relief, she stumbled into the corridor, leaned against the wall, and threw her handkerchief aside like it contained poison. Air—she needed air!

Tears rolling and nose on fire, she turned toward the dining room where servants were still clearing away dinner, hoping for directions to a lavatory. Instead, she ran smack into a tall, dark-clad form that grabbed her by the shoulders.

"Ye gods. You look terrible." Reynard drew his chin back.

"Thank you so very much," she snapped as she swiped at her wet face, realizing belatedly that her gloves were now infused with a peppery scent, too. She sneezed helplessly. He offered her his handkerchief and she grabbed it as if it were a life preserver.

"What happened to you?" he asked as she blotted her eyes.

Desperate to rid herself of every trace of the offending pepper, she peeled off her gloves and dangled them before her in disgust.

Puzzled, he took them from her and waved them under his nose.

"*Odeur de poivre?*" he pronounced, then looked at her quizzically. "Never heard of pepper being used as a fragrance."

"Desperate times call for desperate measures," she said, stuffy and nasal, sounding like she had a terrible case of the grippe. "I had to escape."

"From—ahhh." Reynard chuckled as he realized what she'd done. "A case of the cure being worse than the ill, then."

"Yes, well . . . I'd much rather be out here gasping for breath than in there, wedged between Mama and His Un-graciousness."

"Come, let's find you a place to freshen up."

He gave her his arm and led her straight to the Kessings' butler, who was overseeing preparations for aperitifs and sweets to be served when the music ended. The man was horrified to hear she had a reaction to something in the dinner—she was the second person to say so that evening.

She assured him it was more embarrassing than serious, and he ushered her quickly to an out-of-the-way lavatory room used mostly by servants.

Reynard followed, declaring he would assist her. The butler seemed uncertain, but in the end was relieved to leave it in his hands.

Frankie splashed her face and scrubbed her hands with soap, which helped her flushed face and red eyes, but did little to relieve her swollen nose. When she reached for something to dry her face, Reynard lifted her chin and gently dabbed her with a towel. It was a sweet, unexpectedly intimate moment that sent a curl of pleasure through her.

"I must look a mess," she said, turning her head. He turned it back.

"Your nose is the size of a melon and your eyes could pass for archery targets, but you're still the most interesting woman I've ever met."

"Silver-tongued devil," she said, more than a little chagrinned. She had brought it on herself, after all. "What were you doing in the hall?"

"I was seated at the back, listening, when I saw you leave. You seemed to be in distress." He brushed a wisp of hair back from her face. "I confess, it was something of a quandary . . . checking on you or staying to listen to Claire's music. Your sister is a marvel, you know. Beyond excellent. I've heard her play before, but never quite like that. She would put any violinist in Britain to shame."

"It's Julian. He brings out the passionate 'classical' in her." She took the towel from him, dried her hands, then handed it back to him. "Have you learned anything more about him?"

"He is unmarried, if that helps. My contact in Paris sent word that he has not registered with a wife. His father has built a successful concern in textiles, both produced and imported. But his older brother is of an entrepreneurial bent and has gone into carriage making—is starting to install engines to propel them, like that Benz fellow, eliminating the need for horses. Doubt that will ever catch on. Anyway, Julian seems to be the 'artiste' of the family. He apparently used the last of his come-of-age funds to build his orchestra here."

"And?" she asked, searching his handsome features and wishing her face didn't feel like an unbaked roll left to rise too long.

"That's the sum of it, I'm afraid."

"That's all?" She sighed and rubbed her hands together. "A few more details, but still not a ringing endorsement of character."

"Character? Since you are so concerned about that, one would think you might have a few questions about your Prussian, considering his sudden appearance in London and questionable business practices."

"He is hardly *my* Prussian." She frowned. "And what do you mean 'questionable' business?"

"He makes a practice of finding and buying people whose debts have gotten away from them."

"You mean, he buys people's debts," she said.

"Sometimes the people and the debts are so entwined, he ends up owning both." He watched her closely. "Like Sir Marion Tutty. He now owns Tutty's house and most of Tutty's holdings, but he also has Tutty's family firmly under his thumb."

"The duke told us he bought their house."

"And now you know how he bought it. And why Tutty and his family are staying in a house they had to forfeit to a creditor. He owns them . . . lock, stock, and barrel."

Shock bloomed in her face. The thought of people of

such stature being coerced in such a degrading way was alarming. Not that the Tutty girls couldn't use a bite of humble pie. Wait—he owned them, too? "You mean, even Marcella and Ardith?"

"There are rumors," he said, "of an unkind nature."

"But he is so strictly mannered and so—" She remembered occasional lapses in that fastidious Prussian restraint, and the possessive nature of his gaze that betrayed a hunger for more intimate access to her. Until now, she hadn't wanted to call it what she felt it was: lust. That was the tension she always sensed in him, the press of desires straining to be unleashed. She shivered, thinking of the duke's attentions in a new light.

"Where did you learn all of this?"

"Most of the Tuttys' servants have been sacked, and some have stories to tell," Reynard responded. "Unpleasant ones."

He watched her struggle with the idea that the duke was underhanded and callous with those he could control.

She shook her head, as if reluctant to accept his words as truth.

How could he convince her without revealing that her uncle was now one of the unfortunates who had fallen into the Prussian's clutches? Gazing into her clear sea-blue eyes, he imagined the hurt and disillusionment that would cloud them if she learned that her own future and well-being had been jeopardized by Red's gambling.

Words came to the tip of his tongue, but he couldn't make himself utter them. Red was like a father to her, she adored him. Not even his fears that she might be called upon to make good Red's debts could justify inflicting such pain on her now. He had promised to protect her and once again swore privately to do that, no matter what the consequences. This was one secret he would not let come to light.

He squared his shoulders and escaped back to the problem of the musical lovers.

"If it helps, I went in early and watched Claire and Fontaine together as they tuned their instruments. I've never seen a man so deeply entranced. The way he looked at her—the way he struck notes in perfect harmony with hers—" He cleared his throat, realizing that he might be revealing too much by such a description. "Pure mush, actually. The man's up to his ears in it. You don't have much to worry about where he is concerned. I believe him to be sincere. Your sister, on the other hand . . . women can prove fickle when their prospects for comfort and security are at risk."

"My sister is not fickle. Nor is she overly concerned with comfort and ease. Bumgarten women don't give their hearts easily, but when we do . . ." She paused and looked away.

He turned her face back to him.

"But when you do?" he asked, his voice lower and softer. He wanted to pull her against him, to hold and protect her. And he was doing it again, deluding himself. He wanted her sixteen ways from Sunday. Wanted to sink his hands into that soft hair and kiss her to within an inch of oblivion. Wanted to caress her skin and bare her creamy breasts and feel her warm curves beneath his naked—

"When we give our hearts, it's for a lifetime," she said, then held her breath.

He was looking into her eyes, searching her with a lost and hungry look that roused every sensual impulse she possessed. His beautiful gray eyes were silvering again but were somehow darker, shimmering with the need he covered so well and the passion he kept under lock and key.

Touch me. Sweet Heaven above—just reach out and touch me.

He ran his hand down the side of her face and neck, then dragged an exploratory fingertip across her collar-bone to the rim of her bodice. She stood perfectly still, afraid to give in to her shivers of pleasure lest she break the spell he was weaving over her senses.

"You kissed me that day," he said, barely above a whisper.

"I did."

"And?"

She swallowed, sensing what was coming.

"I might be tempted to repeat it."

"When?" His head was lowering toward her.

"Now."

Her face was tilting to meet his when the duke's irritable tones slammed into them like a runaway brewery wagon.

"Fräulein? Frances? Where are you?"

They both jolted back a step, and Frankie's face reddened furiously. She turned to the sink and opened a tap, splashing her face with cold water. Ottenberg arrived in the hallway just outside the lavatory room and peered through the doorway. His surprise quickly turned to displeasure.

"Your mother was concerned and asked me to see if you were well. I see I needn't have worried." When she turned from the sink, his gaze swept her critically, then turned on Reynard, who stood nearby. "Though, perhaps your mother should have."

That was the moment she decided she would have nothing more to do with the arrogant duke. No matter what her mother wanted, she would not continue to accept his attentions or his company. The sooner she made her determination known, the better.

"Something in the dinner disagreed with me," she said, reaching for the towel Reynard held and dabbing her face. Her heart thudded as she braced herself to face him. "Mr. Boulton was kind enough to help me locate a place to collect myself and recover."

"So I see." He drew out the words and glanced between her and Reynard.

Furious at his sly and insinuating manner, she turned to Reynard. "Thank you, Mr. Boulton. You were most kind. A quality that unfortunately is lacking in many of elevated rank."

With her head held high, she strode out of the lavatory and headed for the grand drawing room. From the corner of her eye, she saw Reynard striding for the great hall and waving for a footman to retrieve his hat and gloves. He was leaving. Her heart was pounding such that she didn't hear the duke's footsteps behind her until she was nearly at the drawing room door. He grabbed her arm and her momentum carried her around to face him.

"Really, Your Grace"—she was caught off guard—"I must insist you release me."

His eyes took on the cold, dark appearance of flint. "And I must insist that you behave in a more circumspect manner. I cannot have my future wife dallying with known reprobates."

She inhaled sharply, shocked that he would presume so much, so openly. "I believe you labor under a misapprehension, Your Grace. I am no one's future wife, let alone yours. Furthermore, Mr. Boulton is not a reprobate. He is the heir to an old and venerable title."

"You are indeed mine," the duke said flatly, his features coarsening as his temper threatened to ignite his self-control. "I have spoken with your mother this very evening. She has promised you to me in marriage."

Her heart sputtered as the sense of it sank through her. Her mother had promised her to him? Without her consent? Without even consulting her? She pushed against his hold, but could not free herself.

"Let me go."

"I would have the matter settled before Michaelmas, when I must return to my estates in Germany to fetch my mother and sister. Even now I am preparing my house for you." He freed her arm only to seize an even fiercer grip on her shoulders. "As for Boulton—you should know, he will never inherit. Even now, he cannot marry or buy property or even settle his own debts. He is cut off from his uncle's fortune and title. He claims to be the keeper of secrets"—his superior expression took on a cruel cast—"but the secret he most needs to keep is that of his own birth."

"What a vile thing to say," she said, her thoughts racing. Reynard had mentioned that he and his uncle didn't get along, that his uncle thought little of him and the feeling was mutual. But a secret about his birth? If there were problems in the succession, why would he still be known as the heir of Tannehill?

"The truth is never pretty, fräulein. His uncle knows the truth and intends to reveal it," he continued.

"How could you learn such things?" She pushed back in his grip. He was hurting her. "His uncle is a recluse. He never leaves his house."

"But he is master of an empire of properties and investments, all of which require management. The viscount has lawyers and clerks aplenty. Some are willing to talk, for a price." He smiled as he delivered a final blow against the man he now considered his rival. "My dear, Reynard Boulton is a bastard."

She froze, grappling with that damning word and what it meant to Reynard and his future. As she stumbled mentally for footing, the duke swooped down to capture her lips in a forceful kiss that gave no quarter. Stunned, she took a moment to respond and break that contact. She pushed back trembling with outrage, and he laughed.

"Don't worry, my sweet. You'll soon learn to appreciate my attentions." He released her, but his grip seemed to have seared itself into her nerves and sinews.

"I very much doubt that," she said, trying to shake off the lingering sensation of his hands on her as she recovered her wits. He had stunned her with his claims and his physical assault, but she vowed silently that he would never catch her unprepared again. "Unlike women who are nobly born, I have an aversion to pain."

He did not try to prevent her from reaching for the salon doors.

"Oh, I will have fun with you, Frankie Bumgarten." His tone oozed satisfaction as he sauntered behind her into the drawing room. "Wait and see."

Chapter Fifteen

The musicale was a smashing success, and as guests crowded forward to congratulate mother and daughter, Claire could see her mother was giddy with pleasure. They would be at the top of the list now, for invitations and social precedence. Her daughter had demonstrated rare accomplishment, and she was receiving acclaim from some of the most important people in London. Lord and Lady Kessing declared that it would be the talk of the season.

Elizabeth was so caught up in accepting congratulations from that elite company that she seemed annoyed when Claire dragged her bookish pianist and the second violin player over to introduce them.

"Yes, yes, Monsieur Maubrey." She extended a hand to the pianist. "Your accompaniment was excellent tonight. I'm sure, as a result, you will be in great demand."

"And this is Julian Fontaine, Mama, conductor of the orchestra Soliel," Claire said, her face rosy and eyes bright with expectation. "You remember, the orchestra that played at Ardith Tutty's ball."

"What a debacle that turned out to be. Not that it was

your fault." Her mother looked him over and chose not to offer him her hand. "You make an excellent second violin, monsieur. Someday you may even play as a soloist."

"Mama, he is the conductor of an orchestra," Claire said, dismayed by her mother's blatant dismissal of him. She placed her hand on the tall violinist's forearm, unwittingly drawing her mother's narrowed gaze to the gesture. "He generously agreed to play second part with me on the Bach sonata and the Russian scherzo."

"As a conductor, he no doubt wishes to be associated with such extraordinary talent." Elizabeth turned on Julian with an arch look. "Claire, however, is not interested in playing publicly. Her gift is meant for more discerning ears." She seized Claire's hand from his arm and used it to pull her daughter along. "Come, my dear, there are people you simply must meet."

Reeling from her mother's behavior toward Julian, Claire glanced back at him with a desperately apologetic expression. The disappointment and longing in his luminous eyes tugged at her heart.

"Mama, how could you?" she whispered as she pulled Elizabeth to a halt at the rear of the grand parlor. "You were rude to Monsieur Maubrey and Monsieur Fontaine."

Her mother was taken aback by her charge. "Are you calling me account for my behavior toward *musicians*?"

Claire stared at her mother with dismay that gradually gave way to understanding. Frankie had said again and again that her mother would be furious to learn she was involved with a musician, but she hadn't wanted to believe it. She knew Julian as so much more than a musician that she couldn't imagine her mother truly rejecting him.

Now the truth of it came crashing down on her. Frankie was right. Her mother's whole life was based on insinuating them into a fiercely stratified society . . . in which lowly musicians did not mix with heiresses who wore designer gowns from Paris and dined with earls.

"Mama," she said, her throat constricting, "*I* am a musician."

"Don't be absurd, Claire. You are a wealthy and accomplished young woman who happens to have an extraordinary gift for the violin. That is a far cry from scrambling to make a living on scraps and fees from anyone willing to hire you."

"Please, Mama"—her eyes widened and her shoulders sagged—"if you would just talk with him, listen to his plans for—"

"I have no intention of associating myself with a musician in any way," Elizabeth said, glancing around to be certain no one was listening. When she focused on Claire again, her gaze was sharper. "And I will not allow you to do so. I believe you've been spending too much time with this music teacher."

"No, I haven't." She backed away a step, though her mother still held her arm. "The monsieur has been wonderful. He has opened up a whole new world to me."

"You do not need a new world, Claire," Elizabeth snapped. "You need to learn to content yourself with the one you are in." She straightened and looked around the grand parlor with a little smile meant for anyone other than her daughter. "We will discuss finding you a new music teacher later." She grabbed Claire's elbow and turned her toward the other guests. "Right now, you have a number of important new admirers to greet."

Simmering, Frankie did her best to ignore the duke, who shadowed and pressed her until she was desperate to escape him. She caught sight of the same misery in Claire's face and knew something had gone wrong. She looked around for Julian and the pianist, only to discover they had withdrawn from the gathering. Their mother was trundling Cece around from one knot of noble cronies to another like a prize pony at a gymkhana. She escaped the duke by hurrying to her sister's side. Peeling Cece from their mother's clutches on the pretext that she looked a bit pale and should take a moment, she ushered her to a bench by the stairs outside the grand parlor.

"When will this be over?" Cece collapsed on a bench, looking dazed.

"Not soon enough to suit me." Frankie settled beside her. "What happened with Julian and the monsieur?"

Cece told her quickly about her mother's pointed dismissal of Julian and his bereft expression. "He left shortly afterward. You should have seen the look on his face. I fear you were right—Mama will never accept him or allow me to see him or, if it comes to that, marry him."

"She is determined to see us rich and miserable," Frankie said.

Those words fell like a pall over them, creating a dispirited silence.

"Then she is destined for disappointment," Claire said, stiffening. "If she thinks she can just order me to ignore the call of my heart and soul, she is badly mistaken."

The set of Claire's jaw worried Frankie.

"We'll find a way, Cece," she said, putting an arm around her sister. "Promise me you won't do anything rash."

"Frankie, have you ever known me to do anything outside the bounds of Mama's will?"

It was the way she said it that gave Frankie a bad feeling in the pit of her stomach. Hurt. Angry. And beneath that, quietly determined.

On the way home in the coach, Elizabeth lectured them

yet again on the importance of making advantageous connections, and stressed the need to seize an opportunity for advancement through marriage. Frankie ground her teeth. Opportunities for noble marriages were rare and not to be stubbornly, stupidly ignored, Elizabeth declared, drawing no response.

Claire, whose spirits were drowning in unshed tears, finally gave in to a surge of despair. With every tear that rolled down her cheeks in the darkened coach, Frankie grew more furious with their mother.

Her hands were clenched around bunches of her skirts to keep them from shaking when Jonas met them in the main hall to take their wraps. Bridges hovered at the top of the stairs, eagerly awaiting news of her mistress's triumph.

"Go to bed, both of you," Elizabeth said with a dismissive wave.

"Not yet, Mother. I need to speak with you," Frankie declared, sweeping past Elizabeth into the darkened parlor. By the time her mother followed, she had turned up one of the gas lamps enough to illuminate one end of the long room.

"Claire is devastated," she declared. "She said you have forbidden her to see Monsieur Fontaine for lessons."

"It is for her own good. She is becoming too independent and self-absorbed. She must get her head out of the clouds and remember her place and her responsibilities." Elizabeth began removing her twenty-button gloves, inch by inch, growing steadily more irritable.

"The monsieur is a wonderful teacher," Frankie countered. "You heard, tonight, how she has blossomed under his tutelage. You cannot deprive her of this chance to follow her heart and develop her gift for music. Music is her destiny."

Elizabeth plopped her gloves on a side table and turned

on Frankie, stalking closer, her countenance fierce with indignation.

"*I* decide what her destiny is, not some dime-a-dozen fiddler. And I say her destiny is to find a wealthy, respected husband and become a pillar of society." She swept Frankie with a furious look. "You could use a few reminders of that yourself. Abandoning the duke tonight to run off to God-knows-where."

"I had a reaction to something in the dinner," Frankie declared, "and I had to leave to keep from spoiling Cece's performance. The duke followed me out and told me that I am to become his wife. That you agreed to it and promised me to him in marriage. Is that true?"

She stared at Frankie for a moment, seeming a bit surprised, then mechanically smoothed the front of her dress. "He asked permission to propose and I gave it. I told him I would be pleased to have you wed him. Dukes do not grow on trees, Frances. There are only a handful in England. He clearly wants you for his wife. Such a proposal is not something one can refuse."

"Well, I do refuse it. I cannot marry a man who tells lies about others and takes liberties with the daughters of his host. I cannot marry a man whose lustful approaches make me want to scrub my skin with lye soap." She stepped closer, her eyes blazing. "Would you have me marry a man whose hands leave bruises on my skin?"

"How dare you accuse the duke of such vile behavior? Where have you heard such—" Indignation turned quickly to deduction. "It's that Boulton miscreant. He's filled your head with nonsense about the duke. Ottenberg is a proud nobleman with manners to put the queen herself to shame. Reynard Boulton has always been jealous of us. He can't bear to see anyone in our family do well, so he makes up poison to spew about."

"Well, he hasn't made up these." Frankie yanked down the shoulder of her dress to reveal the marks left on her shoulder by Ottenberg's punishing grip. "It is my own experience that makes me reject him. His manners may be impeccable in public, but in private the duke is a harsh and unprincipled man. I'll have nothing more to do with him."

Her mother sputtered, staring at the bruises on her upper arm that could only result from the punishing grip of a hand. "I cannot believe that a man so cultured and refined would . . ." She looked up to find Frankie staring at her in righteous defiance. Her face reddened, and she fell back a step before recovering her determination. "It was *you,* wasn't it? You were headstrong and defiant with him. What did you do to make him set hands to you?"

Frankie's jaw dropped. Her mother was blaming her for upsetting the duke and being manhandled?

"I told him that whatever deal you made with him, whatever permission you gave him, I was not his future wife." She drew a deep breath and squared her shoulders. "I will not marry him."

Her mother's hand was coming forward before Frankie realized what was happening. Her face stung from the slap and she staggered back a step. For a moment, Elizabeth's eyes were wide, almost as if she were as stunned by her action as Frankie was. She took in Frankie's trembling chin and clenched fists, and looked at the bruises on her daughter's shoulder. Frankie could see her weighing and sorting, coming to a decision.

"Ottenberg is a duke, a rank that places him next to royalty. Surely you know by now that women must sometimes . . . make accommodations to . . . men of importance." Her chest rose and fell quickly as Frankie made no apology or excuse. "Fine," she snapped. "I told you what to expect if you refused to make yourself amenable to suitors.

Now I must deal with two ungrateful and rebellious girls. Perhaps you will feel different after you've been banished from the luxuries of life in England."

She turned away, rubbing her hand, and Frankie hoped it was still stinging from the slap. Elizabeth drew herself up with maternal authority, though her voice wavered slightly.

"Go to your room, Frances, and think on the disgrace of remaining unmarried and unwanted for the rest of your life."

Her mother's ambition trumped all else in her life and their family. With her cheek still burning from that slap, she gathered her skirts and fled the parlor. In the privacy of her room, she gave in to the fury that she had to vent or explode. She threw and bashed the pillows on her bed until she was breathless and unable to continue.

Then came the hot, angry tears.

Breakfast trays were delivered to Frankie's and Cece's rooms the next morning, with news that they were confined to their rooms for now. An hour later, Jonas the butler supervised the delivery of steamer trunks to Frankie's and Cece's rooms and assigned upstairs maids to assist them with packing.

Red, who was dragging himself up the main stairs after spending the night at a gentlemen's club, had no idea what had happened. But like a true prospector, he read the mood of the house as surely as he read white streaks in ore that betrayed the presence of silver.

When he spotted the servants hauling the trunks into the girls' rooms, he demanded to know what was going on. The footmen shrugged and said they guessed somebody was traveling. Before Red could reach Frankie's room to find out what was happening, Elizabeth appeared in the upper hall and demanded he join her downstairs.

Soon, there were loud voices from behind the closed parlor doors.

"What the bloody hell, Lizzie? Have ye lost ever wit ye had?" Red roared. "Sendin' the girls back to th' States?"

"It's what they want," Elizabeth gritted out. "They hate it here!"

"They do not hate it here." Red jammed his thumbs in his vest pockets and leveled a hard look on his sister. "They just hate all the needlin' and naggin' about how they gotta land a blue-blooded husband to make you proud. I got to tell you, Lizzie, I'm damned tired o' hearin' about it too. That's all you ever talk about. Dukes this, and earls that. Lord Got-rocks and Lady Gimme-more. It's all about money an' it's all a bunch o' horse manure." He halted for a moment, realizing what he'd just said. "See? You even got me so I quit using good ol' '*horseshit*.'"

"That's crude and beneath you, Redmond Strait," she charged.

"That's another thing. Since when did I get to be 'Redmond?' I grew up with you, remember? I knew you when you were just plain little Lizzie Strait. And I knew ye even after ye become Elizabeth Bumgarten. You were a good and lovin' woman to Jonny Bumgarten and yer girls. But I don't reco-nize this stuck-up, sharp-tongued 'Mrs. Bumgarten' who can't think of nuthin' but tradin' her sweet girls for the fool's gold of a fancy title."

"That's what you think I'm doing here? That's what you think of me?" Elizabeth was practically vibrating with hurt and anger. "It is, isn't it? That's what you all thi-ink . . . of . . . meee." Her voice broke and a moment later her tears were rolling like Sherman's caissons through Georgia. Just about as unstoppable.

Red watched her crumple and saw the tears scalding her cheeks. He had lived by and cared for his sister all his life, and the sight of her so overcome and distraught was nearly unbearable—especially knowing he was the one who pushed her to the brink.

He took her sobbing form into his arms and led her to the settee, where he settled beside her and gave her his broad shoulder for her tears.

"Go on, Lizzie, jus' cry it out." He stroked her fancy hair awkwardly and patted her shoulder through her puffy mutton-chop sleeve while she snubbed and gasped and talked into his chest.

"Why can't they understand I just want what's best for them? Can't they see that they need a future, a family, a place to be?" She lifted a tortured expression to him. "I'm all alone."

"That ain't true, Lizzie. You got me." His gut twisted at the thought that he had betrayed his love for her and her trust in him time and again.

"But I'm the one who has to make sure they come out all right," she wailed. "Jonny died and left it all on me. For years, I've tried to do right by them, but they won't listen. I don't think I can do it anymore, Reddy . . ."

He shushed and comforted his Lizzie, while he thought about what could be done. The girls were headstrong and probably needed a yank of the tail now and then to keep 'em on the straight and narrow. But Lizzie was the last person they would listen to at this point. If there was somebody else who could talk some sense into them—maybe help 'em find some middle ground—

Her face came to him. Her face always came to him in emotional moments. She was the one he had admired and teased and finally courted. But he'd been an eighty-proof idiot and lost her.

The Countess of Kew. Evelyn Hargrave. Evie.

She had managed to get Lizzie's eldest, Daisy, sorted and married to the right bloke. She knew how to get girls to listen because she listened to them.

"Lizzie"—he felt a weight lift from his heart—"I got an idea."

Chapter Sixteen

By the time Elizabeth emerged, red-faced and looking frayed by the encounter, a plan had been laid. She headed straight for the writing desk in her room to compose a letter to the countess asking for her help.

Meanwhile, Frankie had defied her mother's order and hurried down the hall to Cece's room. She found her sister anxious and pacing.

"I sent Julian a message," Claire said, wringing her hands and kicking the still-empty trunk with a growl as she passed it. "Dorsey the kitchen boy took it himself. But Julian wasn't at his lodgings or at the rehearsal hall. I sent him back to wait for Julian, and it's been three hours. Where could he be?"

"He's studying a score or recruiting musicians or scheduling some performances for the orchestra. He probably has a million things to—"

Claire shook her head. "You didn't see his face, Frankie. He looked devastated. He knew Mama was dismissing him like he was a kitchen boy. She heard how he played and I told her he was the maestro of Soliel, and she still acted like it was beneath her to speak to him."

Frankie pulled Claire to a seat on the bed beside her and put an arm about her.

"It will be all right, Cece. We'll find a way to make Mama see that he's a good man and a musician with a promising future."

Frankie prayed that she could deliver on that promise.

Red broke the news to Frankie and Claire that they were being sent to stay with the Countess of Kew, Lady Evelyn Hargrave. Neither was especially happy with the news, but since the alternatives they had conjured in their minds during their seclusion were so much worse, neither argued against it. In truth, the genteel countess was loved and respected by everyone in the Bumgarten family. It would do them good to have a change of scene.

Frankie spent the rest of the day in her room trying not to think too much about the future as she packed warm clothes, boots, and sensible hats. Country houses were notoriously drafty and it was better to have that quilted petticoat with her, even if it did take up too much room in the trunk.

Claire spent the time thinking and pacing. It was fully dark and a chill had invaded her room when the housemaid entered with her dinner tray. She had no appetite, but after the girl left, she noticed an envelope tucked under the cutlery and linen on the tray. She seized it and carried it to the table lamp, her heart fluttering. It was from Julian—she now knew his broad masculine script on sight. She tore it open and melted at his greeting.

*My beloved Claire, I so long to see you and express
the fullness of my heart to you. But this poor letter
will have to carry to you my sweetest confession—
I have come to love you with all my heart. Your*

gentle spirit and your astonishing music are the air I breathe and the nourishment that sustains me. Thus, it is with great pain in the depths of my being that I must tell you that I have nothing of value to offer you. I have no money, no home, and no prospects except for my poor orchestra that struggles to produce a living for its talented and selfless musicians.

I am not worthy to ask you to risk your life and your future on me. Had I the power, I would climb to the moon and pluck the stars from the sky to weave in your hair. I would write you a symphony that never ends—only changes with the seasons of my love and adoration of you.

May the angels turn their backs so they cannot witness the pain this letter will cause you. I have matters to settle and duties to face at home in Paris. Forgive my cowardice at not saying this to you in person—I could not bear to see the hurt in your beloved eyes. I hope to see you again when I have something of substance to offer you. Until then, know that I will carry you with me always, in my heart.

> *Yours in love and faith,*
> *Julian*

She gasped for air as her heart skipped beats. When she was able to breathe fully again, a rush of blood pounded furiously through her head and heart. He was leaving. She thought for a moment she might faint. Everything darkened on the edges of her vision and the letters on the page blurred and ran together. He was leaving *her*.

She read the script again and again, clutching the paper tightly, as if to force more words and fuller meaning between the lines. He said he had nothing to give her, that was why he departed for France. She could guess where that notion came from: his ambitious family and her ambitious mother. But they were wrong.

He had everything important to give her—love, companionship, inspiration, passion, faith, and support for her dreams. He had everything but the courage to face the world with her and take life as it came.

Well, she could live with that. She folded the letter into a small packet and tucked it into her bodice, over her heart. She fought back tears, refusing to give in to despair, and felt determination welling in her. She could live with it, because she had courage enough for both of them.

The next day, Frankie finished her packing and sat down to write a letter to her sister Daisy, in New York. She explained that she and Claire were being sent for a corrective "visit" to the Countess of Kew and, despite a niggling feeling that she shouldn't say more, she explained the reason: a musician and a duke, one wanted and one despised, and their mother not pleased with either situation.

Before she prepared it for the post, she slipped down the hall to Cece's room to ask her if she wanted to add anything. Claire wasn't in her room, which was tidy and eerily empty-feeling. Her closed trunk sat in the middle of the floor, waiting. As she was leaving, Alice, the upstairs maid, appeared, bringing a tea tray.

"Where is she, Alice?" Frankie asked. "Claire would never defy Mama to leave her room."

"I have no idea, miss. All I know is, she didn't touch her dinner tray last night, nor her breakfast tray this morning."

"What? Impossible. Claire loves food."

She enlisted Sarah to help search the lower floor while she searched the upstairs—bedrooms, bathing room, WC, and the small sitting room that faced the sun. Claire was nowhere to be found. She had just decided to descend the back stairs to find Uncle Red when Jonas the butler appeared at her door with news that the coach would be ready at ten the next morning to take them to the countess in Bedlington. Almost as an afterthought, he produced a note he had been instructed to bring to her at six o'clock and not a minute earlier.

> *Dearest Frankie, please don't be angry and don't be worried. Julian has gone home and I have decided to go too. I promise I'll be careful and will send word of where we are in Paris as soon as I can. Please, as you love me, do me one favor—keep Mama from learning I've gone for a day or more, until it is too late for her to do anything about it. If possible, let her believe I've gone to visit the countess with you.*
>
> *Please, dear sister, pray for us as we make our way together in a world that does not believe our love for each other or our passion for music to be worthy of respect. With Heaven's help, we will find our way.*
>
> > *My love and deepest regrets for any pain my actions may cause,*
> > *Cece*

Frankie staggered back to the bed and sat down with a plop. She read the note again, hoping that those words would have changed or that she had misread them. She shook her head in disbelief; that devastating message stayed the same.

How could Cece have gone off with Julian—eloped with him? Yet in the letter there was no mention of marriage or of making her home with him in Paris. Had he proposed honorably? Or did he convince Cece to go with him on the strength of their forbidden love alone?

Frankie could barely breathe. Out in the world, Cece would be a lamb among wolves. Who knew if Julian could protect and provide for her? Did he even have money for passage across the channel?

She had to do something—tell—who? Red? He would make a terrible scene and go storming out to search for her. Mama would learn about it and her fury would be downright biblical, complete with floods, plagues, and pillars of salt. She sighed miserably, feeling the weight of the situation settling hard on her shoulders. She would have to go after Cece herself, make her see reason, and bring her home. However, she wasn't much more familiar with what such a trip involved than Cece was.

She needed help.

A flush of anticipation warmed her. There was only one man who both knew Paris and owed her a favor.

That was how she came to be standing in the dimly lighted center hall of Tannehill House, wrapped in a dark cloak that was dripping water on the immaculate marble floor. It was a foul night outside; rain was coming down in buckets and the pooling wetness absorbed the light, making everything seem pitch black. She had taken a cab to the square, trusting the cabbie to find the right house. He didn't. After being redirected by a testy houseman who answered a nearby door, she walked a full block in the rain and got a proper drenching.

"I am Frances Bumgarten," she told the tall, dignified-looking man who answered the knocker. "I've come to see Reynard Boulton on a most urgent matter. Is he home?" She read dismay in his face. "I'm sorry, but the cabbie let me off several houses down and it's a frightful mess outside."

The majordomo looked for a moment as if he might turn her back out on the street. Instead, he scrutinized her face and the quality of her cloak, coming to a decision. The stately fellow strode to the rear of the hall to summon a footman and send him to fetch "Master Reynard."

With relief that the first hurdle was past, she lowered her hood and produced a handkerchief to dab her face as she waited. A trickle of water ran down her temple and she wiped a few wet strands of hair back from her face with her glove. When she looked around, the butler was watching her and after a moment, he offered to take her cloak and tend to it. She refused.

"I wouldn't want to inconvenience his lordship," she said earnestly, praying that the viscount wouldn't see her and assume the worst. She knew what it must look like— a bedraggled woman on a miserable night, seeking out the controversial heir to a title and fortune. It was a wonder the butler had let her through the front door.

"It would be no inconvenience to his lordship, I assure you." The man had a watchful air; he apparently didn't take things at face value.

Several minutes passed before she heard footfalls and turned toward the rear of the hall where a familiar form appeared.

He was halfway to her when the scowl on his face was replaced by surprise. "Miss B. It *is* you. I couldn't imagine—" He paused a few steps away as he took in her wet cloak and hair. "You're soaked."

"I don't wish to intrude, Mr. Boulton, but I needed to seek your advice on a matter that will not wait," she said. Just the sight of him in his evening clothes, looking worldly and capable, was reassuring. The knot in her chest began to ease.

"Don't be ridiculous, Miss Bumgarten. I am pleased to help you in any way I can." He came straight for her cloak and handed it to the butler. "Bailey, bring some hot tea for Miss Bumgarten . . . in the main parlor."

He ushered her through a wide archway, into a large, ornate room that contained a grand piano, numerous portraits, and a lot of silk drapes and French furniture. There was a musty chill to the air, as if the room hadn't been used in quite a while.

"Mr. Boulton . . ." She removed her gloves as she turned to watch him light a splint from the gas light and carry it to an oil lamp on a nearby table.

"Whatever it is, it must be bad if you're calling me Mr. Boulton," he declared, pushing back his coat and propping his fists on his waist. "Good Lord, you look half drowned."

She sent a hand to her chignon, but dropped it without touching her hair and sat down hard on the settee behind her. "I don't have time to parry insults. I'm in a terrible spot and I need your advice." She took a deep breath and looked up at him. "I'm leaving for Paris at first light and . . . well . . . I'm not quite sure how to get there."

"You are full of surprises, Miss B. You come in a driving rainstorm to ask my advice on travel arrange—wait—" He searched her for a moment. "Going to Paris? Accompanied by your family, surely. Your uncle, at the very least." When she winced and shook her head, he came to sit on the settee beside her. "What's happened?"

"It's Claire. She's run off with Julian to Paris. She left a note for me, saying she couldn't live without him and she just left. I don't even think she took many clothes with her." She felt tears pricking the corners of her eyes and blinked to banish them. "I'm going after her, to bring her home. Well, not exactly home—we're supposed to be going to the Countess of Kew's house in Bedlington. So, when I find her I'm going to tie her up if necessary, and haul her back across the channel before our mother finds out she's missing."

He stared at her for a moment, blinked, then grabbed his head between his hands.

"No. Tell me you're not heading to Paris on your own to find your romantically misguided sister and abduct her from her elopement."

"I can't tell you that. Because that's what I intend to do."

"Sweet Jesus." He stared at her. "Are you stark raving mad?"

"Probably. If there were any other way, believe me, I would take it. I can't tell Red or Mama or anyone else—Cece's future is at stake. I just need some advice on what kind of boat to take across the channel and the name of an inn on the other side where I can get a horse to ride. Then there is Paris—I hear it's kind of risky to be alone on the street there. I'll need a hotel—I have some funds, but I'll have to be frugal—"

"You're serious about this."

"Of course I am." She had recovered enough to glare at him. "Why else would I have sneaked out in a driving rainstorm to see you?"

Just then Bailey appeared with a tea tray and placed it on a low table before them. He had thought to bring a small snifter of brandy, in case the lady required something stronger. Seeing the color in her cheeks, he picked it up to head back to the kitchen.

"Leave it, Bailey," Reynard ordered.

The butler turned back, set the brandy on the tray, and left, but not before Frankie saw his raised eyebrows.

Reynard grabbed the brandy and downed it, leaving her to pour her own tea. She held the full teacup between her hands, absorbing its warmth, and later sipped from it as if it contained the nectar of the gods.

"Let me get this straight." It was all he could do to keep from grabbing her and—"*And*" was the problem; he had no clue what to do with her. "You plan to waltz down to the London docks, negotiate for passage, make a quick voyage across the channel, rent a horse, and ride hell-bent through town and country to Paris . . . where you will, by some miracle, locate your sister, talk sense into her, and then you and she simply reverse the process to return home."

She sensed that agreeing was tantamount to declaring herself insane, but she nodded anyway.

"A journey to a country where everyone speaks French. *Parlez-vous français, mademoiselle?*"

Her face flushed as she guessed what he had said. "No, I don't. But surely there will be people in France who understand the jingle of coins."

"There are. They're called thieves, cutthroats, and brigands." He crossed his arms and glared at her. "A woman alone—a pretty woman—is an invitation to every bad element in society. And you, Frankie Bumgarten, are a very pretty woman!"

She drew back, looking struck by his raised voice.

"You make it sound like a hanging offense."

"It could be worse than a hanging offense in some precincts of Calais, Paris, and many parts in between. You haven't a clue what you're getting yourself into."

"Which is why I came to you for advice," she snapped, looking at him with equal parts embarrassment and determination.

"And if I refuse to assist this mad venture?"

She put her cup on the tray and rose, swaying slightly.

"Then I have wasted your time and mine, and I will be on my way."

He rose and captured her gaze in his, even though he knew it was dangerous. Those haunting blue eyes. That lovely, worried face. He was turning to mush inside. Julian Fontaine was a tower of strength compared to him. He was in over his head with her and there was only one way for him to keep her from throwing herself in harm's way.

"All right, I'll do it."

"You'll help me?" Her face brightened.

"Absolutely not." He looked away, trying to ground himself, and fixed his gaze on a piano leg. "I'll go for you. I'll find her and bring her home."

"What?" She was honestly shocked by his gallantry, he thought. Then she continued: "You'd have to abduct her from Julian's side and then spirit her back across the channel and down to Bedlington . . . being alone with her . . . in compromising situations . . . for days . . . if you can handle her."

Every word she spoke rubbed his pride the wrong way.

"I believe I can make her see reason," he said shortly.

"Reynard, she won't come willingly . . . leaving her beloved Julian to journey back to London and Mama's wrath. And certainly not with a man whose stock and trade is secrets. She's no idiot."

"So, a woman would have to be an idiot to listen to me and trust me?" he said irritably. How dare she ask his help one moment and disdain it the next? He leaned closer. "What does that make you?"

"Desperate." She leaned closer to him, practically nose to nose with him. "Desperate enough to seek help from you, knowing how little you think of upstart Americans who follow their hearts instead of their heads."

His eyes warmed and his lips felt hot. She was upset, angry, desperate, and close . . . so very close. The way she was looking at him, into him, with hope and expectation and a hint of admiration, said there was more to her presence here than sisterly worry. Whether she admitted it or not, she wanted help from *him*.

Part of him was suddenly drunk with the pleasure that thought brought him. In that moment, he would have braved lightning, or faced armies, or fought dragons to render whatever aid she needed.

God. She had reduced him to a sappy, boneheaded St. George.

"Very well," he said, his gaze drifting to her lips. "Have it your way. I'll go to Paris with you."

"That isn't necessary," she said, swallowing hard.

He clasped his wrist behind his back. No use giving temptation an opportunity. "Yes? How will you find a ship berth that won't beggar you? A captain or bursar will see a young woman traveling alone as a perfect gull, ripe for the picking. And if not them, somebody in the crew who works with pickpockets and skivers on the docks will spot you and you'll be lucky to even make it aboard a boat with your belongings. You want to hear what happens to unwary travelers in Calais when a ship docks?"

"Not really." She bit her lip and glanced aside, weighing his logic and her diminishing options.

"Well, it's important that one of us knows," he said, his voice softening. "Frankie . . ."

She looked up at him with a vulnerable expression he'd seen only once before. He wanted to pull her against him and hold her until she was warmed and bold and confident again. Instead he took her icy hands in his and pulled her to a seat on the settee.

"You came to me because you know I can see you and your sister return home safely. And I'll do it because I've lost half of my wits in recent weeks and can't resist the challenge."

She bit the corner of her mouth, which soon turned up in a tentative smile. A deep breath later, her response turned a little saltier.

"That, and you owe me a whopping big favor."

Chapter Seventeen

The coach arrived at the Bumgartens' house promptly at ten o'clock the next morning. Trunks were bundled down the stairs and two cloaked figures descended to the hall carrying hatboxes and leather satchels of personal items. Claire hurried out and climbed aboard the coach while Frankie paused to wait for Red and their mother.

"Your things are already loaded?" Their mother came out of the dining room with Uncle Red and looked for a moment like she might extend her arms to Frankie. Instead, she clasped her hands and assumed a stoic expression. "You have thinking to do, Frances. Make the best of this time with our dear friend and heed her advice."

"Aww," Red growled, annoyed at Elizabeth, and barreled forward to engulf Frankie in a bearish hug. "You take care, Frank."

"I will, Uncle Red." She felt a lump in her throat as he released her. "And you'll take Aramis out for a ride now and then?"

"I promise," he said, looking as forlorn as she'd ever seen him—even more than when the countess rejected his proposal of marriage.

"Where is Claire?" Elizabeth asked, glancing back at the stairs.

"She's already aboard," Frankie said. "She asked me to say her good-byes." When her mother scowled, she added, "She's a bit overcome."

Elizabeth straightened and nodded.

Moments later, Frankie was climbing aboard the coach and settling her valise on the seat beside her. The hooded figure leaning against the far window of the coach reached out for her hand and Frankie gave her gloved fingers a reassuring squeeze. They hadn't counted on Elizabeth coming out on the step to wave to her younger daughter.

Frankie held her breath as she waved for both of them and then settled back as the coach began to move. They were silent for several minutes, measuring the blocks and then the miles before "Claire" lowered her hood and looked at Frankie.

"We did it." Sarah's face was aglow with the excitement of their deception. "You're away free."

"Thank God," Frankie said, peering out the window as if expecting an angry mob in pursuit. Finding no such thing, she turned to Sarah. "Now, you remember what to do? Take the coach to the train station, have a porter send the trunks to the countess—you have the money, right?— and then get back to the house before Mama realizes you've been gone."

"Easy as pie," Sarah declared. "I slip in and out all the time without her knowing it."

"Well, you'll be the sole recipient of her attention now that we're out of the house, so be careful."

"Count on me," Sarah said, grinning, and a small mound rose beneath her cloak and started to move from her lap up to her shoulder. Frankie watched in both horror and relief as she retrieved her pet ferret from beneath her cloak and stroked the little creature's head.

"For Heaven's sake, don't let that thing loose in my room while I'm gone," she said. "The little beast steals everything in sight."

Reynard was waiting for her at one of the less desirable berths at the docks. He had secured them passage on a wooden steamship that had seen better days and now carried light freight between London and Calais.

"I don't suppose they have a first-class berth," she said, looking at the peeling paint and salt-crusted windows of the aging vessel. He wrested her larger bag from her hand and ushered her toward the gangplank.

"Any ship with a first-class anything would demand to know who we are," he said, leaning close to her ear. "That would mean putting us on a passenger manifest that would go to a bursar's office and be subject to prying eyes. You do want this mission to be a secret?"

"Of course," she said with an uneasy feeling as she stepped around a sizeable hole in the gangplank and looked down to see an oily strip of water between quay and ship. *Please God, let the gangway be the only place there are holes in this boat.*

He headed for what looked like a small flat-roofed house that had been plopped down on the weathered deck. "Just so you know . . . I thought it best that we stay together. The captain said weather is rolling in and there was only one cabin to let."

She stopped stock still, scowling, and he turned back to usher her toward the most prominent opening in the cabin section. A grizzled old fellow in a faded blue coat and a military-style hat missing some of its braid stepped out of their target as they approached.

"This must be the missus, then," he said with a grin showing gapped, tobacco-stained teeth. He tugged at his hat brim and looked her over with a gleam in his eye. "Pity it's such a bad day fer sailin', ma'am."

"My dear, meet Captain Mercy." Reynard gave the old fellow a nod.

"You say it is a bad day for a crossing?" she said, resisting Reynard's urging toward the main hatch.

"Aw, yeah. Terrible." The old boy's grin broadened. "Wind'll be comin' up to gale and rain'll be comin' down in sheets. Welcome aboard."

The captain reeled off to bark orders at his crew.

She turned on Reynard.

"The missus?" she said through tightened lips.

"It would hardly do for us to share a cabin as Mr. Boulton and Miss Bumgarten, would it? For now, I am the mister and you are the missus. Safer all around to have everyone think you're a married woman."

"I have to be married to travel safely?" she muttered.

"If you weren't so abominably pretty, it wouldn't be a problem."

She gave him a wicked smile. "I'll try to look uglier."

This trip was going to try every nerve she possessed.

Her last glimpse as they stepped through the hatch into the cabin area was of several faces turned their way. Hard visages. Weathered tough. With eyes that shone the way the rats' eyes in a cellar glow when light hits them. She shivered.

The cabin was bare except for a narrow bunk with a stained and threadbare mattress, a washstand that looked like it hadn't been used in a decade, and a battered lantern that swung from a gimbal overhead. The light in the cabin was as dingy as the small window that admitted it.

She stood for a minute, clutching her satchel to her, looking around.

"How long does this crossing take?" she asked.

"It depends," he said, setting down her valise. "Tide, wind, rough water—could be eight hours, could be two dozen. We're under steam, so we'll get there . . . sooner or later."

She frowned, thinking. "Claire and Julian had to make this crossing."

"He's done it before. He'll know what to expect." He took her satchel from her, set it on the floor beside her valise and his, and removed a blanket from atop his valise to spread over the bunk. "May as well get comfortable."

Her frown turned on him. "How comfortable?"

"Sitting down, comfortable." He sat on one end of the bunk and then leaned over to pat the other end. She contemplated it for a moment, reluctant to make contact with anything in the cabin.

"What is that smell?" She wrinkled her nose at the moldy odor.

He sniffed. "Rot of some kind, I expect." He flicked a bit of curled paint and possibly wood from the window behind him. "She'll hold together until Calais. That's all we need."

"I believe I'd rather pass the time in the dining room with the rest of the passengers." She was out the door before he could stop her.

She found the dining room down the hall and down a couple of steps. It was in fact the ship's mess . . . a modest space lighted by small, high windows and containing a pair of tables bolted to the deck. Old sailing memorabilia was nailed to the wooden shiplap walls. Oars, nets, and gaff hooks, dusty signal flags, and faded posters listing sea-going timetables hid some of the weathered paint. Pegs along one wall held mackintoshes for the crew, and rubber boots lay in haphazard piles under the windows.

There didn't seem to be other passengers, unless she counted two men in a far corner who were smoking pipes. One wore a reasonable-looking pinstriped suit and the other a bulging set of tweeds. Around the tables in between sat several roughly clad men nursing mugs of coffee or something a mite stronger. Their weathered faces turned with interest as she entered and paused just inside the doorway. There wasn't another female aboard, she realized, nor another gentleman. She began to reconsider her determination to avoid being alone with Reynard.

"Well, well. Wot we got 'ere?" A tall, rangy fellow wearing a coarsely knit sweater and cap looked her up and down, and the other men present followed suit. He shoved to his feet and sauntered toward her, smug and openly appraising. A second fellow joined him, a short, brawny fellow with dusky skin and eyes as dark as his coal-stained hands. This one's arms were thick; heavy muscles protruded from ripped shirtsleeves—a stoker, she realized. Three others looked ready to join them in whatever they had in mind for her.

Frankie swallowed hard, but stood her ground. She knew this kind. Like timberland wolves and coyotes on the plains, they could smell fear and were attracted to it. Sometimes, like now, they sought it out.

"A fine slip o' muslin," the stoker said with an ugly laugh.

"Whaddaya want, sweetness?" the tall one said, edging close enough to touch her, but not yet attempting it.

"I was hoping to find a cup of tea to warm my bones," she said, realizing belatedly that mentioning "bones" was probably a bad idea.

"Aw, missy, I'll warm yer bones fer ye." The tall one moved even closer. There was bawdy laughter and some low muttering she was glad not to understand. "Truth be— we'll all take a turn at it."

"Thank you, but no thank you," she said with a fierce little smile, bracing and raising her chin a notch. "I'll settle for tea."

She felt her throat tightening and every second stretching to include a small eternity. At best, they wanted a bit of rough entertainment. At worst—Lord, she didn't want to think about worst. What possessed her to leave the safety of the cabin?

Reynard stood just outside the doorway, his fists clenched, but he wasn't sure who made him angrier, the salt-pickled sailors or Miss Too-Independent-for-Her-Own-Good. She seemed to be holding her ground, but the slightest tick of movement could start something he might have to finish in a bad way. And they'd be a few hands short to make a safe crossing.

He stepped into the mess behind her with an icy glare, and flicked back the left side of his coat to reveal the pistol he wore in a shoulder holster. Only one man in the room recognized it as a quick-draw "naked" holster from America, and that man had seen that very gun and holster in use a time or two.

The two ringleaders froze at the sight of Reynard's un-spoken threat. The change in their faces and the direction of their attention caused Frankie to glance over her shoulder. He quickly flipped his coat back over the gun.

One of the pipe smokers at the back—a muscular fellow with a blocky face and a bent nose that gave his face a dangerous cast—rose to break the tense silence.

"I believe the cook can find you a spot o' tea." Grycel Manse, Reynard's friend and sometimes informant, turned and gave a couple of hard raps on the nearest wall with a meaty fist. The apron-clad cook appeared at the galley hatch with a scowl, and he politely asked for "some tea for the lady."

The cook surveyed the room, took in Frankie's appearance with surprise, and disappeared back into the galley.

"Perhaps you'd prefer to wait for it in your cabin," Manse said, glancing between her and Reynard.

"I would. Thank you, sir," she answered, then turned to exit past Reynard. His heart was thudding as she moved past him and up the hallway to their cabin.

By the time he paused outside the door for a deep breath and entered, she had decided to sit on the bunk after all, her arms wrapped around her waist.

"Did you learn what you needed to learn?" Reynard said, stopping before her with his hands propped at his waist.

"That we don't have a dining room or much chance of getting anything edible on this vessel? I did."

"I was referring to the potential dangers aboard this ship."

She looked him in the eye. "Was that a gun I saw under your coat?"

"You saw that. Fine. I am carrying a gun." He crossed his arms and spread his feet a bit since the deck was starting to tilt, ever so slightly.

"May I see it?"

"Hell, no. The thought of you with a loaded firearm in your possession gives me palpitations." He had a quick and alarmingly erotic vision of her standing in her nightgown with a gun aimed straight for his . . . heart. "If anyone needs shooting, I'll be the one doing it."

"Fine." She didn't look like she thought it was fine. "I could always use an oar. They have a couple of spare ones in the mess."

He stared at her, remembering all too well her grit that first night and her dead-on aim with a bread paddle. A laugh escaped him, and he was a little surprised. Tension, he told himself. Some people laughed like hyenas when they were in danger.

A knock on the door made him spin around and reach for the latch. Outside stood Manse with a tray bearing two steaming mugs of tea. "Good," he said, "thanks." She slid from the bunk and was beside him before he could close the door.

"That was quite lovely of you, sir. We appreciate your kindness."

"Anytime, missus," Manse responded, playing his part well. "Crew's a bit rough. You'll want to keep to the cabin." He glanced at Reynard. "I'll look in from time to time to see if you need anything."

"You do that," Reynard answered, registering the twinkle in Manse's eye as he took the tray and shut the door.

"You might have been more courteous to that gentleman."

"He's no gentleman," Reynard said, trying to decide whether to tell her that Grycel was along for the journey. "I suspect he might be quite put out to hear you label him one. He thinks gentlemen are selfish, mean, and lazy. Present company excepted."

"You know him?"

"I do. He's a business acquaintance." Something made him add, "And a friend." He turned that last part over in his mind, deciding it was true. He was a friend and a good one at that.

"He looks kind of dangerous," she said, sipping from her mug as she settled back onto the bunk.

"He is." Reynard settled at the other end of the bunk and leaned back on one elbow to sip his drink. He was relieved to find it was simple tea. No need to lower inhibitions with spirits when he was stuck this close to the desirable Frankie. "Grycel Manse was a bare-knuckle fighter for a few years and put a number of men's lights out. None permanently, but it was a close call once or twice. I met him at Mehanney's Gym. We sparred a few rounds one day and when I quit seeing stars, we went out for a drink at a nearby pub and started a fight with some locals. Since then, he keeps his eyes and ears open for me. He knows a lot of people."

He watched her drinking in that story and could almost see her adding that piece to her assessment of him. Something in him wanted to say more, to tell her more—personal things—ideas, information, conclusions.

"So that's how you get your 'secrets.' People like Mr. Manse."

He studied the tea in his mug.

"Sometimes. Sometimes it's just an unguarded word here or there, sometimes a dinner with a well-placed acquaintance or a favor for someone who needs it. No lurking at keyholes or scaling walls to peer in second-story windows."

"I wouldn't have expected that." She grinned. "You're too . . ."

"Too what?" he asked, watching her sort through a

number of descriptions she either refused to assign to him or refused to reveal.

"Cultured. Elegant. Maybe a bit too superior," she said.

She clearly wasn't one for gilding the lily, he thought. "All true. Honest and yet, not unkind. A rare and admirable combination of traits."

"Much like yourself," she said, letting her eyes linger a bit too long on his sprawled frame.

"Me? Admirable? Beware, Miss B. I am a gossip hawk, after all."

"Just when did you become a gossip hawk?" When he shook his head, she pressed on. "What was your first 'secret'?"

He sighed and finished his tea in one gulp, thinking back. "I believe it was when George Rector wet the bed in our hall at school. Smelled horrid. It was the dead of winter and he was a plebe—a new student—eight years old and missing Nanny. He was in tears and so frightened—I claimed it was me—said I peed in his bed because he was a proper toff. He was forever grateful."

"That's terrible." She gaped at him.

"Not really. Since he'd supposedly had a hard 'welcome to,' the older boys mostly left him alone after that. And I earned points for being a right little bugger. So, we both came out like daisies." He sighed. "Never told a soul it was him. Until now." He frowned, thinking that he was in danger of opening more of himself to her than was wise. "And that secret taught me a lesson that has served me well to this very day."

"Which is?"

"Secrets are valuable. Everybody has secrets, and most people would go a long way to protect them."

"Even you?" she asked, and he felt a curious spur of emotion and looked up into her warm blue eyes.

"Especially me," he said, unable to look away.

"About your family?" she said.

"Why would you say that?" He sat up slowly.

"Isn't that where most secrets start? Look at my family—chock-full of things we'd rather other people didn't know. Some things—like the reason for this mad dash to Paris—we'd rather members of our own family didn't know."

There was something in her gaze and weighting her words, something left unspoken.

"My heritage is fairly well known: only child of Gareth Boulton, the second son of the previous viscount. The first son, my uncle Ormond, had no children who lived, so when my father died—I was all of two years old—I became his heir. My mother was a good woman, but not especially hardy. She died not long before my seventh year.

"I was sent away to school after that. I was small and underfed, scrawny actually. My smart mouth got me into trouble routinely and I probably wouldn't have survived my first two years if not for your brother-in-law, Ashton Graham. He was a scrapper and stuck up for me and for his older brother, Arthur. I owe him more than I can say. Which is the whole reason—"

He looked down, then away, wishing he could take back that last part.

"The whole reason you're here?" Frankie was taken aback, and felt a sinking in her chest. "You're paying a debt to my brother-in-law. And here I thought it might be my too-pretty face and charming conversation."

She took a deep breath and chided herself for reading romance into the odd but intriguing relationship developing between them. Soaring passion? Soul-deep communion? A love to last the ages? Clearly, her mother was right about one thing: she had read too many novels.

"Well, it doesn't matter why you're here," she said, trying to convince herself as much as him, "you're here and helping me. Whatever the outcome, I will always be grateful for that."

Chapter Eighteen

The night was dark and rain pounded the streets and pavement, making Red think he should probably turn around and head back home. But with Frankie and Cece gone, there was too much quiet in the house and too much of a martyred air around Lizzie.

Sarah escaped to her room each afternoon, supposedly to read or stitch—both considered "improving activities" for well-bred young ladies. In fact, she slipped out her window and shinnied down a drainpipe to head to the stable and her dogs and fancy new horse.

But Red had precious little to do that didn't involve spending or losing money. Horse races, betting windows, card games, bawdy houses—everywhere he went somebody had a hand out—or in his pocket. Worse, he was constantly on the lookout, dodging the duke who held his markers. Sooner or later, he knew, the greedy bastard would catch up with him and make demands he couldn't meet.

He stepped inside the Chancery and looked up at the mezzanine from which Beulah MacNeal ran her lucrative concern. There she was, watching as usual. He tipped his hat to her before handing it off to the hat check and heading to the bar.

His beloved Irish whiskey tasted oddly flat and the music seemed louder than usual and slightly off-key. No, he told himself as the barman offered him another, it was he who was off. He declined, feeling restless and miserable and closer to worthless than he'd ever been in his life. The Fox said he'd find a way to help with the debts, but Red hadn't heard from him in days. As he turned, leaning on the bar, to look around for Boulton, he was struck motionless and his mouth dried.

Coming straight at him were the Duke of Ottenberg and a couple of his hired knuckle-bangers. Red's first impulse was to escape, but he could feel his knees locking up, so he just stood, watching doom descend on him.

"Good to see you, Redmond, old friend." Ottenberg's greeting was oil and water—meaning and tone distinctly separate. "In for another bid at Lady Luck's favor?"

"Naw. Just havin' a sociable splash o' the Irish." Red straightened to his fullest height, but Ottenberg still towered over him. He glanced at the heavily muscled head-thumpers, seeing boredom in their eyes. A dangerous thing, boredom, in men used to violent activity.

Ottenberg waved the others farther down the bar and took a place beside Red. He motioned to the barman and as the drink was delivered, he leaned close to Red's ear.

"I want my money, Strait." His voice, already low, seemed to drop an octave. "*Now.*"

"I ain't got it, Yer Grace." Red's voice wavered in a way the duke detected. He could tell by the predatory gleam in the Prussian's eye. "But anytime now, the assays will be back an' we got us another mother lode o' silver."

"I know," the duke said unctuously, "you have your

problems. But I have mine. And right now, I need cash or another form of payment."

"Like what? I got some fine breedin' horses that'll make up at least half the twelve. Though, it'd near kill me to give 'em up. An' we got a load of fancy silver stuff in th' house."

"There's only one thing you have that I want." He smiled like the snake he was. "Your niece." He even hissed as he said it. "Frances." Another hiss. "I have proposed, but it seems she is being what they call 'hard to get.' She keeps me waiting, and my patience is running thin."

"You want Frankie, you gotta talk to her. That girl's as headstrong as a Missouri mule."

"No, no, my friend. *You* will talk to her. And you will persuade her to see reason and accept my offer within the week . . . or . . . you will find it hard to ever ride your handsome horses again. Broken backs, I am told, do not heal." He waited a moment for that to sink in before continuing.

"I will call tomorrow. You will tell her to receive me and to be more accommodating."

"I can't." Red's throat tightened. "She's visitin' an old family friend, the Countess of Kew. Out in Suffolk."

The duke studied his anxious face and must have decided he was telling the truth, for he asked, "When does she return?"

"She an' her ma—they're feudin' an' she's not likely to be back for some time."

"Then you will go to see her. And tell her whatever you must to bring her back to the city and to her senses. Five days, Redmond. You have five days left to use your persuasions to save your legs."

Red felt the blood drain from his head as the duke walked away and motioned his hirelings to follow. The pair of brutes slowed to eye him as they passed and produced nasty smirks that let him know they savored his dread and looked forward to their next meeting with him.

By the time he was steady enough to have the doorman call a cab for him, he had only one thought in mind. The Fox. He had to see Reynard.

Exeter Square was dark and quiet except for the thuds of his fist against the impressive door of the residence he assumed was Reynard's. The butler informed him that Master Reynard could be found in the carriage house out back. He was so harried that he didn't stop to wonder why Reynard lived in a place usually allotted to servants. He rushed through a dark, twisty garden of some kind and was soon pounding on an upstairs door, calling for the Fox to open up.

There was no answer. After a while, a young footman came running from the rear door of the main house to say Master Reynard was not at home—that he had left for Paris that very morning. Something about a young lady who visited a night or two ago.

"This gal—what'd she look like?" Red demanded, grabbing the fellow's jacket and hauling him closer. "Face like an angel? Chestnut hair? Spoke American?"

The youth nodded. "I believe so."

Red released him and began putting two and two together. Frankie had come to see Reynard, and the Fox had taken off for Paris immediately afterward.

He was on his own.

He left Exeter Square with his thoughts reeling. That damned low-down kraut-suckin' Prussian. Demandin' he hand over Frankie like she was a mare of the herd. Thank Heaven she was sent off to stay with—

He stopped dead in his tracks. Ahead, he could see carriage lights that promised a cab stand, but suddenly all of his energy was focused on the realization that he'd just told

Ottenberg where she could be found. The Countess of Kew's house in Suffolk. It wouldn't be hard to find if . . . if the bastard decided not to wait five more days for him to persuade Frankie. Oh, God. What if he decided to just go and get her? Make her marry him . . . force her to his will and his bed?

"Devil take that sonuvabitch!"

And he began to run.

Red stopped at home to write a note to Lizzie, saddled up at Trinity Livery, and then rode through the rest of the night to the countess's Suffolk home. By mid-morning, he was riding up the lane to the gray-stone country house the countess had purchased with the fees she had earned sponsoring Daisy through her courtships with the Duke of Meridian and his charming rascal of a brother.

Red recalled his last visit here, the proposal he'd made, the haze of disbelief he'd carried with him for days after she'd turned him down. She didn't give him reasons, compounding his pain and distress. He had thought she shared his feelings—she certainly seemed to at times. It took a while, but he eventually recognized that she had given him hints that his indulgences and free-wheeling behavior were things she could not reconcile with her respectable soul. He drank too much, gambled, bragged, flirted, and generally made himself the center of attention—some positive and some *not*.

He fought through those heart-rending memories and the mistakes he'd made, forcing himself to concentrate on Frankie's and Cece's peril. If anything happened to them . . .

He knocked on the weathered door under the narrow

portico, and then again. Those sharp, urgent raps brought a housemaid to answer.

"The countess . . . she at home?" Red barreled past the young woman, sweeping the familiar main hall and empty parlor with a glance, then turned back to her. "My girls, where are they? I have to see them right away."

"Begging your pardon, sir." The maid looked at him as if he'd lost his wits. "What girls?"

"Frankie and Claire. They arrived yesterday and I have to see them." It struck him she hadn't been there when he was visiting the countess regularly. "I'm Red Strait, a friend of the countess." Still she stared at him. "Jus' go get the woman, girl. There's trouble."

With a dubious look, the girl left him banging his damp hat against his mud-spattered trousers and hurried up the stairs to inform her mistress. Moments later, Evelyn Hargrave descended the stairs to the first landing and stood transfixed, staring at Red.

His eyes ached at the sight of her: tall, regal, lovely as the day was long. There were a few additional streaks of gray in the hair around her face, but she maintained her youthful figure and sense of style. She wore a day dress of rose-colored wool that accentuated her rosy cheeks and dark hair. But it was her eyes, those big beautiful brown eyes that drew Red to the bottom of the steps.

"It *is* you," she said, her voice a bit thick. "When Molly said there was a 'red' fellow in the hall insisting on seeing me, I couldn't imagine . . ." She descended the steps slowly, focusing on him as she gripped the railing.

"Evie." Red's face heated as he took her in. For a moment, his mission was forgotten. She was every bit the proper and commanding lady he had loved and lost. When she neared him and extended her hand, he had flashes of memory of her reaching for him with affection. He took her hand and was surprised to feel a faint tremor in it.

"I don't mean t' disturb you, but I have to see my girls. It's a matter o' life an' death."

"Your girls?" She stepped down off the last step and settled before him. "You mean Frankie, Claire, and Sarah? Why would you come here to see them?"

Red was thunderstruck. "We sent 'em off to you just yesterday. Lizzie wrote you they were coming for a visit."

"I got no such letter." Alarmed, she turned to the housemaid Molly. "Has there been anything from the post?"

"I don't know, milady. I'll check." The maid hurried off while Evelyn explained.

"Albert, my houseman, was taken ill a few days ago. Things have been chaotic ever since."

"If they ain't here, where are they?" Red grew more anxious and rubbed the back of his neck. "Evie, I'm worried sick. I rode half th' night and they're not even here. They should've got here yesterday—tea time at the latest."

"Come in and tell me what's going on." She slipped her arm through his and ushered him into the parlor. There was a welcoming fire in the hearth and the place was much as he remembered it, soft, soothing colors and comfortable seating that didn't make a man feel like he'd crash something if he plopped his saddle bones on it. He pulled up a winged chair beside hers and told her what happened.

"Oh, Elizabeth," she said, shaking her head when he finished. "She tries to control everything. It's a hard lesson to learn . . . letting them take the reins of their own lives . . . giving them guidance, not orders."

"That's why we thought o' you." He held out his palms to the fire. "You were good for Daisy. We figured you could talk sense into 'em. Bring 'em round to th' idea of gettin' married."

"I'm not sure I would have much influence. Your girls have always had more freedom than English girls have." She shivered and rang for coffee. "Or perhaps you'd rather have something stronger."

"Nah," Red said, looking at the wheezing logs. "I'm not much fer spirits these days."

She stilled and turned a searching look on him.

"There's more, Evie. That duke Lizzie's so determined to have fer a son-in-law—he's a bad one. I told him they were visitin' here, and I'm afraid he may come for 'em— if he hasn't already." He thought about that. "Wait—I saw 'im last night and he didn't know they left town. He must not have them. Then where could they be?" He closed his eyes for a moment and pinched the bridge of his nose. "I'm so tired, I can't think straight."

Her brow knitted with concern. "Just rest a bit. We'll figure it out." Without thinking, she stroked his arm and clasped his hand briefly as she rose to see to some breakfast for him. Red's head sank to one of the chair's wings and his eyes didn't open again for some time.

He snuffled awake, startled by a pop in the renewed fire, to find a lap blanket over his knees and a plate of food cooling on a small table that had appeared beside his chair while he slept. Across from him, Evelyn was reading Elizabeth's letter, which had been found tucked away in the butler's pantry.

"She says Frances is being stubborn and unrealistic about the situation." She scowled. "That the duke is a powerful man used to getting what he wants."

"He's a varmint—greedy and underhanded," Red said. "He buys up debts and uses 'em to force people to give 'im things he's got no right to."

"That's deplorable," Evie agreed.

"Worse than that. He wants me to tell Frankie she has to marry him."

"Why would he think you would do that? Especially since you know Frankie has refused to have anything to do with him."

"Yeah, well. I got debts too." He made himself meet her gaze for a long minute and was surprised to see understanding, not condemnation, in her eyes. She studied his somber mood and continued to make connections in her mind.

"Who among us hasn't had them?" she responded. "You know what a spot I was in when I met you and Daisy. The Kew estates were sold for debts before my husband's body was cold. If it hadn't been for Daisy's letter . . ."

Silence descended for a minute, then Red sat forward, his eyes widening.

"She claimed the Fox owed her a favor and she went to his house to ask him somethin.' Just after, he took off like a shot fer Paris." He looked at Lady Evelyn with dismay. "You don't suppose she's gone off with him?"

"Surely, Frankie wouldn't be so rash," Evelyn said, scouring her memories of the girls. "What about Claire? Would she go with them?"

"Milady." Molly appeared in the drawing room with a puzzled look. "There's fellows from the train station here with trunks. Says they're supposed to deliver them to us."

"The girls packed trunks and took off with them on the back of the coach." Red untangled himself from the lap blanket and charged out into the hall to find his nieces' trunks being deposited on the marble floor. Evelyn appeared at his side and stared at them.

"Why would they send their things here and then go someplace else?"

Red shrugged and turned to Molly. "Bring me yer lady's ring o' keys. Let's see if we can get these beauties open."

That was where they found Claire's note to Frankie. Frankie had hidden it beneath her cool-weather wraps and sensible shoes. Evelyn dismissed the servants, then sat down with Red to read it aloud.

"Paris," Red echoed when she finished. "Claire's run off with some music fellow. That new violin teacher . . . has to be. And Frankie's gone after her." He scowled, trying to think how they'd managed to fool their mother and him. Probably with the Fox's help. That was why Frankie went to see him—to get him to help her go after Cece. Smart girl. From his stories, the Fox seemed to know his way around Paris. Then he realized: "Lizzy will have a heart attack when she finds out. I had a time talkin' her into sendin' them to you instead of sendin' them back to Nevada."

"Then, she can't find out," Evelyn said with a determined expression.

Red studied her for a moment.

"You're right. I reckon I'll have to go after 'em an' get 'em back here before Lizzie finds out they're gone."

He looked up as Evelyn rose and rang for Molly and the other servants.

"What are you doin,' Evie?"

"I'm going with you, Redmond," she said with a finality that brooked no objection. "Sounds to me like you will need a touch of respectability along to set things right. And if there's one thing I'm good at"—her tone turned self-deprecating—"it's being respectable."

Evelyn paused in the middle of issuing Molly orders. "Besides, it's been too quiet around here. I think it's high time for a dose of Bumgarten girls."

While Red was shown to a proper bed for a bit of rest, Evelyn packed what she considered essentials for Paris, had Red's clothes freshened, and made arrangements for her household. The sun had already set by the time they boarded a local train bound for London. Their arrival made them too late to catch a passenger ship or ferry across the channel. The pair could hardly go to his home, so Red found them rooms in a hotel far enough from the waterfront to be respectable.

Promising Evie he would be careful, he ventured out into the night to seek information on Reynard's movements. He visited several dockside taverns before finding a barman who not only knew Reynard, but had seen him two days before inquiring about discreet passage across the channel. He wasn't sure but he thought he had heard Reynard mention Calais.

It was something to go on. The next morning, Evelyn joined him to visit passenger booking stations and then the harbormaster, seeking news of freighters that might have left for Calais within the last two days. A folding fiver made the clerk step away from the ledger, and one freighter in the list stood out. It was headed for Calais and its manifest listed four passengers, two of whom were single men and two were a young married couple. No names.

Red used his lucky gold piece to pry any additional information from the clerk. All he learned was that the captain, a bloke named "Mercy," had said the young fellow and his wife were in a hurry, an' he slipped Mercy an extra tenner. He also mentioned the wife was quite a "looker."

Chapter Nineteen

"This soup is awful." Frankie peered into her bowl through the lowering gloom. "There are dark bits floating around in it. Is that tree bark?"

"Dried beef, more likely," Reynard said, practically inhaling his soup. "Or maybe dried sausage. Depends on where they provisioned last. Beef in London, sausage in Calais." He watched her poking at the contents of her bowl. "Try holding your nose."

She gave him a scalding look and he laughed. A full, resonant sound that made her stare at him in wonder. What a marvelous laugh. Why had she not noticed it before?

"The food will be better the closer we are to Paris," he said, grinning.

"I've heard that French food is a marvel," she said, setting her bowl on the floor and climbing back onto what she had come to think of as her half of the bunk. "So where do we get horses to carry us to Paris?"

"About that . . ." He set his empty bowl down and pushed back on the bed so that his back was against the wall. "I think it would be faster and generally safer to catch a local train to Lille and then take one of the main lines to Paris. They run frequently—we should be able to get there from Lille in a few hours, as opposed to a couple of days collecting saddle sores."

"A train?" She looked at him in dismay and he raised an eyebrow.

"I believe from Lille to Paris they have first-class cabins."

"Oooh. Lille it is." But she had another thought. "Wait— how much does it cost?"

"You'll have to fill out a special form"—he seemed quite serious until he finished with "promising them your firstborn."

She narrowed her eyes. "*My* firstborn. What about *your* firstborn?"

"My firstborn is already spoken for. I assume yours is still available."

"It is. But how would they collect a twinkle from your eye?"

"I beg your pardon." He looked at her as if she'd sprouted a second head.

"Don't tell me you haven't heard the phrase 'I've known him since he was a twinkle in his father's eye.' It's one of Uncle Red's. It implies—"

"I know what it implies." He frowned slightly, concentrating. "So, you think your firstborn is a twinkle in *my* eye?"

"Well, it has to be in somebody's eye," she said, with as straight a face as she could muster. "It could be you or any one of a hundred fellows I have yet to meet. Don't take it personally."

"Good God." He seemed genuinely flummoxed. "You are the most outrageous female I have ever met."

"Likewise." She met his gaze with a steadiness that surprised her.

"What does that mean?"

"It means you say things that astonish and puzzle me on a regular basis. You're warm and inviting one moment and cool and condescending the next. You make arrogant pronouncements, and then turn around and say something that is downright funny and endearing. I don't know how to deal with you. *Yet.* But I will. It's on my list of things to accomplish before I die."

"Assuming you know me for that long."

"I will. I plan to have a long, eventful life."

He pulled his chin back and gave her a dubious look.

"I don't know how I feel about you planning your life around me."

"Good Lord, Reynard. It's not like I've asked you to marry me or something." She sniffed and tilted her chin. "Back to this train from Lille. What are the chances we'll have to ride in a boxcar with the livestock?"

He seemed truly unmanned by her quicksilver changes of subject. "I'll be stark raving mad by the time we reach Paris."

"If it's more than four pounds sterling, we'll probably have to walk."

She sighed internally. Her plan to keep him at arm's length was working, so far. But the longer she stayed cooped up in this cabin with him, the harder it was to not stare at him and want to touch his handsome face and explore his long, lanky body.

"If only we had a deck of cards," she said, rousing a triumphant "Ah-ha!" from him. He slid off the bunk and delved into the side of his valise for a small box that turned out to be playing cards.

They agreed on rummy and began to play. Several rounds of cards had Frankie well ahead in points and Reynard growing frustrated by her luck.

"Perhaps we should try another game," she said. "I've

always been terrible at euchre, but I'll try it if you'll refresh my memory of the rules."

She turned out to be abominably lucky at euchre, too.

With a huff of disgust, he looked up at her.

"You, Frankie Bumgarten, are impossible."

It came out because she just couldn't keep it in any longer.

"That's the problem, Reynard Boulton. I'm all too possible."

His gaze locked with hers and lightning struck along that visual connection. Seconds later, he was up and launching himself across the cards, headed straight for her lips.

She didn't move, didn't gasp, didn't brace to resist. When his chest made contact with hers and pushed her back onto the bunk, she wrapped her arms around his neck and parted her lips in invitation. He accepted with a heat and urgency that answered every question her heart could ask.

Sweet Heaven—it was like every part of her body cheered at those long-awaited sensations. Her face tingled from her lips outward, her breasts heated and their tips became tight little bundles of anticipation. His weight against her was divine and his kisses were long and positively liquefying. She was turning into a pool of exquisite, swirling sensations that seemed to have no beginning and no end.

He touched her face, her hair, her throat, and groaned at the barrier her dress presented. With a nod from her, his clever fingers went to work and soon freed her chest and the tops of her breasts to his ministrations. She was almost delirious at the feel of him kissing and nibbling his way across her chest and up her throat. Such sensations, such pleasure . . . she'd never imagined . . .

When at last he paused to look down at her, his eyes

were that lovely bright silver again, glimmering with pleasure, and his lips were curved in a delicious smile that she traced with her fingers.

"I've never felt anything like this," she said, not bothering to shield the emotions that accompanied her awakening passions. For the moment, she didn't care about anything but the warmth and pleasure of having him against her, loving her. And it was *loving*. His touch was gentle, his kisses were lush and inventive, and his face—his features glowed with a tenderness that took her breath.

"I will never, ever say you are too pretty again," he said. "Because you are far beyond that. You're beautiful. I never realized there were feelings so far beyond words. Feelings you can only show by touching, holding, giving." He dropped light kisses from her forehead down her nose to her lips. "Do you know how many times I have wanted to kiss you like that?"

"I hope it is as many times as I have wanted you to," she murmured.

He smiled softly and in that moment, she wondered if that was what angels looked like. Eyes glowing, face alight with passion and caring. And she understood, finally, what Daisy had meant when she said there were no words to truly describe the depth and joy of love between a man and a—

Love. Her breath froze in her throat, as if an icy draft from the tempest outside had brushed her bared soul. She stiffened with shock.

He read the change in her, and whether or not he sensed what caused it, he responded with a withdrawal that dimmed those beautiful eyes.

He sat back, straightened his coat, and began to pick up the cards.

She rose and with clumsy fingers began to re-button her

bodice. *Love.* A thousand different thoughts and feelings clamored for attention—but the ones she chose to recognize were regret, disappointment, and anxiety that he would think less of her for what just happened. For starting something between them and then stopping something between them.

He said something about needing fresh air as he left.

She focused on the door as it shut, feeling limp and empty, like a balloon with the air let out. And yet, she knew if it had gone further—if they had indulged their true desires—it would only have complicated things. Their lives, their futures were complex enough as it was.

As she sat on the bunk feeling the ship shuddering and shouldering its way through the heavy seas, she realized her emotions were as chaotic as the weather outside. And for the second time in years, her eyes filled with tears.

The ship rolled and tossed in the dark, making sleep impossible, and when the waves and spray drenched the deck and cabin, the temperature dropped enough to set Frankie shivering. The lantern overhead swayed and jerked against the gimbal, dousing the wick and leaving the cabin in darkness. She stood on the bunk and tried to reach and relight the lantern, but she lost her balance twice and decided it was useless to fight such churning elements.

He didn't return to the cabin for some time, and when he did, he brought a chair and sat in it with his feet propped on their valises. She lay on the bunk, cold and miserable. He must have heard her teeth chattering—it was certainly loud enough—and he delved into his valise for a coat to put over her. She was so grateful that she didn't object when he lay down beside her and pulled her into his arms, fitting himself against her.

"Don't you need your coat?" she stuttered.

"No. I'm cold-blooded. Ask anyone in London."

He was back to his sardonic, self-disparaging mode. She sensed that it was a form of protection for them both, but it dealt a bruise to her heart all the same. His breath was warm against the nape of her neck, and she shivered.

"Still cold?" he asked.

"I'm getting warmer." She paused. "Thank you."

"Think nothing of it. And for Heaven's sake, don't let word of it get around. It would wreck my reputation as a heartless scandalmonger."

There was a softness, an intimacy in his voice that took some of the sting from those words. In spite of her best intentions, she snuggled deeper against him and allowed herself to absorb the pleasure of his embrace while it lasted.

Warm and secure against him, she fell into an exhausted sleep, and didn't feel the sweet press of his lips against her hair in the dark.

The ship seemed to have stopped moving when she awoke. There was light in the cabin and the bunk beside her was empty. She stood for a moment, brushing her clothes while adjusting to the lack of motion.

Today began the next phase of her mission. Her thoughts were crowded with potent impressions of the previous night, both pleasurable and agonizing. She was falling in love with Reynard Boulton and couldn't seem to stop. No amount of reasoning or good sense could persuade her heart not to want things he was not prepared to give her. The duke's dark words were ever in her mind; Reynard was not who he appeared to be. He had troubles of his own. His help with finding her sister was already more than she had a right to expect.

Her task, then, was to make sure it went no further, to barricade her heart against feelings that would never be returned.

When Reynard appeared in the cabin with a cup of tea, a hunk of dry bread, and a plateful of overcooked, brown-edged eggs, she was mostly prepared and greeted him with a barrage of questions.

As she picked at the food, he answered. They were in the harbor, waiting for a berth at the quay, which accounted for the minimal motion. The captain said they would be docking soon and Reynard had already inquired about train schedules.

"Excellent," she declared, leaving the plate on the now bare bunk. "Then we'll have time to get some real food."

In the end, they had no time for food. The closest departure time for Lille was barely an hour from their docking. They hurried down the gangplank and across the dock to a place the captain had said they might find a cab to the train station. British coin was accepted for tickets, but Reynard negotiated an additional exchange of currency that he was pleased to say was in their favor.

They were seated in the train's one and only passenger car, when Grycel Manse entered and stowed his satchel on an overhead rack. He took a seat at the rear of the car, propped his hat over his eyes, and appeared to nap.

Frankie looked to Reynard and he nodded, letting her know that he was aware of his friend's presence. She drew a deep breath, reassured. Reynard had been to France a number of times and spoke French fluently. It did worry her a bit that he had arranged for head-cracking help in case they needed it.

Lille was a bustling city much larger than Frankie expected. The train station, the Gare de Lille-Flandres, was still under construction in places, but managed to accommodate a great number of travelers daily. They found the ticket windows and purchased tickets to the Gare du Nord in Paris.

No firstborns were required.

They settled into seats in first class and Frankie was too occupied with thoughts of what they would do in Paris to realize that Reynard was watching her closely. She couldn't decipher the trend of his thoughts in his carefully neutral countenance, and decided to come right out with it.

"Is something wrong?"

"No," he responded, setting the newspaper he'd acquired aside.

"You're staring." She tried not to let him think it was important to her.

"You are a better traveler than I would have expected. Kept your stomach down on that abysmal crossing last night."

"It was empty. I travel better on an empty stomach," she said. "I'll be ravenous by the time we reach Paris." She studied him for a moment. "So, what is really on your mind?"

He took a deep breath and looked out the window at the passing fields and farms. "I'm just wondering what you will do when you find your sister and Julian. She made the choice to leave her home and family and the rest of the English-speaking world to come with him to Paris. What do you think would convince her to return home with you and submit to your mother's will?"

"I've been thinking about that myself. I fear it won't be easy. Julian has the lure of the exotic and the forbidden on his side. Not to mention music in all of its magnificence, which is a big part of Cece's heart. Hopefully, she will have had enough experience on this impulsive journey to see that running off like this is not going to solve their problems, it will only create new ones." She smoothed her skirt over her knees. "She claims not to care about money and comfort, but she's never known anything else. A taste of the reality of a lowly musician's life may change her mind."

She followed his gaze out the window. "There is also the possibility that Julian may not seem quite so desirable once he is in a sea of Frenchmen—just one of many. She has known him for mere weeks. I doubt he has shown her his worst moods, habits, and qualities yet."

"And you think such things may disenchant her? The way he loses his temper over small things, the way he belches during a meal, his penny-pinching or free-spending ways, whatever else he does . . . if you believed you were deeply, eternally in love, would such things discourage you?"

He seemed to be asking about more than Cece's devotion, but she wasn't sure what he wanted. "Perhaps not." She bit her lip, thinking. "Cece always looks for the best in people, and some men hide their flaws better than others."

"Very true." He turned a searching gaze on her. "Your friend the duke, for example."

"Yes." Once again, she felt the burden of the rumors the duke had shared—or invented—about him. "He is all smiles and manners at first, but is too arrogant and impatient to hide his true nature for long. And I will tell you that he says the same things about you."

"Me?" He thought for a moment. "Of course. He sees me as a rival."

"Worse," she continued. "He tells stories of gossip you spread that ruined careers and humiliated families. That you are not so concerned about the truth of the gossip as the juiciness of it. That you are not to be trusted."

He shifted in his seat growing more intent, and then sat forward.

"Part of what he says is true. I was responsible for the downfall of certain men. I can make no excuse for it, except that I was young and arrogant. I felt justified in wielding such power and believed they deserved what they got, not thinking that such actions would reach further than the wretches themselves. I never intended families or business partners to be unjustly injured by my actions. I know in some cases, it happened. An older and wiser man would have been more judicious. I now hold many secrets I will never reveal, for that very reason."

She glimpsed pain in his face, but only briefly, as it was mastered and hidden. It was always there, she realized, just below the surface, masked by a façade of wit and indifference. She began to see the toll that collecting and keeping secrets had taken on him. Reynard—the Fox—bore more of that burden than anyone in the realm. Perhaps she should warn him. . . .

"There is one more thing the duke said, one that I found difficult to credit, but believe you should hear." She paused. "He says you will never inherit, because of your birth. He said . . . you are base born."

He looked like he'd just been gut-punched. A moment later, he rose and walked out of the compartment without a word.

He was wounded by that allegation, more so than anything else the duke had said. The duke's sneering smile rose in her mind, and she realized with a sinking heart that wounding Reynard was probably the very reason the duke had told her. She had just, unknowingly, been the duke's foil in an ugly strike against his prime rival.

For a long while, she sat staring at but unseeing the countryside passing by the window. She wouldn't blame Reynard if he got off the train, headed back to London, and didn't look back. It took a while for her to collect the nerve to go and look for him. She found him just before she reached the dining car. He was returning to their compartment bearing a tray filled with food.

As he stood in the passage holding that tray, searching her reaction, she could see the man inside him, a man tempered enough by time and trial to acknowledge his mistakes and take responsibility for them. But in doing so, he allowed others the same freeing, life-giving honesty that he had chosen. Painfully aware of his flaws and shortcomings, he was now more accepting of imperfections in others. In *her*. It was a lesson in the meaning and power of forgiveness that she would not soon forget.

"Hungry?" he said, glancing down at the linen-covered tray.

"Absolutely," she said, feeling tears pricking her eyes. Blinking them away, she turned back to their compartment with a heart suddenly filled with stubborn and defiant joy. For this moment, for however long it might last, she was with the man she wanted more than anything else in her life.

She had just fallen completely and irrevocably in love with Reynard Boulton.

Chapter Twenty

Paris was huge, busy, and fascinating. The views from the train windows were hardly the most picturesque the city had to offer, but even the modest neighborhoods and brick streets near the rail tracks seemed quaint and somehow uniquely French.

The French loved to eat. Every corner had a green grocer or café or *patisserie*—pastry shop, Reynard explained. When they reached the street, she hurried to look in the window of the nearest one with such delight and longing, that he laughed.

"God help anyone standing between you and a bit of pastry."

Despite the need to conserve their dwindling coin, he stepped inside and purchased a light, sweet pastry filled with crème. The look she gave him when he handed it to her made him laugh. Her eyes glowed with such pleasure, he felt a disconcerting thump in his throat and his heart beat faster.

They walked for a while through the city, savoring the sights, sounds, and delicious smells. There were open-air restaurants, booksellers that lined the bridges, and barges that allowed people to cruise the rivers while dining in comfort. Musicians plied the streets, sometimes drawing appreciative crowds, sometimes standing alone and playing haunting melodies. It was so different from London— the window boxes that overflowed with blossoms, the shaped trees that lined boulevards, the fanciful ironwork on buildings, gates, and courtyards.

Everywhere, the faint scent of something edible was in the air, hints of foods that would tantalize the palates of sophisticated Parisians. And one very hungry American. Frankie felt her stomach growl.

She was so enthralled by the sights that she didn't stop to think about what their next step should be. It was only when Reynard bustled her into a cab and gave the driver a street and house number that she realized *he* had thought ahead and had a plan in mind.

"Are you going to tell me where we're going? This ride is using up part of our hotel money." She watched him settle back in the carriage, put his feet up on the opposite seat, and lace his fingers together over his midsection.

"To a friend's house."

"What friend?"

"I hope he's still a friend. He was before I had to leave Paris quickly on my last visit."

"Why? Did something—what happened?"

"Nothing really. Some drinking, some swordplay. A little blood may have been drawn. My memory is a little unclear on some of it."

"Perhaps we should just try for a cheaper hotel." She looked uneasy.

"No, I'm sure it will be all right." He smiled and gave a jerk of a nod. "The marq is a sterling fellow."

"How did you come to know this 'Mark' fellow?"

He smiled. "He is actually my mother's younger brother." He paused for a moment. "My mother was French, from Paris."

"What was her name?"

"Lillianne. She was a beauty and when my father came to study at the Sorbonne, he met her brother, the marq, who introduced them. They were married not long afterward and she went back to London with him."

"So, when you came to Paris, you saw him," she continued for him.

"I did. We became friends as well as relations. Don't worry, it will be fine." He stroked his chin. "I suppose I could have sent a telegram to say we were coming."

Frankie groaned. "I don't know much about French customs, but I believe that's probably good manners in any country."

The anxious feeling in the pit of her stomach only worsened when the carriage rolled onto a circular drive leading to a large stone mansion in one of the most exclusive sections of the city. Footmen met the carriage and house servants ushered them into a grand hall and reception area—one that branched off into a long hallway lined with suits of armor and elaborate displays of blade weaponry.

Reynard gave his name to the head manservant, who brightened with recognition and hurried off to find the master of the house. He looked around the grand entry with its marble pillars and massive curved staircase, and he turned to Frankie with a deeply satisfied sigh.

"Some things don't change." He smiled.

The tension in Frankie's stomach was just starting to unwind when a man appeared on the landing of the grand stairs and paused to study them. He seemed tall and had distinguished streaks of gray at his temples, but his frame was solid and athletic-looking. He was dressed casually in trousers, vest, and shirtsleeves and she didn't see the sword in his right hand until it came up to point menacingly at Reynard.

"You!" the man roared as he flew down the steps brandishing the blade.

Frankie's lungs froze as Reynard bolted down the hall of arms to their right and shed his coat as he went for the swords displayed on the wall. He ripped one out of its mounting and turned to meet the fury of his would-be host.

Without another word "Mark" charged and the sound of blades meeting rang in the great hall. Frankie could barely breathe as Reynard met him with equal force, parrying and thrusting back and forth with precision and power that even she could tell held back nothing.

Servants came running at the sound of blades meeting and a much older man in a dignified frock coat came from the other wing of the house, leaning heavily on a cane. "Please—do something!" She begged them to intervene, to stop this terrible assault on a visitor who was also a relation, but all were absorbed in the contest and showed no inclination to call a halt to it.

Up the stairs Reynard and Mark went, and once on the landing, each scored hits on his opponent's sleeves. She could see no blood, but it was clear the battle was taking a toll on both men. They were sweating and working to control their breathing as they concentrated on strategy and technique.

The old man edged closer to Frankie, watching the contest critically, but clearly aware of her distress. When she started forward, he put a hand on her arm to restrain her and kept it there until Mark slipped on a step and went down on one knee, giving Reynard the advantage.

Suddenly all was still and Reynard's blade point was an inch from his opponent's heart. "Mark" dropped his blade on the step beside him and Frankie would have run to Reynard if the old man hadn't held her even tighter. Mark broke into a laughter that was echoed by every manservant in the hall.

"You have not lost your edge, *mon frère*!" Mark said as Reynard withdrew his blade and offered his opponent a hand up. "I believe I see new twists and techniques in your form."

"I practice," Reynard said, grinning and slapping an arm around the older man as they ambled together down the staircase. "And I give the English a taste of French blade work whenever possible."

"And when did you start wearing one of those filthy things?" Mark tapped the holstered gun Reynard had not had time to discard before their bout.

"When I discovered how dangerous Englishmen can be."

Frankie watched in disbelief as the men reached the hall floor, arms around each other's shoulders.

"What are you doing here?" he said to Reynard in lovely, accented English, then waved away his own question. He turned an appreciative smile on Frankie. "Never mind that, who is this ravishing creature you bring with you?"

"My good Marquis, let me present Mademoiselle Frances Bumgarten, from America." Reynard turned to her. "Frankie, this is my uncle, the Marquis de Burbonne."

The marquis, the marq—not "Mark." Frankie would have strangled him if she'd had the chance. How dare he not tell her exactly who they were visiting and what kind of blood-curdling reception to expect?

But the next moment, the marquis was kissing her hand and gazing at her with lovely humor-filled eyes and some of her pique drained.

"Lovely to meet you, your lordship. I only wish Reynard had been more forthcoming about your unusual mode of greeting guests." She turned a glare on Reynard, who joined the marquis in hearty laughter.

From the top of the stairs a woman's voice echoed down to them.

"Henri! You madman! What are you thinking—welcoming guests with a rapier and frightening us to—*Mon Dieu*, is that Reynard?" The lady was robed in a morning gown with lace flourishes that made her seem to float above the steps as she descended. "Beautiful" could scarcely describe her raven hair, big hazel eyes, and delicate features. Frankie watched in amazement as the lady embraced Reynard like a long-lost brother calling him "*mon cher.*"

She managed a polite greeting for the marquise as they were introduced, and was surprised when the woman took her by the shoulders and kissed both of her cheeks. Their friend the Countess of Kew greeted her and her sisters that way, but she had never experienced such familiarity from others.

To the inquiry as to what brought Reynard to Paris, and in such lovely company, Reynard discreetly responded, "A mission of great importance."

"Then we must do what we can to help with this 'mission,'" the marquise said with a chiding look at her husband before she turned back to Frankie. "And you must stay with us, *oui*? Henri and I will have it no other way." She took Frankie by the hand and pulled her toward the stairs, while tossing orders over her shoulder. "You smelly, annoying men—go have your drink and make yourselves presentable."

Frankie already liked this woman, who insisted Frankie call her by her given name, Isolde. But when she was taken to a lovely guest room, provided with a bath, and treated to a trip through the marquise's wardrobe, she began to feel as if they'd known each other for years. A few questions about Reynard's time in Paris didn't seem out of line.

"Ah, Reynard," the marquise said with a smile as she perched on the foot bench while Frankie soaked in rosewater. "My husband's nephew—but more like his brother. He was sometimes here for holidays from school, and more often when he was at university. Every chance, they were drilled in blade work by the old marquis." She shrugged. "To be expected. The men of the House of Burbonne are known as blade masters all over the Continent. For centuries, they were armorers to nobles and kings. So, with Reynard, it is in the blood, *oui*?" She laughed. "He is *formidable*. The only one who can truly test my Henri."

Then she eyed Frankie. "*Pardonez-moi* . . . who are you to Reynard, mademoiselle? His lover, perhaps?"

"*Non*." Frankie flushed from her breasts to her hair. "We are just friends. He was at school with my brother-in-law and has become a friend of my family. When my sister . . . when Claire decided to follow her beloved to Paris without vows or my mother's knowledge, Reynard agreed to help me find her and take her home."

"This sister, she is in love, eh?" She sighed. "A forbidden love?"

Frankie nodded, wondering what had gotten into her, discussing such personal matters with a perfect stranger. All right, a stranger who was giving her a bath and whose clothes she soon would be wearing.

"Forbidden love is the sweetest, *mon amie*. It will be hard to pull her from his arms. I do not envy you this 'mission' of yours. But *famille* must be served, eh?"

That afternoon, over luncheon in a splendid rococo dining room, more of Reynard's Paris escapades were revealed. Some he was proud to claim, others turned him crimson with embarrassment, which Frankie found utterly charming. He had learned from, grown with, and formed great affection for his French relations, and they had accepted him without reserve. They had taught him many things besides blade work—appreciation of art and music, architecture, the great French philosophers, and a penchant for fine cuisine. During these revelations, she watched him settle into belonging and wondered why he ever left these people and this beautiful city for England's cold, damp climes and his uncle's grim hostility.

Famille, she realized. He was there to fulfill an obligation to a father he couldn't remember and a lovely mother who trusted her duplicitous brother-in-law to see to his future. When talk turned to their purpose in Paris, the marquis and marquise showed no judgment of Claire's rash decision to follow her love. At the revelation of the musician's name, Fontaine, their hosts did exchange looks of surprise.

"Julian Fontaine? The son of *the* Fontaines?" the marquis asked.

"They are Fontaines, but I have no idea if they are the ones you may know." Reynard sent a hopeful glance to Frankie before continuing. "I believe this Julian's family is involved in textiles."

"Then it *is* him." The marquis looked to his spouse, who nodded.

"It must be he," she responded. "Their younger son was a musician and there was talk he went to London to pursue a career in music. His mother was devastated."

"Then you know them," Frankie said, gripping the edge of the luncheon table. "Do you know where we can find them?"

"We know them by reputation," the marquis said. "But it should not be difficult to find their home. We have acquaintances in common."

"I do not know if they will help us locate their son and your Claire," the marquise added, "but I cannot think of a better place to start."

"Rest this evening," the marquis said, speaking mostly to Reynard, "while I make inquiries and I will accompany you to call on the Fontaines tomorrow morning."

That night, as Frankie settled into her warm and comfortable bed, she thought back over the day's events. She had never seen Reynard so genial and relaxed. His humor was not as sharp-edged and his willingness to accept teasing and return it with good nature revealed an entirely new side of him. He was at home here, with people who valued him and took pleasure in his company.

His every roguish look, every double-edged comment, every adorable laugh plunged her deeper into dangerous territory. She tossed and turned, seeking sleep but thinking again and again that each revelation of his true self only made it more difficult for her to resist her desire for him. Worse . . . seeing the banter and obvious affection between the marquis and the marquise made her wonder if she and Reynard might someday—

"No." She closed her eyes and did her best to refocus her thoughts on her sister Claire and the man she loved enough to give up almost everyone and everything she had known. "Oh, Claire—please God—I pray he is worth it."

The next morning, the marquise dressed Frankie in a fine sky-blue woolen walking suit and a hat that made her feel almost as extravagant as the beautiful Isolde looked. When she descended the grand stairs to join Reynard and the marquis for the visit to the Fontaines, both men seemed quite taken with her appearance and said so openly. She blushed in spite of herself, pleased especially by the admiration in Reynard's eyes.

The ride in the marquis's carriage was surprisingly short, though it encompassed two bridges and several turns that would have been confusing to those not well versed in Paris geography. The Fontaines' home was a fine old villa made of light stone and set with long windows that lent the imposing house an air of graciousness. The carriage turn that led to the front doors was set back from the boulevard and contained several boxed hedges that added to a thoughtful and genteel presentation.

Reynard rapped the massive knocker, but it wasn't a minute before the door swung open. The marquis stepped forward to present his card and ask to see Monsieur and Madame Fontaine on a matter of some importance. On the strength of the marquis's respected name, they were admitted and shown into a grand parlor decorated in an eclectic style that suggested additions had been made through generations of noble residence.

Frankie clasped her again and again, grateful for Isolde's beautiful gloves that warmed her icy hands. Reynard sensed her tension and gave her hands a quick caress. She drew a heavy breath and began to wander the elegant room, wondering at the volatile passions that sent a young man from such a home, to make his fortune in another land. It seemed an echo of her sister's decision; similar choices that would forge a closer bond between them.

Monsieur Fontaine arrived wearing a somber black suit, a pair of gold-rimmed spectacles, and a puzzled expression. Madame was not long behind him, dressed in a sedate purple woolen dress draped with pearls that were clasped to her shoulder with an ornate silver brooch. They greeted the marquis as if honored by his presence.

The marquis then introduced Reynard as the Viscount

Tannehill, and Frankie as Miss Bumgarten of America. An unusual assembly, Monsieur Fontaine observed as he invited them to be seated. Madame Fontaine rang for the butler and ordered coffee to be served.

Frankie seated herself on one of two settees facing each other before the fireplace, and Madame took the seat beside her, leaving Reynard to settle on the opposite settee. Monsieur Fontaine remained standing, facing the marquis.

"We have come on a matter of some importance to your family and to Mademoiselle Bumgarten," the marquis began. "Your son, Julian, is a musician of some repute, I understand."

The monsieur's face tightened and his posture stiffened.

"My son has chosen to dissociate himself from his family," Fontaine said in French that his wife translated and, with some distress, emphasized to Frankie, who gave her a small, sympathetic smile.

"He left us to pursue his own path," Fontaine continued, clearly still aggrieved. "We have not heard from him in years."

"He has been in London for some time," Reynard spoke up. "He has formed a small but highly regarded orchestra and has begun composing and arranging music. It was in his capacity as a conductor and music teacher that he met Miss Bumgarten's sister Claire Bumgarten."

Both Fontaines turned to look at Frankie and she felt her heart sink.

"My sister is a gifted violinist who met Julian through music. We were hoping that you might have seen him since he returned to Paris." She looked from mother to father, hope dying in her as they shook their heads in dismay. "Then we need not trouble you further," she said miserably, coming to the edge of her seat. "We must seek them elsewhere."

"Them?" Julian's mother reached for her hand to halt

her. "You must tell me—what has happened. I must know what my son has done."

Frankie swallowed hard, striving for composure she did not feel. "He has come home to Paris, saying he has matters to attend here. He wrote my sister a letter telling her how much he cares for her." She cleared her throat. "I assumed, wrongly it appears, that the matters he spoke of would include his family."

"It is of great importance that we find them," Reynard said, searching the madame's anxious face.

"Them?" Fontaine straightened, shocked enough to use the English he apparently knew. "You mean this young woman's sister? He has lured her from her home and brought her here?"

"It appears so," Reynard answered.

Madame Fontaine gasped and brought her handkerchief to her mouth in horror. "He was raised to be a moral and decent man. He was always sensitive and artistic—a good and gentle soul. I cannot believe he would be so selfish and thoughtless." Tears formed in her eyes and she swallowed them back.

"*Mon Dieu!*" Fontaine cursed and stalked one way and then another, before turning on his wife with surprisingly fluent English. "He has always been selfish, Monique, and you have refused to see it. Abandoning his family, he puts himself and his *music* above all else, chasing daydreams when he might have had a good life and a fine living from our concerns. Now he has blackened the name and honor of this family and blighted the life of a young woman he claimed to esteem."

Silence fell as the monsieur halted his explosion of bitterness and Madame's tears would no longer be held back. She began to weep quietly and Frankie's heart ached for her. She reached for the woman's hand and Madame clasped hers tightly.

After a few awkward moments, the marquis cleared his throat and apologized for bringing such unpleasantness into the Fontaines' home. Reynard rose as Frankie did, but he could not leave without one last request.

"If your son should come to see you or contact you," he addressed Monsieur Fontaine, "would you please tell him we are in Paris, at the marquis's villa, and that Claire's sister is desperate to see her."

After a tense moment, the proud Fontaine closed his eyes briefly and nodded.

They left quietly and by the time they returned to Henri's villa, Frankie's spirits were low and her thoughts were running in dismal circles. It took Reynard's stubborn determination to convince her there was still hope and that they should begin to search places that musicians would gather. Concert halls, music halls, the opera, the ballet, cabarets—they should look any and every place musicians might seek work or gather to play.

After some strong coffee and a pastry or two supplied by Reynard, Frankie was ready to try. Henri and Isolde, who were known supporters of the arts, promised to contact music-minded friends and ask if they had heard that Julian Fontaine had returned to Paris. Reynard and Frankie took the Burbonnes' carriage to the Champs Elysées and set off on foot to locate as many musical venues as possible in the heart of Paris.

They stopped musicians arriving at music halls and supper clubs to ask after Julian, then sneaked backstage at the Paris Opera House during a rehearsal to inquire about him there. There were concerts planned in several halls—some by string ensembles and others by amateur or professional orchestras. One or two had been cancelled, but there were enough to check that they began to run together after a while. Frankie's eyes and feet both ached by the time Reynard insisted they stop at a lovely café for some hot chocolate.

"It's such a beautiful city, Reynard." She looked out the café windows to the street and buildings beyond. "I wish I could be here under better circumstances, to enjoy the many things Paris offers." She traced the handle of her cup again and again. "What if we don't find them? What if they've decided to go to Vienna or Rome or Madrid?"

"Julian is a Frenchman," he said, placing his hand over hers on the marble tabletop. "He said specifically he was coming to Paris. I think we should take him at his word. We will continue searching, sweetheart, until we find them."

Chapter Twenty-One

It was nearly time for dinner when they arrived back at the Villa de Burbonne. Henri and Isolde had cancelled other plans to dine quietly with Frankie and Reynard and spend the evening discussing the day's findings.

They had just finished in the dining room and removed to the salon when a commotion rose in the main hall. The marquis glowered in the direction of the noise, but decided to let their capable butler handle it . . . until the sound of scuffling and raised voices invaded the salon itself.

The butler and a strapping footman were struggling with a frantic dervish of a fellow who kept saying he had to see the marquis or Miss Bumgarten.

Frankie shot up from her seat like she'd been fired from a cannon.

"Julian?"

At the sound of his name he stopped fighting and looked around.

"Miss Bumgarten—I must speak with you!"

She hurried to him with Reynard just behind her, while Henri motioned to the servants to release him.

Julian was rumpled and tousled from the struggle, but it was his wild expression that stopped Frankie cold.

"Where is Claire?" she demanded. "I must see Claire."

"That is what I came to ask," Julian said, looking from Frankie to Reynard and then the marquis and marquise. "She is not with me. I came to Paris alone. When I went to my parents' house, they said you had been there, looking for me and Claire. They said you told them we came together, but we did not. I know nothing of her coming to Paris. I swear to you—I have not seen her since the night of her performance at the earl's home."

Frankie was struck speechless. Reynard, however, found his voice.

"That is absurd, Fontaine. She left Frankie a note saying she was coming to Paris with you."

"But she did not. And if she did not, where is she?" Julian was beside himself. "I know she has the strong will, but if she came alone—the docks and streets and rail stations—they are not safe for a beautiful young woman. I cannot live with myself if Claire has come to harm. Please, help me find her."

Frankie fought through her shock to go to Julian and take his hands. "You are sure she didn't sneak aboard a ship with you—follow you here?"

"I came on a freight ship. She would have been too noticeable on such a vessel for me not to know. Please, you must believe me—she is on her way here, or is somewhere on the streets of Paris . . ."

He couldn't make himself finish that and neither could Frankie as her thoughts careened through those beautiful streets and boulevards that changed so alarmingly at night. There were thieves, pickpockets, and procurers abroad, not to mention drunken gangs and even moneyed gentlemen looking for flesh-sport—or worse. From the looks on their faces, everyone else in the salon was thinking the same things.

Frankie turned to Reynard. "I know she came. After writing such a note to me and taking her violin, she would not have turned back. She was headed for Paris and Julian." Fear seized her chest, making it hard to breathe. In blind need, she reached for him. "We must find her, Fox."

"We will find her, Frankie, I promise." He wrapped his arms tightly around her, and as she clung to his hard, capable frame, she could feel his heart beating almost as frantically as hers.

The Gare du Nord was crowded the next morning as Red and Evelyn stepped off the train from Lille and confronted a vast terminal filled with clicking departure boards, food vendors, travelers, conductors shouting orders, and tracks full of engines venting steam under the grand glass roof of the main station.

Red hardly knew where to start, but Evie pointed to the stationmaster's office and he took it on himself to make a path through the crowds for her to that destination. They had no luck getting the stationmaster or head bursar to help them locate records of passengers arriving from Lille in the last four days. Evie was shocked at their callous refusal to help locate their "poor, dear niece who was traveling alone."

Red, however, was not one to give up easily. He sat Evie down at a small café with their bags while he slipped in a rear entrance to the offices and prowled the halls until he found a likely candidate for a bit of bribery.

The small, hungry-looking clerk's eyes widened at the sight of a hundred francs waving before him. He darted into the bursar's office and soon returned with a ledger containing summaries of the ticketed passengers arriving from Lille. Unfortunately, the records only held ticket numbers, not names, which disappointed not only Red, but his greedy little informant.

Red joined Evie at the café and told her the bad news. Their only recourse now was the laborious task of canvassing the railroad conductors, porters, and attendants for anyone who might recall her. Then he had an idea: Reynard was fond of gentlemen's clubs. If he could find the names and locations of several, he might be able to cajole or bribe the porters—or whatever they were called in France—to get a message to Reynard.

Evie had been to Paris several times, most recently with Red and his eldest niece, Daisy, as she prepared for her husband quest. Alas, she reported, she had never had reason to investigate clubs for gentlemen in Paris. Just as she was making a list of people she might call on to ask for such information, Red grabbed her writing arm hard enough to make her pencil rake across her writing paper.

"What on earth—" She looked up, but Red was on his feet already and waving frantically. She peered around him to the most welcome sight she had beheld in months. Frankie and Reynard Boulton were hurrying toward them with surprised and hopeful faces.

"There you are—you troublemakin' female!" Red engulfed Frankie in a hug so tight that her spine popped in two places. He released her and gave Reynard a punch in the shoulder that caught him off guard and rocked him back a step. "And you, rapscallion—makin' off with not one of my nieces but *two*!"

He looked around, expecting to see Claire, and when he glanced back at them with a puzzled expression, their faces had changed. "Where is she?"

"You haven't seen her either?" Frankie asked anxiously, reaching for the countess's hands.

"We thought she would be with you," the countess said, looking around at the crowd. "Didn't you and Mr. Boulton come to Paris to retrieve her?"

"We did come to take her back to England," Frankie said, her countenance falling. "But she is not with Julian. Apparently, she set out for Paris on her own."

"Surely not," the countess said with a gasp. "A young woman traveling alone? These are such perilous times—what could she have been thinking?"

"We finally located Julian last night and he hasn't seen or heard from her," Reynard added. "He and my Parisian friends are helping us search every place she might be. We came through Lille on the train, like you, and thought perhaps she might have come through the Gare du Nord."

"Perhaps if we checked with the stationmaster," Frankie suggested, looking past them for the office.

"Tried that," Red said with a disgusted expression. "No dice."

"This 'Julian,'" the countess said, "surely he must have an idea of where she might go. Friends he has mentioned . . . his family . . . other musicians . . ."

"He is searching for her too, but he has had no luck either," Reynard put in. "With two more pairs of eyes, we can cover more ground."

"Sounds smart," Red said. "As soon as we get set up in a hotel, we'll hit the streets an'—"

"Bring your bags," Reynard ordered, reaching for the two largest valises. "You will stay with us at the villa of the Marquis de Burbonne."

"Really, we cannot impose on your friends," the countess said.

"Not a bit of it." Reynard was already several feet away and drawing them along with him. "Henri and Isolde would be devastated not to meet you. They've heard so much about you." He paused to let them catch up and flashed a wry grin. "Besides, the marquis is not just a friend, he is family. And he owes me a favor or two."

Some distance away, Claire was swaying on a horse-drawn caravan seat, beside an older woman with fierce dark eyes and graying hair put up in braids around her head. There were numerous bracelets on her arms and gold hoops in her ears, much like those of the other women in the caravan of wagons making its way toward Paris. A grizzled older man in a dark vest and coat that almost hid his embroidered shirt drove the caravan with a pipe clenched between his teeth.

The woman was Domka and her husband was Silvanus, the "Rom Baro" of the small traveling clan. Domka saw the way Claire leaned forward as if yearning to leap from the seat and into the new life she would find in Paris. She smiled and reached for Claire's hand, holding and patting it in a gesture that said "patience, my child"—a phrase she had heard several times in her nearly four days of traveling with the Romany.

Julian would never believe her, Claire thought, when she told him how she came from Calais to Paris. How she was spotted and followed by two men as she left the ferry and inquired about the train station . . . how she saw them coming after her and ran . . . how they pursued her. She tried to disappear around corners and down alleyways and once even climbed a metal fire escape and hid in a door-way above an alley. She finally gave them the slip, but then found herself totally lost and in a part of Calais that had seen better days.

She tried to ask directions of a man she saw and he turned to her with dark eyes and an even darker glare.

He backed her into an alley that led to a group of men gathered around tables littered with cards and dice and earthen wine jugs. A man playing a guitar stopped the moment she appeared.

Soon she was surrounded by dusky men with sharp eyes, who began to talk all at once and terrify her with words she couldn't understand. A couple of them pushed her into another's arms and she screamed. Silvanus had appeared, assessed both the situation and her, and in his presence the others halted in expectation. He walked around her, looking her over, and when his gaze fell on the violin case strapped to her shoulder, he stopped dead.

Coming closer, he looked her in the eye, searching her, contemplating what he saw. He said something in what seemed like French. She shook her head, barely able to breathe for the fear constricting her throat. Then he said in heavily accented English, "You play?" and gestured to the violin.

When she nodded, he looked around at the other men, then turned back to her and commanded: "*Play. Now.*"

He stepped back, folded his arms, and assumed an air of judgment. The other men grinned, muttered to one another, and copied his stance. They would see what kind of pale music this frightened young English girl made.

She dropped to her knees and, with trembling hands, opened her violin case and took out her instrument. Her knees were weak as she rose and straightened her spine. She couldn't think what to play, what would pacify this hostile group—something that might allow her to escape. She closed her eyes to concentrate and Julian's beloved face rose in her mind. She seized the image and drew her bow across the strings. Him. She had to play for *him*.

The music flowed from her violin, resonating with the

passion she had for music and for the love her music had brought her. His sweet brown eyes filled her mind . . . playful, then passionate, and then deep with understanding. Her playing became rich and soulful as she unspooled her heart and hopes in that shabby rear yard, before those hostile men.

The joy of playing, of becoming one with the music, slowly returned. She finished one piece and transitioned into another, livelier piece that expressed the fullness of her heart and set her foot tapping. With her eyes tightly closed, she was with Julian in her thoughts and was strangely reassured that someday soon she would see him again and they would find a way to be together always. Whether it was fate or destiny or simple happenstance that brought him to her, she would not surrender him and her hopes for the future without a fight.

A third piece, short and bright, finished her command performance. She took a deep breath, calming her racing heart, and opened her eyes. She was surprised to see that women—and what women!—had appeared at the edge of the group and stood watching her, listening. Their dark hair was loose and flowing and they wore colorful blouses and skirts embroidered with fanciful patterns. At their ears were golden hoops and their wrists were stacked with bracelets that jangled as they moved.

An older woman with graying hair and features that even decades past youth were clear and striking swayed forward into that circle of men. She confronted the big man in a language Claire couldn't begin to place, and sounded less than pleased about something.

She turned to Claire with a cool, commanding smile and said in halting English, "I am Domka." She pointed at Claire. "You . . . ?"

"Claire," she answered, feeling like her tongue was stuck to the roof of her mouth. Domka repeated Claire's name and said it to the other women, who looked at one another and tried out the name. Some made a moue of ambivalence, others smiled and nodded in approval. Then Domka took her by the hand and turned her toward the barren lot where several colorful caravans were settled.

Despite that rocky start, they welcomed her into their camp. That evening she shared their food and listened to their singing and their stories, though she caught only half the words. There were children of all ages running around the central campfire, and animals galore—dogs and goats and big, fancy-colored ponies—were kept at the edges of the circle of caravans.

They asked where she was going and where she had been in her travels. Being travelers themselves, they had an interest in new horizons. She told them of her first home in Nevada and of the great, wide-open spaces of western America. Then she spoke of New York, a big and complicated city where money and enterprise shook hands daily. They made faces like they smelled something awful and after some interpretation, she learned they had an aversion to cities and the great, tall buildings that the rest of the world considered monuments to man's ingenuity.

She described the ships she had sailed the great ocean on, and the horses her father had bred. They loved horses and asked her to describe them in great detail. Then she told them about Julian, who was waiting for her in Paris.

They smiled and sighed, and it was time for her to ask questions.

They were travelers, they said, "Romany" who came from the east many generations ago. They lived as their ancestors had; unencumbered by possessions, not planted in the land. They were free to travel and experience the world in all its confusion and contradictions and glory. And they made their living as they could . . . bartering, working at odd jobs, providing services not usually available to the "planted" people, like fortune-telling and palm reading.

Claire knew the English called them "gypsies," but she saw the pride they took in the name they had for themselves and from that day on would only refer to them as Romany or travelers. Being travelers, they had no objections when Domka proposed they travel to Paris to see Claire safely to her Julian.

Each night as they traveled, she played music with Domka's husband, Silvanus, who was a self-taught violinist of some skill. He introduced her to wonderful songs and the stories behind them as they sat around the fire at night. Together they played for the others to dance, until the women pulled her violin from her hands and made her dance with them. The music's rhythm invaded her blood and she danced as she never had before, laughing and feeling connected to these women and through them to the whole world.

On the last night before they reached Paris, the women took her aside and, with Domka translating as best she could, they gave her advice on men in general and husbands in particular. They laughed and drank wine and listened to the music the men made in their absence. Claire went to bed on her pallet beneath Domka's caravan with a prayer that she would find her Julian before another night fell.

When they stopped on the outskirts of Paris the next afternoon, the women came to her with a plan to escort her into the city and help her find her Julian. She was doubtful, but the women were determined to help and seemed well versed in moving through city streets unnoticed. She watched them don dark-colored skirts with no adornment and simple blouses. They hid their bracelets under their sleeves and their hair in braids beneath shawls and hats. Claire wore her usual dark woolen suit and carried her violin on her shoulder. The rest of her clothes and belongings she had left with the travelers in partial repayment of their kindness.

By the time they reached the center of the city, twilight was sliding into night. Streetlamps had been lighted and the traffic of commerce was giving way to the traffic of the night; carriages and coaches, cabs and horses. They kept to the boulevards and the shadows of the buildings, where Domka paused to consult with ragged, wraithlike characters who directed them onward. In every city, Domka said, there was a network of unnoticed people of the streets who knew things that were valuable and who would share for a price.

When Claire asked what the price was, Domka shushed her and made a sign in the air. "Bad luck to ask."

Their destination turned out to be the Paris Opera House. They watched from across a broad street as carriages queued up to unload their passengers for a performance. The women turned their sun-burnished faces from the ostentatious display of wealth and power trooping up the grand steps to the entrance. It wasn't long before the steps were empty and the carriages had departed to wait elsewhere for a summons at the end of the evening.

Quiet fell and with it went Claire's spirits. She had searched the arrivals for a glimpse of Julian, but found no match for that beloved face. She sat down on a step at the side of the entry, feeling deflated.

Domka and one of the others pulled her to her feet and walked her into the side street that ran along the opera house. There they took down her hair and with a comb from one's hair, freed it from all constraint. It fell in thick waves around her shoulders and made her feel oddly exposed. Then they removed her fitted coat to bare her blouse, insisting that she must cooperate if she wanted to see her Julian again. Each woman unsheathed an armful of bracelets and selected two to slide onto Claire's wrists. Each said something quietly as they did so, and Claire had a strange feeling they were blessing the bracelets somehow . . . or casting a spell on them.

"Circles . . . trap good luck," Domka said, patting her cheek.

The others smiled and nodded. "You wear always," Domka said and the others echoed: "always."

Claire felt a growing expectation as they worked to make her ready for . . . whatever they expected to happen. It was as if they were stripping away the artificial and unworthy of her, to leave her with only the essential and valuable. A slight breeze played with her long hair, a lovely sensual feeling she hadn't experienced since she was a girl. Moments later, they removed her violin from its case and handed it to her. Domka ushered her back to the steps of the opera house, positioned her at the top of them, and commanded: "*Play. Now.*"

Claire was confused and a little annoyed. She was to play here, outside this imposing monument to music? She almost laughed. What did one play for one's debut as a street musician?

Still she had come this far. Perhaps there was something more here, something she did not see but the travelers did. She recalled a piece she knew Julian loved—an arrangement he himself had written.

Closing her eyes and picturing his beloved face, she began to play.

Chapter Twenty-Two

"**D**id you hear that?" Reynard asked Frankie as they walked the darkened pavement of the entertainment district, hand in hand.

"Hear what?" She paused, frowning.

"It was just . . . I could have sworn . . ." He shook his head. "I have acute hearing, you know. I can discern whispers at a hundred paces."

"A very useful ability in your . . . avocation," Frankie responded dryly. She knew he was trying to lighten her mood, but three full days of scouring these same pavements and returning over and over to these same concert halls and music venues was taking a toll on her. She was beginning to think Claire could walk past her on the street and she wouldn't know it.

A light breeze was picking up and after a moment he halted and pulled her to a stop, listening intently.

"There it is again. I could swear I hear music." He expelled a hard breath. "And it's gone again."

Julian's long legs usually carried him quickly, but tonight, as he walked the district he knew like the back of his hand, they didn't seem to function normally. It was as if he moved in molasses, one weighty step after another.

For three long days, he'd searched for her, stopping in every church or cathedral he passed to light a candle and pray for her safety. She was nowhere to be found. Images of her lying injured or ravished in a ditch somewhere made sleep impossible and took away his usually robust appetite.

It was his fault, he knew. If he had met with her, explained to her what he intended . . . asked her to wait at home, in safety, while he came to Paris to see to his future . . . *their* future . . .

He closed his eyes and curled his hands into fists. If anything happened to her he would never forgive himself. Every place he visited he saw someone he had played with and was invited to "sit in" with the ensemble or orchestra. But he had never felt less like playing an instrument in his life. The sound of music mocked him. Without Claire, without the music she stirred in his heart, would he ever want to play again?

With his hands shoved deep in his trouser pockets and his collar turned up against the descending chill, he gritted his teeth and went on, seeing the lights from the open doors of the clubs flashing across the pavement in front of him. He was losing heart. He was tired and . . .

A wisp of sound teased his ears, then was gone. He slowed, cocking his head and listening, feeling a bit ridiculous. He was hearing things. A light breeze brushed his cheek and swirled around his right ear, bringing with it a snippet of sound. He could swear it was strings. He had spent most of his life attuning his hearing to the intricacies and peculiarities of stringed instruments. When it came again, stronger but still brief, he recognized the source as a violin. It hit him like a blow to the gut. Longing boiled up in him, potent and bittersweet.

It came again, a sad, sweet strain that was somehow familiar. The capricious breeze brushed it from his senses before he could quite identify it.

A few more steps and it came again. Several notes. A combination he did know, and knew *well*. Galvanized by that familiarity, he put his ear to the breeze, frantic to determine the direction it came from. Pieces of it slowly fit together, drawing him farther down the street with tiny increases of volume.

He stopped at an intersection, watching a paper flyer on the street tumble in the gusty breeze. Suddenly, he heard an entire phrase that was played exactly as he directed it . . . exactly as Claire played it for him.

He walked faster in the direction of that elusive music. His music. His arrangement. His heart gave a fierce thump and began to race. His legs, without instructions, followed suit. He began to run.

He turned this way and that, listening, heartened by the fact that those marvelous strains were growing louder, closer. He jolted to a stop, reading the street sign and realized where he was: two blocks from the plaza in front of the Paris Opera House.

It was here—he ran into the great square—the music was here! Searching frantically, he spotted a lone figure on the step before the grand façade, bathed in lamplight. It was a woman—her hair loose and flowing, her violin singing with an almost human voice. He knew that expressive piece and the one playing it like he knew the back of his hand.

"Claire . . . *Claire* . . . *CLAIRE!*"

He ran across the plaza, breathless from calling her name, but halted abruptly a dozen feet away, his chest heaving and eyes burning with emotion. He wanted to adore her, absorb her, to make sure she was real. A torrent of dark hair was wrapped around her shoulders and waist, and her beautiful green eyes glowed with joy and disbelief as she lowered her violin.

"Julian!" She covered a sob with her hand and then rushed into his open arms.

Frankie and Reynard stopped on the plaza, their hearts pounding as they watched Julian running to Claire and saw that moment of recognition and reunion. Frankie gave a choked sob and would have run to them, if not for Reynard's hold on her. He reeled her close and wrapped his arms around her, bending to murmur into her ear.

"Give them a moment." His voice sounded suspiciously thick as he held her tightly against him. "Hug me instead. I know it will be a sacrifice, but sometimes we must do so in the name of humanity."

He felt her surrender, lean into him, and slide her arms around his waist.

"It's *her*, Fox. We found her." After a few moments, she looked up into his gaze. Her face was wet and her eyes shimmered in the light of a nearby lamp. "She's well and back with us and—I'm going to explode if I don't get to hug her right now!"

He released her with a laugh and watched her run to her sister and throw her arms around both her and Julian, squealing with excitement. He followed at a more measured pace that gave him time to flick a bit of excess moisture from his eyes. Soon enough, he was shaking Julian's hand and giving Claire a brotherly hug. But his face was ruddy with pleasure and there could be no doubt that he was deeply pleased at the outcome of their search.

After a few moments, Claire looked around for her violin case and found it propped against one of the arches behind her. As she put her beloved violin away, she glanced around the side of the great building, into the darkness. She was looking for something—someone.

"What is it?" Frankie asked, helping Claire to her feet.

"They're gone," she said with a wistful expression.

"Who is gone?" Julian asked, coming to put an arm around her.

"Some friends, who helped me find you." She put her hand over his as it lay on her shoulder. "I'll tell you about it later."

Reynard found a cab lurking near the opera house waiting for a fare, bundled them all into it, and ordered it straight to the Villa de Burbonne.

Frankie fired questions at Claire on the cab ride, demanding to know why in Heaven's name she had taken off by herself to find Julian. Claire explained that she was distraught over Julian's departure and perhaps not thinking clearly—at which point Julian defended himself by saying he hadn't abandoned her. He had always intended to come back to her . . . only with a position and prospects befitting a young woman of her standing.

"Hogwash," Claire called it. She shoved his shoulder and told him she'd better never hear such nonsense from him again. He reddened, pulled her closer, and confessed to being an idiot in need of strong guidance.

"Speaking of which," Frankie said with understandable pique, "how did you get here? And where the devil have you been for the last five days? We've been worried sick. We've scoured the city for you three times over."

Claire said she'd found trouble in Calais before she found the train station. She'd gotten lost and encountered some traveling people who were strange and a bit frightening at first. When they saw her violin, they demanded she play for them. They were smitten by her music and began to warm to her. An emotional lot who believed in the magic of music, they were charmed by her story of unrequited love and decided to help her get to Paris. They left her at the opera house with instructions to play like her heart depended on it. She had remembered Julian's wonderful arrangement and the strains of it drew him to her.

There was more to the story, Frankie sensed, but for now it seemed she owed her sister's return to some traveling people with hearts big enough to take in a vulnerable young woman and see her safely to her goal.

That was the story Claire retold to Red, Lady Evelyn, Lord Henri, and Lady Isolde when they arrived at the Villa de Burbonne. They hugged and welcomed her, and Red, as expected, snatched her off her feet and whirled her around and around, laughing, his eyes wet with joy.

Lady Isolde, when introduced to Claire, took her by the shoulders and kissed her on each cheek as if she were already a beloved friend.

"I can see why you searched so hard for her," Isolde said to Reynard and Frankie. "She is a jewel. So very lovely."

"Wait 'til she puts a bow to those strings of hers," Red said proudly, giving Claire's chin a loving tweak. "She'll melt the heart right out of you."

The marquis ordered his finest champagne opened, and they celebrated with more hugs and glasses of the bubbly wine.

Afterward, Frankie, Lady Evelyn, and Lady Isolde pulled Claire from the company and ushered her upstairs for a bath and some rest. As the bath was filled for Claire, Frankie brushed her tangled hair and spun it into a Gibson-esque bun atop her head. The marquise disappeared into her extensive wardrobe once again, and emerged with several garments that would make Claire quite presentable. Then, while Claire soaked in the warmth of lavender-scented water, Frankie, Lady Evelyn, and Lady Isolde perched nearby on chairs and a foot bench to hear more of her adventures on the way to Paris.

She told them of her fear as she ran from the men pursuing her, then of her desperation when she first encountered the men of the group of travelers.

The marquise gasped at that designation. "These *travelers*, they were gypsies, yes? *Mon Dieu*—you are fortunate indeed that they decided to help you. They can be dangerous to those outside their bands."

"It was the women who took me in," Claire said. "They are amazing, these women. Strong and wise and generous . . . and superstitious." She raised her arms, which still wore the bracelets she would not allow them to remove as she prepared for her bath. "But most of all, they love music and use it as if it is a language . . . to tell stories and express their anger and joy and pride and love. I will be forever grateful to them for showing me that." She gave Frankie a soft, glowing smile. "And for bringing me back to Julian and to you."

Later, as the great mansion settled into slumber, a door in the upper hallway opened and closed with stealthy purpose. Slippered feet padded down the marble hallway, careful to make no sound as they approached a threshold they had never crossed before. The door creaked as she opened it to a candlelit room and a bed where covers were still tucked beneath a fully dressed form sprawled across them.

Red's head popped up at the sound of the door opening, and he rose to a sitting position. He stared in amazement at Evie, who wore a frothy silk and lace robe and the little pink slippers he had decided long ago were the most arousing thing he'd ever seen in his life. He looked her up and down and slid from the bed, dumbstruck, unable to decide how to move.

"I thought we should talk about Claire's future," Evie said, clasping and then wringing her hands. "I think she and Julian are admirably matched and that we should do what we can to see them wedded honorably."

"I—agree," Red said, finding all of his easy words used up and the more difficult words hard to put together. "He's a right good sort, for a musician."

She nodded. Her words seemed to be coming slowly too.

"He's quite talented. He works hard. And he's devoted to Claire," she said. "What do you think of a marriage?"

He stared at her, his heart pumping fast and his skin heating.

"It's fine," he said. "In its place." Then he realized what he'd said and gave an embarrassed huff that was part laugh. He was as lost as he had been the first time he'd tried to talk to a girl at a barn dance.

"I meant for them," Evie said, smiling, seeming a bit nervous herself.

"Oh." His wits thawed a bit. "Seems right enough. It'd make 'em happy as clams."

"Well, I think we should go and talk to his parents, get them to agree and to help sponsor the match."

"That sounds like a job. From what I hear, they ain't the coziest of folk."

"Still, it is our task. Seeing to their welfare and future. Right?"

"Lizzie won't be happy," he said, rubbing his mouth and chin. It was hard to concentrate with all his juices flowing.

"With a marquis, a marquise, and a rich industrialist

family lined up with the lovebirds, she'll come around. She has always been impressed by nobility."

"Too true," Red said, hoping that wasn't all Evie had on her mind.

"Tomorrow then," she said. "I'd wager we can get Lord Henri and Lady Isolde to go with us—and Reynard. He's all but a viscount. I think we could just move up his inheritance a bit. Might tip the scales in our favor."

"And a countess."

"Yes"—her eyes sparkled—"I will be there too." She swayed for a moment and looked like she might head for the door. He held his breath, wondering what he was supposed to do next, when she took a step closer.

"You didn't have any champagne tonight." She seemed less certain now.

He frowned, thinking back. "I guess I didn't."

"In fact, you haven't had anything stronger than French coffee since we left England."

"Ain't much for drinking, lately. It just don't taste like it used to."

"And you're not gambling like you used to," she said.

"A waste o' time and money." He caught her gaze in his, sensing hope for him in every question she asked. "I reckon I'm at a time in life where I should quit wastin' things, an' start savin' things. Precious things. Like my girls." He swallowed hard. "Like you. You're about as precious as they come, Evie. I was a fool to waste my time and yours the way I did."

"No more a fool than I was, Red. Worrying about what people would think, upholding my precious reputation, but for whom? I have no children, no family. The few friends I have don't give a fig for my place in society. I've spent my life trying to live up to a standard that is little more than a mask that people wear to hide their flawed natures. Who is there in my big, empty house to disappoint or impress?"

"Evie," he said, anticipation rising, scarcely able to believe this might turn into a second chance. "My feelin's haven't changed."

"I was hoping you'd say that—you outrageous, adorable old prospector." And she was across the floor and throwing herself into his arms before he could meet her halfway.

He laughed and picked her up as he always did his girls and swung her around until one of her pink slippers flew off. Her lips met his as he lowered her to the floor and she kissed him the way she had wanted to for years. He murmured into her ear and she laughed and nodded. He whirled her again before setting her on her feet and feasting on the sight of her glowing face.

"You realize, after this, I'll be a 'soiled dove' if you don't marry me," he said with a wicked falsetto.

She beamed as she sank onto the bed and pulled him down with her.

"Don't worry. I'll make an honest man of you."

Chapter Twenty-Three

It was too quiet in the Bumgarten house in London. For days, the only excitement had come from the growls, yips, chirps, and scrambling of the animals Sarah had collected about her. Four dogs, two ferrets, a parrot, and one long-eared rabbit at last count. The Good Lord only knew where she found that last creature, Elizabeth declared, and why she refused to let Cook toss it into a stewpot. She finally put her foot down and made Sarah move the lot to the nearby Trinity stables. After extensive wheedling and negotiating, she was persuaded to allow Sarah to keep one dog at the house.

Something was going to have to be done about that girl.

Unable to bear the deepening silence, Elizabeth threw herself into a round of entertainments that were, at best, temporarily diverting. She had heard nothing from the girls since their departure for Suffolk, which probably was to be expected, seeing that they were sent to Suffolk for correction.

"But I've had not a single word from Lady Evelyn, either," Elizabeth said over tea with Mrs. Conroy, the handsome Martin Conroy's mother. "Surely the countess would not have been so annoyed by an unexpected visit that she refuses to respond with a simple note."

Sarah popped up from her chair with a shocked expression.

"But you had a letter, did you not?" She placed her cup on the tea tray and looked puzzled. She frowned as if trying to recall. "I remember telling Jonas I would take it to you." She went over her movements, pantomiming them as her mother looked on in irritation. "I put it into my pocket. Then Oxford surprised Alice as she was making up the bed and she screamed and I had to rescue him. . . ." She ran out of the parlor, leaving her mother calling after her. She returned shortly with a damaged envelope bearing a badly smeared postal mark and teeth prints where the stamp should have been. She held it out to Elizabeth with a wince.

"I am so sorry, Mama. Oxford got to it and squirreled it away in his cache." She looked to Mrs. Conroy apologetically. "Oxford is one of my ferrets and I'm afraid he is a bit of a thief."

"Wretched creature." Elizabeth snatched the letter from her and ripped it open using as few fingers as possible. Reading quickly, she took a deep breath and looked to Mrs. Conroy in annoyance. "It seems the countess had planned a bit of travel and says she hopes I won't object if she takes the girls with her—to Paris—for some shopping." She planted fists at her waist. "Can you imagine? To Paris for *shopping* when they're meant to be contemplating their disobedience and amending their attitudes? I expected better of Lady Evelyn." She narrowed her eyes. "If Redmond were here I'd have his ears on a platter for suggesting I send Frankie and Claire to her."

"Oh? And where is Mr. Strait?" Mrs. Conroy inquired.

"Off hunting somewhere up north, with that scoundrel

Reynard Boulton. Just took off one morning. Left a note saying he'd be back in a week or two. I tell you, when he returns, I'll have a thing or two to say to him."

As Sarah left the parlor, she heard Mrs. Conroy commiserating with her mother on the unfairness of it, and she grinned. Her mother was always so preoccupied with her older sisters and her hoity-toity friends that she had no idea of the depth and breadth of Sarah's hidden talents, such as her covert artistic streak. With a bit of practice, she could copy anyone's handwriting. And her mother had helpfully kept all her correspondence from the countess, which made perfect templates. She headed for the library with a spring in her step. Easy, really. And it had come in handy more than once.

As she pulled a book from a shelf she had not yet explored, she began to think of what payment she would extract from her older sisters for saving their precious hides, yet again.

To be fair, the Marquis and Marquise de Burbonne did send notice to the Fontaines that they would be accompanied by friends when they called the next day. Still, it must have been a surprise to have a half dozen people descend on them midafternoon. And what people! In addition to the Burbonnes, the Fontaines found themselves facing a viscount, a countess, an heiress, and a silver magnate from America in their drawing room.

The subject of their visit was a prickly one, especially for Monsieur Fontaine: their son's relationship to Claire Bumgarten. Madame Fontaine was receptive to the idea of a marriage, but she could only look to her adamant husband for approval.

"He has no business with a wife," Monsieur Fontaine declared, clearly irritated by the weight of so much determined influence being brought to bear on the matter. "He has no position, no income, and no integrity."

"The first two can be easily remedied," Reynard said, rising in cool rebuttal. "The third is a judgment that the good people here would eagerly contest. Your son had no part in luring Claire to Paris. He chose to come by himself to seek a position in the world of Parisian music. He hoped to make a future here for himself and Claire, and then return to England to ask for her hand honorably."

"We had no idea she would follow him on her own," Frankie said. "We assumed, wrongly, that they would be together. But for the last four days, Julian has helped us search every street and byway of Paris for her. He was devastated to think her lost or in some distress. We found her last night, safe and unharmed, and were overjoyed to see her reunited with Julian. They are very much in love."

The monsieur harrumphed and folded his arms, looking like a stone wall. "Love," he snorted. "What does that matter?"

Frankie was struck dumb by that callous and obviously deeply held belief. She glimpsed grief in Madame's expression as she turned her face away, and realized Julian was not the only one to suffer from the monsieur's cold dismissal of that most vital of human emotions. But the rebuke to the monsieur's attitude came from an unexpected quarter.

"I'll tell ye what love matters," Red said, shoving to his feet and approaching Julian's father. "It's the difference between feelin' rich no matter how much is in yer pocket, and having yer pockets lined with silver but feelin' flat

broke. Between livin' and just breathin'. Between goin'
through life alone an' miserable, or with folk who'll back
ye through yer ups and downs, no matter what comes.

"Ye talk about integ-ri-ty? Doin' the right thing? Holding yer head up through thick an' thin? Well, there ain't
much point to that if all yer doin' is makin' halo payments
on Heaven's balance sheets." He stalked closer to the old
man. "The Good Lord ain't gonna ask ye how many times
ye beat yer claim-jumpin' rivals in life. But He sure as hell
will ask how many people ye loved enough to open yer
purse for and to name in yer prayers at night."

Frankie stared in amazement at her rough-and-tumble
uncle, who had just made a declaration that would have
made an erudite cleric proud.

"I believe my uncle is saying that love makes life worth
living," Frankie said, moving to stand proudly beside Red
and take his arm.

"If you have not yet learned that your son is a good man
who wishes to make you proud," the countess said, joining
them and taking Red's other arm, "now would be a very
good time to do so."

The marquis and marquise said nothing, but the way he
slipped an arm around his wife as she nestled at his side
conveyed their agreement.

Reynard rose and came to stand by Frankie. "We came
to offer an honorable and equitable way for Claire and
Julian to marry and make a life together. If you were to
offer them support in finding a suitable residence here in
Paris, that would be an excellent start."

Madame roused with interest. "And if we were to
arrange a house or suitable residence, what would the
young lady's family contribute?"

Red flushed and glanced at Frankie. "O'course, that
would take some discussin'," he blustered, avoiding Reynard's

eye. "But you can bet we'll come up with a figure to set 'em up good an' proper."

"We would, of course, hope to have the nuptials in London," Frankie said, watching a trickle of excitement growing in Madame Fontaine. She clearly supported the idea of her son being wedded and settled nearby. "My mother would insist on having a hand in arranging it all."

"We have not even set eyes on this headstrong girl." The monsieur skirted a flat refusal. "How do we know she is suitable for Julian's wife?"

Frankie gasped at the audacity of it, while Reynard stepped closer to the man. She could tell from his voice that his eyes were that molten silver again.

"You may rely on our judgment, monsieur. Her sister, Frances Bumgarten, is cut from the same cloth, and I would defy you to find a flaw in her deserving of your notice. The countess, the marquis, and the marquise have all met and come to know Claire Bumgarten. If you prefer, we will abandon all efforts to include you in their lives and futures and will see that they return to England where they will be treated with generosity and respect."

Madame Fontaine shot to her feet, her face blotched with suppressed anger as she confronted her husband.

"We *will* meet this young woman, Monsieur Fontaine," she declared with determination. "I will see this young woman who risked so much to be at my son's side. And I will give her the respect she deserves as a young woman of character." She paused to take a calming breath. "I would see the rents and tears in this family healed before I am too old to enjoy the pleasure of grandchildren."

Fontaine stared at his wife, taken aback by her outburst, but not entirely unaffected by her words. When he looked away, his gaze caught on the butler standing in the doorway to the parlor. He nodded to the man, seeking a distraction, any distraction.

"*Pardonez, monsieur*," the butler said, "but Master Julian has just arrived, with a young woman."

"Put them in the solarium," the monsieur ordered. "Madame and I will be there shortly."

Frankie objected to being excluded from this meeting, but Reynard reached for her hand and held it, halting her protest. As the Fontaines left the drawing room, Reynard used her hand to draw her closer.

"We have done all we can for now," he said quietly. "It is Claire's and Julian's place to make peace with his family, or not. We just have to await the outcome, and pray for the best."

There was little conversation in the parlor as they waited. Red began to pace and the marquis tapped rhythmically on the table where he and the marquise had taken seats. Frankie headed for the settee beside Lady Evelyn and paused by Reynard on the way, muttering, "If only we had some cards . . ."

He grinned.

Reynard watched her settle beside Lady Evelyn, remembering her pride in her family when Red announced that they would make a substantial contribution to the couple as part of a marriage settlement. His heart hurt for her. She had no idea they were sinking in debt and no longer had the resources her uncle had just boldly promised. She was so good-hearted, so deserving—she should have a fine marriage and a future without fear and uncertainty. And he knew he could not be the one to provide that for her.

For the first time in his life, he truly wanted to be with

a woman, share with her, live with her, *marry* her. He wanted Frankie Bumgarten with every arrogant, unworthy part of him. She was unlike any woman he'd ever known. She made him think, laugh, and *love*. He couldn't imagine his life without her.

What Red said earlier to Fontaine had gone like an arrow to his own heart. That was how he felt around Frankie—rich and blessed and grateful, even though his pockets were all but empty. The gossip about him and his quest for the truth of his birth paled when compared to the pleasure of her presence. For days now he had not even thought about his inheritance, had felt free from the cloud of spite that dogged his life in London. She was responsible for that, he realized with an ache in his chest, and he would always be indebted to her for that priceless glimpse of freedom.

He watched her with eyes full of emotion and didn't care that Red or Evelyn might see and realize the state of his heart. For a moment, he didn't care if Frankie saw—until he realized that would be unfair. She didn't need to know how he felt. That was one secret integrity demanded he keep.

Then she looked over at him, and he felt that determination melting. Deep inside him, his resolve to protect her warred with his desire to love her, to be with her. With a silent groan, he got up to pace the far end of the drawing room with his gaze trained strictly on his feet.

Half an hour later, footsteps sounded in the hall. Everyone in the room came to their feet and stared at the door in expectation. Claire appeared, arm in arm with Julian's mother, who wore a soft, radiant smile. Behind them came Julian bearing a leather music folio and beaming with relief. Last to return to the drawing room was Julian's father, Maurice Fontaine.

Frankie and Red were the first to reach Claire, who told them all was settled; the Fontaines had given their blessing and a promise of support.

Claire turned to Julian. "Tell my family your good news."

"I came to Paris to see about a post with the Société Nationale du Musique—the SNM," he said, brandishing the folio he carried. "I showed them my arrangements, the programs my orchestra in London played, and met with their concertmaster and principals. The board was most enthusiastic. They have offered me the post of musical director of the orchestra, a post of real importance and a chance to make a fine career in Paris."

"When did all of this happen? Why didn't you tell us?" Frankie asked.

"I received the offer the day before I came to my parents' house and discovered Claire was missing. I suppose it seemed pointless to mention it when the very reason for desiring such a position had disappeared."

"Well, she's here now. Congratulations, Julian!" Frankie didn't know whom to hug first, so she put an arm around both and embraced them together. The others crowded around to congratulate Julian and hug Claire.

Madame Fontaine ordered refreshments and insisted on everyone staying to luncheon. While the dining table was being laid and luncheon prepared, Madame ushered Claire to a seat beside her in the drawing room and began to talk about their family history and Julian's childhood and introduction to music. Their acquaintance deepened over luncheon as Red volunteered stories of Nevada and cowboys and mining, which roused even Monsieur Fontaine's curiosity. Frankie and Claire spoke about their family's history with horses, Claire's music, and went on to describe their other sisters.

Through it all Julian gazed across the table at Claire with such outlandish happiness that Reynard caught Frankie's gaze and privately rolled his eyes. She chuckled softly and gave him a half-hearted frown.

By the time luncheon was over, Julian's mother had decided there was one thing Claire must have from Paris, even if she were being married in England: a wedding dress from the house of couturier Charles Worth.

"Charles Worth?" Red leaned to peer down the table at his niece's future mother-in-law. "Why, he was an old buddy of mine. He's the one Evie had make our girl Daisy's clothes when she wanted to marry that duke." He chuckled and reached for the countess's hand atop the table. "I prob'bly spent more time in his showroom than any woman in Paris."

"Alas, Monsieur Worth has passed," Madame Fontaine said sadly. "But his House of Fashion is as vibrant and marvelous as ever."

Chapter Twenty-Four

In the days following Claire's return and Julian's rapprochement with his family, Reynard spent time fencing with Henri and joined Julian in showing Frankie and Claire the sights of Paris. Claire was enthralled to think such a beautiful and vibrant city would be her new home, while Frankie was thrilled to think she would soon have a sister in Paris to visit the way Reynard did the Burbonnes.

"This is marvelous!" Frankie gasped as the door closed on the lift that would take them up to the first-floor esplanade of the Eiffel Tower. She grinned at Reynard, who took it as a sign to begin recounting facts about the design and construction of the tower. She was completely engrossed by the time they reached the esplanade and the lift doors opened. She pressed her hand to her heart as they stepped out onto the first floor. People were pressed against the railings, and she had to squeeze her way through the crowd to reach the view. Amazement was a pale description for reaction to the view.

"What they say is true," she told Reynard when he managed to join her. "It *is* the eighth wonder of the world."

He pointed out the Arc de Triomphe, the Tuileries, and

in the distance the Bois de Boulogne. She was flushed with the pleasure of discovery.

"Let's go higher!" she said, grabbing his arm and leading him to the lift that would take them to the second level. Once on the upper level, she stood for some time looking up into the latticework of iron soaring above them.

"This is remarkable—unbelievable," she said, then hurried from one side of the viewing platform to another. There were fewer people here to impede the view, and this time she could point out the landmarks herself. She didn't see a lift, so she looked for an attendant to ask where they could find the stairs to climb to the top.

Reynard was horrified. "It would take at least three or four hundred steps to get to the third level," he protested.

"A thousand, give or take a few," the uniformed attendant supplied. "But you cannot go to the top, madame. Is not for *le grand publique.*"

Disappointed, Frankie headed for another side of the second level to see what lay north and east of the tower. When Reynard joined her to look out over the city, she turned to him with a frown.

"Do I look like a 'madame' to you?" She crossed her arms. "He called me 'madame.'"

"I heard that," he said. "He mistook you for a married woman."

"Really." She crossed her arms with an irritable expression. "Does that mean he mistook you for my husband?"

"Good God." He looked distressed, straightened his coat, and ran a hand back through his hair. "Do I look that haggard?"

Her mouth opened, then closed. When he grinned at her reaction, his face seemed so boyish and adorable that she couldn't stay angry at him.

"You really are enjoying that too much," she said, strolling farther around the railing. After a few moments she declared, "I'll have you know, I would not be a terrifying harridan of a wife."

"I know that," he said, hardly repentant.

"Or a free-spending harpy that would beggar a man," she continued.

"You were the soul of thriftiness on our trip to Paris," he responded.

"And I don't mind a nip of whiskey or a good cigar," she protested.

"Open-minded and remarkably tolerant," he conceded.

"I put up with you for days on end."

"So you did." He was starting to sound patronizing.

"And I'm not averse to a bit of friskiness now and then."

"Friskiness?" He raised one eyebrow.

"Figure it out, Reynard." She stared flatly at him.

"Oh, *that* bit of friskiness." He nodded. "I'm with you now."

"I'd make a reasonably good wife. Am I safe in assuming that?"

"You are."

"I've been thinking. I may have to reconsider this whole 'marriage' business. Watching Claire with Julian . . . they're up to their eyeballs in love and romance . . . can't keep eyes or hands off each other."

"A bit overboard, actually," he opined.

"But they do make it seem . . . kind of . . . wonderful."

"Like eating a whole bowl of icing, I imagine," he said with a wince. "Not so wonderful once you've done it."

"Tell you what," she said with a show of sudden inspiration. "I'll get married when you do. How's that for a plan?"

"Dismal, I should think. Since I won't be getting married anytime in the next decade or so. By which time you'll be a prune-ish spinster and I'll be entering serious 'codger' territory."

She stepped closer to him, studying his soft gray eyes and parted lips.

"Then, there's no time to waste." She grabbed his lapels, pulled him closer, and kissed him like he was air and she was drowning. Dearest Heaven. Her whole body caught fire, and every whisper, innuendo, and salacious secret she'd ever heard regarding human mating suddenly made brilliant sense. Her parts and his would fit together like . . . girders and rivets . . . paintings and frames . . . corks and wine bottles . . . hands and gloves. The list, like that kiss, could go on . . . and on . . . and on . . .

But the people staring at them openmouthed and covering their children's eyes suggested that they shouldn't allow it to go on and on *here*.

She pulled back and looked up. He seemed to be having trouble focusing his eyes. When she could see straight, herself, she grabbed him by the hand and braved glares and whispers to drag him to the stairs down to the first floor.

Three hundred and forty-one steps later, they wobbled from the steps with burning legs and went straight to the lift that would carry them to the ground level. In the crush of visitors, they were pressed against each other in the lift and she felt his hand moving on her waist. She looked up to find him looking away with a faint smile, and she bit her lip with a smile that matched his.

In the enclosed cab on the way home, he pulled her into his arms and kissed her like he meant to leave an impression that would last a lifetime. His hands drifted over her form and her hands invaded his coat. Soon they were working buttons and lifting petticoats.

Her very skin felt hungry for his touch—and not through layers of quilting, cloth, and boning. She wanted to rip open her jacket and feel him against her naked breasts, have him kiss and nibble her bare throat like he had aboard ship the night of their crossing. His lips were so gentle that the occasional nips of his teeth were a delicious contrast up the side of her neck and beneath her open collar. She shivered and seconds later her whole body sizzled as if struck by a bolt of electricity. More, she wanted more.

But the cab was slowing and the street sounds were falling away. Reynard froze and listened intently. She watched him, admiring the subtle bronzing of his face under the influence of desire, and telling herself it was probably a good thing the ride to Villa de Burbonne was so short.

By the time the cab stopped fully, their clothes were restored, and he helped her down with perfect manners. They met Red and the countess in the grand hall and exchanged a few distracted pleasantries about the Eiffel Tower and its spectacular views. Frankie excused herself to her room to wash her face and collect herself, and Reynard headed straight for the billiards room.

Red looked thoughtful, then turned to Evie. "There's somethin' going on between them two. I'd stake my best saddle on it."

Evie smiled. "I agree."

Frankie sat on the bench at the foot of her bed, trying to make sense of Reynard's behavior and her own. Her responses weren't much of a mystery. She was crazy about him and was aching to be with him and experience the possibilities of loving that she glimpsed whenever they kissed. The way he looked at her and held her, the tenderness in his touch—he wanted those same things. But every time things got personal between them, he turned clever and sardonic, and put distance between them again.

He felt the way she did, she was sure of it. She had seen his gaze soften, felt his body harden, and listened to his heart beating double time in their embraces. He had even offered to come to Paris in her place to keep her from putting herself in harm's way . . . which no amount of gallantry or nobility could truly account for. Then on the trip, he had sheltered and protected her, even against her own poor judgment, and brought her to his Paris family.

She had begun to think that marriage might have some value for women, after all . . . with the right man . . . the *one* man. In her case: Reynard Boulton. She couldn't imagine him ordering her about like a servant or ignoring her counsel or refusing her the opportunity to vote— should that ever come about. Neither of them was exactly perfect, but it was becoming clearer by the day that they were perfect for each other.

Unfortunately, whenever the subject of matrimony came up, he was quick to declare he would not marry until he had inherited fully. The ugly rumors the duke had shared— or started—about his birth gave some legitimacy to his concern over his future. Did he really believe his uncle would try to deny him the title after he had spent virtually his entire life as the old man's successor? Given her admittedly limited knowledge of English laws and tradition, that didn't seem likely. But if it were not possible, why was he so fixed on it?

Men had their pride, she knew. Annoying prats. She would just have to convince him that his inheritance didn't matter. She was an heiress and had money enough for both of them. What *did* matter was that he was up to his neck in love with her. That whole "I'll not marry until I'm the viscount" nonsense was just one more obstacle she would have to overcome to make him see they were meant to be together.

That night at Villa de Burbonne, there was a wonderful celebration: a feast of Dionysian proportions and more champagne than was probably prudent. It was no surprise, later, that bare feet padded along the darkened upper hallway and doors creaked indiscreetly as they opened and closed.

One of those pairs of feet belonged to Frankie as she sought out Reynard, intent on something she had never imagined she would do . . . seducing a man. Outside the door, she paused to take a deep breath and calm her pounding heart, then slowly turned the knob.

Reynard sat before the fire, his coat and vest shed, his stockinged feet crossed on the warm hearth, and his head leaning on the upholstered wing of the chair. He didn't respond to the creak of the door, so she cleared her throat. He turned with a start.

"What are you doing here?" he asked, rising to face her.

"I've come to say thank you for all you've done," she said tentatively.

"I was merely repaying a debt," he said, looking around for his shoes.

"I don't believe that for a minute." She stepped closer, and he took a step back. "I saw your face as we searched for Claire and again when we found her and she and Julian came together. It meant something to you."

He studied her for a moment, then looked down and began shoving his feet into his shoes.

"All right. I was pleased to help two good people overcome some obstacles and find a way to be happy. Happy?"

"Yes," she said, watching him prop one foot after the other on the chair to tie his shoelaces. "It's taken me a while to admit it, but you're a very good man, Reynard, despite the effort you put forth to make it seem otherwise."

"You mustn't give too much credence to my behavior of late," he said, straightening, looking more comfortable now that he was properly shod. "It's Paris. The place has an impact on me that defies reason. I get mushy and sentimental and behave in ways contrary to my custom."

"I understand that." She strolled toward the draped tester bed and ran her hand up and down a bedpost. "It's happened to me as well. I don't know if it's the light or the wine or the clothes or the food—everything seems softer, sweeter, easier here. Even sin seems more tempting and less . . . sinful."

She saw him swallow hard as she continued her stroll and trailed her fingers along the edge of the bed.

"Precisely why one should always be wary of decisions made in Paris. The minute you set foot on a ferry back across the channel, regret and remorse set in. And once you're home . . ." He folded his arms. "Indiscretions in sunny Paris seem even more sinful when viewed under London's cold, sobering rain."

"That sounds like experience speaking."

"It is."

"So, you're saying once we leave Paris you'll lose all desire to kiss me?" she said, settling her bottom on the edge of the bed. He looked a bit rattled—whether by her location or her statement, she couldn't tell.

"I am saying, I suspect neither of us will feel quite as free to indulge in such behavior once we're back in our homes and among our usual influences."

"So, you'll still want to kiss me," she concluded. "You just won't do it."

"I didn't say that."

"I know. And I don't think you're being honest with either of us." She pulled her bare feet up and curled her legs to the side. She could have sworn his eyes darkened. "I, on the other hand, freely admit that when we were in England I wanted to kiss you. I certainly wanted to kiss you here in Paris. And when we're back in England, I'll probably want to kiss you again."

* * *

Reynard found himself mesmerized by her bare feet as she tucked them beside her. God help him, he couldn't recall ever seeing a woman's bare feet outside of a house of . . . hell, even there, shoes and stockings were mandatory attire! His whole body was suddenly charged with heat. Her outrageous talk was making him remember the satin of her lips and wet velvet of her tongue, the way she trembled as he slid his hand up her silky stockings and nibbled his way down her half-open blouse.

"'Ohhh, Reyyyynnnard . . . I'm yours,'" she said in an uncanny imitation of Marcella Tutty's attempt at seduction. There was devilment in her eyes, those big blue, decadently fringed eyes. "'Everyone knows what a wicked boy you are.'" Her voice dropped half an octave, vibrating every nerve in his body. "'Come and turn me into a wicked girl.'"

His mouth was suddenly dry and his limbs seemed to move him forward of their own accord. She was there, on his bed, a fevered dream come true. He knew as sure as he knew the sun would rise, that he was going to kiss her witless and pull those flimsy nightclothes from her and devour her naked body inch by voluptuous inch. He whipped off his shirt and toed off the shoes he had just carefully donned. He caught her gaze in his and gave her a glimpse of just what she was asking for.

"Ohhh, Reynard," she said in her own voice as he pressed her back on the bed with his bare chest until he braced over her on his arms. He paused to memorize the way she looked, hair tousled and shoulders mostly bare, lying in a sensuous swirl of silk chiffon and lace.

"I will always want to kiss you," he said, struggling against a rush of emotion and a deluge of words he could not allow himself to say. "Paris . . . London . . . geography be damned."

Then he did kiss her, twelve ways from Sunday, nestling against her body and between her parted thighs. He caressed her breasts and explored her body until she was quivering with arousal. Then he pressed his sex against hers and thrust slowly, firmly, seeking just the right pressure. Her legs wrapped around his waist and it wasn't long before she groaned and then gasped as she seized and arched beneath him.

There was more, she realized as her senses cleared. This was only the beginning, a lush and tantalizing hint of what could be between them. She reached for him, and he caught her hand and held it motionless away from the bulge in his trousers.

"No," he said softly.

"But we've come this far . . ."

"And no further," he said, his jaw clenched and his eyes molten with unquenched fire. "I will not cross that threshold with you, sweetheart. I will not give you something to regret."

"Shouldn't that be my decision?" she said, searching his face.

"It should be *our* decision. But only if we can be sure there will be no lasting consequences. And I don't think, just now, that we could be sure of that." He gave her a wry smile. "You do know this is how babies are made?"

She smacked him on the shoulder. "Prat."

He laughed wickedly and shifted to lie beside her. The cool air that replaced him against her skin made her shiver. He lay on his side and pulled her back against him, sheltering her as he had before on the ship. He stroked her face and hair, even as she touched his face and studied the lean muscles of his arms and shoulders.

"This is lovely," she said, sinking into a warm haze of

comfort in his arms. "I don't think I've ever felt as good as I feel right now."

He gave a soft laugh and nuzzled her ear. "Remember this the next time you want to strangle me."

After a while his voice called her back from the drowsiness she enjoyed.

"I want to tell you about it . . . the marriage business. I want you to understand."

She turned in his arms and faced as serious an expression as she'd ever seen on him. He cupped the side of her face and kissed her nose. He was deciding what and how much to say.

"My uncle, Ormond Boulton, is a hard man. He never was close to anyone that I know of, including his wife, who died just a few years into the marriage. They had no children and he never remarried. My father was the younger son, but at least he managed to beget me. Both of my parents died young and, being the presumptive heir, I was left in Ormond's hands.

"When I was twelve, I was caught sneaking liquor from his study and he was furious—called me a thieving little bastard and knocked me halfway to County Cork. Since then, that has been his word for me—bastard. He swears that my mother never married my father and has held it over me, to bully and belittle me. Whenever I have challenged him on it, he has said he has proof and that on the day I am supposed to inherit, I will be discredited . . . because of my birth."

"If it is true, why would he not bring the proof forward and have done with it?" she asked, glimpsing the pain and rejection he had lived with for most of his life. "Why let you be presumed his heir and let you live in his house?"

"Not exactly *in* his house," Reynard said, with a tinge of bitterness. "When I came of age, he banished me to the carriage house, which is where I live to this day."

"That's despicable. It's as if he wants you around to torture . . . using your own hopes against you." She thought for a moment. "But couldn't you have searched for proof of the marriage here, in Paris?"

"I did. When I reached university and came to stay with the Burbonnes, I went in search of the place they were married. Henri was quite young himself when it took place, and from what I understand, the old marquis refused to attend. When I asked about it, Henri found a few documents regarding a modest marriage settlement, but nothing else. When I searched for the record, I found the parish register had been lost in a fire . . . along with many other records of that parish. There was no legal registration of the marriage."

"But Henri was there—surely he could have helped you find witnesses."

"I never told him what was happening. He did not react well when he found out I was continually short of funds. He thought my mother's legacy should have been kept intact for me and threatened to go to London to confront Uncle Ormond. The old marquis, my grandfather, was in perilous health and had never been happy with Lillianne's marriage to my father. I couldn't bear to raise Ormond's foul charges against his beloved daughter. And over time, it seemed best to let it lie." He expelled a heavy breath. "Shortsighted . . . looking back on it now."

"It couldn't have been more convenient for your uncle if he had planned it."

"Precisely," he said with a pained smile. "Now I will not know if I am trueborn or a bastard until I inherit and whatever he has planned for me occurs." He lifted her chin on his knuckle. "How could I possibly ask the woman I love to chance being disgraced so and tossed out on the street? How could I ever subject you to such humiliation and loss?"

She heard that word—*love*—and stored it away in her heart. Was that truly meant for her? This was not the time or place to demand clarification.

"I don't care about your title or your money, Reynard,"

she said, pouring all the love in her heart into her gaze. "I have all I could need or want. In fact, I have enough for both of us." She stroked his face, wishing she could take some of that burden from him. His eyes seemed so sad, and he pulled her into a tight embrace, holding her as if he would never let her go.

"I've thought of walking away a thousand times," he said, murmuring into her hair. "But I have to know who I am, Frankie. I need to know my mother was the good and loving woman I remember. I need to put to rest the secret that has haunted me for seventeen years."

She put her forehead against his cheek. There were so many questions, so much left unsaid. But right now, there was only one thing she wanted him to know.

"Do what you must, Reynard." Her throat tightened. "I'll be here for you when you're done."

It was hard saying good-bye to the Burbonnes, and Paris. When the time came for departure, Henri and Isolde promised to come to London for the wedding, and Frankie, Reynard, Red, and Evie promised to return for visits with them.

But who knew what the future held, Frankie thought. Who would have guessed the circumstances and events that brought them all to Paris would bring a happy solution to Claire's and Julian's problems? Who would have imagined that those same events would lead her to a love that was as challenging as it was pleasurable and intoxicating?

As they boarded a train for Lille, she found herself dreading the return to England and all the questions and demands she would face. Their plan was to go straight to Lady Evelyn's house in Suffolk and send Elizabeth an invitation to join them in a week or so. There, they would introduce the idea that they had gone to Paris, where Claire had met her violin teacher, Julian, and had gotten to know his family. When Elizabeth had recovered from that shock, they would spring the bigger news of a wedding to plan and of a French marquis and a wealthy industrialist to invite. Only when all of that was settled would Julian arrive, fresh from Paris, and announce his new position with the SNM and that the newlyweds would make their home in the City of Light.

It would be a lot for Elizabeth to take in. They should probably have plenty of smelling salts on hand.

If it weren't for the countess's steadiness and confidence, they probably wouldn't stand a chance of pulling it off.

Strangely, though Lady Evelyn had always been the epitome of rectitude, she seemed quite happy with her role as mastermind and coconspirator. Some of that, Frankie realized as she watched Lady Evelyn and Red sitting with their heads together, probably could be laid at her wily uncle's feet. She had been so caught up in her own situation that she hadn't noticed how personal and affectionate things had become between the pair. It made her feel warm inside, seeing that Red had renewed his connection with Lady Evelyn—they looked pleased as punch to be together. Another bit of Paris magic, she realized.

On the train, the five of them filled a first-class compartment, paid for by Red and Lady Evelyn. Frankie sat with Claire and pretended to read a book, while stealing looks at Reynard and trading smiles with him. She didn't see Red watching her and had no idea the play of glances between her and Reynard was validating a suspicion her uncle had been harboring for a while now.

Still, Red waited until they were on the small passenger ship crossing the channel to mention it. The sun pierced thin clouds to warm the cold autumn day as she stepped out onto the upper deck to take in some fresh air. Red appeared beside her and offered her his arm for a stroll.

"So, you and th' Fox, you're pretty cozy lately," he said, glancing at her from the corner of his eye and reading fluently the hitch in her step.

"He's not quite what I thought he was." She continued to walk. "He's a good man . . . considerate and thoughtful, and he puts others' welfare above his own."

Red halted with a dubious expression. "We talkin' about the same fella? Tall, fair-haired, always got his nose in the air an' a story on everybody?"

"Uncle Red"—she felt herself blushing—"he's not like that."

"Yeah, he is," Red said with a chuckle. "Just not with you." She saw the knowing glint in his eye. "Ye've gone soft on 'im, Frank. Admit it."

She took a deep breath and did just that. "I have, Uncle Red. But I'm afraid I'm way past 'soft.' I'm downright melted."

Red gave a soft whistle. "That bad, eh?"

She nodded ruefully. "I'm crazy about him. He's strong and gentlemanly and honorable and unselfish. He is loyal to a fault and goes out of his way to help a friend. Without him, I'd still be floundering around some railway station, trying to figure out how to get to Paris." She paused by a wooden bench and pulled him to a seat with her. "I hope you're not upset. I know you have your own opinion of him, but—"

"Frank, Frank, Frank . . ." He took her hands between his. "I've come to know the Fox a bit myself. He's a good man an' a better friend. Honorable. Knows how to keep a secret. Loyal to his friends and civil to his enemies. I think of 'im like family, and I could think of no finer fella to trust with you." He patted her hands. "Still, if he breaks yer heart, I'll have to break his legs."

Frankie laughed and gave him a hug, only realizing later that he might not have been kidding.

Chapter Twenty-Five

It took longer than expected for the ship to dock and unload its passengers onto the quay. Frankie stood by the railing on the upper deck, watching the other passengers stream down the gangway, and spotted Reynard below on the dock, already making arrangements for a four-person growler to carry them all the way to Suffolk. He intended to stay in London to check on his uncle and see if there was any gossip concerning their absence. He promised to join them later at Lady Evelyn's house.

Before he left, he took a moment to say good-bye to Frankie privately. They stood close together on the empty upper deck, and he held her hands.

"I'll keep an ear your way," he promised. "If there are any whispers regarding Claire or you, I'll squash them immediately."

Frankie could hardly breathe, much less speak. She nodded and forced a smile, feeling like a part of her was being ripped away. He had said good-bye to her already—twice. Each time she found herself close to tears, wanting to hold him and to kiss away the strain and regret that had descended on him the minute London came into view. But he had family matters of his own to attend. She worried that while he was protecting her family's interests, he might need some help himself.

He brushed off Red's earnest offer of assistance anytime he should need it, and she realized her uncle was taking their parting harder than expected. The seriousness of what they planned became quite real. They would tread a fine line between truth and fiction that could blow up in their faces.

Still, the countess's confidence was comforting, and Frankie prayed that it would see them through.

Before he left, she gave him one last, impulsive kiss, memorizing its warm and loving sensations to hold in her heart.

Then he was striding away to find them a cab and she picked up her leather hatbox, a parting gift from Isolde to hold the hats she had been given from the marquise's extensive collection. In a haze of misery, she made her way down the steps to the main deck and joined the line waiting to disembark.

She knew where the cab was and turned in that direction as soon as she stepped from the gangway. Some rude persons behind her began to push and she quickened her step and hurried toward the side of the nearest building to get out of the way. Still, they pushed, and she turned to glare at them.

A large, muscular man, dressed more like a dock worker than a passenger, glared back with a nasty smirk. And the next thing she knew a beefy hand clamped over her mouth from behind and a steel band of an arm clamped around her waist. Her hatbox was ripped from her hands as she tried to scream and resist, but she was dragged forcibly into an alley, bound with rope, and gagged with a cloth. Seconds later she was hoisted up over a shoulder and after a few steps was tossed unceremoniously into the hard bed of a wagon or floor of a vehicle. A blanket descended, covering her entire form, and the vehicle lurched and began to move.

Frantic, she tried rolling and bucking, trying to free her face, but she was wedged between what felt and smelled like sacks of grain and soon had to devote all her energy to simply breathing. Panic set in as she worked to find air, and it seemed like an eternity before she was able to turn and raise her head enough to breathe.

. On the dock, Red was busy helping Lady Evelyn and Claire into their hired coach. He mentioned with a wry glance at Evie that Frankie was still saying her good-byes. He climbed aboard and they waited several minutes before he scowled and exited again to find Frankie and speed her along.

He didn't see her anywhere. The crowd from the passenger ship had mostly dispersed and he had a clear view up and down the wharf. It took another long, searching look for him to spot a round leather case lying at the edge of the street. He headed for it before realizing what about it alarmed him. It looked like—it *was* Frankie's hatbox. He rushed to pick it up and looked all around for her, calling her name. She was nowhere to be seen.

He hurried back up the gangway and grabbed the purser standing shipside at the end of it. No one had re-boarded the ship, the fellow said adamantly. He had been there on watch since they docked. Frantic, Red rushed back to the coach to deposit the hatbox and tell Evie and Claire that he couldn't find Frankie, that he thought she was probably with Reynard. He sent them to the hotel he and Evie had stayed in that first night on the way to Paris, the Golden Tulip, saying he was going to stay and look for them.

He didn't find Frankie, but he did find Grycel Manse, who recognized him and rushed up to grab his arm.

"Is th' Fox with you?" Grycel demanded in a growl from between split lips. His face was bruised and swollen and blood was drying in streaks down his neck and in blotches on his shirt. He wore no coat, but his heavily muscled body fairly steamed with heat in the cold air.

"What th' hell happened to you?" Red stared at him in dismay.

"Nothin' that matters." Manse glowered, though it clearly caused him pain. "Where's the Fox? Is Miss Frances with you?"

"She's gone missing. And I got no idea where to find Reynard—he left us a bit ago."

Manse considered that for a moment. "I got an idea where he might be."

The tavern was half full just past noon. Reynard sat at a table in a corner, nursing a drink he didn't really want, waiting for Grycel. His friend had departed for London two days before him and had agreed to contact him here when he arrived. He had asked Grycel to keep his ear to the ground regarding Frankie's family and to check on the duke's movements. Last night at their hotel, an increasingly anxious Red had told him about the duke's demand for Frankie as payment for Red's debts. He hadn't slept a wink after that.

Now he looked up to find Grycel's damaged visage and a furious Red Strait headed his way and sensed that his worst fear had been realized.

"What's happened?" he demanded, rising to meet them.

"Frankie—she's gone. I think somebody took her," Red said. "Her hatbox was just layin' in the street—by an alley. She was carryin' it herself to make sure it didn't get damaged."

Reynard looked to Grycel and handed him a handkerchief. "You all right?" He watched as Grycel dipped the cloth in his unconsumed whiskey, and wiped cuts on his battered face, wincing at the burn of the alcohol.

"I've been worse," Grycel said. "I think Ottenberg's got her. Met up with two of his knuckle-bangers last night. They wanted to know where she was. He's been scouring the docks, spreadin' a bit of coin about for news of you or her. Somebody pointed me out to him and his boys took turns makin' my acquaintance and askin' after her."

"What did you tell them," Reynard demanded, coiling inside with tension.

"That they're pulling their punches at the end and swingin' their arms too much—wastin' impact. They're crap fighters."

"About *Frankie*!" Reynard was ready to do some punching himself.

Grycel gave him an indignant look. "Have you ever known me to give up information just because of a little tap on the chin?" He snorted. "I told them nothing. I closed my eyes for a few minutes—bored stiff—and they must've thought I passed out. I heard the Prussian come in and say he'd found her. She'd just come in on a passenger boat and he wanted her picked up and bundled for shipment."

"Shipment?" Red looked to Reynard with alarm. "He's takin' her somewhere."

"Yeah, but where?" Reynard started to pace, trying desperately to put himself into Ottenberg's state of mind. "He'll want to take her somewhere she can't be found. Trains aren't much of an option—too public. A coach or wagon of some kind, maybe. Where would he take her here in London? He owns a house, but he'd know we will look there." The others stared at him, alarmed by the number of possibilities. "He knows as soon as we realize she's missing, we'll move Heaven and earth to find her. Then he may try to spirit her out of the country." He clenched his fists, struggling for control. "They're already on the docks—maybe he's got a boat of some kind." He took a deep breath and his gaze caught fire. "Somebody has to have seen something. These docks have eyes. And a lot of those eyes owe me favors."

Dim light filtered through the coarse blanket they had thrown over her. She had arched her back and wriggled to the top of bags of grain she lay among. At least she was no longer in danger of being crushed with every jerk and jarring drop of what she guessed was a wagon. She could breathe easier now, but her heart was pounding loud enough in her ears to compete with the sound coming from outside. What she did hear seemed to be wheels turning on rough pavement, crates and containers moving and scraping, and shouts from voices some distance away. Her calls for help and thumps were muffled everywhere but in her own head. After a few frantic minutes, she realized they were a waste and sank back to breathe and wait for whatever came next.

Time alternately stretched and compressed—she couldn't tell how long she'd been moving or where she might be. Eventually, the vehicle slowed and came to a stop. There were voices, deep and rough, and they hauled her, feet-first, out of whatever had transported her, making certain to put their hands all over her. Her furious struggles only produced crude laughter and she could have sworn she heard them say something about a boat. They carried her down what sounded like a wooden walkway or bridge.

Water sloshed against something hard—a dock or pier—
and she heard grunts and felt the men carrying her sway and
correct their positions, as if unsure of their footing.

She was almost upside down for a moment and cried
out, thinking she was falling. Then she was horizontal
again and was soon dumped on something comparatively
soft. They tore the blanket from her and she sucked a
precious breath before snarling every furious epithet she
knew into the cloth stuffed in her mouth.

Two of the biggest, ugliest men she had ever seen were
looking her over with lustful intent. She braced for their
attack, but a moment later, they heard and answered a
voice from above in what sounded like German. Then,
with a glower of disappointment, they thumped back up
the stairs they had just brought her down. It was a hatch,
she realized, and the high windows and subtle motion of
the large, well-furnished room said she was on a boat or
ship of some kind. She managed to sit up and wiped the
part of the cloth sticking out of her mouth against the back
of the sofa, pushing it with her tongue again and again.
After numerous tries, it began to loosen and give.

When her mouth was finally free, she sagged with relief
for a moment, then swallowed hard and tried to scream. No
sound came out; her mouth and throat were dry as a desert.
She needed water badly, but could do nothing about it;
her hands and feet were tightly bound. They were also
throbbing from lack of circulation. She had no hope of
freeing them without help. She tried to summon some spit
to free her voice, and her attempt to speak came out a
raspy croak.

"Hel-lo? Is any-bod-y th-ere?"

There was no response at first, but she kept calling and
trying to attract someone's notice until she finally did. A
pair of legs appeared on the steps and as they descended,

elongated to include a broad chest, a pair of formidable shoulders, and a square, muscular face that all but stopped her heart.

"Well, well. There you are, my little American vixen." The duke paused with his fists propped on his waist to assess her. "I hope that mindless ox and his witless brother weren't too rough with you."

"They were disgusting," she rasped. "I can hardly feel my hands and feet. I insist that you release me immediately."

"How adorable you are when you are angry," he said with a smirk as he strolled toward her, running his gaze over her. "We will soon be underway and then you will be freed to enjoy the amenities of my lovely new yacht." He gestured at the elegant teak-and-brass clad cabin around them. "She is beautiful, yes? She once belonged to a wealthy banker, but now she is mine. A beautiful boat to carry a beautiful woman."

"You have abducted me, taken me against my will. That is a crime."

"Is it a crime to steal some time with your intended wife?"

"I am not your intended wife. I've told you that." She couldn't believe this was happening. He believed, after her earlier refusals and after he had *abducted* her, she would even consider marrying him? The man was mad!

"You are still the 'hard to get' one, I see." He gave her a patronizing smile. "But this will change."

"They will know I am missing and will search the docks top to bottom to find me," she protested, though every word cost her parched throat.

"I doubt that, my dear. By the time they guess where you are and try to come after you—*if* they come after you— we will be outside British territorial waters. 'Freedom of the seas,' an old tradition recognized by all civilized nations. Your inspectors, your police, your navy . . . they can do nothing there but wish us a delightful honeymoon."

He strode closer and gripped her chin. She tried to pull away, but his grip tightened to a painful pinch that—bound as she was—she couldn't escape. "You see, your mother has agreed to our marriage—has promised me your *co-operation*."

"I am of age. My mother has no right to—"

"And your uncle has promised you to me."

That staggered her for a moment.

"My uncle?" She could hardly believe her ears. "Red would never do such a thing. If you're going to lie, Ottenberg, at least make it convincing."

"Oh, *meine Liebling*, this is no lie. Your uncle and I have an agreement."

"That's absurd. Red would never even consider handing me over to a man I despise." She braced for a slap or worse, but he merely laughed. It was a harsh, grating sound that somehow reminded her of the bruises he had left on her shoulders a couple of weeks ago. A chill went through her.

"*Nein, fräulein.*" He released her and crossed the cabin to a writing table where a number of documents lay weighted to the desktop. He picked up several papers and carried them to her, holding them up for her to see. "Do you know your uncle's signature?" His smile twisted into a triumphant sneer. "Do you see the name of the witness who signed the marker?"

She stared in disbelief at Red's signature on the papers . . . Ottenberg dragged one after another across her vision. They documented various sums that together would total thousands and thousands of pounds. The witness on most of them was Beulah MacNeal, proprietress of the Chancery, a known and respected entity in London's gaming world. She felt her bones going soft, and an icy wave of fear stole strength from her limbs. How could this be true? Uncle Red had large gambling debts that Ottenberg had—she looked up into the duke's satisfied expression and realized it was true. He had bought Red's debts.

And with them he believed he had bought Frankie, body and soul.

A flush of horror went through her as she recalled Reynard's warning and his revelation that Ottenberg bought not only debts, but the men who owed them . . . and their families. She had scoffed, she hadn't wanted to believe it.

"You bought Uncle Red's markers?" She scrambled to think what could be done. "We'll buy them back," she said frantically. "Let me send word to my mother, our bank— we'll buy them back from you."

"With what, pretty Frankie?" He looked almost reptilian as his lips curled away from his teeth . . . like a snake baring its fangs. "You have no money. Your family's accounts are empty. The very house your mother sleeps in at night is soon to be sold to repay loans made to your uncle."

"What loans?"

"These markers"—he held up that revolting fistful of papers—"are only part of his debt. I bought what I could, but there are more—many more. The bed you slept in, the horse you rode, the very clothes you wear today belong to London bankers. Your family is . . . how you Americans say . . . *broken*. My delectable little *fräulein*, you are now your family's main asset."

From above, someone yelled down that they were getting underway and the duke snapped a look at the hatch, torn between continuing this conversation and being on deck for the initial voyage of his new yacht. Making his decision, he tossed the markers on the broad sofa beside her.

"Think on this," he ordered sharply. "And we will talk again."

The afternoon was waning when Reynard returned to the tavern where they had agreed to rendezvous. He had sent dockside acquaintances to visit local taverns while he checked shipping companies and the harbormaster's office, asking the same questions and hearing the same useless answers. He'd had no luck, and now had a burning weight in his stomach that felt like a white-hot anvil. He sat at the table where they found him earlier, trying desperately not to think about what could be happening to her.

Ottenberg was not a man who took "no" for an answer, and Frankie was not a woman who would submit to a man she found brutish and controlling. It was oil and water. God knew what would happen when a clash of wills ignited between them, but given their size and power differential, he couldn't imagine Frankie coming out on top.

If only he had stayed with her, if only he had listened to her and quit dwelling on his damnable uncle and his cursed inheritance. Faced with losing the one woman in the world he wanted—he *loved*—he had to finally stare the truth of his situation in the eye. He'd been wasting his time, his life, on the inexplicable anger of an old man and the forlorn hope that he might be absolved of a sin he had no part in, except for being born.

What an idiot he was, withholding what she meant to him, refusing to say he loved her as if his refusal to speak the words would somehow protect her—and him—from pain and disappointment. She honestly didn't care about his inheritance. Was it just his own perverse sense of pride that made him decide he could only share a life with her when his rank and resources exceeded hers? He saw it so clearly now that it was slipping from his hands. Only a fool traded passion, companionship, and love for a life of hunger, loneliness, and regret.

Grycel returned, looking winded and dispirited as he fell into a chair across from Reynard. One look at each other and they knew where they stood.

"You heard from Red?" Grycel winced as Reynard shook his head.

Reynard didn't trust himself to speak at that moment. He waved over the barman, who brought two glasses and a bottle. Neither had the heart to open the bottle and pour. They just stared at it, while trying to think of another way to find Frankie and bring her home.

"Where the hell is Red?" Reynard snarled.

"Mr. Strait! I thought that was you." The pasty-faced fellow in the pinstripe suit, expensive bowler, and thick spectacles stopped in Red's path outside the *Daily Guardian* on Fleet Street. On a hunch, Red had run by the newspaper's office to see one of his gambling pals—a fellow with his ear to the ground in the financial world— who might have a clue about Ottenberg's plans, or recent acquisitions. The fellow wasn't in and Red was just heading back to meet Reynard and Grycel when this fellow accosted him.

"How good to see you." The man extended his hand and relieved the awkwardness by providing his name. "Lawrence Fielding. Martins Bank."

"Ah." Red shook the man's hand, more than eager to get away. He owed Martins Bank money. "Fielding. Good to see you."

"I was just talking with someone about you a few days ago," Fielding continued as Red started around him.

"Really, I must be gettin' back to—"

"Now, who—ohhh—the Duke of Ottenberg was in to sign papers to take possession of a boat. A shame, that. Smithfield having to sign it over. But the duke asked after you . . . if you had been in lately. Said he kept meaning to pay a call on your family, but heard you were traveling."

It hit Red between the eyes. "A boat? Ottenberg's got a new boat?"

Fielding nodded, then leaned in. "Seems a bit crass to call it a mere boat. A yacht, actually. A sixty-five-footer. Smithfield looked like he hated to give it up, but . . . needs must." He gave a very banker-like smile. "The duke did ask me to let him know if we heard from you."

"Won't be necessary." Red clapped the little banker on the back with genuine pleasure. "I'll be seein' him tonight." He fixed the fellow with a look. "Say, where did old Smithfield keep that yacht? I'm thinking about doin' a little sailing myself."

Reynard and Grycel had given up on Red and were heading out for another round of searching when Red blew through the tavern door and nearly bowled them over.

"A boat!" he said, clutching his chest, breathless. "He's got a boat!"

A quarter of an hour later the threesome stood on the wooden dock in a small, private marina upriver a bit, staring at a dark, empty berth.

Red's heart sank.

"He's gone. Took 'er right out from under our noses."

Reynard looked around, his face grim. "From here

there's only one place to go in a seaworthy yacht. Down the Thames and into the channel."

"From there . . . he could reach Amsterdam, Bergen, Hamburg . . . anywhere."

"If I was him—I'd head straight to Germany," Grycel said.

The ramifications of that sent a chill through the group.

"Then we can't let him reach open water," Reynard said. "We have to catch him before he reaches the channel."

"In what?" Grycel looked around at the sloops and ketches bobbing nearby. "I ain't a sailor, Fox." He jerked a thumb at Red. "I doubt he is either."

Red stared in dismay at the boats. "I never been on a boat that small."

"He's got a head start." Reynard looked like his thoughts were racing. "They may have been under sail for three hours." He turned his face to the river, studying conditions. "But there is little wind.

"I know someone with a Priestman—a boat that runs on a motor," he said, coming alive. "He's half mad and a machinery fiend. Tinkers with motors and brags that he can beat anything under sail. But if he's had a pint or two, I can talk him into anything." His long legs set a wicked pace as he struck off for the mad tinkerer's location.

Red looked at Grycel as they set off after Reynard. "Is there anybody that boy *don't* know?"

Chapter Twenty-Six

The boat was hardly moving, Frankie thought. A sailboat needed wind and she could tell by the lazy flap of sails and the curses of the crew that there wasn't enough. Current alone seemed to be carrying them. She prayed for dead calm and struggled to find a position that would relieve the strain on her shoulders, wrists, and legs.

The daylight was waning when the duke returned to the cabin in something of a temper. She had heard him barking orders at the crew and guessed he wasn't pleased by their performance. But he took a deep breath and exerted more control before producing a knife and approaching her. He must have seen the way her eyes widened, for he chuckled as she shrank from him. He grabbed her arm and rolled her onto her side to reach her swollen feet and hands. He cut her bonds and ripped away the ropes, then helped her to sit up.

"There. Much better, yes?"

When she had difficulty moving her hands and fingers, he perched beside her on the arm of the sofa and reached for one of her hands. As he rubbed her fingers and palm, blood returned to them along with throbbing pain. It took a moment for her to realize that his touch caused part of it. She yanked her hands away from him to massage them herself.

"My poor fräulein, you have had a bad start to your *Flitterwochen*," he said with a sly smile. "But I will make it better." He headed to a bar built into the wall cabinets to pour her a glass of water. She was so thirsty that she took the glass eagerly and drank it without thinking what else it might contain.

Toward the bottom of the glass, she stared into the liquid and then stopped drinking.

"No, fräulein, I put nothing in your drink." He seemed amused as he came to stand over her. "You are a suspicious one." He lifted her chin on his fingertips, digging his nails into her skin. "I want you awake, *Liebling*." His face tightened as she jerked away. "To enjoy every moment with me."

"I will enjoy nothing with you," she said, watching him light a pair of sconces set in gimbals on the walls. The light revealed more details of the handsomely appointed room, but gave her no comfort. "You may as well set me ashore somewhere. I am not now, nor will I ever be yours."

"You are wrong, my dear." He strolled across the room toward her, and she felt her heart lurch with dread. "You will learn to crave my touch, my kiss, my admiration. Starting now."

For such a big man, he could move quickly. Like a dart to a target he grabbed her face in one of his thick hands and ground his mouth against hers. It was a crude imitation of a passionate kiss that practically drowned her in wetness. She pushed him and strained away, but his assault didn't end until he broke it off himself and stared with what seemed amusement at her reaction.

Her lips felt bruised and throbbed with heat. She tried to slap him but he caught her wrist as if he had expected it.

"You didn't like my kiss?" he said with false dismay. "Then you must show me what you do like."

She frowned, not quite certain what he meant, not trusting his demand.

"Kiss me," he ordered, his eyes lidded with pleasure. "*Now.*"

When she refused to move, he produced a sly smile and seized her hand. "You will not obey? Then we will do it my way."

Again, he mashed her lips with his and then took her lower lip between his teeth, holding her to him by that appalling intimacy until she couldn't bear it any longer. Desperate to make him release her, she raked her nails down the side of his face. He grabbed his cheek and sat up with his nostrils flared and eyes glittering. She scrambled back on the sofa, thinking he would punish her for that.

"You see? You learn to please me already," he said, not bothering to hide his arousal. "Love is a battlefield, *Liebling*. In the end, you are either victor or vanquished. But ah, the fighting in between . . ."

She flung herself from the sofa and struggled to her feet, feeling light-headed and faintly nauseous.

"That is not love, Ottenberg, it is madness." She wanted lye soap to scrub the taint of him off her skin. "Whatever you do to me, you will not have my obedience or respect. And sooner or later, I will find a way to be free."

"We will see about that," he growled, rising and reaching for her.

She stood, braced and stone-like, as he pulled her against him and pressed another revolting kiss on her. Her first response was to fight back, but she stayed that impulse long enough to realize that was exactly what he wanted.

Her fierce and unmoved calm was a greater disappointment than any resistance she could have mounted. He proved her right when he broke off his assault and shoved her back.

"I will have your passion. And you will marry me." He touched the red scratches on his face as if savoring them. "And you will be my obedient wife."

"Not if I have anything to say about it." She raised her chin.

"Oh, I think you will be grateful to be my bride once you see the alternative." He backed her toward a door leading into another part of the belowdecks cabins. "Perhaps when we marry we will invite your mother and pretty young sister to my estates in Germany. What was her name again? Sarah? I would love to show her the special delights of my—"

"You leave them alone," she demanded, panic rising.

"Perhaps." His eyes burned with passions he had yet to unleash. "Perhaps not. It is up to you."

He grabbed her against him, binding her with his arms, and forced her through the door and through a passage she could barely see in the growing darkness. There were steps he forced her through and she stumbled and fell through a low opening into water.

"Think on it, my lovely fräulein. There is only one death. But there are thousands of ways to hurt."

A hatch closed with a metallic clang. She tried to stand up in the darkness and bumped her head. She was somewhere in the ship's belly. With trepidation, she put out her arms to learn the limits of her prison and discovered cold metal that slanted toward the ship's pointed keel beneath her feet. Water had collected in the bottom and she prayed it would rise no higher. She found a way to wedge herself on the cold, metal slope and soon began to shiver.

No one knew what had happened to her or where she

was, she thought. She was alone and defenseless, at the mercy of a madman who would threaten her family to make her serve his vanity and twisted passions.

In the cold and darkness, she pulled her knees up into the dry part of her skirts and wrapped them with her arms. How had she come to this?

Red's signature was on those markers, she couldn't deny that. But the duke said her family was in debt and about to be turned out into the streets. Would Red have wasted all of their wealth and beggared them without so much as a word to her mother?

She thought of Red's somber moments in Paris, the way he seemed to have something on his mind. She had put it down to his fears for Claire, but now she wondered if it had been more. And the way he'd joked when they went to order a gown for Claire's wedding—that the couturier shouldn't assume Red was made of gold—he was just a *silver* man. Was that a hint that he worried about money?

Her spirits sank as those dismal thoughts swirled in her head. Ottenberg was despicable, twisted. Hints of it had been there from the beginning, but she had wanted to be fair and, truth be told, she had been fooled by his elegance and courtly manners. "Rottenberg," Reynard had called him. He had seen beneath the manners and Continental polish to the truth of the man.

Reynard. An image of his face, his beautiful gray eyes and wry smile, rose in her mind. She recalled his tenderness and determination, his droll sense of humor. One of the things he liked about her, he had confessed, was the way she made up her mind and then took action, no matter how crazy it was.

What could she possibly do to help herself now? If she got out of this water-logged prison—no, *when* she got out of here—she would find a way off the ship. Her spirits rebounded. She had to find a way to free herself even if it meant pretending to go along with the duke's intentions. And when she was free of the duke, she would search for the truth of her family's finances.

There was enough rising moon to brighten the water and make boats and barges tied up along the channel plainly visible. Most traffic had stopped for the night, giving their small launch a clear path down the broadening river.

There was so much machinery in the midsection of the motor-driven boat that there was little room for passengers. Reynard sat in the front with his collar up searching the river ahead, while Red huddled in the back watching mad Terrance McGraff tinker with the motor running the boat's propeller. Grycel, after seeing the vessel, had agreed to stay behind to make a report to Lady Evelyn at the hotel and then to the authorities.

"She's goin' swell—got 'er wide open! We'll catch 'em!" Mad Terrance yelled in order to be heard over the motor. "This beauty's built to run on kerosene, but I got me own special brew. She's forty percent faster than a regular Priestman." He pointed with pride to the open motor belching noise and exhaust. "This here's the way o' the future, it is!"

It was the better part of an hour and a half and they had had to refuel the motor with Terrance's special brew twice before they caught sight of a ship wallowing along in mid-channel. Her sails were deployed and she had running lanterns fore and aft, but the canvas hung limp, leaving the boat at the mercy of the current.

Reynard rolled to his knees and hauled out Terrance's

spyglass for a look. His heart rate picked up as he saw the markings on the pale stern and squinted, concentrating on what looked like a large round letter—an *O*.

"It's them," he shouted over the motor noise, pointing frantically to the boat in the distance.

"Yeah?" Red looked ready to swim to the ship if necessary. "What's the plan?"

"We board and go in and get her," Reynard answered, feeling like an idiot for not coming up with something better. Still, there wasn't much room for stealth or cleverness when you were trying to catch a sixty-five-foot sloop in a noisy, smoke-belching fourteen-footer with an inebriated Scotsman at the helm. "They'll hear us coming. Don't be shy about cracking a skull when you get the chance."

He looked back and saw Red grinning like a demon. He pulled a weighted truncheon from his jacket and held it up, admiring its mayhem-polished surface. "Courtesy o' our friend Grycel."

"What's that?" Ottenberg demanded of the crewman at the tiller as he looked back over the stern of his yacht, searching for the source of that noise.

"Sounds like an engine . . . or one of them motorboats," the fellow said. "What kind of fool would be out on the water in one of them things at ni—"

"Steer toward the banks and let them pass," Ottenberg snapped.

"But this part of the river—there's sandbars, an' the tide's goin' out."

"Steer over and let them pass!"

The wheel turned and within moments, the ship itself was turning toward a stretch of moonlit water outside the channel markers. Seconds later, a small, noisy boat followed their course, steadily closing the gap.

Ottenberg uttered a curse and made his way forward to where his two muscle-bound henchmen lay snoring on the deck. He kicked one and barked orders to see no one boarded. Then he headed back to the main hatch and descended to get a weapon. "This," he said with a hint of pleasure, though there was no one to hear it, "could be interesting."

By the time Reynard tossed a grappling hook over the railing of the yacht and pulled them closer to the larger boat, he was ready to explode into action. He climbed up the rope and was aboard even as Terrance cut the throttle to match the movement of the larger boat. When he turned to give Red a hand, a bull of a man wielding a huge fist appeared out of nowhere and would have knocked him over the railing if he hadn't ducked. It took some fancy footwork, but he managed to stay out of reach while drawing the brute away to allow Red to climb aboard.

Something knocked him on the head from behind. He remained upright, but saw double, and it took him a minute to realize that he wasn't just seeing double—there really *were* two men the size of mountains coming at him. He retreated along the edge of the deck toward midship.

"Where is she?" he demanded. "Frankie—what did you do with her?"

"Yer fancy piece o' tail? We dumped 'er overboard some ways back," one said with a laugh. "Wore out, she was, when we got through wi' her."

The taunt was meant to enrage Reynard and it worked. But the pair hadn't counted Reynard's experience as a bare-knuckle fighter. When he sprang at the closest one, the brute's instinct was to scramble back to avoid the punch and he backed right into his twin, who fell backward. Reynard got in two solid blows before the second bruiser got to his feet and went to work on him, too.

Red had managed to make it to the railing and hung on for dear life, struggling for footing and trying to catch his breath. He could see a nasty ruckus midship as he climbed over the metal railing, and muttered to himself that he'd given up saloon fights long ago. He managed to get his aging bones aboard and held on to the railing as he lumbered to the Fox's aid.

The blows this pair could deal were staggering, so the trick was to not let them land, Reynard realized. Sooner or later, that much raw power was going to wear him down. Mobility was their weakness, so he shifted to lower body kicks and found them more successful than straight head or gut punches. He managed a blow to one of the brutes' knees and sent him pitching sideways, howling. Twice he was clipped on the chin and nearly went down for the count.

Where the hell was Red? Heartbeats later, Frankie's uncle appeared, smacking Grycel's lucky truncheon against his palm.

"Better late than never," Reynard panted, dodging another haymaker.

Red sized up the situation, crept to the side to stay out of sight, and delivered a blow from behind that sent one of the mayhem twins to his knees. It took a second, harder blow to send the man facedown on the deck.

"I take that back—good timing," Reynard called, bracing

for another round as the one still standing channeled his surprise into a grisly roar and a bull rush. Red plunged in and two-on-one evened the odds a bit. By the time the second twin was down, both Reynard and Red were panting and glad to be alive. So, apparently, were the three crewmen Ottenberg had acquired along with the vessel. They surrendered with their hands up and sat wearily on the deck under Red's watchful eye. The duke, they said, had gone below.

"Come down, Boulton," the duke's voice came up the hatch as Reynard paused at the top step. "I prefer to do my killing face-to-face."

Reynard looked to Red, who gave him a nod, and then descended the steps into the main cabin. Ottenberg stood in the middle of the cabin holding a sword that glinted in the lamplight, but it was the figure on the sofa that claimed his attention.

Frankie sat in a heap of wet skirts with her arms wrapped around her and her sodden feet and shoes propped on the sofa. She was shivering and barely reacted to his presence. Anger ignited in him and he could feel a change come over him, one that separated the man he was from the fury possessing him.

"She will live," Ottenberg said, then twirled the tip of his blade in a circle aimed at Reynard's core. "The question is, will you?" He gave an arrogant shrug. "But I am a sporting man, and I recall that I owe you a debt. So, I will give you a chance. Have you ever killed a man with a blade, Boulton?"

Reynard watched the glow of anticipation in the Prussian's eyes, sensing Ottenberg wanted to draw it out, to savor his control of the moment.

He spoke to Frankie instead. "Are you all right?"

She struggled to focus, then nodded.

"There is something uplifting in sending a true swordsman to his final reward. But you would not understand that. You English—you have lost the art of the blade, and with it have lost your true warriors. Still, I offer you a blade with which to defend yourself." He glanced at the desk behind him.

Reynard circled him, moving toward the blade, and when he picked it up and felt the grip, the weight, and the balance, he smiled, recognizing the feel of a Burbonne blade. He glanced at Frankie, praying she would understand: "Don't worry. I'll get you out of here."

With that he delivered his first lunge, surprising Ottenberg and sending him crashing back into a small table not bolted to the deck. A moment later, the cabin filled with the ring of blades clashing, but there was not enough room for such a heated battle. Reynard backed to the steps and up them to the deck, parrying Ottenberg's strokes until he was obliged to leap back from the top steps to avoid injury.

Ottenberg came roaring out of the hatch, stung by Reynard's unexpected skill with a weapon that he considered to be beyond all but a few.

"Where did you learn the sword?" Ottenberg demanded furiously as they circled each other, each probing for weaknesses in their opponent.

"From Gerard, Marquis de Burbonne. My uncle." He took pleasure in Ottenberg's expression, knowing that the duke's own hubris had betrayed him. "Yes, *that* Burbonne. The House of Burbonne. My mother's family."

Ottenberg leapt at him with a snarl that combined both anger and fierce pleasure. Reynard scarcely had time to parry, lock their swords, and shove him back. The Prussian's technique was formidable; he was surprisingly graceful for a man of his size. But Reynard had been trained to the exacting standards of master swordsmen and kept his movements simple and precise. After years of being schooled by the old marquis and his son Henri, Reynard's subtle precision was as natural as breathing—a perfect strategy with an overconfident opponent who relied on intimidation to enhance his blade work.

At times, their thrusts, slashes, and parries seemed dance-like as they sallied back and forth, but their eyes were deadly serious, filled with a desire for domination . . . victory . . . blood.

In years of blade work, Reynard had never intentionally harmed another swordsman. Occasionally a thrust went too far or a cut fell too quickly in the rhythm of a match, and a halt was called to tend a stab or minor slash. But now, with all his being, he wanted to see Ottenberg done— laid out on the deck and unable to rise—unable to hurt Frankie or any other woman ever again.

As they pivoted and clashed, steel slid against tempered steel to bring them face-to-face. Both wore a grimace of effort, but Ottenberg laughed as he wiped sweat from his eyes and Reynard wanted to finish him all the more.

It was stubborn, uncompromising will that drove Reynard to take greater chances and begin fighting with a cunning that came from the London streets—like a downward strike at Ottenberg's legs as he rolled his blade through an arc. He drew blood with that one, surprising the duke, but it was not enough to seriously hinder the man's attacks. With an odd sense of calm, a rightness in his core, he pressed Ottenberg until that smirk of superiority vanished.

Both men were panting, nearing exhaustion yet refusing to yield, when nature provided a nudge in the form of a lowering tide that drove the bow of the boat into a sandbar. A shudder and groan went through the vessel. The deck vibrated and lifted, causing the duke to stumble. He ran into a raised hatch cover and the point of Reynard's eager blade at the same moment.

Down he went, with a look of surprise and horror at the rapier thrust upward into his chest. Then he looked at Reynard and the spark of fury died in his eyes. He fell forward, running the blade farther up and through his heart. And it was over.

Reynard staggered, exhausted and desperate for air. He grabbed the nearest railing to work his way back to the main hatch. He didn't see the big man moving quickly across the deck with death in his eyes. One of the duke's knucklers had recovered enough to desire revenge. He rushed Reynard and was soon hammering him with blows that forced him to the deck. Reynard was nearly unconscious when there was a "crack" and the big man went sprawling on top of him.

When his vision cleared, Reynard pushed that mountain of flesh off him and looked up. There stood Frankie in her French pantalets, holding an oar with both hands and wearing a fierce expression. He'd never been so happy in his life. She was all right! More than all right—she had just saved his worthless hide from a savage beating!

He pushed to his feet, opened his arms, and staggered toward her. She still clutched the oar, even as she flew into his arms and buried her face in his shirtfront. He held her for a moment before recognizing her shuddery movements as shivers and realizing she was still half-frozen. He ushered her back into the cabin, where her wet skirts and petticoats lay in a heap on the floor. He set her down on the sofa, pried the oar from her hands, and disappeared briefly to find blankets to wrap and warm her.

"How is she?" Red called from the steps of the hatchway.

* * *

"*She* is j-just f-fine," Frankie answered for herself. She was wrapped soundly in blankets and then in Reynard's arms. She could hardly believe they had found her, saved her. To prove it to herself—right there in front of Red—she pulled Reynard's head down to hers and he gave her the sweetest, most tender kiss of her life.

It was real, all right.

Relief flooded her as warmth returned to her body and heart and she settled gratefully into his arms. She was almost asleep when she heard Red say, "Better just let her rest. An' Fox, what do we do with the body?"

Chapter Twenty-Seven

Dawn was breaking before they reached the docklands and were welcomed by Grycel and a contingent of London's law enforcement officers, including an inspector and a superintendent. The crew testified, the scene was examined, and the two bone-breakers were taken into custody. Red and Reynard were released to take care of Frankie, whose statement would be taken later. All were cautioned not to leave London.

They carried her straight to the Golden Tulip Hotel where Lady Evelyn and Claire had waited up all night for word of their search for Frankie. The minute she was carried through the door by Reynard, fatigue and fears were forgotten and they threw their arms around Frankie and shed tears of relief. They wanted details, all and sundry, and were soon hearing the story of her rescue and the duke's fate.

"So, he's well and truly gone?" The countess reached for Red's hand.

"He is," Reynard answered, with some relief. "There are witnesses to say it was honorably done. According to the inspector, it is unlikely that any charges will be brought against me."

The Golden Tulip's proprietor bustled to meet Reynard's demands for hot tea, food, and water for Frankie's bath. By the time she was warmed and fed, she could no longer keep her eyes open. No one objected when Reynard carried her sleeping form to bed, tucked her in, then sprawled on top of the covers nearby, but Claire gently scooted her over and crawled under the covers beside her to make it proper. Evie and Red found a settee to curl up on and slept in each other's arms, and Grycel talked the proprietor into providing him a small room of his own.

They slept the clock around, and it was early the following morning, during breakfast in the hotel dining room, that Claire mentioned starting for Suffolk and Lady Evelyn's house.

Frankie halted in the middle of consuming a savory dish of eggs and ham and put down her fork. "I want to go home," she said, looking somber. "I need to go home."

"But what about yer ma, Frank?" Red asked, frowning.

"It's time she heard the truth about the duke," Frankie said, then glanced at Red. "The truth about a lot of things."

"She won't like it," Claire said, thinking hard about the options and coming to a conclusion. "But I think Frankie is right. She needs to know the truth about that monster and how narrowly Frankie missed being held prisoner in a nightmare of a marriage."

"The truth," Frankie echoed. She looked at Reynard, who sat across the table from her, his gaze thoughtful but unreadable. He had awakened from his heroic rescue quieter and more distant than he had been in weeks. He was keeping his own counsel, she sensed, preparing once again to leave her. She recalled his words to her on the ship as they parted—he would listen for any whispers about her family or their mad dash to Paris, and would see they went no further. He would keep her family's secrets.

She was sick to death of secrets. She held too many of them and after a while they became exactly what Reynard had called them: a burden.

"Sooner or later," she said, "secrets will come out. Who knows, Mama may be more hurt later to learn we distrusted her so much that we deceived her. It is time for honesty in our family. Honesty is a part of caring for one another and trusting and loving. If we cannot be honest with one another in things this important, then what kind of family do we have?"

She glanced from Claire's tear-rimmed eyes to Reynard, who nodded, and then to Red, who looked down at his plate and then nodded as well.

Lady Evelyn leaned across the table to squeeze her hand.

"Well said, Frankie." The countess beamed. "Well done."

The Bumgarten house was quiet as a churchyard when they arrived. The sound of several voices greeting Jonas brought Elizabeth from the parlor. She quickly pulled her spectacles from her face and tucked them away in a pocket as she took in the group.

"You're back," she declared, seeming puzzled by the arrival of Red and Reynard in company with the countess and her two elder daughters.

"Yes, we are," the countess said, stepping forward to give Elizabeth a brief Continental kiss on each cheek. "How good to see you, Elizabeth. We've brought your girls home, and there are some things they need to tell and you need to hear."

"Red?" Elizabeth caught her brother's gaze, looking a bit alarmed.

"Let's go inside, Lizzie." He stepped forward to take his sister's arm and turn her back to the parlor. "You may need to be on yer saddle bones for this."

"I must say, I was quite disappointed to hear you took the girls to Paris," Elizabeth said to the countess as the women seated themselves on the facing settees and Red and Reynard pulled over chairs from the nearby card table. She had sensed something important was happening and decided to strike first. "After my request that you help them see their responsibilities, you took them on a shopping holiday."

"Not exactly," the countess said. "We were in Paris to settle the matter of Claire's marriage to Julian Fontaine."

"Her what?" Elizabeth almost came out of her chair. She looked at Claire, who nodded.

"Julian and I are betrothed, Mama. Uncle Red has already given us his blessing and we're hoping you will give us yours . . . when you hear about his prospects, his family, and his connections."

"What connections?" Elizabeth demanded, turning to Red. "How do you know anything about this?"

"I was in Paris too," Red said, looking a bit uncomfortable. "I met the boy's folks—they're rich as Croesus an' hoity-toity, but we got things settled, right enough. An' the marquis and his lady will be comin' to the wedding."

"What marquis? Will somebody please tell me what's going on?"

"Did you not listen, Mama?" Frankie said with an edge. "Claire and Julian Fontaine are to be married. When in Paris we met his family, and got to know them. Julian— the conductor of Soliel, remember?—has been given a post as the artistic director of the SNM, France's premier symphonic orchestra. It is a position of great importance in Paris. His family is purchasing a beautiful house for them in Paris and we have set the nuptials for March. We even ordered a wedding gown from Charles Worth, while we were there."

Elizabeth's jaw dropped farther with each revelation.

"Wi-without consulting me?" she sputtered. "You arranged all of this without my permission?" She looked from Frankie to the countess to Red.

"They got *my* permission," Red said, after a prodding glare from Reynard. "It's a right good match, Lizzie. Truth be told, it'd likely happen without our permission. So, I figured to make the best deal we could and let the kids get on with their life."

"And the wedding will be here, Mama," Claire said, sitting forward, her face taut with worry. "We wanted you to be able to plan it and to enjoy hosting the marquis and marquise. We stayed with them in Paris. You'll love them."

"Who is this 'marquis' you keep talking about?" Elizabeth snapped.

"That would be my uncle," Reynard spoke up. "Of course, titles are no longer official in France, but custom requires he be acknowledged as such and that his title become part of his name. He's rather well known, actually."

"You were in Paris too?" Elizabeth was now roundly annoyed.

"I was. As an escort to your daughter and"—he glanced at Frankie—"something of a tour guide."

Frankie could have sworn he winked at her. And she had never wanted to kiss him more than she did at that moment. He was such a perfect "nob."

"Frances"—her mother turned on her angrily, desperate to reclaim her parental authority—"I cannot countenance you flitting about Paris in the company of this Boulton fellow when you have a known commitment to another. The duke paid me a visit while you were gone and was emphatic that arrangements be made as quickly as possible. He will be calling on you as soon as he hears you are home."

"No," Frankie said, clenching her hands into fists at her sides to keep them from trembling, "he won't."

Reynard came to the edge of his seat and Red rose, watching Frankie with a devastated expression. Elizabeth was too intent on exerting her will on Frankie to pay attention to the others.

"He most certainly will. And you will be accommodating and receptive to him."

"No, I won't," Frankie said, her eyes narrowing. "He's *dead*."

It took a moment for Elizabeth to make sense of what she had said.

"Don't be absurd, Frances. He was just here . . . two days . . . ago." Then she did look at the other faces watching her. They were filled with tension, anger, and worst of all, pity. "What are you talking about?"

"He's dead, Lizzie," Red confirmed. "And not a day too soon."

Frankie felt anger and frustration and pain building to unbearable levels in her. She had to get it out—the whole terrible, degrading story—or she would burst.

"He abducted me," she declared, her eyes burning with forming tears. "His thugs tied me up and carried me onto a boat that he intended to sail to Germany. He tormented me and imprisoned me in the bottom of the boat where I nearly froze in the bilge. If it hadn't been for Reynard and Uncle Red, I would still be there . . . violated and abused . . . or dead. They found and rescued me, but not before Ottenberg tried to kill them. Reynard fought with every ounce of his being to free me. I owe him my life. And if you care anything at all for me, you owe him a debt you can never repay."

With tears burning down her cheeks, she fled the room and headed blindly back through the main hall. She found herself in the study and released the sobs that, if not freed, threatened to stop her heart. She leaned against Red's desk with her face in her hands, breathing in spasms between sobs.

Somebody approached quietly, turned her, and pulled her into his arms. Her knees almost gave way as she recognized Reynard's scent and strong, comforting arms. She wrapped her arms around him and held on for dear life.

After a few minutes, her sobs ceased and her tears quit falling. She took a deep, shuddering breath and looked up at him.

"Thank you," she said, searching his soft gray eyes. "I meant what I said. I owe you my life."

"Then we're even," he said, brushing her hair back and then running his fingertips down the curve of her cheek. "Because I owe you my heart."

They stood for a long time, holding each other, listening to the way their hearts began to beat in time. This was the moment she would carry in her heart for the rest of her days. This was the moment she loved him in a way that would take decades of living and loving and sharing to express. In that moment, she refused to think about losing him.

There was a sound by the door and Reynard loosened his hold on her.

"I think you need to talk to her," he said into her hair, then released her.

As he walked out of the room, he passed Elizabeth

standing in the doorway looking a bit lost. She couldn't meet his gaze as he passed.

"I'm sorry, Frankie. So sorry." She came forward with a hand out, but as Frankie stepped back, she dropped it. She seemed to be just now understanding how much anger and distrust lay between them. "I didn't realize . . . I didn't know how bad . . ."

"Yes, you did," Frankie said, wiping her wet face, then meeting her mother's gaze with a fierceness that made Elizabeth stiffen visibly. "I told you what he was like, that he was harsh and vile and dishonest, that his manners and pleasantries were a lie and you refused to believe me. You believed *him* because you wanted him . . . his title, his looks, his charm, his wealth . . . as a trophy . . . as proof that we're worthy, that *you're* worthy. But of what? What was so much more important than my happiness, my safety, my very life?"

"I—I just wanted you to be . . . comfortable and secure . . . to be respected . . ."

"You saw the bruises he left on me. Was that evidence of respect? He had no care or consideration for me—I was a possession to acquire, someone to break and bring under his control, something to vent his twisted lusts on. How could that ever make me comfortable and secure? You said I should accommodate him . . . let him do what he wanted. Did you expect me to let him abuse me just so you could have bragging rights about your daughter the duchess?"

She watched the horror and guilt building in Elizabeth's face.

"What kind of mother are you?"

Moments later, she returned to the parlor to find that Reynard had gone. It was a blow. There was so much she needed to say to him. He probably believed it all had been said in Red's study. She had saved his heart. What did that mean? That he cared about her, that he wanted her? If that was true, that desire would always be second to the problem of his birth and inheritance.

Claire joined Frankie on the stairs minutes later, and they went straight to her room. It seemed empty and devoid of the intimacy and security she had always felt in its sheltering walls.

"I'm sorry, Claire," Frankie said, wiping a few stray tears from her cheeks. "This should be the happiest time of your life and I'm all tears and woe."

Claire pulled her to the foot bench and put an arm around her.

"You've been through a nightmare, Frankie. There will be plenty of time for me to celebrate," Claire assured her. "Right now, I want to make sure you're all right."

Frankie thought for a moment. "After what I just said to Mama, I may have to find a new home. Know anyone who needs a governess or secretary?"

Claire laughed through the prisms of tears forming in her eyes.

"I have never known anyone less suited to governess work than you, Frances Bumgarten. I'm afraid we'll have to find you another destiny." She gave Frankie a jiggling hug. "Perhaps you can come and stay with Julian and me in Paris."

Frankie sniffed, looking wistful. "That sounds wonderful. I love Paris."

Sarah burst into the room and threw herself on Frankie, engulfing her in a desperate hug.

"I heard. Everything," she said, looking grave and very adult in her concern. "I'm so sorry, Frankie. Is there anything I can do?"

"How did you hear?" Claire demanded.

"I listened in at the door's edge." Sarah looked at her as if she were daft. "How else can I learn what is going on?"

Frankie looked up into her little sister's glowing face and melted a bit inside. She cradled Sarah's cheek with her hand. "I'm going to be fine. It will just take a little while, that's all."

Sarah breathed a sigh of relief and brightened with mischief. "That's good, because you two owe me favors from here to forever . . . for saving your bacon."

Later that night, after resting and taking a dinner tray in her room, Frankie went in search of Uncle Red. She found him in the study, alone and in an uncharacteristically pensive mood. The countess had just retired to one of their guest rooms, he told her. "Evie" was staying the night with them, but was scheduled to depart for Suffolk in the morning.

"Are you two getting along?" she asked, recalling their sweet intimacy on the trip from Paris.

Red nodded. "We're fine. Better'n fine." He looked up from his folded hands. "She forgave me. I was an idiot. A selfish fool. I didn't deserve to have her ever speak to me again. But wonder o' wonders, she did. An' we come to a right sweet understandin'. I'm goin' to visit her in a week or two."

He rose and came around the desk to plant himself before her, looking like he faced a firing squad.

"I got another confession t' make. An' this one may be harder to forgive. If ye can't, Frank, I'll understand." He swallowed hard. "It was my fault, that bastard comin' after ye. I owed him money, lots of it. He said he'd forgive my debts if I made you marry him." He shifted his feet and looked away.

"I told 'im you wouldn't marry him, and I couldn't make you even if I wanted to . . . which I didn't. He demanded I make you agree, an' give me a few days to make you come to heel. That's when I found out you and Claire were gone, and Evie and I struck off for Paris to find you. He figured I reneged and he came after you." His eyes began to water and his voice thickened. "I'll regret that every damned day for the rest of my life."

Frankie watched her uncle struggling with his flaws and transgressions. Yesterday she had wanted to kick him into next week, but now all she felt was a bit of sadness for him. In the last few years, robbed of meaningful work and purpose, he had become a drinker, a gambler, and a high-living rascal. But he was also the man who taught her to walk and held her hand as she learned to ride and told her stories when she had the measles and refused to let fancy society drum the spirit out of her. He had also braved darkness and violence and possibly death to help rescue her in her darkest hour. No matter what he did, she always knew he loved her. And she would always return that love.

"Uncle Red"—she settled her own heart as she reached for his big hands and lifted his gaze into hers—"you weren't any more to blame than I was. He marked me as his from that first night at Tutty's ball. If it hadn't been your debts, he would have found something else to hold over me. Or he would have just taken me anyway. I said no a dozen times and he didn't listen to a single one.

"In fact, I think my stubbornness was what he liked most about me. He wanted to break me like a wild horse, bend me to his will. Once he had . . . the pleasure would be gone and who knew what he would have done to me then?"

She reached out to stroke his shoulder. "I don't blame you, Uncle Red. Really and truly."

It wasn't said just to make him feel better, she realized. She didn't blame him, or herself, or even her mother anymore. She thought of Elizabeth's guilt-ridden expression and genuine horror at what happened to her. One way or another, they were all victims, taken in by the mask of nobility and affluence Ottenberg had crafted. All but Reynard, who saw danger coming and tried to warn her.

When Uncle Red opened his arms, she slid into them and hugged him tightly. They stood for a few moments, savoring the restoration of their loving relationship. Until Frankie remembered.

"How broke are we?" she asked.

Red set her back and looked into her reddened eyes. He realized she knew the whole of it and enlarged his confession.

"Pretty broke. And that *is* my fault, pure and simple. I gambled and drank and wasted tens of thousands . . ."

"Do we have to move out of the house? Ottenberg said we were penniless and that the bankers were about to foreclose."

Red sighed. "I took a loan not long ago from Martins. It will tide us over for a little while. But if that new vein don't come in soon, we're gonna have to start sellin' Lizzie's silver doodads."

"So, we are broke." A horrible thought struck. "Do we have enough for Claire's marriage settlement?"

"If we cut back and sell off a few horses . . . maybe cash out of the New York house . . . we can get her married off proper."

Frankie took a deep breath. "Does Mama know?"

"Lord, no," Red said, looking terrified by the prospect of Elizabeth's reaction. "I kept it from everybody."

"Except the duke," she said, scowling.

"I didn't say a word t' him, I swear. He bribed somebody at th' bank to tell him. The only one I told was the Fox."

She tried not to gasp. "He knows?"

"Yeah, but he won't say nothin.' He promised and he keeps his word."

"So he does," she said, feeling an ache begin in her chest. *He knew.* "When did you tell him?"

"Didn't have to say much. He knew I was in trouble th' night he brought me home from Beulah's place. I guess she told him."

"He knew from the beginning?" She felt a sickening wave of chagrin at the number of times she'd flaunted her wealth in talking to him. He knew all along and refused to call her on it.

"Well, not all of it," Red continued. "It was when I went to him for help that he found out th' worst of it. He said he'd do what he could, but he don't have much money. From what I hear, he's just as skinned as we are. You know, that uncle of his makes 'im sleep in a damned carriage barn. Somethin' must be wrong with that man."

The despicable duke was gone and Claire would soon be happily settled with her beloved Julian, but the family was quietly, privately still in trouble. Through another sleepless night, as Frankie tiptoed down to the kitchen to make warm milk, she thought about the mountain of problems they faced.

Their prospects for the future were bleak. There was no money for a marriage settlement for her or for Sarah. Now that she'd finally come around to thinking marriage could be a wonderful thing, vengeful Fate had ripped that possibility from her future. And her scrappy young sister might be right that she would be forced to live with and tend Mama in her dotage.

She shared her conclusions with Red after he had taken the countess to the train station the next morning. He agreed that keeping their word to the Fontaines and supporting Claire were most important and that they should keep word of their predicament between the two of them for now.

She told herself she was beginning to reconcile herself to her fate when Reynard called that afternoon to see how she was feeling and to assure her that no legal charges would be filed. One look at him and her mind and heart went into a helpless downward spiral. She managed a cool tone and when her mother left the room, she told him that there were "factors" that made their continued presence in England untenable. They probably would be leaving soon.

"It's a relief, really," she said, imitating her mother's hauteur. "The dreary London weather always wears me down this time of year. I find myself yearning for the sun and the wide-open spaces of the West."

Reynard responded with a characteristic quip.

"I'm sure the cowboys and 'little dogies' have missed you terribly."

But his expression had little of its customary insouciance. As the comment fell flat between them, she sensed he was just as miserable as she was.

As he left, she told herself she should not see him again. Her main attribute in society had been her wealth and now that was gone. With money, she might have had a chance of changing his mind about marriage and making a life outside of the noble ranks. Without it, she hadn't a coffer to stand on. And if perchance he did inherit, he would need a wealthy lady wife to bring him both status and substance. As a ruined heiress, she could provide neither. Worse, as a penniless heiress, she had no prospects and that meant she had no place in England at all. It hit her between the eyes. If the house in New York was sold, then going back to Nevada was their only option.

She would never see him again.

Her knees weakened and she sank onto a settee in the parlor.

The thought of leaving him while he was at the mercy of his devious uncle was intolerable. She owed him that much and a great deal more. Her heart ached and she struggled to think of a way to help him. Strangely, she came to realize, being penniless was somehow freeing. If she were already ruined, nothing she did could make her prospects much worse.

She thought of his predicament and his uncle's threats.

She would not leave England without at least trying to do something about it.

Chapter Twenty-Eight

Dressed in Claire's best walking dress and a cloak borrowed secretly from her mother's closet, Frankie set out in a cab for Tannehill House. She wanted to confront the viscount and tell him how his nephew rescued her. She wanted to make him see Reynard as the man she had come to know. If that went as hoped, then she would entreat him to tell Reynard the truth of his birth—for better or worse.

In her mind, she rehearsed phrases to express her respect for Reynard and to describe his gallant efforts to rescue her from a tyrant. But when she arrived on the doorstep of the mansion and clacked the knocker, her mouth dried and her hands became clammy.

The majordomo, Bailey, answered the door and she could tell he recognized her immediately. He admitted her to the hall, saying, "I believe Master Reynard is out at the moment, Miss Bumgarten."

"Well, it isn't him I came to see," she said. "I came to see his lordship, the viscount, on a matter of some importance." When the majordomo scowled in surprise, she hurried on and it just slipped out: "I am Reynard's intended, and I believe it is time I meet his lordship and we have a talk."

A whopper of a lie, clearly, but told in a good cause.

"I had no idea, Miss Bumgarten," Bailey said with a marked warming in his face and mien. "Felicitations on your upcoming nuptials." He paused a moment, looking over his shoulder at the stairs, seeming unsure. Then he made his decision. "Let me take your cloak and you can wait in the parlor while I see if his lordship is awake."

Reynard exited the renowned White's Club with a folio stuffed with markers he had bought up from sundry gentlemen in clubs around town. He had most of them, he felt sure, and when combined with the ones the duke had possessed, they should give Red some relief. Never mind that he'd had to go to a friend at Coutts Bank and take out a personal loan to pay for them.

He could do nothing, however, about the much larger loans Red had wrangled out of Martins Bank and a couple of private lenders.

Every time he closed his eyes, he saw again the pain in Frankie's face the day before when he called on her. She was cool and distant and there could be only one reason— she now knew the financial straits they faced and was putting up defenses against the humiliation of it. The one thing that he could do to help her and her family might be helping them out of the frying pan and into the fire. If he knew that someday he would inherit the Tannehill title and fortune, he could propose to Frankie and find a way to stabilize their finances.

There were plenty of bankers willing to lend him sizeable sums. They assumed that as the heir of Tannehill he would be good for it when his uncle passed on. But what good would it do to marry her and find he couldn't inherit and pay them back? His so-called solution would only pile debts upon debts.

With flagging steps, he turned toward Tannehill House.

Frankie stood in the doorway of the old viscount's bedchamber looking in dismay at the pale figure in the bed and the two black-clad men attending him. They spoke to each other in quiet tones as they put metal cups connected to tubes in their ears, to the old man's chest. They were listening, Bailey whispered, for the old man's heartbeat. Seeing her confusion, he went on to say that the viscount had suffered a stroke some weeks ago, and since then, he had grown steadily worse.

"Can he hear me? May I speak to him?" she whispered.

"When the physicians leave, we shall see," Bailey said. "He sleeps most all of the time now."

The physicians nodded to each other, concurring, then packed up their equipment and reported to Bailey, who stepped out into the hall with them.

In his absence, she edged closer to the bed, where the old man's head lay perfectly still and serene on the pillow. She searched those illness-distorted features and sunken eyes for some similarity to the face she loved, but could see nothing of Reynard there.

"Your lordship?" she said, softly at first. "Your lordship, can you hear me?" His eyelids fluttered faintly but did not open. "I am Frances Bumgarten, a friend of your nephew Reynard. I have come to petition you to . . ." She halted as Bailey reentered the room, followed by a nurse in a striped uniform, white apron, and cap. The woman came to stand beside Frankie, checked on her patient, then took her watchful place in a chair beside the bed.

"My lord," Bailey declared as he took the nurse's place beside her. "Master Reynard's fiancée is here to see you. Can you open your eyes to her?"

Again, the eyelids fluttered, but they quickly ceased moving and stayed closed. Bailey looked to her and shook his head.

"He will be like this, they say, until the end. He hasn't fully awakened for three days now. We cannot even get him to take sips of water." He looked sad. "The doctors say he cannot go on like this for much longer."

He caught her look of distress and gestured to the door, suggesting, "Perhaps we should get you a cup of tea."

Her hopes for anything meaningful from the old man sank. She nodded and followed Bailey out and down the broad staircase to the parlor.

"Please be seated, Miss Bumgarten. I shall be back shortly with something to brace you up."

Too anxious to sit, she wandered the room instead, running a hand over the beautiful piano, the exquisite tapestries, and the carved and gilded figures around the fireplace. The windows were tall and draped with French damask that someone had selected with an artist's eye. The edges of the settees and chair cushions showed no signs of wear. Clearly, the room was little used.

She paused by one of the long windows to stare out into what was once a lovely garden, but now was on the verge of chaos. Someone needed to take it in hand soon or the whole thing would have to be chopped back to twigs and started over.

Bailey arrived with a sizeable tray holding a teapot, cups, and a plate of biscuits. He set the tray on the table between the settees flanking the fireplace and surprised Frankie by sitting down on the settee across from her and pouring. This was a familiarity she would never have expected of the tall, distinguished majordomo.

He creamed and sugared her tea to her taste, handed it to her, and then sat back without pouring himself a cup. He would only presume so much and not a whit further.

"I have worked for his lordship for thirty-five years," he said, watching her. "I was a mere pup, newly come to service, when I first met him. He seemed older than his years, with a barren wife and a younger brother who had always been the favorite. I saw and heard things I shouldn't have, but I quickly learned to hold my tongue and see only that which was helpful to my position."

He offered her a biscuit from the tray and she declined.

"What was he like? I have heard stories that he was difficult."

"At first he was quiet and particular in how he liked things. He and his wife were mismatched and had little to do with each other. There was only one person he seemed to favor with smiles and confidences." He glanced away and after a moment, went on.

"He became increasingly stern and exacting, especially with Master Reynard. Too harsh, the staff felt, though we had naught to say about it. Some took it upon themselves to help the boy in small ways. Cook especially was a soft touch—was always slipping him extra food. He was a skinny little thing. Minded his manners. Adored his mother." He smiled sadly. "Now there was a beauty. Master Reynard favors her strongly. There was once a picture of her in his room. It . . . got broken."

She sipped, wishing with all her heart she could have seen that picture.

"Did you know Reynard's father?" she asked a moment later.

"I did, but mostly from a distance. He spent a good bit

of time in France." He moved to the edge of his seat with his hands on his knees, preparing to rise. "If I may say, Miss Bumgarten . . . I am most pleased that Master Reynard has at last found someone who cares about him and wants to share his life. He has had a hard go of it from early days. Viscount Ormond was never suited to be a father, much less to a boy with such a sensitive spirit. I hope when the young master is lord, this old house will hear laughter and music and the sound of children playing again."

Frankie had a sip of tea in her mouth and a sudden constriction in her throat made it almost impossible to swallow. The thought of Reynard's beautiful children—borne by some wealthy society girl—was crushing.

Determined footfalls from the hallway caused her to turn her head toward the doorway, freeing her throat enough to swallow.

Reynard appeared in the arched doorway wearing his overcoat, gloves, and top hat. His face was reddened from the cold, and he held a leather folio in one hand. The sight of them sitting together clearly jolted him. She had never seen him speechless before.

"I . . . came to . . ." she began, floundering.

"To visit his lordship," Bailey said, rising quickly. "Unfortunately, the viscount is unable to appreciate visitors these days, so I took the liberty of serving Miss Bumgarten some tea. It is still hot, Master Reynard. Perhaps you would like a cup yourself."

As Bailey strode out, Reynard removed his hat, gloves, and coat. Then he clasped his hands to the silver teapot and sighed softly at the warmth it gave. She could almost see his mind racing.

"What are you doing here?" he asked as he poured himself a cup of tea.

"Meddling," she answered, reddening. "I came to see your uncle on your behalf. To tell him what you have done for me and to ask him to give you the answers you need to get on with your life."

He set the teapot down with a bang.

"You what?"

Before she could utter a word, there was a cry from somewhere upstairs and they heard servants running.

"What the hell?" Reynard bolted out into the hall and saw Bailey rushing toward the source of that sound: his uncle's room. Instantly he was down the hall and taking the stairs by twos. He made his way past the servants collecting in the upstairs hallway, and into Ormond Boulton's sickroom.

Frankie was not far behind him, until she reached the top of the stairs, where she paused, telling herself she should probably leave now and save herself the embarrassment of facing him after she had tried—and failed—to interfere in his future. But she couldn't make herself turn and flee.

For one single heart-stopping moment, she had seen a light in Reynard's eyes . . . pleasure at seeing her, hope, desire, yearning. That was all it took to make her realize that not seeing him ever again was more devastating to her than anything the duke could have done.

Bailey emerged from the sickroom and sent a footman running for the physicians. She crept to the door and peered in. Reynard stood at the foot of the bed, gazing down at the old man who had overshadowed so much of his life. She could tell that he was struggling with his emotions. Daring more on his behalf, she went to his side and slipped her hand in his. He said nothing, but closed his hand around hers with a gentle squeeze. It was a wordless request for her to stay with him.

They stood together, keeping watch, deep in thought but joined in concern, until the physicians arrived. Reynard excused himself, saying that he would await their conclusions in the parlor. His possession of her hand meant she went with him downstairs. Only then did he seem to realize he had pulled her along. He released her and stood for a minute looking around him as if baffled by everything he saw and unsure of what to do next. She took his arm and ushered him to a settee, taking a seat beside him.

"It's over," she said, and he looked into her gaze with disbelief.

"Or just beginning," he said, his voice thick. "He told me I would never inherit."

"He's gone, Reynard." She took his hands and collected his gaze in hers. "Come with me to the States. Forget all of this nobility nonsense and come, make a new life in the wide-open territories out West."

His rueful smile gave her a little hope. "And do what, Frankie?"

"You could be a rancher, a cattle baron. You could learn to punch cattle."

"I have nothing against cattle—why ever would I punch one?"

It was a thin quip but promising.

"You could run for sheriff." When he scowled, she explained, "Pretty much the same as here, except for the collecting taxes part. You'd keep the peace."

"A constable then."

"Sort of." She guessed that wasn't very appealing to a man who loved swords. "But they'd let you wear your gun and lock up lawbreakers."

"A gaoler. My heart's ambition."

"All right, then, how about mining? We have lots of land

that needs to be explored. There would be mines to open and lucrative deals to make."

He studied her for a moment, and then stroked her hands with such tenderness that it nearly broke her heart. She read his answer in that touch.

"Frankie. My dear, sweet Frankie. My life is here. Whatever happens, I have to face it and learn the truth. There is too much I don't know . . . too much that has been kept from me."

"I . . ." She bit back the words "love you" and substituted, "am so sorry, Fox."

"I know you are," he said, and she could have sworn he was making that same substitution when he added, "I am . . . sorry, too."

The doctors made quick work of confirming that the old viscount had passed on, and agreed to make arrangements for the viscount to be embalmed and interred in the family mausoleum. Next, Bailey sent a footman next door to request that a telephone call be made to Sir Harold Rowantree, the old viscount's solicitor. Then he joined Reynard and Frankie in the parlor.

"Before Sir Harold comes," the majordomo said quietly, "I think you should know that your uncle kept a hidden safe in his office."

"A secret safe? How do you know about it?" Reynard asked.

"I was privy to its installation many years ago. I know that the old viscount visited it from time to time, and always in the strictest privacy. I was never permitted to see him access its contents."

"Then we should have a look, by all means," Reynard said, gesturing for Bailey to lead on. His grip on Frankie's hand indicated he wanted her with him as he delved into his uncle's tightly held secrets. She felt her heart begin to pound, moments later, as they stepped into the murky study.

The old viscount's private sanctuary was as Reynard remembered it, dark, slightly musty, and filled with the aura of the old man's stifling and antisocial habits. Bailey drew back the drapes to admit light and then went to an antique tapestry on one wall, rolling it up and tying it with its own presentation cords to reveal a substantial metal safe recessed into the wall.

They searched the old lord's desk for anything that might indicate how they could open the safe. In a hidden drawer, they found a small leather ledger containing numbers and dates, some of which Bailey was able to identify as purchases made by Ormond. Toward the rear, there were what appeared to be groups of numbers. Bailey knew nothing about those, but Reynard seized on several repeating sequences of three numbers that he suspected might prove to be a combination. He had Frankie read the sequences as he spun the dial and entered them.

One combination caused clicks behind the safe door and when he tried the handle, it gave and the door swung open. Bailey turned up the gas light and then lighted an oil lamp on the desk to give Reynard a better view of what lay inside.

Stacks of folios and ribbon-wrapped documents comprised a majority of the contents. There were several posh leather jewelry boxes, numerous stacks of gold coins, and at the rear was a flat pasteboard box of old papers. They carried all but the coins to Ormond's desk and Reynard felt his hands trembling as he opened the first folio, looking for something pertaining to his origins.

"Do you want me to help you look?" Frankie asked.

He looked into her sky-blue eyes and told himself he might not have the courage to do this without her. Her presence, here, at this moment, mattered more than anything that safe might hold. The fact that she had come to confront the old viscount on his behalf said everything he needed to know about the state of her heart.

He handed her a folio to examine and she untied the ribbon and scowled as she worked to make out the legal script. She reported it was a certificate of ownership of a company that produced copper wire and heavy cable of the kind used by telegraph services. He showed her certificates of ownership in mines in several countries. Bailey stood by, watching, saying nothing until they had completed their search of the documents detailing many of the viscount's holdings.

The jewelry boxes held stunning pieces containing diamonds and other gems that made Frankie's jaw drop. She touched them reverently, then quickly handed them back to him. One piece, a diamond and sapphire ring, stopped Reynard cold. He stared at it, feeling a pull it exerted on his emotions. After several moments, he closed the box and set it aside.

The desk was all but lost under layers of deeds, ownership documents, and engineering drawings. The only thing left was that battered pasteboard box filled with papers. As he opened it, Frankie edged closer to him and put her hand on his back as if offering him support. She must have sensed, as he did, that this might be the most important piece of all.

Some of the papers were letters in what Reynard recognized as the viscount's hand. Others were correspondence bearing the viscount's unbroken seal. Farther down they found letters still in velum envelopes and several old photographs, a few of which were in poor condition. One had streaks and gouges across it, as if the glass of a frame had broken against it. The subject was a beautiful woman with light hair and soft gray eyes. She wore a white summer dress and stood by a table that held a stack of books and a globe.

Reynard felt his chest constrict. He knew this woman, this picture. He held it up for Bailey to see.

"Who is this?" he asked. "I feel I know her."

Bailey approached with a melancholy expression. "You should, your lordship," he answered. "That is your lady mother. Lillianne of Burbonne."

Frankie leaned closer to look at the photograph, then looked up at him.

"Good Heavens—you look like her." She studied him even as he studied the picture. "Exactly like her. The resemblance is amazing." She pointed to Lillianne's hand. "And look at the ring she is wearing."

"It is her ring," he said, remembering snatches of images and staring again at the picture. He picked up the smallest jewel box, and opened it, holding the ring against the photo. "This picture," he said, holding it up to Bailey. "I've seen it before."

Bailey took the photo gently from Reynard.

"This photograph was in your room when you were a boy. The frame and glass were broken somehow and the next thing I knew, the picture had disappeared. I never found out what happened to it. His lordship must have . . ."

"He took it from my room," Reynard concluded for him. He delved more urgently into the letters and documents in the box. "A clipping from the *Times*—my father's obituary, naming Ormond, my mother, and me as his surviving family." He lifted a thick piece of velum with elegant engraving. "An announcement of the marriage of Lady Lillianne de Burbonne to Monsieur Gareth Boulton." Still another piece of memorabilia: "My birth announcement." He stared at it for a long moment. "Didn't say much besides the fact that I was born."

Near the bottom was a packet of letters, some bearing a London postmark and others apparently never sent. They were addressed to Mademoiselle Lilly Burbonne. He opened one and began to read.

> *My dearest, fairest Lilly,*
> *It is dreary here and I long to come to Paris where your presence brightens even the City of Light. Alas, I have responsibilities here and cannot come until the weather breaks in April or May . . .*

He read silently until he reached the signature. He looked up with his eyes wide. "This is from Uncle Ormond . . . to my mother."

Bailey nodded, handing her picture back to Reynard.

"In my early days here, I heard whispers that his lordship had courted Lillianne before your father met her. When Gareth traveled to Paris to study, he visited the Burbonnes and became smitten with Lillianne. They fell in love and were wedded in Paris, against her father's wishes. The next time his lordship saw her, she was his brother's wife."

He was so swamped by emotions that he had difficulty putting all the pieces together. "She married my father, the younger brother, for love?"

"Then she came back to London with him and moved into the family home," Frankie said thoughtfully. "That must have been awful for your uncle: having to see her constantly, having to watch the two of them together." She looked to Bailey. "But the viscount married after that, did he not?"

Bailey nodded. "An arranged affair. Not a fruitful union. She was a bit sickly and he was not one to coddle what he saw as weakness."

"I can testify to that," Reynard said irritably. He sorted through the letters, setting them aside, then came to a larger envelope that contained a number of pages. What arrested him was the familiar script of his uncle's hand on the front, stating simply: "The Boy."

He held it in both hands, staring at it, feeling a sudden pressure in his chest that made it difficult to breathe.

Frankie looked over his arm to see what disturbed him so and froze when she, too, glimpsed those words.

"The truth of my birth," he said, his mouth dry and forehead wet.

"Reynard, are you sure you want to see what is in there?" Frankie asked.

Bailey stepped around the desk to stand beside him. "You are the heir, Master Reynard. It has always been said, and I cannot think anyone would contest it now."

"Except possibly Sir Harold, the old man's lawyer," Reynard said.

"Who has always been passing fond of you, my lord. You know he has."

Frankie pulled the envelope from his hand and weighed it in her fingers. "What good will it do to open it now? Now that you are already seen as the new viscount?"

"By everyone but me," he said. "And anyone who hears a scurrilous bit of gossip and decides to pass it along to half of London. There are some who would love to see me exposed as a fraud and brought low."

She carried the envelope to the oil lamp and removed

the painted glass shade and the hot chimney. "You could walk away . . . start a new life . . . become your own man," she said, holding the envelope above the flame, awaiting his decision. "Or you could just be the Viscount Tannehill everyone expects you to be." She caught his gaze in hers, and he read there no judgment, no coercion, only support for him and the hard decision he had to make.

Strangely, now that it was in his grasp, he was reluctant to learn the truth. It was a question that had tormented him for years, and tonight it came to an end. What would he do tomorrow? Who would he be tomorrow?

He had to know.

He took the envelope from Frankie, sliced it open with the old boy's letter opener, and finally saw the truth.

On top was a page ripped from a French parish register, detailing a marriage between Gareth Boulton and Lillianne Burbonne. "They were really and truly married!" he cried, and the next moment was adamant. "Well, of course they were. She was a lady from a prominent Parisian family and he was the son of an English nobleman. They wouldn't have disgraced their families by anything less. But this record—the proof of those nuptials was stolen and brought to London."

Did the viscount steal the record of their marriage in order to throw doubt on his parents' integrity and his own legitimacy? How else would it come into his possession?

Again, he looked over that fading paper, feeling angrier. "All of the time I wasted, all of the sleepless nights and anguish, the penury and deprivation . . . all because the almighty Ormond Boulton was disappointed in love. *Love*, of all things." He turned to Frankie and raised his arms, then lowered them to run his hands through his hair as if he were considering pulling it out by the roots. "My life was all but ruined because of *love*!"

He paced this way and that, and nearly ran into Sir Harold in the doorway.

"I am so, so sorry about your loss, Reyn—your lordship." Sir Harold extended his hand to Reynard.

"Did you know?" Reynard ignored the hand and confronted Sir Harold. "That he stole their marriage record and lied to me for years about my birth?"

"Wh-what?" Sir Harold looked to Bailey, then Frankie in shock.

"What did he tell you to do when he died?" Reynard demanded furiously. "Find this record and burn it? Was that his grand plan to see that I never inherited?" He was ready to explode. "I trusted you—all of my life, *I trusted you*!"

Chapter Twenty-Nine

The genuine shock in the lawyer's face couldn't penetrate the fury from the betrayal Reynard felt. He charged out of the study, then out of the house, then out into the world in a mindless explosion of motion and action.

He started with Mehanney's Gym and a punishing round of bare-knuckle sparring, then made a mad slog through several dockside taverns, where he dealt out nasty cuts and bruises before Grycel appeared and rescued his unfortunate opponents.

Grycel nearly acquired a few new bruises himself, before he got Reynard to calm down and go with him to the bar at the Cecil Hotel. Together they imbibed enough whiskey to drop an ox, but Grycel still managed to get him into a cab later and carry him home. Reynard was alert enough to insist on going through the front door of the house, but had to be carried up the stairs by Grycel and Bailey and dropped in one of the gilded bedchambers that hadn't been used in decades.

Frankie had watched as his eyes turned that furious molten silver she had seen before and for a moment she held her breath, praying he didn't mean to challenge Sir Harold. Then he charged out of the room and the house, into the cold twilight of the streets. She would have gone after him, but Bailey held out his arm across her path and shook his head sadly.

"Let him go. He's had quite a shock."

She let Bailey summon a cab for her and went home to a quiet house and an evening of reflection that made her think about how similar Reynard's situation was to hers. She still felt anger at her mother, but for some reason was drawn to wonder if her mother's motivation was as selfish as she believed.

There had been times—granted, in years past—that Elizabeth had been warm and loving to her daughters, that she had taken great pride in their discoveries and achievements and taken true pleasure in their company. What would it take for them to have that kind of feeling between them again?

When they brought a supper tray to her room, she sent it back to the kitchen with orders to set her a place at the family table. All of them were present for dinner that night: Elizabeth, Red, Frankie, Claire, and Sarah. Despite a few nervous exchanges, the gathering settled into a surprisingly pleasant meal. Afterward, Claire played for them in the parlor, and Frankie went to bed that night with bittersweet memories floating on music through her head.

For the third time that week, she cried herself to sleep.

Reynard awoke the next morning in a strange gilded bedchamber that belonged either in a Russian palace or a Parisian bawdy house. Beside him in a chair with his shoeless feet propped up on an ottoman was Grycel Manse, who eyed him with concern.

"Where the hell are we?" Reynard demanded, clapping his hands to his head, trying to silence whoever was banging a kettledrum inside it.

"Your house." Grycel winced as if it hurt to speak louder than a whisper.

"My house?" He looked around. "Then what are you doing here?"

"Oh, I'm here to keep you from thrashing the servants and generally behaving like a drunken barbarian."

"Oh." The fact that such an answer seemed reasonable to Reynard was evidence that he had spent a very strange night, and his morning wasn't going to be much better. "Well then." He looked around the ornate room. "I don't recall ever seeing this place in my life. I live over the carriages and I'm pretty sure I've never had gilded cherubs above my bed."

"You need some hair of the dog and some food," Grycel said. "Put some clothes on and we'll get Bailey to find us a belt and something to eat."

Then it came back to him. Bailey and Frankie . . . his uncle . . . the safe . . . *he wasn't a bastard.* Events after that were fuzzier. His jaw and fists were sore as the devil, and he felt like he'd gone a dozen rounds in the ring with Grycel.

When they entered the dining room Reynard stopped sharply. There sat Sir Harold Rowantree, sipping coffee and reading the *Times.*

"What are you doing here?" he asked, as Grycel grabbed a plate and served himself a small mountain of food from the sideboard.

"Waiting for you," Sir Harold said, folding his newspaper and ringing for assistance.

"This early?" Reynard said, heading for the sideboard

himself. He learned long ago not to take news on an empty stomach. "I never imagined you would be so eager to deliver bad news. Before breakfast, even. That must be a first." He piled his plate full of eggs, sausages, kippers, and potatoes.

"I am not the bearer of bad news, your lordship. I am here to execute instructions from your uncle to the letter. It is my sworn duty." Sir Harold looked up as Bailey entered and came to stand beside him.

"You have already inherited the title of Viscount Tanne-hill. That is quite done. In fact, despite what your uncle apparently led you to believe, that was never truly in question. The fortune that accompanies the title, however, is a different matter. It has been entailed by your uncle." He looked at Grycel's puzzled frown and explained, "He placed requirements on it."

"Hey, Fox, you gonna be rich?" Grycel asked with a mouthful of food.

Reynard turned with his half-filled plate to stare at the lawyer.

"Normally such things would be discussed well after the burial and in a more decorous fashion," Sir Harold continued. "But there is a time constraint imposed by your uncle's will that must be considered. Therefore, I must inform you that to inherit the considerable fortune left by your uncle, you must be wedded within thirty days."

"What?" Reynard sat down with a plop and his plate hit the table with enough force to send some of his food flying up and over the plate's edge.

"Wedded. Married. You must marry within thirty days a woman of superior character and sound reputation. And . . . it must be a love match."

"A love match." Reynard was stunned. "This from an old

codger who never had a moment's affection or tender—
oh." The irony—the pure cussedness of it—struck him like
a cannonball in the chest. His stomach churned and he
grabbed it. "I believe I need some hair of the dog."

Bailey raised an eyebrow, but exited to see to it.

"The question is, your lordship," Sir Harold said with a
grave look, "how can you find, court, and wed a suitable
bride in such a brief period of time?"

Clearly, Ormond intended this codicil to be the fatal
stroke to Reynard's hopes for a future. He believed Reynard had no possibilities for an honorable marriage, much
less a loving one, and believed the one requirement that
would ruin his heir's life would be the one thing that he
himself had failed in life. *Love*. He truly intended one last
stab of vengeance to embitter Reynard beyond all recla-
mation.

And he might have succeeded if his wayward nephew
hadn't become helplessly entangled, heart and soul, with
Miss Frances Bumgarten.

Her lovely face rose in his thoughts. Who else had he
ever wanted to marry and love and shelter and provide for?
Good God—she had practically proposed to him yesterday! He'd marry her in a heartbeat. This was a dream come
true! A hazy grin spread over him.

Then he remembered how he'd stormed out of the house
without a word to her . . . her cool dismissal of him just a
few days ago . . . her pride and her penniless family and
her determination to go back to Nevada . . .

He grabbed the glass of whiskey Bailey set before him,
tossed it back, and grimaced as it hit his stomach.

"*Merde*."

That night, after a day immersed in contracts, ledgers,
and legalese that left his head spinning, Reynard escaped

to his club for a semblance of normalcy. What he got instead was a bizarre combination of consolation and congratulations; a black armband and sympathy that his uncle has passed, and brandy and congratulations on ascending to the title.

The king was dead; long live the king.

He still hadn't accepted the sea change of his status, but what wore on his mind and heart was the new requirement hanging over his head. There was only one person in the world he wanted to talk to about it and only one person in the world who could help him meet his devious uncle's codicil . . . and they happened to be the same woman. Even mentioning it to her would make him seem like the biggest bounder in the world.

Marry me, dear, so I can get rich. Wed me to save my inheritance. He could just imagine her possible reactions. Rolling eyes . . . crossed arms and long-suffering sigh . . . "so now you need me" grimace of distaste . . . all of which would be preferable to being tossed out in the street, especially if her uncle Red was doing the tossing. He finally had to face the fact that he was terrified.

What if he asked her, face-to-face, and she said no?

What if he asked her without telling her the whole truth?

He nursed a drink or two in the bar until the barman brought him a fresh one and some nuts to nibble. A boisterous voice entering the bar made him cringe. He looked up to find Red Strait bearing down on his table, looking hale and hearty and none the worse for their adventure of a few nights ago.

"Good God," he said as Red took the chair across the table, "they've gotten so they admit just anybody to this place."

"Not really. I had to bribe 'em," Red said, reaching for

the nuts. "What are you doin' here, Fox? I figured you'd be out celebratin' your fancy new name."

"Title," Reynard corrected. "And it's actually old as titles go. A fancy *old* title. What are you doing here, Redmond, seeing as how you're neither a member nor an invited guest?"

"Oh, I just had to get outta the house. You know. And since I had to give up the cards and the game tables and the horses . . . that don't leave too many options for a cowpoke my age."

"Cowpoke?" Reynard winced at the term. "So, how's the family?"

"If by 'family' you mean Frankie, she's okay. Talkin' about Nevada a lot. How she misses it. How she misses the smells of dried sagebrush, and the corrals after the cattle go through, and brandin' time . . ."

Reynard was half listening. The mention of Frankie being unhappy had set off another round of memories that caused that infernal ache around his heart again. He rubbed his chest.

"Beats the heck out of me, but I think what she misses most is . . . you."

"What?" He came back to the present with a jolt. "Me?"

"Lord, what an idiot." Red shook his head. "She's crazy about you, Fox. I thought you'd figured that out by now. Lord knows, she give you enough hints. That girl don't go around kissin' just anybody."

"No, she doesn't." Reynard felt a familiar stirring at the thought of holding her, kissing her. She came to him in Paris, wanting to love him and share herself with him, and he got all noble and honorable. . . .

"I have been an idiot," he said to himself, but aloud.

"Now you're joinin' my club," Red declared. "The Stupid Fool Who Don't Know When to Shut Up and Kiss Her Club. Oh, and we got one o' them fancy aux-hillarys:

The Jackasses Who Don't Propose and Lose the Love of Their Life Forever So-ci-ety." Red's deepening glower was a clear indication he had just enrolled Reynard in both.

"It's a bit more complicated than—"

"Hell, son, it's always complicated. Life is complicated. People are complicated. But love—love is easy. You're either in it or you ain't. You get to decide. The only thing is, you may not get to decide in yer own sweet time. Remember she gets to decide too. And if you wait too long . . ."

Reynard felt something as strong as desire pushing him toward the edge of action. It was hope, and Red's next statement sealed the deal.

"My Frankie is one sharp gal. If you got problems, there ain't nobody better to talk 'em over with."

The morning dawned bright and cold and absolutely dreadful, as far as Frankie was concerned. Already, it had been a day and two nights since Reynard learned the truth he had sought for years and stormed out of the house as if he wanted to give the whole world some bruises. She hadn't heard a word from him since. Maybe he was furious at her for trying to interfere. Maybe he had had bad news of some kind. Maybe he'd been drunk for two days. In his younger days, Red would occasionally go on a bender that lasted a while. She shook her head. No, Reynard wasn't a drinking man.

"What's the matter, Frankie?" Elizabeth asked.

Frankie looked up at her mother, who sat at a writing desk by a sunny window in the small upstairs parlor. Elizabeth and Claire were both staring at her strangely.

"What makes you think something's wrong?" Frankie said, lowering her gaze to the ladies' journal on which she was trying desperately to concentrate.

"You were shaking your head," Claire said.

"Was I?" She shifted in her chair and pointed to the open page. "People publish the most ridiculous things these days. Downright nonsense."

"Well, perhaps you should write something sensible for them to publish," Elizabeth said, returning to the letter she was writing. "You've always had a way with words."

From downstairs came the sound of the door being answered and of a pack of dogs running and barking to greet whoever had just arrived. Moments later, Jonas arrived in the solar, brushing dog hair from his usually immaculate trousers.

"Excuse me, madam." He straightened, clearly aggrieved. "You have a caller. I have put him in the parlor."

"Him?" Elizabeth rose, pocketed her spectacles, and hurried out after Jonas. "Who is it?"

Claire grinned. "Mama has a gentleman caller?"

"Probably someone asking her to sponsor a charity," Frankie said.

"Good luck to him," Claire said. "Mama's not exactly been in a charitable mood lately."

They settled back into their reading and were surprised when Elizabeth came rushing up the stairs, minutes later, flushed with excitement.

"Now, Frances!" She pulled Frankie up out of her chair. "You must go down to the drawing room, straightaway. His lordship has called and wishes to see you."

"Who?" Frankie had the alarming feeling she had experienced this very thing, not long ago, and it had not turned out well. "Who is calling on us?"

"The viscount. He's here and he has asked to see you . . . privately."

"The vi—you mean Reynard? Reynard is here?"

Her mother nodded and began to fuss with her bodice

and worry aloud if "Frances" should take the time to change her dress.

Frankie was almost as stunned by the fact that her mother was urging her to see him as she was by his presence . . . here . . . downstairs . . . waiting for her.

She ran for the stairs and only when she reached the floor in the main hall did she pause to take a breath and collect herself.

Steady, girl.

He stood by the parlor window, wreathed in sunlight, his hands clasped behind him and his feet spread. It was a determined stance and she paused just inside the door to search his manly, eye-pleasing form for clues to the reason for this visit. But when he turned, all of her suppositions were knocked in a cocked hat. His gaze was steady and warm and the way he smiled as he came to take her hands made her heart skip. He was nothing short of beautiful.

And he was looking at her as if her eyes weren't still a bit puffy from crying and her nose wasn't still a bit red from blowing.

"Your lordship. How lovely to see you."

"I suppose I should get used to that," he said, taking her hands in his and looking her over as if he were memorizing every line and curve of her. "But I don't want to get used to it from you. I want you to always call me . . . Reynard or Fox or Handsome or Dearest . . . 'Dearest' would do nicely for all places and occasions outside of Buckingham Palace."

She gave a puzzled laugh. "What on earth are you talking about?"

He drew a deep breath and gathered his lordliest mien.

"There are things a man must learn in life, Frankie," he said, drawing her with him to the sofa at the far end of the parlor. As they passed the parlor doors, Jonas was pulling them shut, something that she'd never seen before. In fact, she hadn't noticed they *had* parlor doors until now.

"How to tie a proper four-in-hand," he continued. "How to drive a Phaeton, how to don one's own boots when there is no valet available, and of course, how to escort a lady into dinner, onto a dance floor, and into a compromising position."

"Ye gods, Fox, are you drunk?" She interrupted with a slightly nervous laugh. "It's ten in the morning and you sound half stewed."

"If I am drunk, Frankie, it is with your beauty."

He looked her in the eye as he said that, and she felt a delicious shiver run through her. And he continued meeting her gaze with those beautiful gray eyes that were slowly darkening the way they did when—

Heaven above, he was wooing her.

"What happened after you found out about your parents that evening?" she said with a faint quiver to her voice. "Where did you go, what did you do? Is everything settled, with the estate and all? Care for some coffee? Tea? A belt of whiskey?" She halted and glanced at the parlor doors. Her mother was undoubtedly outside with her ear pressed to the crack where the doors met.

"I do not want coffee or tea or whiskey"—he leaned closer to her, practically nuzzling her hair—"unless I can taste it on your lips."

"Holy buckets" was her response.

Reynard sat back and took a deep breath. Casanova, he was not. But he was the Fox and he could be charming. Why couldn't he be charming *now*?

"This is not going the way I planned," he said, truly perplexed.

"What is not going the way you planned?" she asked, equally confused.

"Do I have to spell it out? Because that kind of ruins the mood."

"Please, do not tell me you're trying to seduce me . . . here, in my mother's parlor at ten o'clock in the morning on a Tuesday."

"Tuesday's a bad day for you? I could come back to-morrow."

Frankie had never seen him like this. A little off his game and easily rattled. It was kind of cute. She started to giggle and it turned into a laugh.

"Well, this is a fine kettle of fish," he said, trying to look insulted. But one corner of his mouth betrayed him, curling up, and the sound of her laughter did the rest. A moment later he was chuckling himself.

"You are seriously undermining my dignity here," he said, sobering.

"I am," she said, biting her lip. "And I apologize. I was just so shocked to see you here and couldn't imagine why you came."

He turned to her with an earnestness that grabbed her by the heartstrings. "I came because . . . I've missed you. It's been nearly two full days since I've seen you and even though I spent one of them getting soused proper and starting fights with perfect strangers in taverns—"

"You didn't."

"I did. And it still felt like I'd been away from you forever. I think Paris . . . all that time with you . . . spoiled me."

He looked at her and for one dazzling, splendid moment, she saw straight into his heart. Longing and desire and delight and chagrin and naked hope . . . it was all there, just as she had glimpsed it in his room that night in Paris. Only this time, he gave it to her voluntarily, openly, inviting her into his heart.

"Paris spoiled me, too," she said, barely above a whisper.

He turned the rest of him toward her, searching her face the same way she searched his. The barriers she had worked so hard to erect were now being demolished by a force more powerful than pride or fear or any pressure society could bring to bear.

"I'm in love with you, Frankie Bumgarten. I love you all the way to my marrow, and I can't imagine my life without you."

He leaned into her and she threw her arms around his neck and met his kiss with a hunger that surprised even her. A few moments and a storm of kisses later, she dropped her head back and said, "Yes, yes, yes!" And he began to dispatch her buttons and cover every inch of skin he revealed with eager hands and kisses. She gasped as he bared her breasts above her corselet and stroked, nuzzled, and nibbled them. The sensations sent vibrations down through her body to her sex and made her draw tight, anticipating, yearning for what she hoped came next. He rose to throw off his coat and vest and returned to her to help her remove her jacket and blouse.

She froze for a moment listening, and could have sworn she heard dogs in the hallway outside the parlor. She pointed anxiously, and he strode to the door where he found and flipped a latch with a triumphant grin.

When he came back to her she pulled him down with her and began to explore his body as he did hers. Soon she hiked her skirts and straddled his lap, fitting her body against his and yearning for a time when there would be no clothes to curtail their explorations. She reached for the front of his trousers, searching for and finding buttons. He moved his hands to hers and for a moment she thought he meant to stop her again. But he caught her gaze in his as she wrapped her hands around him and he whispered, "I'm yours, sweetheart. I'll never deny you again. But I kind of think this might be better if we were . . . in a more comfortable situation. Someplace with champagne and silk and all the time in the world."

"Really? You lock the door and seduce me and this is what I get? A few seconds of pleasure—breathtaking though they were—and then it's back to promises, patience, and propriety?"

Elizabeth paced the upper hall, waiting for the parlor doors to open, waiting to learn if he had indeed proposed and what her stubborn daughter's response had been. He had been so courtly and respectful when he'd asked permission to propose to Frances. There truly had been a change in him. Gone were the arrogance and condescension she had always found so objectionable. She halted, listening. She could have sworn she heard the clicking of claws on the marble floor. She hurried partway down the stairs and found Sarah with her ear glued to the seam of the parlor doors.

"Sarah Grace! Come away from there this instant!" she said in a furious whisper as she rushed down the remaining steps and waded through a pack of dogs. She grabbed Sarah's arm, hauled her away from the door, and sent her off with shooing motions and wicked glares. "And take these mutts with you."

The instant they were out of sight, Elizabeth crept back

to the door and put her ear to it, straining to hear what was happening. Their voices were low and she worried that something untoward might be happening.

"Lizzie!" Red's voice gave her a start and she whirled around to find him and Claire standing at the bottom of the stairs. "Come away from there!" He was clearly scandalized. "That boy's a full vi-count now. You can't be eavesdropping on a full vi-count."

Chapter Thirty

"I've never met a woman more determined to be rid of her virtue," Reynard said, holding her tight on his lap, refusing to let her escape.

"And I've never met a man less eager to relieve me of it," she said with a scowl, relenting and staying in her scandalously intimate contact with him.

"Oh, I'm plenty eager, Miss B, but I didn't come here to ravish you on the sofa while your mother listens through the keyhole." He shot a glance at the parlor doors and felt some of the resistance drain from her body.

She glanced at the doors and sagged, ceding him that point.

"Fine." She crossed her arms with a provocative cant to her chin. "What did you come for?"

He straightened so he could see her wonderful blue eyes and smiled with all of the love overflowing his heart.

"Marry me, Frankie," he said. "Make me the happiest man in England. And I swear, I'll do everything in my power to make you the happiest woman on earth . . . including making love to you whenever, wherever you like."

"That's a bold promise, your lordship." She gave an

impish laugh. "Of course, after today, I may need a bit more convincing of your veracity."

He noticed she hadn't exactly said yes.

"Marry me, Frankie. And I'll make you a rich woman."

"Really? How rich? I mean, Vanderbilt-rich or Rothschild-rich?"

Her small, mischievous smile made his chest ache.

"Does it matter?" he asked, and she answered with an insistent look. "All right, more like a Vanderbilt, I suppose. I'm still not sure the extent of it. Won't know until after we have the reading of the will."

"So, enough to help Uncle Red?" She watched his face.

"I'm confident there is more than enough for that."

"Enough for a trip to the States occasionally? Even Nevada?"

"Definitely."

She beamed and gave him a delicious squeeze. He was starting to think he was mad for not giving her what she so obviously wanted, here and now.

"And the most important question: enough for a houseful of children?"

He smiled, feeling every particle of his body capitulating, melting.

"Absolutely. In the interest of full disclosure, however, I have no clue how to raise a child, much less a brood. I'm hoping you have paid attention to such things."

"You're in good hands."

"So, you *will* marry me?"

"Yes, yes, yes . . . a thousand times *yes*." She grinned and kissed him thoroughly. "Was there really any doubt? After all, I practically proposed to you the other day."

"Well, there is always room for the unexpected." He shifted, feeling himself losing all will to address the one last obstacle in their path to bliss. But it had to be done.

"Speaking of which, there is one stipulation. We need to have the ceremony within twenty-nine days."

"That's a little specific." She gave a puzzled frown. "Why twenty-nine days?"

"It's . . . a requirement of the will. Wedded in twenty-nine days or I'm flat broke."

"Well, we can't have—wait—you're marrying me for *your* money?"

"I'm afraid so, at least timing-wise. The old boy learned he couldn't disinherit me and tried to sneak in one last salvo. I have to marry within thirty days and it has to be a love match. Little did he know I had already charmed my way into the perfect woman's heart." He studied her calm face with a tinge of anxiety. "That is, I think I did. Because I know she's captivated mine.

"You're not upset, are you?" he asked, trying to read her response.

"At least you had the decency to tell me about it before you had your wicked way with me." She frowned and pursed the corner of her mouth. "You may have to soothe my injured pride."

He laughed with relief and drew her into a lingering hug. Moments later, he lifted her off his lap and headed for his coat. When he came back, he held out a small leather jewel box that she recognized. She stared at it, clearly in the grip of growing emotion. He sank to the sofa beside her and put it in her hands.

"Is this what I think it is?" Frankie asked.

"Open it and see."

She looked up and found his eyes were glistening. He was so beautiful, so good, so dear . . . her heart ached from being so full. He finally opened it for her. She stared into the deep, reflective beauty of the big sapphire surrounded by brilliant diamonds.

"This was your mother's," she said, her throat tightening.

"It was," he affirmed. "But now it's yours. If you want it, that is. I could buy you one of your own, if you'd rather—"

She took his face between her hands and kissed him gently.

"I would be honored to wear this ring, Reynard . . . my sweet Fox, my *dearest* . . . for the rest of my life."

She held out her hand and he slipped it on her third finger. It was a perfect fit. Like their love, it seemed meant to be.

After they straightened their clothes and let some of the heat fade from their faces, they flung open the parlor doors and had Jonas gather her family.

The announcement of their marriage was met with joy by three of the four family members. The fourth, Elizabeth, just stared at them for a moment, tilting her head this way and that, as if trying to see them going into the future together. She evidently made peace with what she saw, because she gave Frankie a tearful hug and Reynard her hand in welcome. Red snatched Frankie off her feet and twirled her around in pure joy, as he had when she was a girl. Claire and Sarah squealed with delight, then both hugged her, and oohed and aahed over her beautiful ring.

By the time they finished an impromptu champagne luncheon in celebration, Frankie and Reynard were both glowing. As she walked him to the front door, she leaned close and whispered, "Want to hear a secret?"

He gave an exaggerated sniff. "Absolutely not. I am retiring from the 'secrets' business. After all, I will have a small empire to run."

"Really? Are you sure? This one's quite juicy."

He assessed her secretive smile. "All right. One last secret. Just for you. After that, my lips are unsealed."

She pulled him down to whisper, "My bedroom window will be unlocked tonight. I could arrange a convenient stack of barrels."

Reynard took a deep breath, smoothed his vest, and squeezed his eyes shut as temptation swamped him.

"Barrels are noisy," he muttered.

"I believe I could find a ladder," she said with sultry invitation. "It will be quiet and private. My bed is like a cloud. I'll be wearing silk."

He groaned and glanced around them, finding the hall empty before pulling her into his arms and kissing her passionately.

"That is the sweetest secret I've ever heard."

•

It was a clear night, chilly and damp when he climbed that ladder, raised her window, and hoisted himself across the narrow windowsill. It wasn't the most dignified entry into his new life, but it was what she wanted and he sensed it was somehow fitting.

There was a glowing fire to provide welcome warmth and two thick beeswax candles provided soft, golden light as he removed his gloves and overcoat and turned to find her coming from beside the bed, dressed in a white silk nightgown and carrying a small bouquet of flowers. Her hair lay in thick waves about her shoulders and her eyes were bright with pleasure.

He stood for a moment drinking in the beauty of her and the sweet seduction of the setting. When she smiled, he felt his knees weaken.

"Take off your coat," she said softly.

He obliged, grateful for the distraction. He was so immersed in emotion and sensation, he was unable to summon a single word.

"And your shoes." She lifted her nightgown to reveal her own bare feet.

He toed off his shoes, thinking that for the rest of their lives, he would give her anything she asked. Because he trusted that anything she asked would be right and honest and loving. Like this night. This sweet and wonderful night.

When he stood barefoot, in shirtsleeves, she came to take his hand.

"I love you, Reynard Boulton," she said, gazing into his eyes. "I promise to love you with all my heart and to stay by you and encourage and strengthen you . . . to be truthful and faithful and kind to you, to always think the best of you . . . and to share my hopes and decisions and joys with you, in good times and in bad. I will be your compass, your helpmate, your defender, and the keeper of your heart. I will love you as long as there is breath in my body . . . and beyond even that."

Tears sprang to his eyes. She was giving him her vows. Here. Now. With her heart bared and open. Pledging to him her love and her life—so much more than he ever imagined he could have. He could hardly breathe. He blinked to clear his eyes and felt wetness rolling down his cheeks. Never in his life had he experienced such a flood of joy and gratitude. What had he ever done to deserve this gift of pure grace?

It took a minute for him to be able to speak. And when he did, he surprised himself with a flow of words and realized he had been storing them up from the moment he first looked into her eyes.

"I love you, Frankie Bumgarten, with all that I am . . . heart, soul, and body. I promise to stand by you and protect you . . . to be gentle when you need it and strong when you need that. I will be honest with you and faithful to you and I will always think of your best interest. I will set my course by your star and will share my hopes and my decisions, my joys and heartaches with you. You have become the center of my world, the light in my soul. I will do my best to be the faithful keeper of your heart. And I will love you as long as there is breath in my body . . . and well beyond that."

Tears rolled down Frankie's cheeks, even as she smiled.

She opened her arms to him and he lifted her off her feet and kissed her with such tenderness that she felt herself melting in his arms. He carried her to the bed, laid her there, and shed the rest of his clothes to join her. Sharing the powerful emotions of the moment, they simply held each other for a time, exchanging tender kisses and caresses.

"You never cease to amaze me," he finally said, stroking her hair as he gazed down into her eyes. "I never expected . . . this."

She gave a soft laugh. "You thought I invited you here just to relieve me of my virtue?"

"I had no idea what to expect." He smiled. "But I knew with you, whatever happened would be good."

"I wanted to have some time with you, in private, to tell you what is in my heart and to hear what is in yours. This closeness"—she stroked his chest—"is what I wanted."

"And that's all?" he said with a throaty rumble. He

nuzzled her neck and she shivered as he explored her reactions.

"Well, maybe a bit more. Something on the order of this . . ." She took his head between her hands and kissed him deeply, intimately. By the time that kiss finished, they were both warming fast and shedding the last of their clothes.

He came gently to her, fitting himself in the cradle of her thighs, adoring her body with his eyes and lips and hands. She welcomed him with eager hands that explored the hard contours of his frame and the tender places that made him tense and arch with pleasure.

She moved against his hardness, seeking the right angle and pressure to intensify her pleasure and summon his. As her response built toward a climax, they held each other tightly and soon she was gasping and quaking with pleasure and release.

There was more, so much more to explore, and he needed no urging to begin joining their bodies and completing their union.

She was surprised by a feeling of fullness, completeness as he entered her. Steamy, delicious sensations satisfied yearnings she hadn't realized she had. When they were fully joined, they lay together for a few moments, gazing at each other and absorbing the wonder of the moment.

This, she realized, was what Daisy had talked about—the speaking that needed no words—the joining of flesh that changed hearts and lives forever. It was an embrace of body and spirit, a mingling of mind and marrow that called the best of each to reach for the best in the other.

But there was still more. She read in his eyes a hunger that was rising in her, too. Instinct took over and she began to move, undulating against him, producing increasing waves of sensation. He met her movements with slow careful thrusts that propelled her on a tightening spiral of pleasure, until she lost all sense of separateness from him. She seemed to feel his pounding heart, his straining muscles, his intensifying pleasure in her own body. She clasped him tightly with her legs and arms. As her climax approached, she felt him meet her urgency with stronger, deeper strokes until her senses shattered and he became her sole anchor in reality. He joined her moments later, pouring his love and passion into her with exquisite care.

Later, as their bodies cooled and he moved to lie beside her, she gave a moan of dismay.

"Don't worry, sweetheart, I'm not going anywhere." He chuckled. "I just don't want to squash you on our wedding night. Very bad form, squashing one's bride."

"Our wedding night," she whispered, turning it over and over in her mind. "It is, isn't it."

He nodded, looking like he shared her wonder. "Promises made to each other before God, and consummated in flesh. I think that what we just did qualifies."

"So, this isn't one last act of sin," she said, with a blooming smile. "It's one first act of married love." She took a deep breath and paused halfway through. "I don't think my mother or your solicitor will quite see it that way."

"That's why we're going to repeat those vows in front of a bishop and a small crowd of onlookers in a couple of weeks," he said, nuzzling her shoulder and her neck. "There won't be any question about the legality or the propriety of it. And if there is any question as to the 'love match' requirement, I've arranged for discreet testimony that we spent a glorious night together."

"Really?" She couldn't imagine . . . "Who?"

"If things have gone according to plan, your uncle is stationed in the hall a door or two away." She tensed and made to rise, but he caught her by the waist. "If you'll be so good as to step outside, he will hand you a tray bearing chilled champagne to mark the occasion. He agreed to be an accomplice only after threatening me with bloody mayhem if I hurt you in any way or back out of the engagement afterward."

Determined to see this for herself, she rolled away and slid from the bed. He spoke and stopped her as she headed for the door.

"I suggest a robe, dear wife."

She looked down at her naked body and turned fourteen shades of red. He laughed as she headed for her wardrobe and donned a sensible woolen robe.

Red was indeed stationed on a chair, two doors down in the dimly lighted hall. Beside him on the floor was a silver tray bearing an ornate wine chiller and champagne flutes. He started at the sound of her door opening and looked up with a hint of anxiousness.

"You okay, Frank?" he asked with gruff concern, looking her over as he rose and handed her the tray.

"I'm better than okay, Uncle Red." She blushed even more as she met his gaze, then smiled. "I'm downright *wonderful.*"

When she turned back to her room, Reynard was leaning a shoulder against the doorframe, arms crossed, smiling.

Red took a deep breath, and nodded to him. "Fox."

Reynard nodded back. "Red."

Her beloved uncle seemed to be blinking quite a bit as he turned away to seek his own room down the hall. She glanced back to see his shoulders rounded and steps slow. Her throat tightened as Reynard came to help her with the tray.

When the door closed behind them, tears rolled down her cheeks. He took the tray from her, deposited it on her tea table, and then drew her into his arms. He held her tightly against him and she held him just as fiercely as that storm of powerful emotions passed. After a few moments, she took a deep breath and he loosened his hold enough to look into her eyes.

"Champagne or bed?" he asked.

"I have to choose?" She made a face that drew a grin from him.

He scooped her up into his arms to carry her to the bed and she laughed.

Twenty-nine days wasn't much time to arrange a wedding and invite family from both America and Paris. But if anyone could do it, Elizabeth Bumgarten could. There was a dress to buy, a church to arrange, and a wedding breakfast to plan. And of course, there was the honeymoon trip, which Reynard insisted be left up to him.

Lady Evelyn returned to London only a few days after she left and at dinner the first night, Red announced to the family that he and his "Evie" intended to marry soon, also. The family erupted in peals of joy and hugs were shared all around. Frankie whispered to Reynard, who smiled and nodded, then offered to make their wedding a double one. Family would be there and it would be a delight to share a wedding day with her beloved uncle and their beloved countess. There was little discussion before they accepted and there were more hugs and more champagne to toast yet another addition to the family.

Every day that passed in the following weeks was filled with discoveries and anticipation. Sir Harold Rowantree was pleased to certify that the coming marriage was indeed a love match and went so far as to arrange an early release of a sizeable account to Reynard. A proper honeymoon trip required proper funding, after all. And a marriage required a trousseau, which Reynard quietly insisted on funding for Frankie. All of the Bumgarten women got new clothes for the festivities and the house received a needed bit of polish.

But by far, the greatest excitement occurred three days before the wedding, when Frankie's elder sister, Daisy, arrived from New York with her husband, Ashton, and rambunctious two-year-old son, Redmond. It was a joyful reunion and the American contingent brought news of the discovery of another massive silver vein in one of the Silver River mines. Ore was already moving and money was beginning to pour into the family coffers again. Ashton, Daisy said proudly, was proving to be as financially astute as he was brilliant and handsome. He was already being invited to lecture on history at various colleges and universities in New England, and there was talk of him being invited to sit on the board of trustees for two schools.

After dinner that night, the Bumgarten women trailed upstairs to tuck little Redmond into bed and spend time sharing courtship stories and catching up, and Red and Evie withdrew to Red's study for some private wedding planning. That left Ashton and Reynard in the main parlor together, eyeing each other over snifters of brandy.

Things got very quiet between them. Ashton finally spoke.

"I asked you to look after Daisy's sisters, not *marry* one."

"I did my best to avoid the situation, believe me. Avoided them like the plague for more than years."

"But then?"

"It's hardly a story I would tell you . . . who would tell it to your wife, who would tell it to her sisters, who would blab to their mother . . . who would tell it to half of London. Then where would I be?"

"That good, eh?" Ashton seemed to be enjoying Reynard's discomfort.

Reynard gave a sniff. "Suffice it to say: I saw her luscious little body, looked into those big baby blues of hers . . . and my bachelorhood up and snuffed it. I was had. It took a bit longer for her to come around. Dead set, she was, on dying a bluestocking spinster. I imagine your wife was to blame for her low expectations of matrimony." He glared at Ashton, though without much heat.

Ashton chuckled and propped his feet up on the coffee table. "When we got the telegram saying there was to be a wedding and we had to come, I couldn't believe it. Had to read it again and again, and still couldn't believe Frankie was marrying *you*."

"I'm not such a bad catch," Reynard said testily. "Anyway, I got past Red and her mother. That should count for something." He paused.

"You have a point there." Ashton studied him with a critical air. "So, she put you in a whirl, did she? Damn, I wish I could have seen that."

"I imagine there are still lingering traces of it," Reynard confessed. "That woman sets my temper and my passions to boil. And daily makes me wonder how I ever got along without her."

"So, it's love, is it?"

Reynard paused for a moment, thinking of Frankie's many moods and faces, each one more adorable than the last. He was half tempted to scale that ladder again tonight, though he'd sworn to abstain until the legalities and proprieties were taken care of. And she seemed to enjoy making it hard on him. Pun intended.

"Love it is. A glorious madness," Reynard said with a growing smile. "One I will enjoy for the rest of my unexpectedly worthwhile life."

Outside the parlor, in the darkened hall, Frankie stood clutching a note she was trying to decide whether to give to her intended. Her eyes misted and her heart seemed to swell in her chest.

"I love you too, Fox."

Then with a glint in her eyes, she headed back through the house to find Jonas and have him carry that note to Reynard.

When Reynard opened it minutes later and reddened from the collar up, Ashton sat forward with a look of concern. "What is it?"

The note said simply: *The ladder is up*.

Reynard tucked the paper into his inner coat pocket and smiled.

AFTERWORD

Frankie and the Fox have become two of my favorite characters of all time. I hope you enjoyed their story (and the continuation of the Sin & Sensibility series) half as much as I enjoyed writing it.

While the overall plot of the book is not based on a specific historical happening, as Daisy's story was, the writing required a lot of historical research. Here's just a taste:

As Frankie's mother admonishes: there were only a handful of dukes in Great Britain at any given time, and sometimes not even one was eligible. Thus, setting one's cap for an English duke was a very iffy proposition. There were, however, quite a number of dukes on the Continent, many of whom controlled small estates and, like most English noblemen, were in need of an infusion of cash. Daisy didn't catch a duke, but their mother thought Frankie had a chance with a German duke. It must not have occurred to her that marrying a German duke would mean Frankie would probably have to LIVE in Germany and would never see her family.

The Fox's distaste for everything "Prussian" was very much in tune with the prevailing attitude in England during the Victorian period, despite the queen's German ancestry. (Overcoming this and working to legitimize the monarchy was one of the main reasons for Victoria's strict moral code.) However, the Fox's jealousy-tinged comments are his alone and intended for comic effect. In the 1890s Germany had finally been united, but there were still factional loyalties and identities. Prussians continued to think of themselves as Prussians as well as Germans during this time. And yes, Maximillian, Duke of Ottenberg, is purely fictional, as well as "Rotten."

Speaking of rotten, Rotten Row had been remodeled earlier and was paved with sand between rows of trees, and carriage traffic was now separated from mounted riders by a metal railing . . . which I made use of for Frankie's disastrous ride. And as for horses—the closest in coloring to Sarah's "pretty boy" is an Andalusian I've seen pictured numerous times. But the coloring of a white body with black mane and tail is considered to be so rare as to be nearly nonexistent. Watch for Sarah and her pretty boy horse in the third and final book of the Sin & Sensibility series, out in 2019.

Dueling had been outlawed in England for more than fifty years, by the time Frankie and the Fox began their adventures in the 1890s. But Red was not entirely correct to say that there hadn't been a duel in England for fifty years. It was just that there were no recorded deaths from duels during that period. The covert nature of duels makes it unlikely that good statistics exist, but dueling is known and recorded in other countries well into the twentieth century.

As for Reynard's visit to Mehanney's Gym—most fights in this period were bare-knuckle contests between wiry, street-bred fighters. Fighting was seen as one of the few ways a man could elevate himself in the world, and many young men took a shot at fighting for money and fame. Only a few made it to the top, but they became the first widely known "celebrities." During this time, some fighters began to employ padded gloves and became known as "boxers." With this change came the idea to "train" fighters/boxers for strength and endurance; hence, the rise of gymnasiums that trained fighters and also promoted and sponsored fights.

The status of Victorian musicians (except a few great composers) is represented fairly in Claire's part of the story. Musicians were considered part of society's backdrop; to be hired and occasionally appreciated, but not to be welcomed into society, no matter how accomplished they were. Only when they rose to direct well-known orchestras or were granted royal commissions as composers were they given recognition and social standing. Also, in upper-crust salons, there was generally no applause—it was considered vulgar—something the lower classes did in theaters and music halls.

Crossing the channel from England to France in those days was a fairly common event. Ferries and small liners made the crossing daily, the shortest of which was between the east coast of England and Calais, France. But that route was often stormy and fraught with delays. The twenty-four-hour crossing Frankie and the Fox made was not uncommon. And the trains and terminals the two used in France were indeed in service at that time—and still are.

As for Reynard the Fox's troubles with his uncle, the tradition of inheritance of titles was well entrenched, but there could be problems—the prime one of which was illegitimacy. Children and young adults have struggled with issues of identity for millennia. Reynard's questions about his parentage, starting early in life and coming from so forceful a figure as his uncle, could have had a profound influence on his self-image and self-esteem. Titles and inheritance have long been the cause of discord within families, from royalty to "plain sirs."

Quick facts:

A bit of cattle drive lore: "dogies" (as in "Get along little dogies") were orphaned calves that the trail hands looked after on cattle drives. They were vulnerable to being picked off by wolves or coyotes, so the trail hands gave them a little extra attention.

Scott's in Bond Street was indeed one of the premier men's hatmakers in London. A good hat handmade by them was worth a bundle.

Banking was controlled by the state-run Bank of England, which also issued the currency. But private lending institutions like Child's, Martins, and Coutts were created to serve the moneyed classes. If a gentleman needed a loan, that was where he would go. Personal, collateral-free loans were sometimes made to men of substance and good character. And yes, like today's bankers, they did sell off loans that became bad debt and were not always choosy about the buyers.

And finally:

Frankie's confrontation with her mother was not planned to be as volatile as it became. But it was clear to me that Frankie's problem was classic sexual harassment as it would be seen in today's light. She was being forced to suffer Ottenberg's attentions because of his title and position. He knew she didn't want him and in refusing him she became a challenge. He wanted to break her spirit and tame her like a wild horse. Control and domination brought him pleasure. Frankie's mother provided chilling and all too familiar admonitions: "What did you do to make him set hands to you?" and "Women must make 'accommodations' to important men." I did not consciously channel the words of women in the news in 2017–2018, but certainly the message came through. Women have always been at the mercy of powerful or "important" men, and women (like Frankie's mum) have always been complicit in such abuse. Perhaps now that so many women are speaking out, things will begin to change. One thing is certain: it will be no different until women themselves acknowledge the problem and seize the power to make it change.

Come and see me at BetinaKrahn.com, and leave a word about *The Girl With the Sweetest Secret*. I would love to hear from you.

Connect with U s

Visit us online at
KensingtonBooks.com
to read more from your favorite authors, see books
by series, view reading group guides, and more.

Join us on social media

for sneak peeks, chances to win books and prize packs,
and to share your thoughts with other readers.

facebook.com/kensingtonpublishing
twitter.com/kensingtonbooks

Tell us what you think!

To share your thoughts, submit a review,
or sign up for our eNewsletters, please visit:
KensingtonBooks.com/TellUs.